Beyond the Elastic Limit

An Epic Fable
By Howard Loring

Howard Loring

He is also the Author ~~he.~~

Epic Fabl *ing*

Piercing the Elastic

and

Tales of the Elastic L

Howard Loring's books are availa
paperback or eBook format through all ma
distributors

Or find at: **www.howardloring.com**

Become a fan at:
www.facebook.com/HowardLoring

For Paul Stofan

Friend and Human Being Extraordinaire

Gone but not forgotten

TABLE OF CONTENTS

INTRODUCTION
THE EPIC FABLE

Justice is one of those ephemeral terms, like love or beauty. Consequently it must be personally defined, given it's a vague conception that's impossible to describe by any universally accepted standard. Consensus can be rare.

In fact, justice is made manifest most often in the negative. Striking by its very absence, the elusive idea then becomes much easier to see. Someone may not be able to explain love, beauty or justice, but almost everyone can recognize an unloving act, an ugly object or an unjust situation.

So justice is a real thing, it simply, for most people, defies clarity. Yet, in today's interconnected world, identifying justice has real ramifications. It can be tricky.

You have to know just what you mean if you're talking justice on a vast scale. All involved have to be on the same page. If someone says they believe in something, is that something the same as what you believe in, by virtue only of the terms used, and because the concept is couched within the same jargon?

What if they're just lying?

More to the point, is the idea of justice etched in stone? Is it the identical concept today as it was yesterday, and will it be consistent, mean the same thing, tomorrow? How about a week from now, or a year, or millennia?

In other words, does the definition of what's right or what's wrong ever change? Is good always good and evil always evil? And can something bad ever be used to a good purpose, or something good be twisted and used with evil intent?

Is the ancient, and well-used adage, 'Right makes Might' correct, or is the opposite, 'Might makes Right' the better ideal? Can both positions, diverse as they are, be a valid stance? And who says, who makes that determination?

11

Such moral issues never change, only their context, and being universal, everyone must deal with them on a continuing basis. It's impossible not to as there are always choices to be made in any given situation. And of course, even if you decide not to choose, then that becomes your choice.

Such complicated considerations are, for thoughtful people, eternal questions. They frame the deepest issues at the very core of the human condition, and therefore, each succeeding generation must grapple with them. They must be learned, and then learned again, in perpetuity, forever.

However, these elemental, eternal constructs are internal concerns, as well. Everyone must draw his or her own personal boundaries, unless one blindly follows the dictates of others. Even then, you still must choose to do so.

Of course, someone with free will can always decide to exercise it and willingly become a slave, either to a higher power or some godless ideology. History is replete with examples of both occurring. But if they're sincere, then who's to say they're wrong, who determines that?

This book deals with good people forced to choose between bad options, and what happens to them when they do. It's just a Fable, a short "what if" story. But it's also an Epic, steeped in these universal themes unchanged through the ages.

If desired, readers may draw their own conclusions, and also find their own moral. As a species, it is our unending, compelling quest to do so. Choose well.

PART ONE – AFTER THE BEGINNING
CHAPTER ONE
THE LOST ONE

Spencer Hall awoke early, cold, his campfire dead and his woodpile depleted. The first decision of his new day thereby underscored the broader dilemma he faced. In general, he was stable and reliable, but Spencer was screwing up of late and his situation was not getting any better with the passage of time, a valuable commodity of which he had precious little to spare.

Producing some heat in the frosted-over, pre-dawn forest was his first task. That meant gathering fuel and reigniting his fire, which would take him some time, or walking at a brisk pace, which would take him less. Reaching for the heavy footwear that rested beside his backpack, he chose the latter.

Soon he was tramping the crude forest path leading from his base camp to his first test pit much earlier than he had planned, shivering in the bitter cold, and with no hot breakfast, to boot. Grasping for some small measure of comfort, he thought he'd be warm enough by the time he got to the pit, for it was a good mile away over hilly, wooded terrain. For now, he shivered.

As he walked, his hissing lantern illuminating the way, he noticed his feet crunched the crisp, brittle debris of the woodland floor beneath him in syncopated time with his frosty breath. He tried to keep the beat. It occupied his mind, and it was better than obsessing over the daunting problems he faced.

The sounds thus made, his walking and breathing noises, the lantern's hiss and the creaking of his stiff, cold clothing, were Spencer Hall's only companions within the dense forest.

With no breakfast, the man was hungry. He was next to worthless anyway without his morning coffee, always piping hot, and his standard meal of eggs and bacon were missed, as well. Strange, but he could almost smell them all.

Worse, his well-established morning routine was the most enjoyable part of his current field assignment. It provided the time he needed to assess his upcoming labors. Not today.

Spencer began searching for any food on his person. With luck he might have an old candy bar stashed away. The supplies in his backpack all required cooking, but he remembered also an open bag of jerky that he had stuffed somewhere.

As he hiked the trail, investigating his various pockets, he bobbed his head this way and that, dodging low-hanging limbs in the eerie lantern light. It slowed him somewhat, forcing him into a more deliberate pace, and he didn't like it. The man had an agenda, and any delay worked against him.

Still, he held to his speed. Spencer was wearing his favorite winter cap, and every gnarled snag in the canopy above was just waiting, in silent ambush, to snatch it off his near-freezing head. He had to be careful of this, so now and then he bowed to the forest before him, as if in supplication.

He surmised that he was only minutes away from extinguishing his lantern. Morning was coming up fast. It was still very cold, however, and he knew that once he arrived at the pit he would have to start digging right away to keep himself warm.

It sure would be nice to eat something first, even jerky. In spite of himself, Spencer shook his head while realizing that he had only himself to blame. The man never could predict weather in the field, and he had not bothered to gather any firewood after last night's meager dinner in his base camp.

No, the lone researcher had slept late, hoping for a mild morning, but he had been wrong. Just add it to the growing list, and does it ever stop piling on? He could use a piece of that jerky.

The shivering man was wearing his warmest jacket, with plenty of deep pockets, but for all his groping he was having trouble locating any possible breakfast. This failure was not some earth-shattering development, but it grated nevertheless. It was indicative of his whole, dismal field trip thus far.

After blowing into his fist to warm it, Spencer switched the lantern to his other hand, the better to search his other pockets. He did this with resignation. He would not be surprised if the effort also ended with a negative result.

No, that would be the norm on this expedition, not the exception. Weeks of hard work wasted, he feared. Or were they?

At last he was rewarded, producing a rumpled, half-empty bag of old beef jerky. Now at least he could eat while walking and not have to stop to eat in the cold, before digging, after he'd made it to the pit. Small consolation, but at this point the poor man wasn't picky, and he would take what he could get.

Normally fastidious and efficient, in the past, the hard-working Spencer Hall had abundant pride in his excellent use of time. To be truthful he was eminent in his chosen field, and he used to be superb at that kind of thing. But he was preoccupied of late, and he had made some poor work choices because of it.

Of course, it was only after the fact that these actions had caught up with him, and at the worst moment possible. Jerky and no coffee for breakfast had just driven the point home again. His whole situation was spinning way out of control.

At present he was isolated, cut off from everything he knew. In the old days, that fact would have invigorated him, set him free, for in general, Spencer didn't like other people all that much. Time was he had enjoyed working on his own with no interference from anyone, but now things were different.

Now he wasn't just alone. Now he was lonely, and the cold feeling was beyond overwhelming. It enveloped him and affected his every waking action, infusing whatever the pitiful man did.

This was a new and strange feeling for him, and because of it Spencer had once again put off a big decision. It was one that he

15

needed to make, the final approach that he should take to complete his assignment. He had narrowed his options to two choices, but he had been unable to decide which one to choose.

Now he felt as if he had wasted another day, and it wasn't like him to be indecisive. Regardless, he had no days to waste. He had to stop this, he thought to himself, but he didn't know how.

His current personal problems were consuming him, and he couldn't deny it, no matter how hard he tried. The isolated man now found himself quite paralyzed. He couldn't think.

But no, that wasn't quite it. Spencer could think all right, he thought too much, in fact. He just couldn't organize his thoughts, and this was not his usual frame of mind.

The lone researcher was powerless in controlling the rampant images. They were relentless and unending, hovering just below the surface of his every conscious moment, scattering in ever growing and divergent directions, somehow forbidding him from taking charge of his life. But that wasn't all.

The worst thing about the whole situation, and this was the part that galled him the most, was that deep down he was aware of what was wrong with him. He was heartbroken. There was no other word for it and he knew it, even though he had fought hard to hide that obvious fact from himself.

Circumstances beyond his control had driven him to leave his beloved wife, Judith. As a result, he was desperate now, and also depressed. This mood was growing every day, and in retrospect, with all his being he wished that they had not parted.

This stance was foolish on his part as well as unproductive and time consuming. He could do nothing about the situation now, buried as he was within the vast forest. Still his mind raced with scenarios that could have been, of things he could have done differently, of actions and words now too late in coming.

Of course, daydreaming like this was the last thing he desired, for thinking of his marital woes just made him more melancholy.

That was his dilemma in a nutshell, that and the dull, cramping pit in his stomach that of late was his constant companion.

The man was trapped. Spencer knew that he had to think of something else, anything else, hopefully something positive, but he couldn't. He couldn't even begin to.

For his wife, the wife that he loved so much, the wife that he was so dismal without, was the same wife that had compelled him to go in the first place. Devastated at the time, the tortured man had evaded the painful issue as best he could. He plunged wholeheartedly into his professional life and insisted on fieldwork.

Spencer had cut and run, hoping his job would be his salvation, as it had been in the past. Now his work was suffering too, and he knew it no matter how much he wished otherwise. Even in his present state, he was far too savvy not to see that.

He found himself beset by nagging questions over decisions that he'd already made, and he hated to second-guess himself. Before this assignment he never would have. Now, when he did think about his chosen occupation, he worried about the miscalculations of the past, and not the possibilities of the future.

Spencer was seeing the bitter truth at last. His personal life was history, and his current assignment, all that he had left, was in jeopardy as well. It would just crumble away in front of him if he didn't do something fast, and it might already be too late.

He had already committed a number of errors. This was out of character for him also. It was typical of him to see and prepare for any potential problems long before they arrived on the scene.

Yet the man had split his troops, in a manner of speaking. Wishing solitude to mull over his personal demons, he had sent his young assistant further north some three weeks ago in an attempt to multiply their chances of success. At the time, it had seemed like a good idea, but now he wasn't so sure.

True, in the beginning they were in close radio communication, 'were' being the operative word. Soon the two of them lost all contact. Out of the blue, Spencer's regulation issue field radio had become useless, nothing more than a small box of squeaking static.

He didn't know why. He'd checked the machine meticulously. Mechanically it seemed to be in good working order.

Under such an event, standard procedure dictated a retreat in haste back to square one, the home base of his expedition. This was a large and permanent installation located at the very edge of the huge forest. It had a name, or rather an official designation, but almost everyone working there referred to it with fondness as 'Point Zero,' or more simply, just 'the Point.'

He hoped this was where his young compatriot was heading, and with all due dispatch. At least then the kid wouldn't be jeopardizing his own fledgling career. He was just a grunt anyway, a follower, and the responsibility was not his.

Spencer was a different story altogether. Another mistake or no, he wasn't leaving, he couldn't. For this man was no green youngster just starting out his professional life.

He had to produce now or die, in a manner of speaking. Spencer had gone out on a limb with this job, way out. He had fought hard, contesting the heated objections of his superior, and he couldn't return now with nothing to show.

And he was so close to obtaining what he was after. At least he hoped he was, in spite of everything. Spencer needed this find far more than he had ever needed anything else before.

The desperate man was now almost sure, and he wasn't going anywhere, his standing orders be damned. Anywhere but to the pit, and he had better find something there fast. It was the only way left for him to pull out of this one.

Just as soon as he had thought it, Spencer found himself at his test pit. It was in a small clearing that he had chain sawed out of the surrounding forest, located on a steep, heavily wooded hillock. The excavation's raw opening measured about ten feet square and its depth was now at about fifteen feet.

A large pile of discarded earth, the project's innards, was nearby. Beyond this heap lay his meager belongings, toted out on other trips. These were his extra sleeping bag, frying pan, and coffee pot, plus the odd tools and equipment that he had with him.

Included in this list were a chainsaw and gas can, a nearly empty jug of bar oil, an old toolbox with some pliers and a few screwdrivers, assorted small wrenches and such.

Spencer looked around the clearing and, observing nothing had changed in his absence, assumed that it was safe to begin working. This very scene was once what he had lived for, he realized. Now it was just another day at the office.

First, he extinguished his hissing lantern, for he thought it no longer necessary in the growing morning light. Next he dumped his knapsack, packed the night before with food from his base camp larder. Then he climbed into the gaping hole, descending on a ladder that he had fashioned from tree branches.

Yet, once at the bottom, Spencer discovered to his chagrin that it was still too dark to see much of anything inside the deep hole. Now he had to climb out again, in order to fetch the lantern that he had just turned off. More precious time wasted.

"Exactly what I need," he thought, trying to see the irony. The attempt left him flat. His natural sense of sarcasm was normally sharp, but it gave him little comfort now.

The beat-upon man was so exasperated his knuckles turned white as he grabbed at the rungs of the ladder. He forced himself to pause a moment to regain his slipping composure, by taking a few deep breaths, before climbing up with fixed determination. When his shoulders broke the surface, he reached for the lantern, but once he had it he didn't move to re-light it.

"What am I doing?" he asked himself with disgust. His steaming breath cut the words. He didn't know the answer.

He turned his head away from the big pile of dirt. He looked to another pile that he had made, a heap of artifacts stacked with care that he had found in the pit. They were impressive, he knew.

He was almost sure that he was digging in the right place, but only almost. He couldn't decide. It was nearly driving him crazy.

The bureaucrat ingrained in him knew that his original plan of attack, to construct a base camp while working several test pits, was still a good one. It was the same operational strategy that he had pressed on his reluctant assistant some three weeks ago. First, build a crude cabin while taking the time to survey several potential test sites, and then have some measure of creature comforts while excavating the various exploratory pits.

However, Spencer had quickly abandoned his own plan, for this first test pit had proved so rich in artifacts. He'd been camping out at the dig for two weeks now on and off, and every day he had, without fail uncovered more and more of them. All were in pristine condition, each one a thing of beauty.

But the previous day, the lone researcher had stopped his various labors at the pit and hiked back to his base camp. Spencer had gone early in the gray afternoon to escape the bitter cold of the forest's autumn twilight. The base camp, only half-constructed, was now seldom used, but most of his supplies were still stored there and his field victuals had run out.

The unhappy man had tried once more to raise someone on his radio, something that he did from time to time. He ached for human contact and he wished to report in as well, but he needn't have bothered. The radio was still worthless.

He was looking at the pile of artifacts while thinking, what if I'm wrong? What if it wasn't here at all? He hadn't even started on any other pits, and had no time to do so in any case.

But the artifacts had been in this pit, no doubting that. There were a lot of them, too. And he was sure that the newest ones he had catalogued were from the time period he sought, so now he judged himself at the proper depth, as well.

Armed with this well-founded theory, Spencer had begun to widen the bottom of the gaping hole, increasing the pit's circumference with each gradual pass. He was betting everything that the object of his search was, in fact, there, and close by. But was he right in this assessment or just wrong again?

Currently, he couldn't afford to be hesitant, but he wasn't sure. With winter coming on, a wrong decision now could mean a cold morning every morning, and he didn't need that. The man had enough dilemmas looming in his life.

What was wrong with him? Why couldn't he just get it together as he always had before? Where was the old Spencer Hall, the one who had been so calculating and detached, the steady professional who had always been so cocksure of his actions?

Such thoughts tormented him. Of late, he couldn't get away from them, for he had brought this on himself, even the situation with his estranged wife, Judith. Knowing it just made it worse.

It didn't matter what she had done. Spencer knew in his heart of hearts that he was the one responsible, knew that he had caused it, had driven her to it. The fact burned crystal clear in hindsight.

It seemed the length of his crap list increased the more the poor man thought about his screwed-up life. While standing on the ladder and holding the lantern, Spencer realized that he was cold, shivering, staring at nothing and getting nothing constructive done. And all with that nagging pain in his stomach.

He looked below and saw the light inside the pit was now more than sufficient without the lantern. He dropped it without thinking and climbed down again, his eyes filling with tears. He grabbed his well-used pick, and without regard to anything in his way, he employed it with vigor on the excavation's wall.

Again and again Spencer blindly swung the tool, not knowing or caring where he struck. After slashing away a few dozen times, he collapsed in a heap. His arms were aching, and it hurt his heaving chest to breathe the cold air so deeply.

He felt wounded and physically spent. He was lost and alone. He wanted to die, but he was still very much alive, and he knew that his daunting problems weren't going anywhere.

He gazed up at the early morning sky, thickly clouded and gray. The winter birds had started to call out, proclaiming their frosty territory. Life goes on and his would, too.

After a moment, it was back to business. Was he in truth at the correct level? He started thinking about those alive in that period.

Then the irony struck him. Any life twenty-five thousand years ago was sure to have been a hard existence as well. Perhaps it had been harder than Spencer would ever realize.

The caveman was excited as he ran through the woods.

He was forever darting around obstacles in his way, heading towards his camp deep within the forest. Branches and vines were scratching him as he ran, ripping at his face, arms, torso and legs. He paid them little heed, except to run faster and with more agility, hunched over to better evade the thick brush surrounding him.

He was a young man, just approaching adulthood. He had always been strong and brave, but his bravery often bordered on foolishness. Of course, that was not what he thought, but it was the standard opinion held by most of his primitive community.

He was also independent, a rare thing in his Stone Age society. Yet, he was different from others of his kind and had been for a long time. This caveman had been orphaned at an early age.

Although members of his tribe had always looked after him, none there ever had taken him in as one of their own. As a result, the boy had pretty much raised himself. For this reason he was self reliant, and also highly unconstrained.

He was happy with his life in his primeval forest home, but he was unfulfilled. More than anything, the youth wanted to be acknowledged, by his entire tribe, as a great hunter and warrior. This was his largest dream, his obsession.

The youngster most of all wished to demonstrate his prowess in a definitive fashion, and to the very people who now thought him foolish and headstrong. It had always been so. As long as anyone could remember, he had embellished his daily deeds.

He was quite good at it. At night in the village, he would take his place around one campfire or another, and his brazen story of the day's conquest would unfold. His audience was ever receptive, always eager and willing to listen.

If he had been successful in the wood, his rendition never failed to reflect that he was the finest hunter his tribe had ever produced. If he came home empty-handed, his extraordinary tales always revealed how he was the greatest warrior. For in such a case, some spirit or evil thing had made away with his kill, and every time he had fought it off with great skill and cunning.

The tribe didn't believe a word of these stories, but they relished the telling. His outrageous tales were famous and well loved. Several of them had passed into the tribal lore, although as examples of absurdity and not as records of achievement.

It was undeniable that he was a gifted orator. Ever was he brash, excitable and enthusiastic, full of vivid descriptions and exacting details. Still, long ago his people had deemed anything he said meaningless, and so his name was Jargon.

Jargon knew that no one, not even his closest friends, took him seriously. No one ever had. But now they would.

"This will show them," he thought, as he raced with a natural ease through the deep woods. No one could deny him this time. With a silent prayer, Jargon thanked the tribe's unnamed gods that had granted him this wonderful opportunity.

Reports of a new animal living deep within the forest had been dismissed at first, not believed by anyone. No one had ever seen this elusive creature. Many members of the tribe had only laughed at descriptions of its strange and terrifying call.

Still, the reports had continued, with more and more people claiming to have heard the unnerving sounds. Always, in each new recounting, the bizarre cries had occurred only in the most remote, inaccessible areas of the forest. For this reason, the group of elders who ruled the tribe was unconvinced.

These stoic elders theorized that the beast, if there was one, lived a great distance away. So it was not viewed as a direct, nor even a potential threat to the tribe. Until the beast was seen, the elders had declared there would be no hunt.

That position had changed when, at last, someone with an unimpeachable character came forward. He was a respected warrior, and no one ever dismissed what he said. In fact, his stature was among the highest in the tribe.

As a young man in battle, he had been calm and unflinching. His great bravery was renowned by all. He also understood the many ways of the forest, without fail producing far more than his share of the tribe's supply of fresh meat.

Often he had shown his true character, fearless and unbending, and so his name had become Steadfast.

The warrior also was wise beyond his years, holding the entire tribe's confidence. Plus, he was personable as well as successful. Thus he had many wives, and they had given him many children.

However, Steadfast most favored his youngest wife, for she had given him his beloved twin boys. Twins were considered lucky by the tribe, and twin sons even more so. Therefore, it was undeniable that the tribe's unseen gods had smiled on Steadfast, blessing him with many everyday pleasures.

He had been deep in the forest that day, with only his young wife and their boys. Steadfast had been diligently working there, engaged in something else for which he was admired, loved even. He had been growing his annual crop of grubs.

Long ago, the tribe had discovered that if a tree fell into a forest clearing, the grubs would come. They never came to the trees that

24

fell against or among other trees, but only to ones that fell clear of the surrounding forest. Fat and dark green, the grubs were delicious when roasted over a smoldering fire.

Somewhere along the line, the tribe had discovered that the creatures could be farmed. Felled trees dragged into a clearing were all that were needed for them to thrive. The problem then was protecting the growing crop from thieves.

No one could be trusted not to steal the tasty grubs. This was bad enough, but it wasn't the worst. As the largest ones were unquestionably the best, the temptation was ever present to take them too soon, always an added disappointment.

For this reason, Steadfast diligently took another approach. Every year he went deep into the woods, and with nothing more than his stone axe and abundant determination, he created in secret his own clearing. Over the seasons, he had learned just how large an area was needed for a set number of trees.

When the grubs were at their optimum size, Steadfast would harvest them, often with the aid of some eager helpers. For weeks after, if the harvest was a good one, the whole tribe enjoyed the appetizing bounty of his labors. It was anticipated all year, for without fail he grew the very best, the fattest and tastiest.

That day, he was checking on the size of his grubs. The location of this year's crop was still a secret, and he had come with only his young wife and sons. It was then that it had happened.

Steadfast, bent over his logs, had heard the cries of the beast.

Now, Steadfast was at home in the dense forest, and it was all that he knew. Little did he not understand of what went on there, but he had never experienced anything like this. The sound itself was sufficient to stand his hair on end.

At times the angry call continued for long a period, longer than any animal he knew of could make. The cries would grow louder and louder, but somehow the beast never stopped for breath.

Sometimes the cries had been at a lower pitch, short and repetitive, but even then they had sounded angry.

Every so often the unmistakable reverberation of crashing trees could be heard in the distance. Steadfast knew from the sounds that they were big trees. It seemed to him the beast was attacking one tree after another, perhaps feeding on them, he thought.

Telling his family to stay in the clearing, Steadfast for a time had tracked the sound, going deeper into the forest. The cries then grew to such a point that even he was concerned. Of course, he could fight and would not mind dying in the hunt himself, but the man was afraid for his unprotected family should he fall.

Steadfast had hurried home to secure his loved ones. He then wished to return to hunt the unseen beast and, ever dutiful, he had informed the elders of his intentions. However, being cautious men, they had disagreed with his plan.

They wanted his grubs for the tribe, and if Steadfast were killed, they wouldn't get them. Not this year, not ever again, but they couldn't tell him that this was their reason. As a great warrior, such a stand would only insult him.

The elders had needed another option, one that would keep Steadfast unoffended and alive, and his grubs coming. Unfortunately, they didn't have one. Instead, all being true politicians, to a man they stalled for time.

They formed a loose huddle while standing with their heads bowed inwardly, each one engaging in loud mumblings.

Yet, soon the chief elder was compelled to say something. Steadfast was not a man to be kept waiting for long. In the face of such news, action was called for.

However, the old man was still uncertain, having no acceptable course of action to take. He stonewalled, by requesting Steadfast repeat what had happened in his clearing. With great patience Steadfast obliged, and he began to recount the events of the day.

By then, members of the tribe had begun to gather about and more were coming. Rapid word had spread that something out of the ordinary had occurred concerning the beast. Most present had not believed that the beast was real.

At the appropriate moment, Steadfast's young sons had turned blue in the face trying to imitate the lengthy cries of the creature. Some of the tribe had laughed at this display, but others who were wiser had not. The story had sounded like something Jargon would tell, but this time they were not amused.

Steadfast was no Jargon.

Then the eldest elder had formed an idea.

After conferring with his peers, who had all quickly concurred, the chief elder stated in a loud voice that Steadfast would not yet hunt the beast, but prepare the tribe's defenses in case the creature ventured closer. It was plain to see that Steadfast didn't care for this plan. The old man, unfazed, continued.

Someone less important to the tribe's safety would locate the beast and report back to the elders, he explained. Only then would the proper hunting party be assembled. Next, while looking about the crowd with a slow pass, pausing for the most dramatic outcome, the crafty elder had added that when the time came, naturally Steadfast would lead the hunt.

This simple statement had a great effect on the assembly. The relief was obvious. Everyone, before so tense, murmured their agreement while bobbing their heads to each other.

Under such striking circumstances, Steadfast could not argue the point. His pride was at least satisfied, and he did see the wisdom in the elder's overall plan. He first nodded his consent, then gathered his family and left for his new duties.

The old one had then sought out Jargon. He had stated with his toothless mouth that the young caveman had been picked by the entire group of elders to investigate the strange, unknown beast.

This was a great honor for Jargon, and undeniably marked him as an up-and-coming member of the tribe.

Next, with a companion supplied by the elders, Jargon had traveled deeper into the vast forest than either of them had ever gone before, searching for the mysterious creature that had never been seen. At long last, they had heard its piercing cries from a distance. Indeed, the strange noises it made were unlike anything the primitive pair had ever encountered before.

His companion, a huge but stupid giant of a man, was all for turning back. He was no warrior despite his great size. He was terrified by the outlandish sounds made by the creature, and by their unfamiliar location deep within the forest.

All that the pair was supposed to do, the giant had cried, was locate the illusive creature. They had done so. For the frightened mammoth of a man, that was enough.

He had begun to sob and babble. Jargon had calmed him down by offering the following plan: he, Jargon, would scout ahead, alone. His hulking confederate could then hang behind and make camp, while watching their rear and protecting their position.

The two could not go back, the young warrior had stressed, without even seeing the thing first. They had to at least lay eyes on it. There was no other viable choice.

The larger man had agreed, but he was uneasy.

Now, Jargon was running through the forest, most eager to inform the reluctant giant that he had spotted the obscure beast! With luck, the two of them could kill it themselves with no need of a further, delaying hunt. In doing so, Jargon hoped his reputation would be assured, and in an undeniable fashion.

As he ran through the forest unaffected by the whipping brush, Jargon's heart was pounding. He was excited, but his breathing was not labored. His air intake was rhythmic and deep, but drawn and expelled at a slow, determined pace.

All of his youthful senses, each one at peak performance, were wide open and fully attuned. He seemed aware of every little thing about him. This was one of his favorite feelings, but even he, verbose as he was, would be hard-pressed to describe it.

Jargon was now enjoying the primeval thrill of the chase.

Late in the day, Spencer was still working the pit, still using his pick on the wall of the excavation, but his heart wasn't in it. He was just holding it together, viewing himself a monumental failure. His marriage was over and his job was a bust, too.

He had been thinking, of all things, about his father. His father had been a bureaucrat, as had his father before him. In fact, as far back as anyone could remember, the men in Spencer's family had all been bureaucrats of one type or another.

Such a profession was a safe career. No going out on a limb there. His father had wanted him to be one, also.

"It was in the family's blood," he had said. He would grow into liking it, would learn to appreciate it as a vocation. But Spencer knew that he was no paper pusher.

No, he had always taken after his mother who was an artist and a good one, too. And Spencer had always thought that in some strange way, science could be just as beautiful as art. It could be just as elegant, and just as rewarding.

As in art, in science you could always take chances. You could make a statement. In science you could make a difference.

Some difference he was making now, Spencer thought, as he again swung his pick. This was no art. The man was in a daze, only going through the motions, and barely so at that.

He would have made a crummy paper pusher, too.

Then, the lone researcher found what he had been looking for, although he was unaware of it at first. The point of his pick became stuck in the red clay of the pit's wall, and Spencer tried to pull it free. Yet, the stubborn implement wouldn't budge.

Bending down, he began to work the head of the tool back and forth, trying to coax it out of the wall. Then with a grunt, he extracted it, causing a mass of clay to fall in the process. The force involved propelled him backward a few steps, spinning him around and almost causing him to lose his balance.

He caught himself in time to avoid falling, but only by a hair's breadth. He was angry, jarred from his malaise, but not surprised. Just what he needed, he thought as he turned around.

That was when he saw it, still embedded within the clay. Spencer was stunned at first, almost unbelieving, but it was undeniable and staring him in the face. This changed everything!

He thought over the situation, realizing that he had left his camera back at base camp. Should he expose his find now and document it later, or should he retrieve his camera first, and then film his entire procedure? Soon he climbed up to get his camera, but at the lip of the pit, he stopped to consider his options.

He didn't want to waste valuable time if he could help it. Was the camera really that important? Spencer was uncertain and anxious, and his heart was beating fast.

Even so, he felt better than he had in a long time. The pressure, before so oppressive, was off. He saw that his quandary was nothing in the bigger scheme of things.

Spencer sensed a strangeness then, as if he were experiencing déjà vu. He felt lightheaded and airy, but the feeling was not in itself unpleasant. It was quite the opposite in fact, although the man couldn't put his finger on it at first.

Then in a flash, he realized that he was enjoying himself. About time, he thought and he laughed aloud, experiencing something anew as he did so. It felt good.

At last, Spencer Hall was feeling the ancient thrill of the chase.

Jargon and the giant were hiding in the cover of trees, looking at the creature in a small clearing beyond. Jargon was all for chasing it down and killing it on the spot but the giant was scared and disagreed. What if it killed them instead?

The very idea seemed to unnerve the large man, and he clutched at an amulet about his thick neck for luck.

Jargon had seen this strange amulet many times before. The giant always wore it, hung by a short but stout rawhide cord. It was an almost rounded stone, about the size of small wren's egg, and it had the bright color of fresh blood.

One night, while sitting in the village around the campfire of the giant, Jargon had noticed a vivid green speck embedded deep within the red stone. Curious he had asked for a better look, but the big man, who was never without it about his neck, would have none of it. He was having none of it now.

He only wished to travel home to report what they had found. They could then return with greater numbers and kill the beast with ease. That was the plan, after all.

Jargon did not like this line. There was no glory for him there. He drew his stone knife and stated that he would go it alone.

With fear in his eyes, the giant reached out his beefy hand and grabbed the free arm of the smaller man, stopping him with an effective grip. Again the pair looked at the creature in the clearing. It was lumbering back and forth, its massive woolly head bent, as if it was looking for something along the ground.

Jargon was concerned that it might leave the area. The giant did not care if it did or not. With more hunters, they could track it at leisure no matter where it happened to go.

This reasoning impressed Jargon for he saw no valid argument against it. He also was much amazed that such precise formulation had come from the giant, who was not known for his abundant wits. Instead, the large, simple-minded man had merely surprised everyone by his abrupt arrival one day in the tribe's forest.

He was unable to explain his condition or location, but he had a good nature, and with his massive bulk he had proven himself very useful to the tribe. The elders had accepted him into their society at once. Since the giant had seemed to many as burly as a wild ox, almost overnight his name had become Moas.

However, no one had ever asked him his opinion on anything. The very idea would have been absurd, unthinkable. So it was disconcerting for Jargon to find out that he had formed a well founded one with such ease and clarity.

Jargon, known by all as a hothead, was nevertheless a proud fellow, and he did not like the predicament in which he now found himself. Yet he was powerless against the much larger, stronger man. With a stony face, he secured his knife.

The giant then let go of his arm. But after standing, the unpredictable young warrior dashed off toward the creature. Moas hesitated for just a second, and then he also raced down the steep hill, following at a short distance.

After some minutes of pacing back and forth in indecision, Spencer made up his mind. He turned towards his camp and camera but instead of moving he stopped and screamed. Jargon, leaping through the air, collided with him.

Both of them, now hollering, fell shrieking into the pit, plowing through Spencer's neatly stacked pile of artifacts as they did so.

Moas, running downhill too fast to arrest his great bulk, soon followed suit, and also fell into the deep excavation.

After landing, Spencer managed to roll away and scamper to one side of the gaping hole. At a slower pace, Jargon and the giant moved to the opposite side. Spencer's heavy coat and woolly cap had protected him in his fall, but now he saw to his horror that his makeshift ladder had also crashed to the floor of the pit.

Now he was trapped!

Spencer had no illusions, and he was not a brave man, he knew it. Judith had always called him a coward at heart, although she meant it in terms of his refusal to address the daunting personal problems between them. But this man was truly a coward, and now he was close to being paralyzed with real fear.

The three stood there, staring at each other, none knowing what to do next. Spencer moved first, and pulling off his cap, he mapped his skull with his long, thin fingers. His head was now hurting and he needed to check for possible injury.

Jargon saw that his elusive creature was just a man, although one wearing strange clothing not stitched from animal skins. Up close he didn't look so fearsome. He wasn't even armed.

The younger caveman looked to Moas. The giant appeared bored by the whole situation, leaning against the pit's edge with his arms crossed. He was staring up at the overcast sky above, seemingly uninterested in the other two men.

Spencer, mashing himself into the cool earth of the pit's wall, was desperately trying not to shriek. When Jargon attempted to communicate with gestures and grunts, he just dug his fingertips into the red clay behind him. This was beyond all belief.

Attempting to hold his already frayed nerves together, he started speaking to himself, saying in a whisper, "Don't scream, Spencer. Whatever you do, just don't scream." He did though, a few frantic heartbeats after the giant spoke to him.

While nodding at the young Jargon, the hulking Moas looked to the researcher and said, "Relax Doctor Hall, I never let him kill anyone this late in the day."

CHAPTER TWO

THE TRAVELER

If the morning were any indication, the rest of the day would be very hot and dry. Already thermal waves were rising above the dusty floor of the desert, and soon the temperature there would become too unbearable for anyone to stand. Still, a man alone and on foot, was traversing this harsh and unforgiving terrain.

The solitary man looked primitive in dress and weaponry, but not in bearing, as he continued, hiking in the growing heat. He was tallish and well muscled, and he traveled at what seemed to be a leisurely pace. This steady tempo was deceiving, however, as they were determined steps that he took.

He was unyielding, and never for a moment slowed his march.

He had been on the move since midnight to escape the relentless heat of his barren surroundings. He had drunk the last of his water before sunrise, as only a fool would have, and he was thirsty. Thirst and the desert was never a healthy combination.

Yet, the man knew that he must continue onward at all costs. He had a mission, an unending quest, and nothing would halt him. With adamant strides, one foot in front of the other, he advanced through the blistering and obstinate desert.

As he walked, sweat dripping as the heat only increased, he constantly scanned the bleak horizon arrayed before him. The man had seen no one for days, but that meant nothing. In this region, travelers had to be on their guard at all times.

He saw the nomads before they saw him, a small group packing up their evening camp. The Traveler could have evaded them but he didn't, he didn't even try. They might have water, he thought.

One of the band, an adolescent boy, spotted him as he approached and let out a warning cry. The solitary man slowed, but nevertheless moved ever closer. The Traveler saw there were six people in all, four men, the boy, and a woman.

A dozen paces away from them, he stopped his march. Then he held out his hands in what he thought was a non-threatening manner. He wished to be obvious that he wanted no trouble.

One of the nomads, an old man with a gnarled wooden staff stepped forward and asked of him, "Stranger?"

"Traveler," he answered him.

The nomads reacted not at all to this brief exchange. The newcomer looked to each of them in turn. He noticed that all six stared him in the eye, as if to read his possible intentions there.

They were a grim lot with few possessions, and from them the Traveler saw that life in the desert could be harsh. They were dressed in the same loose-fitting outfits that those in the area frequently favored, though perhaps theirs were more worn than most. Yet, even poor people of the desert took pride in the bright colors dyed into their plain, homespun cloth, and the usual rule-of-thumb followed was the brighter, the better.

In this vast and barren landscape, brilliant hues were a definite advantage, helping to avoid unpleasant encounters between hostile parties. They could be seen and recognized at great distances. Still, a glance at the faded clothing of this group was all the testimony needed to prove their dismal state.

The most striking thing about these nomads, perhaps a family, was how gaunt they appeared. Not that they were drawn or sickly looking by any means. Shifting his gaze between the four men, he saw that they were thin, but healthy.

He was relieved they didn't seem to be excited, for they could be a handful to deal with if things became interesting.

The Traveler then tried a more direct route.

"Have you any water?" he asked with bluntness, addressing the question to no one in particular.

The woman, who was the young boy's mother, responded but not to him. She reached out and touched the old man, whispering with urgency. The newcomer didn't catch her words, but it was obvious to him that she was wary.

The old man seemed uninterested in her, and again posed his original question, asking, "Stranger?"

By this time, the boy was standing next to the woman and the old man, but the other nomads had started to fan out in defensive positions. These three were armed with knives and spears, and stony faces. The atmosphere was tense.

"Yes, a stranger here," the Traveler answered. "I'm crossing this wasteland, as you are. Have you any water?"

The old man stepped closer, getting a better look. He had wild, grizzled gray hair. His eyes were almost hidden within deep wrinkles that grew even deeper as he smiled.

"Those are nice boots," he said, almost to himself.

The Traveler fought the urge to grab the knife hanging at his side. Instead, he gave no outward sign of concern. It was a bluff.

"I need my boots," he said as a fact.

"You need water, also?" asked the old man, still smiling.

"True," the Traveler conceded, "but in this desert I also need my boots." And then he quickly added, "Would you deny a peaceful man water, in this scorching heat? If so, just tell me, and I'll take my leave and bother you no more."

The younger nomads didn't like the tenor this conversation was taking, but deferring to their elder, the three did nothing beyond looking nervously at each other.

The Traveler tried another tack.

"I'm on a quest," he said, and he tapped for emphasis a bright, red charm that hung about his neck. If the old man had been closer he would have seen a vivid green speck embedded within the amulet. Yet, what he saw was enough.

This was a well-known tradition throughout the desert, and the old nomad knew it. People engaged in a quest often wore a token of some kind, as a tangible reminder of their pledge and duty. Upon completion of their burden, they were free to discard the symbol, but most kept them as a totem.

"Well then," the old man said without hesitation, "of course you shall have some water." He glanced over to one of the men, a tough-looking specimen. The other two adult males were standing their ground, awaiting events.

The designated man nodded to his elder, then slipped off a pouch he carried on his shoulder. The woman, disliking the transaction, nevertheless produced a small bowl from the sack that she carried. She handed it to the boy, and after the man poured from his pouch, the boy turned, smiled and offered the cup.

The Traveler took a deep breath and crossed over to him.

"Thank you," he said, reaching out for the water. He was very thirsty, his mouth so dry it hurt, but at first he did not drink the precious liquid. Instead, the weary man just looked down into the bowl now resting in his calloused hand.

Made of wood, the inside was inlaid with an eggshell of pearly white. Seeing that the water was crystal clear, the Traveler was amazed. Water found in the desert as a rule was brackish at best.

Trying but failing to savor the moment, he then drank. It was no more than a gulp, but it tasted delicious, and this was an odd thing, too. Desert water was renowned for its foul taste.

"More?" asked the old one, now leaning on his staff.

The handsome boy was excited, and not waiting for an answer, he then took the bowl for refilling.

"Thank you," the Traveler said again. He added, "I'm on a quest, so my name is Onus." This input got him no response.

Once more he accepted the bowl from the now beaming, brown-eyed boy. It was easy to see that the child was pleased with himself for having such an important task. Not yet a warrior, he would grow up fast in his vast desert home.

Onus returned his smile, asking, "Tell me now, where did you happen to come by this sweet water?"

After this brief exchange, the three younger nomads perked up and moved closer as the woman clutched at the thin boy, pulling him towards her. The old man abruptly ceased his smiling. He looked instead very hard and lean.

"No matter," he almost spat out. "You've had all you're going to get from us." He turned, facing away, and Onus could see that he had overstepped his welcome.

He drank the water down, and then held out the empty cup.

"I'm sorry," he said, "I didn't mean to," but the woman cut him off by addressing him for the first time.

"The water is a gift from the Great One," she almost screamed as she pushed the still-grinning boy behind her. The woman then leaned in and snatched the inlaid cup from him, placing the small vessel back into her sack. Only then did she look at the elder nomad and vigorously add, "You were wrong to give him any, Father, he does not even know of the Great One."

Again the elder turned to look at Onus. It was easy to see that the Traveler carried little of value beyond his boots. True, he was outnumbered, but he was fit and looked able to handle himself.

At last the old man said, "He's on a quest."

As if that settled the matter, the group next picked up their possessions and began moving on, heading off in the direction from which Onus had come.

The Traveler watched, but only for a moment. It was getting hotter, and he didn't know how far his ongoing trek would take him. He started again on his original route, and soon was back to his old and deliberate, unrelenting stride.

The temperature later became so intense that Onus was forced to seek shelter in the shadow of an immense outcropping of rocks. It was a few degrees cooler in the shade, but it didn't influence his comfort level much. Hot was hot.

While there, he caught several large lizards, by stabbing them at leisure with his homemade knife as they slowly lumbered by in the searing heat. After, the Traveler sucked out their warm blood, but he didn't eat them then. Instead, the reptiles were stored for later use in the pouch hanging at his side.

He slept some, but not long for it was too stifling. Comfort was not possible. He would awaken with a start, dripping sweat.

Again Onus pushed forward. To turn back now was not an option, for he was driven by his mission, and by the fact that he already had come so far. Turning around now would mean only his certain death in the desert, as well as failure.

Onus cursed the one he sought, the object of his quest, but he knew at the same time that he couldn't stop looking for him. To find this man was his singular task, and dereliction of his duty was not a viable choice. He continued on.

Hours later, after he had thought for the hundredth time how thirsty he was, he saw more nomads. Unlike his earlier encounter, this time they saw him first. The two men were almost on him when Onus spotted them, even though their vibrant clothing had flashed out against the bleak desert backdrop.

By now, the Traveler was so overcome by the relentless heat that he could not stop his determined walking. If he had, he would not have started again. He kept up his steady pace undeterred until he was face to face with the pair.

"Hold on there," said the bigger one he almost bumped into. "Even here in the desert we have manners, you know." His companion only nodded his assent.

"Forgive me," said Onus, as he wiped his sweaty brow, "but I'm so burned by the sun, I was not sure that you were real."

"Water," barked the big man, and water soon appeared in Onus' hands. It was the same clear, sparkling liquid as before, he noticed. The Traveler drank it down and then passed out.

Later he awoke, surprised to be cold. It was evening, and he was in the nomad's camp, their meager fire doing little to warm him in the growing desert night. He smelled something cooking.

Noticing that he was awake, the bigger nomad walked over and asked, "Are you feeling any better?"

"Much, thank you," Onus answered. He sat up. "Lucky you found me when you did," he added.

"Only a mad man crosses the desert with no water," said the second nomad, speaking for the first time. He was only a little smaller than his stocky cohort. He had walked over to the pair with a steaming bowl in his hand.

"I'm on a quest," said Onus in weak voice. The nomads looked at each other, but Onus looked only at the potential meal in the bowl. After sighting it, he realized just how hungry he was.

"Even so," said the big one, employing caution, "one should have sufficient water while crossing the desert."

Onus stared at the food. It was a stew, one of his favorite dishes, with copious amounts of steam rising off plentiful chunks of meat. The sight mesmerized him, but he stuck to the point.

"Yes," he said, "I should have taken more from the Great One before I began my journey through the desert."

The nomads, exchanging a glance, seemed relieved by this answer. After a nod from the bigger one, the smaller one gave the bowl to Onus who began to eat the stew with gusto. It was still warm but he dug in heedless, using his fingers.

"Very good," he said with his mouth full, and then he added in between his swallowing, "Excellent."

"Well, it's true," said the smaller nomad, amused, "after all, your lizards do give it some fine flavor."

Onus laughed aloud at this exchange, and warmed by the food he again fell into a deep slumber.

The next morning, the Traveler awoke refreshed. His companions were eating breakfast, which they shared with him. They also offered to give him more water for his trip.

It was obvious to all of them that Onus could use the water, but he was hesitant to accept any. They had done so much for him, and he didn't wish to impose on them further. The nomads understood his motivation, but again they made the offer.

"Take it," said the big one, pointing off in the distance. "The city of Arret is only one day's walk, but it's a hot day's walk." The smaller one nodded in confirmation that it was so.

Onus smiled, suddenly satisfied. Until that moment he hadn't known for sure the exact location of the famous desert city of Arret. The Traveler had surmised that he was close, but a slight error now would have meant a much greater one later, with who knew how much time wasted in the interim?

He had considered just asking them the true direction to the fabled city, but he hadn't. That request would have gotten him nowhere. The two nomads would not have told him anything, had they realized that he was unsure of the way.

That would have marked him as an outsider, a mystery, and someone to be avoided, maybe even feared. Fear in this region often meant fighting, sometimes bloodshed. Not this time.

Onus was relieved. The two desert natives had considerable bulk between them. Currently that fact didn't matter.

"No," the Traveler said, standing his ground. "I'll make it now, thanks to you." After shaking their hands, he turned and started walking, feeling better than he had in a long time.

The nomads soon headed off in the opposite direction.

Onus had always believed that the one he was seeking, the object of his quest, would be found in the fabled city of Arret. Under the circumstances, that made the most sense. At last, he was on the proper path to that legendary place.

Soon, Onus hoped, he would have his elusive man at last.

He hiked all morning through the vast wasteland, feeling invigorated. The still oppressive heat did not seem so unbearable to him, but at midday he forced himself to stop just the same, to husband his strength. After a short stay, however, restless and unable to postpone his quest any longer, Onus continued.

The determined Traveler was thirsty again as well as hungry, but not terribly so. Having come this far against all odds, he knew that it was only a matter of time before he made it now, no matter what might next happen. That was the bigger picture, where he kept his focus, and he was just too excited to be bothered by such seemingly trivial things as food or water.

After hours of hiking, he saw the outcroppings of the opulent city of Arret. Sprawling settlements complete with lush trees unheard of in the desert, surrounded the vaulted, breathtaking walls of the great citadel. Approaching the outer districts, he soon came to a small flower garden bordered by a low stone boundary.

"Welcome stranger," greeted a short, well-dressed, rotund man. He was standing in the center of the tidy plot, minutely inspecting the work of his grounds man. He then called out for one of his house servants to bring forth some food.

"Come now, friend," the little fat man said, while pointing, "sit here by the fountain and rest yourself."

The low, well-laid garden wall was more decorative than functional. Onus stepped over it, and the two men crossed the brief distance to a pleasant courtyard just past the well-tended and fully blooming flowers. The man, moving with grace, was at ease as he led Onus to a sturdy-looking rock bench, built with pride into the edge of an elevated pool of water.

The pool was conveniently placed in the cool shade under a trellis that cut down on the sun's relentless rays. Located just outside a fine, stout house, the wooden trellis was covered by thick and twisted interwoven vines. The vines themselves were brimming over with small, burgundy flowers, and these perfumed the air with a light and delicate sweet-smelling aroma.

Onus crossed over and gratefully sat upon the offered bench. He then noticed the pool was in actuality a fishpond, complete with a small waterfall. Several large inhabitants, brilliant and multicolored, slowly glided about the enclosure.

He had just traversed, at considerable personal peril, land bereft of any water to speak of, and now he gazed down with envy at fish that were literally surrounded by it. The weary Traveler was tired, dry and parched, and he noticed with interest that the pond was about the size of a large bathtub. Onus had never before been jealous of fish, but that fact had just changed.

The sociable man asked, "You have come far, my new friend?" He was smiling as he handed Onus a mug of water just poured from a nearby pitcher. The cool liquid was clear and sparkling, and tasted just as sweet as it had before.

"Yes," answered his visitor, thanking the little man. "I'm on a quest, so my name is Onus. I have just crossed the entire desert to come to the beautiful city of Arret."

At this pronouncement, the man beamed, adding, "We are lucky, it's true. Our city's patron, the great god Rebus, smiles on us, granting abundant water for all our needs." He then placed the pitcher beside Onus and continued his narration.

"I myself," he stated with a theatrical sweep of his arm, "am in charge of all the shipments of water to the many farms north of Arret, and so my name is Lading." He took a seat across the bench and added, "We are indeed lucky. The great Rebus is a wonderful blessing to all that live here, thank all the gods."

Onus smiled and nodded, looking around admiring Lading's grotto. It was built of perfectly stacked sand-colored stones. The place, not overly large, was very beautiful.

"Yes," the Traveler agreed, "the great Rebus is most generous, and all should be grateful." He then refilled his mug and toasted his host. "Thank all the gods," he added.

As they chatted, Lading twirled a jeweled ring on his short, plump finger. The little, fat man was prosperous and proud, and he was more than happy to extend hospitality to a stranger in his beloved city. Soon the house servant arrived with a platter of food, abundantly loaded with fresh fruit and sweetmeats.

Lading, with apologies, left to attend to his duties. The night shift at the north loading docks was soon to begin, and he was needed. Onus stood and thanked his host for his kindness.

Left alone, Onus ate at a slow pace, thinking. He had learned much in the desert, and even more since he had arrived in the city's suburbs. The people of Arret were kind, and unlike those that he had met before in the area, seemed happy and content.

The water that came from the city gave them security against a harsh life in the desert. Now he knew that it was given by the Great One himself, who resided within the magnificent metropolis. Without knowing it, Lading had also given the weary Traveler another piece of valuable information.

It seemed to Onus very probable that the god Rebus, the giver of water, of life itself in the desert, was in fact the same man that the Traveler had been seeking. He was, Onus believed, the very object of his quest. At least he hoped so, as he didn't wish to think of what would happen next if this were not the case.

Onus soon finished his meal, satisfied with his progress to date. When the house servant arrived to collect the platter, he carried a bucket of warm water and a towel. With them, the Traveler wiped the grit and grime from his pores.

Afterward, Onus walked out into the cool desert evening, but this time only a short distance to seek out a suitable place to sleep. Tomorrow he would rise with the sun and investigate his theory further. It was almost over, he hoped.

The Traveler had come so far, against all odds, and at last he now felt himself very close. He had to smile at the irony of the situation, knowing that only time would tell if his assessment were true. To him that was very ironic, indeed.

The next morning, Onus found Arret a bustle of activity. He entered the city proper through a large gate crowded with busy people. All were bent on carrying out their hectic schedules, and no one there seemed to take any notice of him.

Trying hard not to appear the country bumpkin, the Traveler observed much. Soon he surmised that the entire society was dominated and driven by the water. It was drawn with great ceremony from several stations placed about a circular lake located in the city's center, and from there it was taken away by slaves to various storage areas for later shipment and use.

Handling the water was a big task and those that gathered and dispensed it were not the only people concerned. The rest of the citizenry, shopkeepers and storeowners, planners and tradesmen, all served the ones that tended the water. It provided them a vast commerce, as well as a purpose to their lives, and everyone living there seemed to be in some way involved.

The lake was not large, just an acre or two, and unfed by any river. Seeing how much water was being drawn, Onus knew that the precious liquid must spring from an underground source. This only confirmed his growing suspicions.

Becoming excited in spite of himself, he headed next to the seat of power, the city's opulent temple complex located on the far side of the lake. This was identified with ease by its imposing grand facade. Onus was almost positive that the one he sought, the object of his quest, would be found residing there.

As he walked toward the complex, he noticed the temple's inner sanctum was suspended over the lake itself, held up by a huge central pedestal. Several long stairways placed about its periphery led up to it, collectively looking like the spindly legs of a giant spider. Lines of paired slaves were standing at the base of these stairways, awaiting their turn to climb the steps.

Each slave held a large, empty earthenware container. Once they had completed their transit, the slaves would enter the main chamber by twos, later leaving with their vessels filled. Onus presumed that the water thus received was viewed as distinctive, because the great god Rebus had doled it out himself.

The Traveler observed that while the process was continuous, it did take time to accomplish. Like clockwork, the paired slaves exited the room every few minutes, their jugs filled. Grunting under their new labor, the haulers then climbed down another stairway and dropped off their heavy burdens.

After crossing to their original position, the slaves picked up another clay vessel and patiently waited to repeat their, long prescribed and directed procedure.

All the while, priests dressed in rich, multicolored vestments indulged in an elaborate blessing of the water. Meanwhile, hordes of bureaucrats, also well dressed, were looking on. These functionaries scribbled notations on large clay tablets, keeping detailed records of everything that transpired.

After the ritual was ended, different slaves hauled the water away. The whole thing was very organized. Years of planning were involved, maybe even centuries.

Before walking very far, the Traveler thought of a scheme to enter the temple's inner sanctum. To carry out his plan, he stopped by one of the many trees planted about the lake, acting as if he were pausing only to take in the myriad activities of the city. Then he looked around, making sure he wasn't being observed.

He next climbed the short wall that bordered the lake and slipped into the cool, clear water. Remembering Lading's fish, he realized that they had nothing on him now. Then he took a great breath, and swam underwater the entire distance to the base of the pedestal holding up the towered temple, soaring above.

The swim was so utterly refreshing that Onus thought about a longer soak, but only for a moment. He dismissed the fleeting idea, for this was serious business. The man was on a mission, and his unchanging Mandate was crystal clear, as was the lake's water.

With determination, he climbed up the pedestal into the very heart of the city. Once there he paused, dripping behind a marble column, watching as a new pair of slaves approached the inner sanctum of the fabled city of Arret. They stopped before entering, waiting for the signal, he learned.

This was a resonating, but muffled sound of an inner gong being struck. As the rumbling tone slowly diminished, the waiting slaves marched in. A few minutes later they both left employing another door, each now carting a fresh supply of water.

Onus then sneaked inside, rushing the exit before it closed.

The Traveler found that he was in an enormous, opulent room, with awe-inspiring tapestries hanging about the walls. There was also an imposing throne placed to one side of the vaulted chamber. Resting on a dais, it was raised above the polished stone floor.

His senses were assaulted by the pungent smell of incense hanging in the air, and slits of sunbeam radiating from rectangular openings in the ceiling high above slashed the room in stark contrasts of light and shadow. In the very center of the place, he saw a solitary man who was dressed in beautiful clothing and bathed in a bright pool of sunshine. He stood next to two large earthenware jugs, the same type as the slaves carried.

Humming to himself, he was engaged in filling one with water, using a length of ordinary green garden hose.

"Son of a bitch," Onus said in a loud, clear voice. As the sound of it resonated in the vastness of the room, the man in the bright sunlight glanced up, a puzzled look on his face. Their eyes met.

The Traveler smiled. Success. He had his man at last.

After a beat, he added, "Hey there, brother. Long time no see. Somehow, I just knew it would be you."

CHAPTER THREE
THE CRONE

The echoes in the hall were so deafening, the girl was almost in pain from the piercing noise. As she and her escort dashed along the corridor, she covered her ears with her hands to smother the sharp blasts. This action did help, but not much, for the thunderous echoes were relentless as well as loud.

The girl was wearing a long dress, very plain, and a short, ruffled hooded cape. Both were made from light cloth that produced little sound as she moved. Conversely, her companion was armored in jingling chain mail and creaking leather, with a long sword and a short knife, both clanking, and all of this gear announced their approach as they passed through the castle.

These were the normal sounds of a soldier, she knew, but the echoes in the hallway were from the warrior's heavy boots rapping against the gray stone floor. The pounding rhythm, increasing in tempo as they hurried past, reminded her of unrelenting drum beats. The booming tones reverberated off the hall's rough masonry walls and beamed ceiling with a resounding staccato.

Working hard to keep up with her short but stout companion, she was relieved the hallway was not a long one. Soon, they would be through the worst of the deafening noise. However the man beside her seemed unaffected by the din.

In fact, he was becoming more determined with his strides the closer they came to their destination, adding his puffing breath to the mix. As their speed increased, his footfalls enhanced the echo's volume. Then, becoming aware of her discomfort, the old soldier went faster still, to sooner end her torment.

At last, the two of them came to the end of the lengthy hallway, and the deafening echoes ended. As the pair turned and climbed the narrow staircase there, the wooden steps they encountered forced the excited soldier to slow his frantic pace. The typical jingling and creaking sounds made by the man's uniform resumed, but now accompanied only by his scraping footsteps, with several well-placed grunts thrown in for good measure.

The two began to hear muffled voices as they neared the small anteroom atop the staircase. The voices were loud and heated for they carried through the heavy double doors from the great room beyond. Moreover, by the time the girl and her escort finished their climb, both of them recognized the loudest one.

The most vehement and booming by far, although distorted by the great oaken doors, belonged to the strong and passionate young Duke of Fervent. Handsome and vain, he was indeed much younger than the old man now sitting on the throne, but of late many believed that he would make the better sovereign. The old king's current policy was on the whole disliked, and the young duke's family line did give him a legitimate claim to the kingdom.

The duke's now dead grandfather, the imperiled realm's late monarch, was the present king's sire, but it was Fervent's father who had been the old king's eldest son.

Upon the death of Fervent's grandfather, with the country at war on all sides, the current king had usurped the throne from the infant prince, his own nephew. Of course, this action was distasteful to say the least, and was frowned upon at the time. But it was deemed necessary by all, for the Empire of Am-Rif needed a strong warrior to lead its beleaguered fighting forces.

True, the young prince's father, the former king's first-born heir, had been much beloved by all, but he was long dead on the field of battle. Such slaughter, unending to this day, was a constant occurrence. And all could understand how a baby monarch under such dire circumstances was unthinkable.

The infant prince had been granted a dukedom, and now, these many years later, he was strong and well past his majority. He was viewed by many as courageous, and so to some he looked better every day because of the current, widespread turmoil. The once powerful State of Am-Rif was now experiencing a deep crisis, and the duke was for some the secret, unspoken choice for king.

He was untried, but all knew the failings of the cruel man they had now, and many would not shed a tear if the vigorous young nobleman replaced him. Under the present circumstances, any change would be welcomed by most of the beleaguered citizenry. Yet, neither the girl nor her escort held this treasonous view, as both supported the current sovereign.

Having completed his duty as guide and safe voucher, the soldier turned and pulled on his gauntlets for effect. He smiled at the girl with one bushy eyebrow cocked in question. She knew that he was interested in her royal audience.

As the commander of the king's tower forces he was overworked and always underappreciated, but as a surviving veteran of many a bloody campaign, he still knew a good fight brewing when he saw it coming. He also knew this girl could take it, and more. She confirmed this by returning his sly smile.

She liked this tough, old man, a hardened professional by any standard. In the last year, she had seen him on many such occasions, and always he had accompanied her on this same trek. Although she did not know him well, she did know he was ever busy, yet in each instance he had taken the time to walk with her when he could have assigned another of lesser rank in his stead.

"Once again, thank you very kindly, Captain," she said.

Tonight the captain would have liked to follow her inside, to see for himself what would happen next, but now he only nodded his head and grunted in acknowledgment. Still smiling, the old soldier then turned and descended the staircase without further reply. He would hear soon enough, he knew.

The girl watched him go, but only for a moment. She had other business. She turned and faced the far side of the small anteroom.

The two royal guards stationed there, like bookends to the great double doors, stood to attention. In the last weeks they or their comrades had seen this girl many times, and all knew well their duty. The standing orders were clear, and the girl would be admitted promptly, no matter what time of the day or night.

It still amused the girl, a young woman in truth, how some within the castle perceived her. All there were aware of her unique service to the king, and while all were curious, most acted aloof and somewhat awed by her, young as she was. Looking at the guards, she was not surprised they did not meet her gaze.

It was all so silly, she thought, but at the same time the girl knew that it was all very serious, as well.

The muffled but ardent voices within the room were yet conversing. Waiting for any pause in them, the girl knew, was useless. There was not a better, more opportune time, nor would there ever be, there never was.

She took a brief moment to arrange her simple cape and smooth her long, golden hair. Then the girl bobbed her head staring not at the two men there, but at the ornate doors towering before her. The guards opened them as always, without the benefit of a knock, and the girl strode boldly into the room.

Unlike her previous audiences within the king's chambers, empty save a retainer or two, this time the vaulted enclosure was crammed to capacity, packed with soiled and exhausted-looking nobles. All wore full battle dress, including weaponry, and all bore with pride their family's crest upon their haggard tunics. She couldn't help but notice that many of them were bloodied.

The Duke of Fervent had been caught in mid-sentence, and he turned as all the rest of them did, to look at her when she entered. He soon backed away with a nod of his noble head, to grant her easier access to the royal presence. The young woman acknowledged this with a nod of her own, delivered while crossing the large chamber to stand alone before the throne.

"Well," barked the seated king as the girl curtsied, adding in a deep bow. "What news bring you, lass? Speak."

The room had fallen silent to hear her reply, but it exploded in low, agitated comments when she answered, "Not yet, Your Majesty." And then, over the increasing buzz, she added in a louder voice, "But soon, Your Highness. Very soon."

"My King, this is madness," cried the charismatic young duke, grateful to have an opening once again to state his impassioned case. He crossed the royal chamber to stand before one of the room's large, arched windows. He didn't like what he saw.

Pointing out in the distance, he said, "The city is cut off and under siege, our supplies past running out."

He turned to face the king and the girl, continuing, "By all the gods, attack is now the only true option, Sire, yet we must hold, by your command, and take losses that we can ill afford."

He again looked out through the large, hand blown glass panes of the windows, adding under his breath, "And all the while pulling valuable fighting men from the ramparts, to use as nothing more than moles and gophers."

This line caused some in the assemblage to smile, although no one standing there dared laugh aloud.

"Digging and more digging, the situation is intolerable," the young duke added. "My Liege, we are bleeding and under horrendous assault while holes are everywhere dug, and we do not attack. Time is precious, and swiftly slipping away."

The girl knew that no one in the kingdom believed in the value of the holes. All in the city were dumbfounded by the king's bizarre dictum in this regard. Many in the population were frightened, concerned for the king's very sanity.

She saw that several young nobles, representing with bravery what was left of their family's fighting men, agreed with the duke's

53

grim assessment. In faith she could not blame them, for their great houses had been whittled down by years of gruesome war, and many of their fathers and elder brothers already had fattened the endless casualty lists. First with the old king and then with this one, who himself had grown old in the staggering effort, the years of unending death in battle had continued unabated.

The Empire of Am-Rif, once so vigorous and far-flung, in truth no longer existed. The kingdom itself was now in peril. The besieged city was literally all that was left of it.

The girl was surprised by how young some of the nobles standing there were, with a few of them being only boys. None of them knew what was possible given time, and how could they? They had never experienced a single day of peace.

Sadly, it was too true, for there never had been any present to see. Yet they did see this young duke. With all being old enough to die, some there liked what they saw.

Fervent was well aware of this unmistakable fact, and he used it to his advantage. The dynamic duke decided to hold his stance before the largest, arched window. It framed him well, and added to his effect as he continued his speech making.

"We dig and dig, My King, under constant barrage, against all known wisdom," he said, his strong voice booming throughout the room, "and all on the word of this wench's old mother."

The king said nothing to this. What was there to say? It was the truth and all in the room knew it.

But this young duke was not finished, by far.

He pointed his ornately gloved finger at the girl. All eyes fell on her. When Fervent spoke again it was in a slow cadence, almost spitting the words for a fuller result.

"All on the word of the Crone," he said with heavy sarcasm. Of course, he had stated these views numerous times before, to the king as well as many others, so all knew his leaning. But never before had any seen such drama, and the great room fell silent.

The Duke of Fervent was pleased with the reception his blunt assessment had on the occupants within the vaulted, beamed chamber. Gazing about he saw many there were spellbound. Holding out his arm with its steady digit aiming at the girl, he was expert at looking determined and heartfelt.

In truth, Fervent cared not a whit for the lot of his soldiers. For that matter, he cared not for the peasants or even for the nobles. In fact, this duke cared for nobody of a lesser station, which in his exalted case was almost everyone.

All he cared about was sitting his arse on that royal chair before him, or perhaps one more suitable to his majestic person. He belonged there. He was, after all, the rightful king.

True, his uncle had no direct heirs, and the duke would one day inherit the throne. Yet, the current sovereign, ancient as he was, showed no signs of dying with convenience anytime soon. And because the young royal still lacked the allies needed to take back the throne, he was forced instead into play-acting the part of the faithful vassal to the tired old man.

He was good at it, too. Fervent cut a dashing figure striding to and fro upon the works, barking orders left and right, but the duke knew that he was safe enough upon the ramparts. The chances of death there, for him at least, were scant.

The scheming royal could always leave if things progressed badly, to report in person to the king. The real dying, Fervent was well aware, came in open conflict upon the battlefield, where no quarter was given and none was asked. Yes, on the bloody field in the heat of fierce action, it was ever possible to die with alacrity, as had his own, long-absent, butchered father.

That was why this particular duke had never fought in an open, pitched battle. Neither had he served in a prolonged land campaign. He chose instead to remain detached, and always he had made certain, to linger at the king's side.

There, dispassionately but from afar, he had merely observed the never ending, unfolding carnage, adding to the contest only his choice comments on the current action.

The young Duke of Fervent did know that rebuffing an extended siege was quite another thing, however.

Still, he was not afraid of dying in the event of a breach in the city's wall. He knew that in such an instance, he could always dicker with the victors, and that a ransom of some description could be arranged if the wall did wane. That was the standard transaction, at least for one of his exclusive and lofty class.

Therefore, this duke cared not how many fools perished. It was no matter in the least to him. The more the merrier would be his stand, if he ever even thought about it.

They could all dig holes till Judgment Day if only it got him what he wanted. Once he was king, he could negotiate something or other with the enemy, to be a friendlier and more pliable ally or some such rubbish. And, if Am-Rif fell with Fervent not yet on the throne, he planned to use this line as suasion on the victors, when the time arrived to arrange for his ransom.

A vassal king was a king nonetheless.

Still holding his rigid stance, the duke looked to the girl and was surprised that she met his stare with bold determination. Strange he had not noticed before just how pretty she was, with great blond curls surrounding her high cheekbones and piercing green eyes. She held herself well for a commoner, he saw.

Normally Fervent prized a thing of beauty, especially a woman of lowborn status. They could be used at will and discarded with ease. Now he saw that this one was haughty as well.

That was just the way he liked them, at least at first. It would be an exciting escapade to teach this wench her proper place. He would amuse himself much by doing so.

The young royal then had the distinct feeling that the girl knew exactly what it was that he was thinking, for he could see it in those big green eyes. For just a moment this caused concerned, but then he thought, so much the better. If she knew what was coming, he would enjoy himself all the more.

The Duke of Fervent then dropped his arm and turned his head to face the king. His stance was flawless. Most of the assembled nobility had been awed by his performance.

"Always the Crone," he said, looking appropriately solemn.

"The Crone is a true subject," answered the hard-pressed ruler, loud enough for all present to hear.

The old king was seated while all others in the room stood, each of them awaiting his pleasure. His throne was just a plain, unadorned chair, but it was a stout one, and built well. To serve the royal preference, it had been placed upon a raised dais, only slightly elevated to accommodate several steps.

A normal man sitting there would have been eye level to those standing, but this majesty was tall as well as old. The king looked down on all before him, back straight as he sat. His stance was flawless also, dignified and regal.

But he was tired, and wished only to shed his heavy battle dress. It was similar to what the others wore, save a small but stylish crown placed over his helmet that elegantly conveyed his station. Yet the old king now seemed exasperated with his upstart nephew, and he looked to the floor rather than meet his eye.

"No," replied the duke, continuing, "she lies," and those in the room who agreed with him murmured their assent. But most of the men there were older than this brash young duke. It was honor, not words that meant the most to them.

To a man they were strong and brave, but they were not great thinkers. The exacting details were unimportant. They wished only to be told what needed to be done.

All would then know their duty and carry it out no matter the outcome or consequences. Still, there were the damned holes to consider. Of late, they were everywhere.

But the king was sly, and always thinking. He had to be. He looked up, and waited to see if such an accusation of high treason against the Crone was in fact the truth, or just wild speculation.

"She lies," again stated the impassioned duke, stepping closer and adding, "and with her lies, by all the gods, she buys more time for the enemy. The old Crone deals only in folly. Her sweet words are tender, but stink like rotted flowers."

The king now realized that no telling evidence was forthcoming against the old woman. He stared his nephew in the face. At this, the duke dropped his head in a curt bow.

The currently besieged monarch was well aware that the situation was desperate, that tempers were short and growing shorter. But he also knew that the nobles needed him, at least as things now stood. He bent them to his royal will.

None could deny it, he was an imposing figure facing them, sitting still as chiseled stone. His long arms were thrust out before him as he gripped the throne, resembling the front legs of a reclining lion. Only his piercing eyes were moving, scanning the throng, and demanding its attention by his very bearing.

"The Crone is like the ash tree," the somber sovereign lectured the assembly, "she is small and twisted but tenacious and strong." The nobles understood this observation, and agreed with it. Again they murmured their concurrence.

"Like the ash tree, depending on its use, her fruit may be either deadly or sweet, and so her name is Sorbus," the king added, employing the genus of that astringent plant.

He then looked to the girl. Time was running out, there was no denying it. Everyone there knew it.

By the king's demeanor, the duke now knew that he was beaten for the present. Still, he persisted, to save face with the assembled nobles and to throw more questions on his uncle and his royal prerogative. He again turned to the window.

"At least I must have the diggers back to the wall, My Liege," he said, feigning despair. "I must have them to protect against the coming onslaught, and now, I beg of you, as later may be too late. By all the gods, it must be so."

"Enough," said the weary king, hearing his fill. He raised his hand for emphasis. "I am unmoving, and so my name is Invar."

All eyes in the room then fell to the girl standing before the throne. She normally spoke well, hence her present calling, but now she could not find the proper words. She thought of all that was at stake here, and she thought of her dear mother, Sorbus, the old distorted woman that everyone called the 'Crone.'

Of course, she was not the girl's real parent, but Sorbus was the one and only mother the child had ever known. While just a babe, sickly and near death, the girl had been given to the Crone, in hopes the ancient woman could save her young life. She did, using her vast knowledge of illness and healing.

While growing, the girl was unaware that the Crone was shockingly, physically different from other people. But Sorbus, even with her bent back and wrinkled, toothless face, had always been a loving and tender parent to her. And the girl had always cherished her beyond what mere words could convey.

Things were simpler then, before her mother had begun her years of service to the king. Together they had lived free and unimpeded in a crude but snug hut deep within the wood. Constructed of stones and mud with a sod roof, it had been located on the edge of a beautiful glade by a lazy stream the girl had loved.

In this uncomplicated place they had lived a happy life, with not a care in the world as well as she could remember.

Now and then, people of the forest would come to the glade by the stream, leery, even fearful of the Crone, but also seeking what only she could give. Sorbus had long been known as a healer and a wise woman, rich in knowledge the average person lacked. The old woman was an expert concerning herbal remedies, and those she always unselfishly helped held her in the deepest respect.

59

As the young girl grew, she realized that Sorbus was in large part simply a good cook, and that a sick, ill-fed person often got well with rest and plenty of hearty soup inside them.

The child had quick wits, and soon she had discovered from the Crone all the differing plants of the wood. She learned these lessons well. After a time, she was gathering every component needed by her mother to ply her healing and tasty ways.

Yet what the girl remembered most from those tender and bygone days were the stories. They had started early on, when she was very young. Sorbus had always amused her with all manner of fantastic tales of great kings and high conquest.

Episodes of what they had done and how they had acted had entertained her for many a carefree hour. After a time, the girl could recite them all. It had been an easy thing to do, for she had loved these exciting stories, and her simple life in the forest had lent itself to daydreaming the time away.

Now that she was grown, things were not so simple anymore.

"How much longer must I hold, child?" the king asked her, and all present awaited the girl's reply. Yet she didn't know how to answer him in truth while also serving her mother. He had nerves of hammered steel, but the angry nobles being chewed to bits daily could not last indefinitely, honor or no.

"My Liege," the girl said with her head bent, but she could not continue for she had not the proper words to convey her thoughts. Still, she had to be convincing. There was no other way.

"Good King Invar," she began once again, but looking up at him the girl was stopped once more.

She had known this man since her childhood. Yes, she remembered the day that he had first come with desperation to her mother, at their small hut in the wood. The great king had been pitiful then, a far cry from what he had wished.

The dejected royal had arrived quite alone, for all his fancy retainers had abandoned him. After acquiring the throne through ruthless manipulation, he could do nothing with it save run it further into the ground. The desolate despot had pleaded at great length with Sorbus for her invaluable assistance.

That part the young girl remembered well.

Help me, he had begged of her for long days on end. It was not possible do it alone was his bitter, unending song. At last, the king had broken down and cried, and this the girl had never forgotten.

She recalled that occasion with ease, even though it was now many years in the past. For it had been at that very moment that the girl had realized the truth. However, at the time she could not foresee the hidden import of the situation.

She could not know then of the great changes to come, neither in her life nor the life of her dear mother, but the truth of the matter was revealed to her once the king had wept.

The girl knew then that the wonderful stories she had loved so much, all the stories of kings and kingdoms, of great battles fought and greater victories won, her stories, the stories of her mother, were not just silly legends told to pass the time away.

She knew then that the stories were, in fact, real tales of what would occur, and she knew as well that the Crone had seen them all, even before they had transpired.

The king had traversed a long distance, alone and defeated, and at length he had cried real tears, just as in her stories.

Sitting there, all these years later, was a powerful man before them. King Invar's kingdom might have been in peril, but he was a monarch to be reckoned with just the same. It had taken much time and hard effort, but nonetheless it had happened, just as the stories related to the girl had foreshadowed.

The old Crone had indeed seen it all, and told the tale. Sorbus had known of how they would come and what then would occur. Yet, they were not just innocent fables now, for all of it was indeed happening, and with all too bloody an abandon.

She looked about the large, vaulted chamber and saw desperate men standing there with real fear on their faces. This was life and death, no doubt about it. Everything was at stake here.

The king must not give up, no matter what, not when they were so close. Not when they had come so far. Not now.

It would happen. She knew it would. It had to.

It had been her favorite story.

"Soon," she told her sovereign.

Just then, a commotion was heard outside. The massive wooden doors were opened and a smiling man, a common peasant, burst into the assembly. His escort, the old captain of the guard, was left standing on the landing with his chain mail gloves resting on his hips and his generous eyebrows raised in wonderment.

Without words, the girl asked the man the most important question. He responded by winking at her as he crossed into the crowded chamber. Clothed simply without armor, but with a plain and battered soldier's helmet tucked under his arm, he was still smiling as he went down to one knee.

"King Invar," he said, "thank all the gods, we have found it."

Gasps of surprise escaped from the nobles in the room, but the old monarch just sat with a blank expression on his royal visage.

Stunned, he stared in numb silence at the kneeling peasant.

The man was a lowborn commoner, but in the last year he had addressed the king many times. He had never thought, even in his wildest dreams that this would ever occur, for he had not been raised to think in terms of such lofty heights. Far from it, for he had been bastard born, and though that appellation held little real stigma in the kingdom, he himself had never forgotten the fact.

True, it had made no great difference in his life, save in the law of inheritance, but it had grated nonetheless. He was the son of a prosperous miller, but he would never own the mill. Luckily for him, his father turned out to be a kind and loving man, and the growing boy always had been acknowledged and consistently fed, something of which most could not boast.

His dream in life, therefore, his only lofty ambition had been to own a mill as his father did, the better to continue eating well.

As a lad, working for his father he had labored hard, learning well the various operations involved in the trade. Years later his father, falling sick, turned over to him the day-to-day running of the business. No facet of the operation had escaped his notice.

He had proved himself to be an able administrator. The mill had flourished. However, sad to say, his father had not.

The man soon died, and ownership then passed to a legitimate son. The young miller's dreams had been dashed, but not his will. He had made immediate plans to move on.

There had been no question. He was a simple man, but not a fool. He would start from scratch if he had to, and be glad about it, rather than work hard only to make another prosperous.

But the stepbrother's mother, the new widow, knew a good thing when she saw it, and knew as well her own son had no head for business. She had wanted the mill to continue running, and the profit therein, to continue to flow. This meant that the bastard must stay on, for he ran the place after all, and did so very well.

She persuaded him to hold his stance by an outright gift of half the concern, for half-ownership of a working mill was much better than owning all of one that didn't produce, and she knew his pride would accept nothing less. She also gave him the promise of a free hand, by agreeing to keep out of the business end of the whole operation. The bastard had been astounded at the offer, and he had with great eagerness accepted her proposition.

By doing so the peasant had achieved his life's only true desire, and so his name then became Apex.

Later, the king, finding his forces besieged and cut off, was impressed with this commoner's work ethic and administrative abilities. He then placed Apex over all of the city's bakeries, a position of vast importance. This was because bread was the only staple for most citizens during the terrible siege.

At last, the Crone had raised him further still.

Of late, the hard-working Apex had preferred the simplicity of the mill or bakery, but no longer.

The nobles and soldiers, calling him 'that bastard,' had scoffed as he had directed the various crews of diggers. They would not scoff now, and no one in the city ever would again. The Crone had been factual, and they could all go to hell.

True, he had not believed at first. He had only carried on under orders from the king and the old woman, but he had not thought anything tangible would come of it. Now he knew better.

Yet the girl had known. She always had known the true state of affairs. Meeting with her day by day for the Crone's latest instructions, the beautiful girl often had tried to convince him, to bolster him when he needed it, and she had been correct.

He would be a powerful man now with the girl by his side, and all because of the gnarled old Crone, Sorbus.

Apex stood in pride before the king. He may have been of low birth, but now he held his head high. He had justifiable reason.

"We have found it," he repeated. "We have found the Fortress of Forecastle." At this news, pandemonium broke.

The nobles screamed out in joy. Some walked over to slap him on the back, congratulating him on a job well done. This levity ceased once the king stood.

He was a tall man anyway, but standing atop the raised platform that contained his throne, he seemed immense.

"Show me," he commanded the peasant.

All trouped, en masse, to the lip of the newest hole. One of many scattered throughout the city, this example had just been dug in the castle courtyard. Between soldiers holding blazing torches, they descended freshly carved, crude steps.

64

Next they passed through a set of enormous metal doors that had been newly broken open by the bastard baker's diggers. They continued down a corridor to yet another set of doors, also large and imposing. Here the girl advised the assembly that all must hold fast and await the arrival of the Crone.

The nobles balked at this, but the king silenced them.

The Fortress of Forecastle was real, the Crone indeed a true subject, and all of them would wait, he decreed.

At this point, Apex and the daughter of Sorbus, who were standing on either side of the old king, looked at each other and smiled. The pair had worked diligently of late, and now both were well satisfied. However, the young Duke of Fervent was upset, and this was not his normal, collected nature.

He had never believed in the many promises of the Crone. In fact, he had based all his actions thus far on that very premise. At this juncture, he had no other to fall back on.

"What is this witchery?" he asked, visibly distressed, while looking about the damp, underground enclosure.

They all began then to speak of the mysterious fortress. Who built it and when? How does the Crone know of it?

What ancient secrets does it possess? Was the stronghold a gift from the gods? If so, why, to what hidden purpose?

Many of the nobles, much as the young royal, were uneasy standing there, surrounded by the eerie torchlight.

"I feel no good can come of this, My King," the now agitated duke stated with displeasure, but a voice, strong yet obviously old, answered him from behind the crowd.

"Not so, young Fervent," it said.

The Crone, repulsive to see, had arrived at last. The densely packed group of nobles and guards were startled, and they parted with alarm to give her access and entrance to the king. Only then, with the aid of a stout walking stick, did the old, bent woman shuffle to the head of the waiting assembly.

She was a small person, hunch-backed with masses of stringy gray hair protruding from beneath her plain peasant's wimple. Her blanched face was overly wrinkled, and her eyes were mismatched, with one squinted almost shut while the other, bloodshot, was opened overly wide. Her toothless mouth twitched often, as if she were talking to herself, with spittle always near spilling out of it to drool over her wart-covered chin.

"The fortress shall grant us much, and all of it favorable," she boldly said as she produced a set of keys from a string about her neck. Making a selection, the Crone unlocked one of the great doors but she turned to the throng before opening it. All present were spellbound, each wondering what was next.

"The fortress is alive," she announced, "and not in need of torch light." She added the command, "Follow me, but touch nothing." Sorbus then spun around and entered the doorway.

All in the group save the Crone were dumbfounded to see that the underground Fortress of Forecastle was bathed in bright sunshine. The guards, sharply mumbling among themselves, extinguished their torches and left them in the corridor. Unperturbed, Sorbus next led them into the mysterious edifice.

As they walked along, everyone became aware of a noise, a low humming buzz that permeated the place. It sounded somewhat like a faraway beehive. It was a strange sound, both disconcerting in its newness, but also comforting in its constancy.

Through long halls and down endless stairways the Crone diligently led them. At each descending floor they passed through yet more corridors as if in slow motion, Sorbus shuffling on her ancient feet, with the stilted horde following wide-eyed behind. They constantly passed by innumerable doors, some of which contained large glass panels.

These doors, however, revealed nothing of the rooms beyond, for no sunlight was shining within them. The windows were

66

therefore rendered black as pitch, and each one acted as if it were a looking glass, depicting a distorted image of them as they passed. The whole scene was ghastly and foreboding.

No one had ever seen such strange wonders. Every door they encountered was labeled in neatly scripted, black lettering. The literate ones in the assembly noticed with distaste that the words there were written in a bizarre and unknown language.

At last, they stopped before a set of double doors that looked much the same as all the others they had seen, save these two were somewhat wider. Each contained a larger than normal glass and again the room beyond was dark as night. As the wary group slowly crowded about the Crone, the dim and contorted scene the windows reflected back at them was hellish looking.

The Crone was unconcerned with their reflection. She placed her grizzled hand on the door to the right and chucked to herself. Smiling, she then handed her staff to her daughter.

"Yes, yes," Sorbus said softly.

"Mother," asked the girl, breathless, "what is this place?"

Calmly unlocking the door with another key from the same string about her neck, the diminutive old woman then slowly pushed it open. She entered the room a few steps and stopped, bathed in the spilled hallway sunlight. Sorbus next cocked her hunched head about in rapid recognition, then turned with proud accomplishment and faced the now-crowded doorway.

The Crone looked into the bewildered faces there and clapped her bony, spotted hands together in joy at the sight.

They were all lost in the strangeness of it, she realized. They had no idea of where they were, nor the consequences thereof. Sorbus did though, for she knew everything.

At last it was happening. The game was afoot, no doubting it now. After a happy, satisfied cackle she answered the girl.

"This, my daughter," the old Crone said, holding out her thin, spindly arms, "was once my office."

PART TWO – BEFORE THE ENDING

CHAPTER FOUR
THOSE WHO DIE

After falling headlong in to the forest pit, Jargon the caveman had been afraid. To be fair, he had never before been faced with such an unknown situation, and soon he had forgiven himself for his initial fright. He was at present calmer.

The primitive understood that he would hunt no more this day. For the moment he was content to sit and wait, and observe the other two. The interaction of the strange creature and the giant, both trapped with him inside the deep hole, was bewildering.

Jargon had always thought that his mammoth, hulking companion was nothing more than a colossal idiot. Everyone in his tribe had believed the same thing. Now he found to his amazement that Moas was not only intelligent but also able to understand the abnormal speech of the stranger, as well.

How was this possible, he wondered? Did the giant and the stranger come from the same, unknown tribe? Jargon didn't know it, but the odd one, the elusive beast, who was not some fanciful creature but just a normal man, was equally confused.

Spencer Hall had been terrified after falling into the pit. Being a true coward that was natural enough, for fear of the unknown does run deep in the human animal. Yet now that the giant was speaking to him, he was fighting another feeling altogether.

The lone researcher had been disoriented from his abrupt descent. Now he was experiencing a raging headache as well as a slight case of double vision, but he realized this wasn't his biggest problem. He knew that things in general weren't adding up here, but he couldn't put his finger on the exact reason why.

He did know that he didn't like the feeling, and he didn't think the situation resulted from a bump to his head, either. No, there was more to it than that. Why was this giant man, who was obviously not some primeval caveman, acting like one?

And what's more, why were cavemen even here at all? That was in the past, the distant past. The whole thing made no sense.

All of a sudden, Spencer's brain came into sharp focus and in a flash he realized at least one possible explanation. But, just as soon, he dismissed it, that is, he tried to, for it caused in him another feeling altogether. That feeling was well-founded panic.

It couldn't be true, he told himself; don't be stupid. The whole thing would be inconceivable as well as a real disaster, he knew. Just calm down, he thought, for his fluttering heart now felt near exploding, the beats within were so rapid.

Next he tried to form a credible question for the giant, and then several questions, each one starting with how or why, but he failed in this attempt. There were just too many to ask. The queries forming inside his mind would grow, but then their varied implications would expand, as well.

Each of these would then fly elsewhere, begetting more questions, and before he could even complete a coherent sentence. Soon, he was close to babbling although he didn't realize it at the time. The giant saw his quandary.

After some difficult moments, the big man at last succeeded in calming him down a bit, saying to him over and over, "Hey, it's OK," and "Just let me explain." He used the same patient tone one would use to speak to a lost and frightened child, to reassure them once they had been found. The strategy worked.

After getting Spencer's dazed but full attention, the giant began to explain the situation, and the appalled man learned that his worst fears had all been true! This was bad. This was very bad.

"There's been an incident," said the giant. "At Point Zero. It's time for a new plan, Doctor Hall, and the sooner the better."

Ever the professional, in most cases Spencer saw himself as more than equal to any new task that he might be handed, but this bold news he could not accept. It tore into the very fabric of his ordered existence. Without realizing it, he leaned back against the cool, red clay wall of the pit, feeling lightheaded.

Spencer next began to fight, and then fight hard, the growing urge to throw up. As he tried to focus his concentration, he glanced about the looming excavation surrounding him. The poor man had pushed himself so far, and so hard.

With bulging eyes he wondered, was it all for nothing? He couldn't believe it. Spencer, in shock, was still in denial.

This had to be a huge mistake, he thought. Such a devastating blunder did not just happen every day. He knew there were standard procedures in place, unerring backup stopgap measures, and these precious, time-tested protocols had always assured that a troubling scenario such as this one would never, ever occur.

The mere thought of such a thing happening was enough to frighten him to death. How should one react to such exceptional news? How could one even deal with it?

Yet Spencer was a realist, and he had been trained over the long years to be an unbiased observer. Upon reflection, he saw that there was just no doubting the situation. One look at his out-of-place companions told him that it had to be true, for they were in the pit with him, and there was no getting around that blunt fact.

From Spencer's changed demeanor, the giant could tell that the frightened man had ingested the truth at last. It was a start, but only a start. He continued his briefing, injecting a new point.

"Someone's turned," he added in a low tone.

The giant then looked at Jargon, who was sitting and leaning against the clay wall of the pit. He was watching in wonder as the other two conversed. The big caveman smiled at him, and then looked back to Spencer and continued.

"Best head back now and figure out who it is later," he said.

The giant seemed calm and collected, but Spencer, still visibly shaken was nowhere close to displaying a serene composure.

"Someone did this?" he asked in horror. "Why?" And then, "You're telling me that someone did this thing on purpose?"

The giant hunched his huge shoulders.

"Looks like it," he said.

"This changes everything," was Spencer's quiet comment, as if he were talking to himself. The implications were staggering. They also were unknown, and as such, were unpredictable.

"That's a given," answered the big man, and then he added, "I've been sent to fetch you, Spencer."

This statement passed over the lone researcher. His mind was elsewhere, trying to grasp the implications. He wasn't succeeding.

"Why would someone do such a thing?" he asked.

At this point, the giant was reluctant to complicate Spencer's life further. That would come soon enough, he knew, it was inevitable. But he didn't wish to go into sticky details now.

"Some people have their reasons," was all he said.

After this understated exchange, the hulking caveman spoke no more. There was no need, for he could tell that Spencer's efficient brain was again working overtime, desperately trying to sort out the varied possibilities now in play. The giant had personal knowledge that it was not an easy thing to do.

Spencer had been convinced that his dismal day couldn't get any worse, but this development was light years past his now petty work problems. It even dwarfed his personal ones, he realized. And then, a further realization struck him.

Spencer's spinning mind latched on to another, earth shattering thought so daunting that it took his breath away, and he was horrified anew. In retrospect, it should have his first consideration. He pushed himself off the wall and looked at the large man who was now standing quite close to him.

"My wife," he said with terror frozen on his now pallid face.

The giant, before so concerned, at last seemed relieved.

"Julie's safe," he said, "don't worry, she's OK." He smiled and nodded at the dazed man, trying to be reassuring. "She's at the Point, I've seen her since the incident."

Spencer was physically banged up. Mentally he was very upset. At first he didn't catch the import of this response.

All his concentration had been focused on his wife, and the possibility of never seeing her again. What could be worse? Then realization struck a third time.

No one called her Julie. No one did, that is, but him, 'the' him. Only one person had ever done so.

Her friends and family all called her Judith. Her co-workers and students always called her Doctor Hall. Even Spencer had given up on a pet name for her, for every time she had resisted his many, differing efforts to give her one.

No, she always had always preferred to be called simply Judith.

Spencer slowly looked over the much bigger man standing next to him, as if seeing the giant for the first time. He was huge, and there was no other way to describe his bulky build. Not fat, mind you, but large in the extreme as well as very tall, with massive shoulders and arms that were as big as Spencer's thigh.

Maybe even his waist.

The giant had one of those particular faces that almost looked goofy when relaxed, but would turn intense and pensive once an important issue engaged him. The difference between the two postures was sometimes startling to see. The diametric change could come like a shot, and with no warning.

His coloring was light, almost pale. He had long, straight sandy hair, and his deeply set, tar-black eyes looked small in comparison with the rest of his broad, round face. The big man's overall build was impressive, to say the least.

Spencer glanced at the remarkable size of the man's hands. They were well used it was easy to tell. Hanging there they looked like dangerous weapons just waiting to be employed.

They also looked to be as large as steering wheels, each one having powerful digits, as hulking and as strong as the claws of a great bear. If this was to become a physical contest, Spencer thought, he was going to be on the losing side of this battle. And they were the same hands that had touched his Judith!

Staring with glazed-over eyes, Spencer was unsurprised that the dull pain in the pit of his stomach had returned, and this time with a vengeance. His mouth went dry, and his tongue stuck to the roof of his mouth. The poor man was also dripping sweat although it was now late in the afternoon and getting considerably colder.

The giant misread his cowering countenance, however. He thought that Spencer was still upset only because of the new and engaging circumstances in which he now found himself. He again tried to set the researcher's mind at ease, this time by addressing further a point they had barely discussed before.

He placed one of his beefy hands on Spencer's shoulder and said to him, "Hey, relax, man, I know it wasn't you who's turned."

That line of reasoning struck Spencer as strange. He hadn't even considered that point of view. What a waste of time, and who'd assume such a thing in any case?

"I'm no free thinker," he said at last, the words themselves distasteful, "and I still believe that Primus is supreme."

74

The giant nodded, as if to say that he knew it was so. Afterwards he again looked over at Jargon and smiled some more. He was reassuring the both of them.

Spencer then understood that the giant did not know. That he was unaware that Spencer knew of the relationship between him and his wife, and that he hadn't recognized how Spencer had made the connection between the two of them. Or had he?

He had just said that he had seen Judith. Did that mean that they were still together? Was she waiting for him?

If not, why else would the two of them wind up at the same lonely and isolated location of Point Zero? By his reckoning, Judith should have been a few worlds away, teaching as he used to do. Had the scenario somehow progressed?

After all, Spencer hadn't seen his wife in a long time, and when they had parted it had not been all that amicable. Things had been pretty much left up in the air between them. He had just shipped off on his mission with no time left to iron out the hanging details of what would happen in their troubled marriage.

Had the pair of them, Spencer wondered, together decided things in his absence? And if this were so, was this rescue just a convenient ploy to get him alone with no credible witnesses? The giant could then, under another pretext altogether, easily be rid of him forever, and with no sticky questions asked.

Spencer knew how simple a thing that would be for him, for he was aware of the big man's true occupation. The giant's training had been extensive. He was nothing if not a professional.

But if that were the case, then why did he not just kill him now and be done with it? He could easily do so at this point with little real trouble or future consequences. Realistically speaking, who would there be to argue his account of the circumstances?

But no, Spencer knew that such a situation made little sense. The man was here to help him. He had to be.

There was no other explanation that fit the bizarre facts.

75

But that didn't alter things. The giant was in love with his wife and she with him. There was no doubting that item.

Sadly, it was Spencer's biggest nightmare come to life, and he hadn't even known it. Yet, though it blindsided him, he was not resigned to the fact. Quite the opposite was true, for now he realized that he could never give her up.

"Just who are you anyway?" he asked of the giant, but the lone researcher already knew the answer.

At the question, the giant laughed, showing a mouth full of large, straight teeth. Then, in a flash, he realized that he hadn't laughed as hard in a long, long time. It was a plus that he appreciated the heavy irony hidden in his response.

He said, "I'm an extinct beast of burden, slow but always steady, and so my name is now Moas."

Spencer was not amused by this attempt at humor, yet Moas didn't care. At least he had tried. But he did continue.

"I've been slowly tracking you through the forest for decades," he reminisced, "moving through different groups of grunts," and here, with a nod of his head, he indicated the young caveman on the other side of the pit, "so as not to arouse their suspicions."

The narrator sat on the clay floor. It was damp and clammy cold. This was obviously going to take some time, thought Spencer, and so he sat as well.

"In the last few years," Moas continued, "I knew I had to be getting closer, because by then I had eliminated the rest of the forest region. It was just a matter of time, a needle in a haystack.

Then, some months ago, I infiltrated the locals."

He started to chuckle as he recalled the particulars. He couldn't help it, nor did he wish to. It all seemed so surreal in hindsight.

"Shortly after that, the outlying grunts heard your chainsaw running," he said, "and boy, it really got to them. They'd never heard the like before. You should've listened to the stories some of them told, the descriptions and all."

He shook his head at the recollection, laughing a little louder before adding, "They thought it was some kind of a beast, you see? Something terrible. You're lucky I was there, you know." Spencer nodded, for it was so.

"I was tracking, too," he said.

He leaned over and retrieved one of his artifacts off the floor. It and many others like it had also fallen into the deep pit when he and Jargon had crashed over the excavation's edge. It was a pop bottle so pristine that he could still read with ease the product's label so long ago printed on the light green glass.

"But I was tracking junctions and lines," he said, tossing the bottle back onto the cluttered floor.

"Yes, I know," said Moas, now looking him in the eye. "We need to find the big one, Spencer, and fast, since I've been told it's the only way to solve this thing. You had any luck yet?"

This query received no immediate answer from Spencer. Upon hearing it, he automatically became apprehensive. He didn't like where he thought this thing might be going.

At last Moas said, "It's important, Spencer."

That was it. Spencer had had enough. He wasn't responsible for the whole universe, no matter what anyone said.

He scrambled to his feet but stopped in his tracks when he saw that Jargon had jumped up too, startled into action by the swift movement. Moas groaned. This was not what he needed.

He stood.

His very stature commanded attention. The other two were held in check, with both eyeing him. First Moas extended his hand to reassure the caveman, and then he turned to Spencer.

"What is your problem, man?" the giant asked of him, while using quiet words but determined inflection. "I'm trying to get you home. Don't you understand that?"

"What I understand," said Spencer in an intense whisper, "is that now we just don't know where the larger situation stands." He then realized that he was whispering for no reason. Jargon, after all, couldn't understand their speech.

"Look here, Moas," he continued in a more normal tone, "we have no idea what's changed in the interim. Since the incident, that is I mean there's just no way to know, don't you see?"

Now the exasperated man was again fighting off panic, and as such he was having trouble breathing. He took a second then, to open up the front of his heavy winter shirt, baring his neck and upper chest. This movement revealed his identification tag.

From across the pit, Jargon noted with interest that it was the same reddish amulet that the giant always wore. The two of them were definitely connected, no doubting that now. However, what it all meant remained a mystery for the young caveman.

"Things are different now, Moas," the harried engineer continued, gesturing with his empty hands in hopelessness. "Things have been different for a long time now," he explained. "Maybe even a very long time, we can't be sure."

"Doesn't matter," Moas said, employing a sour disposition.

"How can you say that?" asked Spencer. "It has to matter. At this point, it's the only thing that does matter."

Then he added with real conviction, "Look, if we go back, things will be altered yet again, there's no way around it. It will happen, it has to. People could die, Moas, maybe many people."

The giant's face blanched at this comment. It was not what he had wanted to hear. Moas had assumed the troubled man would jump at any chance to set things right.

Spencer didn't give up.

"We're talking millions here," he said with determination. "Don't you see that? At the very least, their lives will be altered."

Moas considered this, but only for a moment. He had to be objective. The mission was paramount and had to move forward.

With a dismissive shake of his head he asked, "And what if it's war, Spencer, happening as we sit here? What about that? Many more could easily die then."

This stark observation caught Spencer off guard, for he hadn't even considered the possibility. How could Primus ever permit such a thing? Soon, however, he was forced to see the validity of this new, overshadowing viewpoint.

And then he thought, of course, that's it. It all made sense in a crazy sort of way. A new war would explain everything.

Talk about compounding the issue! This was hard to absorb. The complexity of the desperate situation just kept escalating.

After a moment, Moas added another point, saying, "We've got to try, Spencer. It's forbidden not to. You know that."

Sudden Spencer was tired of making decisions. It now seemed to him that he had been doing it forever. He was very weary as well, of always being on the line for the ones he did make.

"How can such a thing be fixed?" he asked with scorn hanging heavily in his voice. It was hard to believe that it could be.

He added, "Who says it's even possible?"

Now Moas was the one getting tired. It seemed to him that he had been answering questions forever, and his patience was wearing thin. Enough was enough.

They were leaving and that was that.

"Give me a break, will you?" the giant protested. "At the time I couldn't understand half of what was being said. But I'm told it's more than possible, according to those that should know."

Moas, big as a mountain, would not be moved.

"It's got to be done, period." He continued. "The Mandate clearly dictates it. Beyond that, there's really nothing else to say."

Spencer knew that Moas was right. The pair of them had to try. It was forbidden not to, and also, he knew that he had no choice if he ever wished to see his Judith again.

Spencer now realized that he had to get back to her, and at all costs. Nothing, literally nothing else in the universe, was as important. Not to him, at least.

He had to make her understand. Somehow he had to convince her, demonstrate to her just how much in love with her he remained. What a revelation, simple but true, and now glaring.

This sentiment was also elegant, and so, from a scientific point of view, it was right up Spencer's alley. Knowing it changed everything. Nothing else mattered.

But he was still a coward, and the last thing he needed in his screwed-up life was any blood on his conscience. The mere thought, Mandate or no, mortified him. On the other hand, he knew that righting this thing was important, a much bigger situation than him and his petty, screwed-up life.

"So," he said, "acting now and killing some is better than doing nothing now and letting others die in the interim?"

Looking again at the young caveman sitting across from them, Moas said with sad resignation, "That's about the size of it, yes."

Spencer knew it had to be. There was no other way. The Mandate, rigid and unchanging, was clear.

"I've already found it," he said at last. "The big one, I mean. It happened right before you two got here."

He then pointed across the pit to Jargon, and this movement was not unnoticed by the young caveman.

"He's leaning on it," he said, "it's right behind him."

Without hesitation, Moas stood. Jargon jumped up as well. Waiting to see what would happen next, Spencer just sat.

Moas stepped to the makeshift ladder, bent over, and grabbed it. With little effort it seemed to Spencer, he placed it back in its original position. Then, with a determined look, the giant indicated that it was time for Jargon to be on his way.

This proud primitive didn't like to be told what to do, and he seldom stood for such a display when it did occasionally happen. But the youth understood well enough that this fantastic situation was beyond his control. He agreed to leave.

However, Jargon did not move until Moas first stepped back a few paces. After that, in an instant he ran for and jumped onto the ladder. Then he bounded up and escaped the deep pit.

For just a second he paused and looked down at them, his hand touching the handle of his homemade knife. He was assessing his next move with care, weighing the options. But with a shrug, he next ran off, already wondering how he would explain this bizarre occurrence to his primitive tribe.

As he moved through the brush, Jargon started to smile. Even then he had begun in his mind to embellish the strange tale and to his own credit. No one was going to believe this one, he knew.

Soon he started to laugh aloud as he ran, for he realized that before long his new name would be Outlandish.

Inside the pit, Spencer asked Moas, "When do we leave?" and the giant answered him, "As soon as it's off."

Both then stepped over to the point in the wall where Jargon had been sitting. Still somewhat embedded within the red clay, the large, previously exposed water pipe junction was clearly visible. Spencer, now resigned, pointed to his well-used pick, but the giant man shook his huge head, declining the offer.

Instead, using his gigantic fingers, Moas soon dug off the remaining clay clinging to the junction. Next, after first smiling broadly at Spencer, he employed both of his strong hands in his task. With his massive arm muscles bulging from the effort, Moas then turned the large metal ring attached to the coupling, and by degrees, he slowly closed the ancient water valve.

"Well, that's done," said Spencer, trying to sound positive and upbeat. It didn't work. He was not relieved.

Neither was his new partner.

"Yes," agreed Moas. "There's no turning back now." He looked to Spencer before adding, "Not for any of us."

CHAPTER FIVE
THOSE WHO HATE

In the desert city of Arret, the two men within the water tower glared at each other. Hard. They shared a stormy history.

One of them was dressed in ornate finery. The other was clothed in nothing more than tattered rags. Despite this stark contrast, a casual observer might think the two were related, for at first glance each of them closely resembled the other.

However, upon a more exacting examination, such an observer would also see obvious and subtle differences between the pair.

Both had short hair of the same deep russet tint, and both had matching complexions, also dark. As well, each one possessed the identical sharp, angular nose and squared, chiseled chin of the other. The two men had similar wide shoulders and strong arms, and even standing apart in the vast room one could see they shared a like bearing, with both of them holding their lean bodies in much the same poised and confident manner.

But the Traveler was much bigger than the opulent man standing in the center of the room, and he had deep brown eyes that now looked even darker next to his sunburned skin. The man with the green garden hose, while being stocky and broad, was much shorter than Onus, and his eyes were a bright and flashing blue. His natural olive complexion now looked somewhat pale, and Onus presumed this came from living inside the vast water tower, away from the bulk of the desert sun's penetrating rays.

Across the large enclosure, the men held each other's penetrating gaze, neither one speaking until the earthenware jug that was being filled overflowed its brim, oozing an ever even level of the clear liquid past the container's lip. The absorbed water altered the receptacle's normal clay color from a light reddish tan into a deeply rich auburn hue. The darker tinge, as if painted on by some invisible brush, glided down the smooth length of the tall vessel and headed toward the polished marble floor.

The well-dressed man cursed at this development, but after moving the hose to the next jug, he said nothing else. Neither did he again meet the taller man's eyes, but instead nervously looked away. However, his agile mind was racing.

The Traveler crossed into the center of the room. A blazing shaft of sunlight streaking through the high, arched ceiling lighted the spot. In short order, Onus stood beside the Great One himself.

After a moment passed, he said, "It's been a long time."

The smaller man laughed aloud at this line, not in any humor at the remark but at its absurdity. This brief action revealed yet another difference between the two of them. His front teeth had a noticeable gap between them while Onus' had none.

"Yeah, I'd say so," he answered, all traces of levity now absent from his face. He then busied himself by dabbing at the spilled water with a small, dazzling cloth that he pulled from within his generous robes. The fabric was a deep red, and contained a broad border neatly stitched with heavy golden thread.

Onus noticed that it matched the man's splendid outfit, and that both items blended well with the room's vivid decor.

Trying again, Onus stated, "There's been an incident."

Hearing this, the well-dressed man looked up, and with a mask of false amazement on his face he said, "No kidding? I've been stuck out here, let's see, two, or was it three thousand years? I can't quite remember, but yes, I'd say there's been an incident."

Disgusted, he looked back to his operation, his broad jaw bulging as it clenched. Again there was a telling silence between them. The splash of water was the only sound in the room.

Onus crossed his ample arms, thinking about his grueling trek to date. He had just traveled through pure hell on his far-ranging and dangerous quest, and during the entire, agonizing time he had thought only of seeking out this very man. He had been consumed by the idea, and it was the only thing that had kept him going during his long, and uncompromising journey.

With each painful step, the Traveler had believed that his biggest obstacle along the way would be in finding him at all. Now that he was found, Onus realized he faced a whole new set of problems. The true adventure was just beginning, he saw.

Both men stood gazing at the jug, now almost filled with the same pure and sparkling water Onus had encountered during his trip through the blistering desert. In spite of everything, the Traveler's lips curled into a sly grin as he thought how little things really changed, no matter how much time might pass in the interim. It always, it seemed to him, came back to the water.

"We've got to talk," he said, and as a matter of fact.

"No thanks," was the curt reply he received.

The Traveler now felt this cold reception was getting old. After all, he was here, and he wasn't going anywhere until things were settled between them. Both of them knew that.

"I've been sent here to find you," he stated, with some impatience now creeping into his voice.

The Great One was not moved by this comment. He carried on with his routine undeterred. He turned off the tap and removed the garden hose from the now-filled jug.

"I didn't think you'd come on your own," he said at last.

Next he coiled the hose, and then concealed both it and the faucet by using a nearby cloth, apparently employed before for the purpose. It was light in weight but beautifully made, with bright, competing colors. It covered everything nicely.

More matching decor, the Traveler saw.

After first checking to see that all was hidden, the determined man then turned and started to cross the massive room, ignoring the newcomer. Onus, growing angry, followed at his heels. He was taller, and it took him little time to catch up.

This whole thing was not going well, Onus thought, trying to master his growing temper. He had always found it hard to hold his emotions in check, but this time it was serious business, and he knew that the whole thing was, in fact, doable. It only had to be handled well, with a delicate but persistent touch.

The Traveler knew that, in the end, it would go his way but he didn't want to fly off the handle. They hadn't seen each other in a long time and the circumstances had changed. Anything could happen between the two of them, it was hard to read beforehand.

He reached out and grabbed his moving quarry by the arm, stopping him in mid-stride just as they approached what seemed to be the far wall of the inner sanctum. In truth, they stood before a huge and breathtaking tapestry so immense that it covered the entire expanse of the great room. The ancient artwork clearly rendered a stylized depiction of the infant city of Arret.

Onus recognized the lake and water tower, although the now mighty citadel had been represented then as little more than a bustling hamlet, embedded in a vast and barren surrounding desert landscape. He wondered how long the Great One had been doling out his precious water to the simple and grateful people in this parched land. And how long had he been doing so since this colossal, ornately stitched spectacle had been created?

The Traveler tried again. He had no other option. Time was ticking by, and there was none to waste.

He said, "I'm on a quest, so my name is Onus."

"I'm a mystery within a puzzle, so my name is Rebus," retorted the other, and here he reached out and held back the edge of the heavy tapestry, revealing a modest bedroom beyond. "It's almost time and I've got to move fast," Rebus told the Traveler. "Step in here and I'll call it a day after this batch is gone."

Onus moved behind the imposing wall hanging and watched as Rebus crossed the dreamlike room to sit upon his marble throne, elaborately carved and placed high upon a covered dais. After settling in a little, he struck a nearby gong. The Great One then leaned back into his majestic seat and waited.

His face was hidden in shadow when two slaves, who had been next in line and only awaiting their cue, entered the vaulted tower. Each was carrying an empty water jug. They made their way to the center of the chamber employing a solemn cadence, unhurried.

They resembled the other water-bearing slaves that Onus had seen earlier, but these two were a particularly well-matched pair. The men, both shaved bald, were thin with no facial hair. They were about the same height, and each wore identical outfits of sandals and a half robe of a rich purple color.

Onus saw this striking costume was well designed, for the material of the robes would only enhance the effect of a deep hue against a dark shadow should it become wet. The duo wore the garments tucked in at the waist, which left their chests bare. A thick, golden armband completed their raiment.

When they reached the exact center of the cavernous room, it was still bathed in a warm patch of brilliant sunlight. The slaves carefully placed their empty jugs down behind the two newly filled ones that were awaiting them. Both men then turned and proceeded to prostrate themselves before their master.

"All praises to the Great One," they chanted in unison, their lips almost touching the polished marble floor.

Hiding behind the tapestry, Onus was impressed. There was lots of practice here. This entire act was just the normal routine for them, the playing out of respective, well-known roles in a flawless fashion employing impeccable timing.

This occasion, however, was soon to be different. Rebus raised his hand for emphasis. It was good to be in charge.

He announced in a loud voice that boomed throughout the room, "Let it be known to all that I am finished for this day and will not be further disturbed until the sun shines tomorrow."

The slaves were much surprised by this unforeseen alteration in their well-established ritual, but each took the news in stride. Who were they to argue with the Great One? The two stood with alacrity, lifted their heavy burdens, and exited the inner sanctum, happy to have the rest of the day off.

After they left, Rebus continued sitting his throne. Pondering, he stared off to the side at nothing in particular. He was slumped, leaning on his right arm, and unmoving except for idly picking at his lower lip with the fingers of his left hand.

Onus had seen this display many times in the past. He knew that the posture represented some hard thinking on Rebus' part. Good, the Traveler thought, let him think.

There were several marble benches placed about the base of the throne, and Onus walked over and sat down on the nearest one. He didn't like the fact that this placed Rebus in a superior position, one from which the Great One could look down on him from above, but, for the moment he was content to sit there and wait. The Great Rebus, he knew, needed time to mull over this novel development in his normal, well-ordered lifestyle.

He did this for several long minutes. He was lost in thought. He seemed unaware that Onus was even there.

Then, still picking his lip he asked of him, "Why are you here?"

"I told you," said Onus, "I'm here to take you back."

"Yeah, right," said Rebus. "I guessed at some point they'd send someone. What I mean is, why was it you?"

The Traveler hunched his shoulders. There was no need to complicate things now. That would come later.

"Someone had to come," he said, "and I happened to be there."

Rebus considered this, but only for a moment. This had to end. He had other priorities and they didn't include Onus.

"Well, I'm not going anywhere with you," he said.

Onus leaned forward with his head bent. He was resting his elbows on his bare knees, his pudgy fingers interlocking. Now it was his time to think, and he used that time well.

He knew that he had to broach another subject sooner or later, and he knew that waiting would not change the inevitable reaction that would then follow. Yet he had no other option left to him. It was out of his hands now, so he looked up, resigned.

"Oh, you'll go," he said, "but, first things first, friend. After all, this could mean war. That's a bigger thing than you or me."

He began to rub his palms together, back and forth, fingers still entwined, giving his statement a moment to sink in.

He added, "Someone from the inside has turned, you see. That complicates things. I need to know up front that it wasn't you."

Rebus seemed stunned by this staggering statement. Although he said nothing in response, his blue eyes were open wide in wonder. This did change everything, and in a big way.

The Traveler now wished to stand, to change their relative positions. He hated to be addressed from a superior stance. But not wanting to be too demonstrative, he just unlocked his hands and placed them on his well-tanned knees.

"I'll get you out either way, you understand," he continued, "but still, I'd like to know." Of course he realized that he had just given Rebus a rather large opening. What he didn't know is whether the Great One would rise to the occasion and take the bait.

He shouldn't have worried. Throwing a tantrum and evading the subject had always been easier for this man than addressing any real problem he might be facing. He didn't disappoint.

"So that's it?" Rebus screamed as he leapt up and bounded down the dais to confront the Traveler face to face. "You've come all this way, just to ask me if I ratted? You need to know if I'm just some heretic traitor, is that what you're saying?"

Onus stood and Rebus realized too late that he had lost his only advantage, for he was now forced to look up at the taller man before him. Onus, feeling better, didn't press the issue. There was no need to now, as things were finally progressing.

"As I said, it's been a long time," the Traveler commented as he moved past the Great One. He headed toward Rebus' private chambers and once arrived, he pushed open the heavy tapestry. Turning, he motioned the object of his long quest inside.

Rebus was angry, and he hesitated a moment before stiffly stalking past Onus and into the room beyond. What else could he do? He threw himself into an overstuffed chair, located so near an overstuffed bed that the two almost touched.

"Look," he said in a terse voice, "I was just a hard working guy, OK, in the armpit of nowhere. I was only doing my mindless job when things went bad. It wasn't my fault."

The Great One then started once more on his lip, his fingers almost a blur. Pinch and pull, pinch and pull, faster and faster each time. It was clear that he was upset.

He paused only long enough to say, "I don't even know what happened," after which he continued his agitated actions.

When Onus didn't respond, he added, "I'm no rat, OK? I wouldn't turn, no matter what. I'm no free thinker."

"Hey, you never were such a hard-working guy," said Onus, as he sat on the mattress, which was much too soft for his taste.

The Great One saw no humor in this snide remark. He thrust himself forward in his chair, and Onus thought for a moment that he might try to strike him. The tension soon passed though, and Rebus eased himself back down again.

"I've worked plenty hard, thank you," he said between clenched teeth. "Do you have any idea what it was like for me then, what I went through to get here? It wasn't easy, you know."

"Hey, I got here, didn't I?" barked Onus. He was now angry as well. His attempt at humor had failed, and he knew it.

All of a sudden, the Traveler noticed how very tired he was. His earlier excitement had worn off, and now reality held the truth of the matter. He also realized that he was quite hungry.

He asked, "So, you got any eats in this plush palace?"

Rebus indicated with a tilt of his head a heaping bowl of fruit on a nearby table. Onus stood and crossed over to it. He grabbed a couple of large, green apples and tossed one to Rebus.

He asked, "Don't you people have any real food around here? I've had nothing all day. I'm beyond famished."

"Sure, no problem there," Rebus answered, "I'll pass the word. These grunts may not know much, but they do cook up one mean suckling pig. It's my favorite."

Onus nodded as he sat. He started eating his apple, but Rebus just held on to his, turning it in his strong hands. His head was bent in thought, and for a moment neither man spoke.

At last the Great One looked up and said, "Hey, you know I wouldn't rat anybody out? I never would. What's the point?"

Onus, busy chewing, didn't answer but thought this might not be altogether true. He knew Rebus was the kind of man that would do almost anything if the possible payoff were enticing enough. Still, if he had turned, that unpleasant fact would not in itself become a pressing problem until much later on.

Onus, after swallowing a mouthful of tangy fruit, said, "OK."

After this exchange Rebus remained both uneasy and confused, for he now had much to consider. Onus' casual arrival, strolling in during what for him had been an ordinary day's work, had been quite a shock. Onus saw that Rebus was trying hard to reason out the possible implications for the Great One was once again, without thinking, pulling furiously at his lower lip.

Onus smiled in spite of himself, for in the past he had always thought the personal habit to be an asinine display.

Beyond doubt, the action was just plain goofy looking. Besides that, it always gave Rebus' strategy away. How could you be nonchalant while doing such a stupid thing?

Nevertheless, the Traveler was pleased to see the gesture now. It underscored their relative positions, and whose agenda was paramount. For all his bravado, Onus knew Rebus was worried.

I'll give him something to really think about, Onus thought.

"We've got plans to make," he said. "We've got to head back to Point Zero. It's the only way to get out of this mess."

Rebus stopped the motion of his fingers on his lip, but he still held his hand ready, just in front of his face, the better to continue pulling if need be. The Great One shot his vivid blue eyes, brows now raised, to Onus. This was big news.

"I'm going nowhere," he said. "Not back to the Point, or anywhere else for that matter. Not with you, in any case."

Onus had been trimming his apple, using small, well-placed nibbles of his un-gapped teeth to sculpt away every morsel of edible fruit. He held up the result of his labor by the stem and inspected his creation with boyish pride. Then he ate it as well, popping the scrawny core whole into his mouth.

"Yeah," he said, smacking and chewing as he stretched out on the overly soft bed, "I could see how easily you'd get used to this cushy place. The whole set up is pretty sweet for a working stiff. It's no wonder you want to stay here."

"Hey, it wasn't always like this," Rebus answered, "it took a lot of time, and it does have its drawbacks. It's the same routine, day after day, year after year, never ending. Sometimes, you know, I think I'm going to lose it if I hear that gong again."

Onus, adjusting his position on the bed, was unmoved.

"Get one of your grunts to make you some earplugs," he said with dry humor. "Why even dole out the water at all? I mean, the city draws most of its supply from the lake anyway."

92

Rebus knew where this line was going, and he didn't like it. The situation could be misunderstood with little effort. Onus had to see that, at the time, he'd had no other choice and that might prove difficult, given that Rebus was losing his temper with him.

Still, the Great One was angry with himself, as well. He had known from the first minute he saw Onus that he would wind up abandoning his normal composure. With Onus, he always did.

In general, Rebus thought of himself as calm and relaxed. Few things interrupted his laid-back lifestyle, but it never failed that when the two of them got together, things always blew up, at least on his part. It gnawed at him that every time, no matter how he wished it otherwise, within minutes he would be screaming.

This always gave Onus the opening he needed to look at Rebus with his big, brown puppy-dog eyes that so well feigned dismay. Rebus would always wind up feeling like an idiot who couldn't hold on to his wits. Onus could then, and with good reason, simply refuse further discussion, thereby evading any consideration of whatever legitimate concerns Rebus might have had.

Not this time, the Great One thought.

He leaned further back into the vastness of his chair and added with less vigor, by way of explanation, "It just completes the whole illusion. It keeps them guessing, like how come I never age. I wouldn't want them to think they could do without me, would I?"

"Oh, no, that would never work," Onus answered, with what Rebus recognized as his best superior air.

It grated all the more that he was so good at it, but Onus was not through yet. The Great One knew the Traveler had yet to play his trump card and he knew also that Onus would not fail to do so. Rebus wouldn't have had their roles been reversed.

"I doubt that Primus Himself lived this well," said Onus, as he crossed his arms behind his head, and worked himself further into the thick mattress. On second thought, it wasn't all that uncomfortable. The pillow was nice, too.

Because he knew this issue had been coming, Rebus was uncharacteristically prepared. So, he didn't scream his innocence or beg to be understood. Those days were long over.

He said, "I'm no heretic and you know it, and what would that get me?" He then reached into his tunic. After some fumbling, he pulled out the identifying tag that he still wore around his neck.

It was a small, slightly rounded, ruby-red crystal that held a deep green speck. This embedded speck encoded all of his personal, pertinent information. It was standard issue equipment, and he knew that Onus wore one just like it.

"Get real," he added. "I'm not Primus and I know it. So just stop putting words in my mouth, thank you."

Onus, expecting an outburst, was surprised by this bland reply.

Rebus continued, pressing his line.

"Look, what do I have to say?" he asked. "I had only one thing going for me. I knew the water tower's location."

Water was life itself in the blistering desert. They both knew that. Without water, and plenty of it, you died there.

"That's all I had to work with," he continued. "I had to come, there was no other choice. The forest was too far away and my supplies wouldn't have lasted me a week."

Onus was again unmoved.

"Well," he began, "I'd say you now have quite a bit more going for you, and all at the grunts' expense, too. You think it's fair to them, to their evolving society, to keep this act up for so long? They are the point of this whole thing, after all, and they deserve better than kissing your sorry butt for all time."

At this retort Rebus exploded, just as Onus knew that at some point he would. He was an easy read. He always had been.

"I can't help it if these grunts turned it into a religion," screamed the Great One. He stood and started pacing in the small room, pulling away at his lower lip as he did so. He was fuming.

Onus pressed ahead, almost running through his newest opening. With luck, he might solve this whole thing fairly soon. Then they could eat some suckling pig.

"Oh, please," he opined, "you live in the lap of all this luxury, without a care in the world, an ever-living god to these misguided grunts and you say that you can't help that?"

Onus snorted his contempt as if he meant it. If the truth were known, he'd have done much the same thing if he'd found himself in Rebus' position. He couldn't say that though.

"I think you had a good deal to do with it," was all he said.

Rebus had to admit that this was so, but he couldn't say that, either. In addition, from his vantage it was also beside the point. He hadn't desired this, any of it.

He said only, "It's not forbidden to live well, at least not the last time I heard. And living well is only my reward for being here. I didn't want this life, it's nothing but a prison."

Onus had to admit that this was true enough, but just as Rebus, it didn't advance his agenda any. The Traveler changed his tack. Facts were facts, and they couldn't be changed.

"Better learn to get over it," he said with feigned resignation, "and argue with the Mandate, not me."

That's what it all came down to in the end. The Mandate was paramount. Rebus couldn't argue with that but he could ignore it.

"We have to get back," Onus added, keeping it simple. "It's the only way. And you know it's forbidden at least not to try."

Rebus had heard enough.

"Well, forget it," he said, standing his ground by arresting his movement. "I'm not going anywhere, don't you understand? Not with you and not with anyone else."

Following this, Onus just stared at him without speaking. It was an old tactic of his and Rebus could never stand it, for he had always buckled in the end. But things were different now.

Rebus resumed his pacing to evade the piercing glare.

"So what if I have a good thing here?" he asked. "I'm hurting no one. I'm just a nothing anyway, in the bigger scheme of things."

Onus let him pace. If he stewed some, he might come to the right conclusion on his own. It was a premature hope.

"Who's to say that this," the Great One asked, his arms held out, indicating everything, "is not the Mandate? Are you a priest now? No, you just leave without me, and thanks anyway."

Onus shook his head.

"It doesn't work that way," he answered. "You and I are paired, see? If we don't both go, then neither one of us gets back."

This caused Rebus to stop once more. He pulled his lip a time or two, considering. It didn't matter.

"Well that's your problem," he said at last. "It's not mine. I didn't ask you to come."

"That's irrelevant," answered the Traveler, "I'm here."

"Listen to me," Rebus almost shouted, "I'm sorry, but I'm not like you. I never was. I'm not a hero."

This was too much for Onus, for it cut to the heart of the bigger, personal problem between them. He reacted before he knew it. In an instant he leapt to his feet, not only grabbing Rebus by the rich fabric of his robe, but also pushing him up against the cool, slightly curved metal wall of the water tower.

However, as soon as this lightning movement was accomplished, Onus thought better of it. Such action was useless and nonproductive, getting him nowhere. He slowly dropped the Great One, realizing too late that his flawless strategy had backfired, as he had been the one to lose his composure.

"I'm no hero," he said quietly, his eyes cast downward.

Rebus was now livid. The swiftness of Onus' performance had caught him off guard, but it was just like the bigger man to react in such an overbearing and heavy-handed fashion. Rebus was shorter by a head, but he was strong as an ox and no one but Onus had ever bullied him and gotten away with it.

The Great One had never put up with such a thing except with Onus, and he didn't like this aspect of their relationship. It never changed between them, it never would. And it didn't help that. Onus was always overly apologetic after.

Rebus fought for control. He knew that nothing would be accomplished between them if this degenerated into a clash of personalities. He didn't like it but he had to move on, to get once and for all past the past that they shared.

He smoothed his robe and stated, "I'm no boy scout then, OK?" Onus didn't answer. He returned to his seat on the bed. Rebus then crossed and also sat as before.

Bending, he picked up the apple that had fallen to the floor during the melee and tossed it to Onus. The Traveler wasn't paying close attention but he did see it coming, out of the corner of his eye, just as Rebus had thought he would. He caught the sphere, loping in a graceful arc, one-handed, almost without trying.

The Great One started to pick some more lip, but before he did he said, "Look, no one's getting hurt here, so why are you judging me? Just get off my back, OK? Just leave and leave me alone."

Onus considered this statement, but only for a moment before saying with stiff resignation, "I'm here to help, not judge. It's time to face facts, friend. It's the Mandate, and you know it."

This time Rebus did the staring. He was so angry now that he couldn't speak, but his eyes were burning into those of Onus, talking volumes. Onus held the look.

"We're leaving," he said with finality, in hopes of putting an end to any further discussion, "and the sooner the better."

That was it for Rebus, the proverbial straw that broke the camel's back. He couldn't help it. He snapped, and in a big way.

"No, you face some facts," he screamed, no longer capable of holding his rampant temper, "haven't you been listening to me?"

97

He exited his bedroom, talking as he walked, and not caring if Onus followed. He needn't have worried. Onus did.

"In the first place," the Great One shrieked, "in case you haven't noticed, we hate each other's guts." He was stalking into the center of the main chamber, gesturing with his arms as he went. The man was so hot now, that he almost let off steam as he moved.

"In the second place," he barked, "you think that I've turned, become a heretic. I'm just another traitor running loose, wreaking havoc. Of course, I can't be trusted."

Onus, following at his heels, couldn't get a word in edgewise. "Next," the Great One added, as he snatched the multicolored fabric off the faucet and hose, "I've got a pretty good thing going here. You may not like it, but that's your problem. After all this time, in spite of everything, it's home to me now."

"Listen," said Onus trying to calm him down, but Rebus was on a roll and cut him off in mid-sentence.

"But I'm not finished with my list," he blurted as he reached for the hose and turned on the tap. "My last point is the best one. I'm not going anywhere as long as I have this sweet, sweet water."

The water, clean, clear and sparkling, gushed from the green garden hose. Then it sputtered, then sputtered again, then dribbled for a few seconds, then it stopped. Neither man spoke.

A minute went by before Rebus became animated. He squatted and tried the faucet again. Nothing.

Next he unscrewed the hose and duplicated the procedure, feverously twisting the tap without reserve this time, but with the same negative result despite his determined attempt.

"Well, well," said Onus, crossing his well-muscled arms, "I wouldn't want to be you when the water in the lake goes. Yes, this could get very sticky. Now, how long do you suppose it will take," he asked with false concern, "to use up the water that's there?"

Rebus didn't answer but he was thinking, and thinking hard. It wouldn't be long at all, he knew. The City of Arret was dependent on the precious water for its commerce as well as its health, and a lot of it was consumed to fill these needs.

He thought of all the surrounding farms and the many nomads beyond. Of course they would come to him. Who else was there?

The Great One was dumbfounded. Despite his best efforts, again he'd been beaten by Onus. His position, so lofty in the past, was now untenable, and he had to do something.

"I'd say we better move fast, big brother," he uttered.

"I'd say that's a good idea, little brother," the Traveler replied.

CHAPTER SIX
THOSE WHO LOVE

The overburdened baker was much pleased with himself.

He was walking to the entrance of the now famous Fortress of Forecastle, to meet once again with the old Crone, Sorbus. Making his way across the castle's crowded courtyard, he passed among many groups of common people engaged in the hard work of rebuilding the city. Now that the devastating siege had been lifted, all waved or spoke a few quick words to him.

After Apex passed, they would look to each other, smiling and nodding in mutual acknowledgment before resuming their respective tasks. Because the baker was a peasant much like all of them, it filled their hearts to see that one of their own had made so fine a showing in this world of the rich and powerful. No one, not even the soldiers, called him 'the bastard' anymore.

Since the discovery of the Crone's vast underground enclosure, the king's demoralized army had beaten back the forces besieging the once-dying city with ease. It did this by using weapons stored within the ancient fortress. The old king, before so bitter in defeat, was now well content, and all in the kingdom knew of the role that Apex had played in bringing about this turn of events.

For some reason unknown to him, the Crone had demanded of the king that he, and only he, was to deliver the terrible items of destruction to the beleaguered troops on the walls as well as demonstrate to them their proper use. This had meant that the baker had to learn beforehand all of their mysteries, and he had done so. With great patience, the bent and toothless old woman had taught him herself, deep within the bowels of the fortress, in a large room that he had first cushioned with many thick mattresses.

Because Apex still held much concurrent, important and demanding business, he indeed had been very hard-pressed at the time. Yet, what else could one in his lowly position do but swallow hard and take on the added labor? As the tenacious old king himself had held out for so long against all odds, the simple baker knew he could not, in good faith, do any less.

And so, as many times before in his life, he had just plunged ahead, and by working hard he had done his duty well.

It had been taxing labor with long and grueling hours. It had been terrifying, too. All the same, it had been a great honor for him, for the humble baker had not been raised to the military life.

And yet, besides the time involved, the most difficult part of the whole venture had been persuading the hardheaded troops to listen to him at all. To a man they had resisted, for whom among them wished to learn soldiering from a baker? That situation had quickly changed, however, when a lazy and slacking tower guard had accidentally killed himself and several others.

Not following the proper directions, he was trying to be funny with one of the Crone's stones. As a result, they literally had all been blown to pieces before their startled comrades. After that, seeing firsthand the awesome and terrible power of the Crone's new weapons, the astonished warriors had listened well enough.

The bitter hostilities that followed had been anticlimactic, exciting enough at the time but just a foregone conclusion. However, one played out in bloody earnest all the same. From the city's towering walls the Crone's weapons were easily dropped from above upon the terrified enemy below, and the exploding stones had performed their function with deadly abandon.

With the successful outcome of the fighting thus far, the baker's heavy duties had lessened. The action was all in the countryside now with the king in the field at the head of his troops. The changes that had taken place were both sweeping and swift.

The once-stagnated army had been transformed by their victories, first at the gates of the city and then in several pitched battles that soon followed in the countryside. After years on the losing side, overnight they were invigorated, and now needed no new weapons from the Crone to kill their fleeing opponents. The old-fashioned ways of halberd, sword and mace, of showers of arrows and crushing cavalry charges were at present more than sufficient tactics needed for the now eager and brazen troops.

The tide had completely turned. As such, the baker had enjoyed an easy time of it lately. He now reported to and fro between the king and the Crone, with others appointed in his stead to see to his old duties concerning food for the city.

He found that he liked riding in the country, even if now it was cluttered with the debris of battle. Apex, having worked hard in the last year, had been enjoying his well-earned leisure. The king's newest Mandate, however, would soon alter that.

Quite by happenstance, as the baker passed through the packed courtyard, the Duke of Fervent espied him. He called for the rushing man to hold his pace but Apex continued on, taking no heed and acting as if he had not heard the command. The baker cared not to converse with this young royal, who was granted command of the city during the king's absence.

He cared not for the man himself and he was, by the king's own dictate, in a great hurry to dispatch his newest task.

Undaunted, the duke called out all the more, much to the delight of his surrounding entourage, who laughed at the display. The baker saw that others about him were taking notice of the screamed summons. He had no other option but to respond.

"My Lord?" Apex said, at last stopping to turn about. The duke, after waving for his retainers to hold, crossed over to the man unattended. This was a private affair.

"Ah, yes, Baker, a word with you," said Fervent, who was resplendent in a new tunic and coat of glistening chain mail.

Apex saw that the fashionable nobleman had ordered his entire wardrobe updated, as the heavy combat had now abated. Well, the baker thought, the duke was not the only one, for he had altered his own dress since the siege had been lifted. The peasant no longer wore his battered helmet.

"You see the wench often," said Fervent, and as a fact and not a question. "I wish you to carry a message for me. And quickly."

"The wench, My Lord?" slowly repeated the baker, looking more confused than he was. In general, he had no truck with this brash and forward duke, who was well known by all for his dislike of the Crone. Yet the quick commoner had a fair idea of what was currently on the mind of this smug nobleman, and he was now very interested in what the young Fervent had to say.

"Yes, you oaf, the Crone's girl," snapped the duke.

This lowborn scum could really be dense, he thought. What a shame it was that from time to time one in his lofty position had to even converse with them. But after all, they did perform the real work, and so it was a natural turn that someone of a higher station had to instruct them in what was needed.

Nevertheless, he was becoming exasperated with this seemingly dull, clod of a man. He wouldn't have bothered under normal circumstances. But the comely lass that held his interest was always well protected by the old Crone.

"When next you see the girl, convey a message from me," the duke commanded, as he noticed with disgust a fresh layer of mud on his new, highly polished armored boots.

"A message, My Lord?" asked Apex in a questioning tone, for no other reason than he knew it would vex the other man.

"Yes, damn you, tell her I would speak to her," stated the infuriated duke. This episode was fast becoming tiresome. Notwithstanding, he leaned in closer and added under his breath, which smelled at the time heavily of onions, "And by all the gods, take care the Crone hears not of this."

The baker was now fighting hard not to show his growing anger for he saw that he had been correct in his base assumption about this contemptuous duke. He knew that no matter what it took on his part, the girl would never meet this one alone. And he was now more than eager to set this arrogant royal aright.

Then, with haste he handled what would have stymied most people in his present position, for he was a bright man, and he had assessed the situation, correctly and at once.

He did indeed hold his emotions in check, the better to best this young and snotty Duke of Fervent.

Moving overly close to the duke's person, he said in a soft tone, with a puzzled look plastered on his strong peasant face, "But, My Lord, once I speak to the girl, the Crone will know," and here he had the effrontery to reach out and touch the duke's richly-clad arm. "The Crone knows all," he continued, with his eyes open overly wide. "And she knows at once, always."

His swift stratagem proved all too perfect to his task, and seeing the young duke's face blanch at the mere prospect was his reward.

"No matter," Fervent barked at him. Then, in a gentler voice the lofty noble added to the lowly commoner, "Don't bother, for I've now changed my leaning. I shall myself attend to it later."

Apex shook his head in stoic disbelief, standing as if rooted to the spot while watching the arrogant young royal strut away, picking up his laughing henchmen in tow as he went.

"And they call me a bastard," he said aloud.

He then sighed to himself and turned and walked on.

Soon he approached the steps leading to the subterranean Fortress of Forecastle. The two sentries posted there greeted him with warmth, for like all of the members of the royal army, they were relieved to no longer be on the losing end of the death and carnage. Of course, as the enemy quit the countryside, the theater of war was now further from the redeemed city each day, and all knew that the battles had been reduced of late to little real action beyond harassing the already beaten, retreating forces.

"What news of the front, good baker?" asked one of the two guards. Not waiting for a response, the other one, who was younger and grinning as he leaned on his well-used halberd, asked while oozing excitement, "Still scampering away? Are they still running in terror as fast as they can?"

"Not as fast as the king would wish," said the baker. He was smiling as he spoke, and the two watchmen laughed at this answer. He then descended into the bowels of the great fortress.

Guards were also posted at the second set of doors of the stronghold, for now the massive installation was seen to be most important to the kingdom. The Crone and the weapons she controlled were viewed as essential to the future of the empire, and, as the king's go-between, many now deemed the humble baker indispensable as well. Two beefy soldiers, who were likewise happy to see this now significant person, admitted him.

Apex was jovial enough with them but he did not linger at the doorway for any small talk. He was becoming more apprehensive the closer he came to his final destination. Under normal circumstances, he was a brave enough fellow but the baker grew uneasy within the mighty Fortress of Forecastle.

Underground, the unique stronghold nevertheless had bright sunlight throughout. Also, a strange buzzing sound permeated the place. The commoner relished his newly found prominence within the city, but he had misgivings once inside this ancient and vast edifice, so he was most relieved when the Crone's daughter encountered him as he walked down the main hallway.

She smiled at him and said, "Good day to you, Apex."

Apex was delighted to see her and smiled as well, but he could say nothing in response. He just stood there, grinning and nodding his head, looking like a mute moron. He knew beyond a shadow of a doubt that he was in love with this pretty young woman but he could never find the words to tell her.

The baker also thought that she was in love with him, but the poor peasant could not bring himself to ask her if this hopeful supposition was, in fact, a true one.

"The king himself bids I speak with the old one," he said at last, blurting it out with much too high a volume.

The girl was disappointed by this statement, for his supposition was true, and she had been wishing to hear other, more personable words from him. This time she was the one who said nothing but she did nod her comely head at him. Once.

She then turned to dutifully search out her mother. Yet the baker wished to describe to her his leaning. He reached out and stopped her, but to his chagrin, he discovered that once more he was unable to convey to her his actual feelings.

Instead, the tongue-tied man said to her with some importance, "The king, being well pleased with me, has changed his harsh ways, and so my name is now Pliant."

At this news she beamed at him, and Pliant was smitten. When she was happy, she appeared even more beautiful. Would she be as happy always, he wondered, with me as a husband?

The girl then led him down the many halls and stairwells of the fortress in search of Sorbus. The two walked in silence, every now and then looking to each other and smiling. He wished to engage her in conversation, but he didn't know what to say.

At last he asked of her, "What is that infernal noise?" Pliant was referring to the droning, ever present hum throughout all parts of the giant fortress. The buzzing was always in the background and most disconcerting to the peasant.

He was taken aback when the girl answered, "Mother says the fortress lives, and the sound we hear is but it breathing."

At last they reached the large double doors of the very room Sorbus had described earlier as her office. This time the space beyond was not hidden in darkness. The glass in the doors was now clear and showed the place to be bathed in bright sunlight.

Upon entering, Pliant saw that the room was an immense chamber filled with many desks and strange-looking equipment, the purpose of which he could not hazard a guess. At first he didn't notice the Crone, but the girl knew where she was. Then the bewildered peasant saw Sorbus behind a barrier of glass that covered the far wall of the large, crowded enclosure.

The old woman, absorbed in her ongoing labors, was unaware of their presence. Sorbus was reading from a thick stack of papers held in her bony hands while seated at a large wooden desk that dwarfed her small, bent frame. She seemed surprised, but much pleased, by the pair's unexpected visit.

"Good tidings to you, son," said the Crone. She pointed a crooked finger to some chairs arranged in a crude semicircle directly before her workstation. "Your visit is much welcomed, for we have much to speak upon, the three of us."

"And a great welcome to see you, as well," answered Pliant while taking a seat. "Even if I am here by the king's command, I always enjoy it." The girl sat also, in a chair next to his.

Sorbus rose and crossed, with her feet shuffling, to the front of her desk. When this was done, she plopped into a chair that was facing the two of them. As she moved, she had steadied herself by placing her thin, spotted hand on top of her desk, for her ancient walking stick was idle, resting in the corner.

Pliant knew his manners. Once he understood her intent, he had wanted to assist her. But with a stern glance the girl had stopped him, and so, with his head bent, he had waited with patience for Sorbus to complete her transit unaided.

"What scolding missives from Invar do you bring to me?" Sorbus asked of the baker, as if she were inquiring about the weather or some other such mundane thing.

It was strange, Pliant thought, to hear the king addressed without his title, and with no deference to his station.

"The king wishes more exploding stones," the peasant answered, referring to the Crone's weapons, employed of late against the enemy forces once besieging the city.

The Crone seemed much amazed at this news and asked him, "Have not the enemies of the king fled from the field in terror?"

"Yes," Pliant answered, "but King Invar now wishes to press the enemy. He has told me that he plans to attack the many forest kingdoms in the north. More stones are therefore needed."

Pliant saw that this information caused Sorbus to concentrate with a heavy contemplation, and misreading the situation he quickly added, "Does not the fortress hold more stones, or perhaps other, unknown weapons of destruction?"

The ancient Crone then grunted in open disgust. This discourse was not what she had wanted to hear from him. That was evident enough by the look on her distorted face.

"The purpose of Forecastle is not to serve the king," she said with a sour tone while gazing at Pliant to read his reaction.

The poor baker was stunned by these unforeseen words. He didn't understand them. Pliant glanced at the girl, but she was looking to her mother, and was therefore no use to him for interpretation of the old woman's strange utterance.

The ancient Crone had long been known, for years now, as a staunch servant of the king, and so Pliant was puzzled by the comment. After all, everyone and everything served the monarch. Was that not the natural and proper order of things?

"The king," he started to respond, but Sorbus cut him off by sternly saying, "This massive fortress has been here, good baker, far longer than any king, and also the reason behind the fortress."

Now Pliant was even more confused. Being an intelligent man, he didn't like the feeling. Still, he knew his duty and stuck to it.

"But Sorbus," he asked, baffled and at a loss, "what is more important than one's steadfast service?"

At this the Crone laughed to herself, saying, "You are correct, of course. Nothing is more important than one's own devotion to duty, especially when that obligation is heartfelt, but I serve only

Forecastle and not the king." Again she stopped and looked at him, the better to gauge his response.

"Why must you do so?" he asked.

"To do otherwise, for me at least, is forbidden," she said. "It is my Mandate. I can travel no other course."

At this pronouncement, Pliant looked to the girl, but she was still staring at her mother and did not meet his searching eyes. He turned back to Sorbus but said nothing. He then looked down and took a deep breath, as if in resignation.

Next, the Crone was the one who misread him. The old woman thought that he was finished, but he wasn't, far from it. She began to speak, but this time he cut her off.

Pliant looked up and boldly asked her, "Pray tell me, Sorbus, who built this grand fortress, and why?"

This question threw the Crone, blindsiding her, for the words were totally unexpected. She had thought the mighty fortress itself would be enough. Yet she had been mistaken in Pliant's case.

This was a strange occurrence that didn't happen often. The old woman was seldom, if ever, wrong. In spite of this fact, she smiled.

She had realized, yet again, that this plain, uncomplicated baker was a conscientious and thinking man. She was pleased with her choice of him over all the others she could have picked at the time. Still, she liked the way she could amaze these simple people.

"The one I serve," she said in her creepiest voice, pausing for the most dramatic effect, "is not of this world."

This ploy didn't work. Her little scheme backfired. Worse, he didn't even seem to notice it.

Pliant persisted, unperturbed, as if she had said nothing of consequence, but she had.

"This one of another world," he asked, "is a god?"

Now Sorbus paused in earnest, to consider the ramifications. Court intrigues were one thing, but what people thought and felt was another thing altogether. Still, she had come this far.

The Crone nodded, saying, "For me, He is the highest god, and so His name is Primus. I serve Him, and Him alone. He Himself conveyed to me my Mandate."

She slowly leaned forward, and pushing aside her wimple, she exposed her wrinkled neck, and then showed him the bright red identification tag that hung there.

"He gave this to me," she added, "as a token of my servitude."

Pliant looked and nodded, contemplating. Here was part of the answer. Now he knew who created the giant structure, but still he didn't know why it was built.

He took another deep breath and continued, "You said you serve this place, but what is the true purpose of the fortress?"

Sorbus stared at him a long moment. The old woman had him now and she knew it. Finesse was everything.

"The purpose of Forecastle," she said, drawing out each word, "is to contain the beast kept under the keep."

"The beast?" he asked, shocked to the core. He had never heard of any such beast. The poor baker was all attention now, his eyes riveted on the bent little woman.

It was true that Sorbus was striking to see. Yet, as he awaited her explanation, he noticed that she was not as repugnant as all the numerous stories about her stated. She was just very old and the long years had taken a heavy toll on her.

Sorbus leaned closer and said, "A ferocious beast is contained within the very dungeon beneath this fortress, but barely so."

Pliant raised his eyebrows at this frightening assertion, but he did not dare to interrupt the Crone.

She still had it, thought Sorbus.

"The beast is fierce and terrible to behold," she continued, "and must be held in check at all costs. That is why Forecastle was erected to begin with. It lives to contain the horrid beast, but now the fortress needs help to live, and I am here to give it that help."

"But the king must be told," protested Pliant.

The old Crone countered him with, "He knows already. He has always known, but he does not understand, nor trouble himself over the far-reaching consequences. King Invar cares for nothing at all but himself and his crumbling kingdom."

She leaned back, continuing, her fingertips just touching.

"No matter," she advised him, "for Invar is unimportant in the bigger scheme of things. Only the terrible beast is important. At all costs, it must not run rampant."

This was heady news, completely unexpected. Pliant didn't know how to react, nor how best to proceed. It was a foreign feeling, for in general this lowly peasant was pretty good at knowing what to do in most any situation.

"I do not serve this petty king," she added, "but this impressive fortress. It must be so. And you must help me in my task or the beast will indeed escape and destroy us all."

Sad to say, she knew that this was true.

The mere thought terrified the peasant. It was a hard thing to hear, that destruction was so close. Still, he wished to know more.

"But what will become of us when you are gone?" he asked.

"Pliant!" said the girl, speaking for the first time, but the Crone raised one cadaverous hand and silenced her.

"Let him speak," she commanded, and Pliant continued, this time trying to choose his words well.

"Sorbus," he said, "you are old and," but the girl was horrified by this thrust. She tried to stop him, to protect her mother anew. Then the Crone leaned in and took the girl's hands in her own.

"My child," she said with tenderness, "you are a clever girl and ever have been. Always you have spoken well, and so your name is Lucid. Tell me now, do you remember, so many years ago, when you first came to live with me?"

"No, mother, I was but a babe," was her answer.

"Yes, yes," said the Crone patting Lucid's hand. "I meant later. Do you remember growing up at our hut in the wood?"

"Of course I do, mother," the young girl said, with her great green eyes open in startled wonder. She thought of those times often. Why wouldn't she remember?

"Think well, my daughter," Sorbus said. She leaned her hunched body in still closer. "Was I younger then?"

Lucid paused but the answer came with ease.

"No, mother," she said.

The Crone grunted and nodded.

She then asked, "And now, my dear child, am I older?"

Lucid understood. The answer now became obvious to her. The implication that followed was as well.

"No, mother," the girl answered.

Sorbus turned to Pliant.

"Believe this, my son," the Crone lectured the stunned peasant, "I do not age and will not die. Beware this king, but pay him no heed. He is not important in the main."

With this proclamation, Pliant felt the hair on the back of his neck stand on end. Such an admonition was indeed shocking. The ramifications were many and unknown.

"Remember," said the old, bent woman, "at all costs, the fortress must live to contain the beast, terrible to behold. It must be so. Only the Mandate is paramount."

She then let go her daughter's hands and again leaned back in her chair. Her demeanor was resolute. The game was on.

"Help me," she pleaded.

Pliant knew what she was asking and it was no slight thing. This was high treason, no doubt about it. Heads could roll.

The baker had come far in the last year, working hard in his honest and diligent service to the king. He had reached great heights. Now such talk risked everything that he had struggled for.

Pliant thought back to the many harsh and taunting jeers that he had put up with while searching for the elusive fortress. Then he thought of his grand reception once it had been found. Next he looked at Lucid, who this time met his eye.

She was so beautiful, and as she smiled and nodded her head, Pliant now saw that she loved him. He took her hand in his own. It felt warm and, somehow, as if it belonged there.

"What must I do?" he asked of Sorbus.

The Crone then stood and shuffled back to her chair behind the desk. She had thought long and hard over the proper measures. Simplicity was always the best course.

After taking a seat, she said to him, "Do nothing now, save act as if all is well, and go about your everyday business. Nothing must seem amiss. Invar's suspicions must not be raised."

Pliant thought this over a moment, and then he asked of her, "And what about the exploding stones?"

"Tell the king," she instructed him, "that I've told you there are no more weapons for me to give. Of course, the king will not believe it, and will then come to me himself. You must come also and we will deal with him at that time."

"And we will kill him?" he asked her in wonderment.

"Were it so easy, but I fear that old Invar will not die with such compliance," she answered. Then to reassure him she added, "No one will die as long as the fortress lives. We will simply hold him here, and you, acknowledged as his official spokesman, will issue any commands that are needed in his name."

"But others may come, wishing to see him," said Pliant, looking for a flaw in the ever-growing arrangement.

"Not to worry," she answered, "for they will hold fast. They are afraid, you see, of the fortress and its many secrets," and here she smiled, "and of me." The old woman seemed to relish this idea.

As she spoke, she fingered a small silver pin on the collar of her dress. It was very plain but also very elegant, and was in the shape of a just-blooming rose. This was an old habit of hers and she often performed such action without thinking.

"And what will happen then?" asked Pliant, wishing to know all facets of their proposed treason.

"As I mentioned before," Sorbus informed him, "the stricken fortress needs much help. I must have the time, unimpeded, to nurse it back to its normal strength. Once that is done, the beast shall not escape and all of us will remain safe."

"So," Pliant continued, trying hard to understand in totality, "you shall then rule Am-Rif in the king's stead?"

At this, the Crone laughed, her distorted head thrown back.

"No, my son," she said. "I shall be busy with my healing ways, and Lucid shall be assisting me in my endeavors. It must be so."

"But Sorbus, the kingdom must be run," said Pliant, trying to be instructive. "Every day decisions must be made and commands issued. The ravaged city is only just rebuilding and the empire itself must be pulled back together."

"So it shall be, Pliant, by your leave," she said, no longer jovial.

"By my leave?" the peasant said. The baker was as clever as anyone, and more so than most were, but he had not yet gained the full import of the Crone's devious plan. He soon would though.

"Why, yes, Pliant," said the old woman with patience, as one would address a child, "you shall then rule the empire."

The girl, who was holding Pliant's hand, now felt him flinch at this profound news. He sat unmoving just for a moment and then

115

he turned his head to once again cast his gaze on her. Seeing Lucid still smiling at him, he smiled back at her, but only absent-mindedly, for he was stunned by what he had just heard.

He looked again at Sorbus but remained silent, for he had nothing further to say. He had never in his wildest dreams conceived of such an unexpected turn of events and the consequences were beyond staggering. Talk about more work!

Sorbus saw that he was in a state of shock. It would pass, she knew. The bent, but determined old woman understood just how to bring the man quickly back to his usual senses.

"Would you rather the young Duke of Fervent?" she asked him.

This time he squeezed Lucid's hand on purpose, to reassure her. Then he squeezed again, to reassure himself. Then, upon more reflection, he thought that it might not be so terrible after all.

In fact, Pliant had considered often of late, almost every day, of how certain things should be changed. Dealing with the inefficient system that was now in place, he had realized how easily it could be bettered with just a few simple modifications. Again the baker increased his grip on Lucid's soft hand.

"I leave tonight to report at once to the king," he announced.

The Crone smiled a wide smile, her toothless mouth twitching and her smaller eye closed. The plan was in play. She was content.

"As you wish," she said to him.

Just then the mighty fortress went black and the ever-present background buzzing of the place ceased to be.

Pliant, ever resourceful, busied himself in the dark by striking a flint and lighting the snub of a candle that he always carried.

"Mother," asked Lucid, "what has happened?"

The Crone was dismayed. She seemed deflated, and looked lifeless. Her already grim face, illuminated by the flickering candlelight, was an eerie portrait.

She leaned forward on her desk, answering, "The power has been shut off." She then looked to each of them in turn. "The beast in the dungeon," she whispered, "is dead."

The young couple was mystified by this baffling turn of events. Not so Sorbus, for she knew everything. Still, the Crone was pensive, consumed by the vast implications.

There was no going back now, that much was evident.

Just how had it all come to this, the old Crone mused?

PART THREE - THE BEGINNING
CHAPTER SEVEN
ALL ABOARD

Archie Spume awoke with a start, unaware until that moment that he had even been asleep. But he had been, and deeply so, with his long, lean body pitched back in his well-worn captain's chair, and his large feet propped up on the edge of his control console. For Archie, this stance was nothing new.

He assumed the position often during such a deep space voyage. He was in command of his destiny as well as his ship, and being alone on his vessel, he often did not bother to crawl back into his cramped bunk that was located just aft within spitting distance. Rather, the man slept and ate and passed the long, lonely hours where he wished, with little set routine to bind him.

He was surprised that he had slept so deeply, almost toppling over backwards when he awoke. Instead, he only dropped the clipboard that had been on his lap. It, not he, had crashed to the metal grid that served as a floor in his ship's command center.

Archie was disoriented, his eyes puffy from sleep. It took him a few seconds to clear his head enough to shut off the blaring alarm that had awakened him. This was nothing new, either.

"Deferent," he said as he stretched his long arms.

"Standing by," came the bland reply from his ship's computer.

"Alarm off," he barked, "I'm awake already."

Archie was never at his best upon arising, and in the past that fact had more than once gotten him into trouble. He had often lashed out at those unfortunate enough to try and roust him from his slumber. It didn't help either, that he always felt bad about it later, after belatedly realizing what he had done.

Then again, screaming at his ship's machinery would, in fact, hurt no one, and as such, Archie now thought nothing of his outburst. Still, it was a good thing that he had held the foresight to order the wake-up call for now he had much to do. If his sleepy brain could just recall what it was, he would get right to it, too.

He retrieved his clipboard from the floor but gave up looking at its contents for his just awakened eyes would not focus. Then, with an abrupt jerk of his head, he remembered his task at hand. He had to check on the progress of his still unfinished, urgent business.

He slumped back in his chair with a sigh.

"Deferent," he asked, "what's the status in cargo bay One?"

"Pressure normal, cargo bay Alpha," was the Deferent's reply.

Archie grunted. That was something, at least. He had been so keyed up over the strange circumstances of the past day, that he hadn't been sure how he was going to pass the time needed before he could safely enter the bay.

The huge cargo hold, one of six on his supply ship, the Deferent, took close to five hours to pressurize. And five hours could be a substantial interim when you were alone. Now Archie realized that he had slept through the bulk of that time.

It was just what he had most needed to calm him down.

At least this whole crazy thing was a much-welcomed break in his long and drawn out normal routine. On a run like this one he had little to do to occupy his all too lengthy and lonely hours. His stock of old movies and computer games had already grown stale, and he never had been much of a reader.

As always on such a distant deep space delivery, Archie's route was preprogrammed into the onboard computer, and, in reality, his ship ran itself. All he need do was monitor the Deferent's already set systems. He simply lived his life in the tiny command center while the rest of the looming vessel, close to a mile long, was locked down tight against the cold universe surrounding it.

Dwell on the bright side, he thought. At this point, two days out from his final destination, his planned itinerary for killing the lingering hours had worn pretty thin no matter how you looked at it. At least now he wasn't bored stiff on this passage.

All of a sudden, Archie felt invigorated.

"Deferent," he asked, "time remaining for the pods to hatch?"

His ship's computerized voice, always calm, always steady, answered him with the usual deadpan monotone.

"Number one cryogenic unit fully operational in ten minutes," it said. Then, "Number two cryogenic unit fully operational in twenty minutes." And, at last, "Number three cryogenic unit fully operational in thirty minutes."

Archie looked over the information on his battered clipboard but it was a wasted movement. He was not concentrating on the many pages it held, instead thinking of his three sleeping passengers in cargo bay One. They would be surprised over being awakened now and not at their final destination, on the small, far-flung planet of Am-Rif Arret.

And Archie thought that he had been groggy. The man knew that coming out of an induced deep sleep was quite an eye-opening experience, to employ the standard overused pun. It was a situation that he seldom observed, however.

Of late, he just dropped off his cargo unopened, then turned around and left with alacrity. These days, none of his destinations was very exciting, and so none was much worth investigating. He could always be bored aboard his ship.

"Deferent," he said, "give us a gallon of hot coffee in bay One." He knew that his passengers would be out of it when they began to struggle through their deep sleep. That would help, at least.

"One gallon hot coffee in Alpha bay in thirty seconds," was the bland reply of the computerized voice.

Archie sat thinking a moment, concentrating hard. He normally did this on the brink of something big. It often calmed him.

He always worked best under pressure, although it had been some time since he'd had any, and now that he was in a situation with some real, palpable tension, he remembered the absent feeling well. So he relished blowing a few moments on himself before jumping in. In the past, doing so somehow had always made him sharper, and besides, it might be quite a while before Archie found himself alone again.

It was funny, the previously bored man thought to himself, how sometimes things work themselves out.

"Be careful what you wish for," he said, smiling.

As he entered the immense bay, only a short distance from the command center via a tunneled bulkhead, the rich aroma of freshly brewed coffee assaulted him. The lingering, pungent odor thickened the newly pressurized air. Just sniffing it settled him down a bit, as if he had already consumed some.

He sat at a console on the fore wall that served as his warehouse office. In truth, all six of the Deferent's cargo bays were just gigantic warehouses attached to the ship's massive engines on one end and Archie's miniscule command center on the other. He swiveled in his console chair and after checking the bills of lading on his clipboard for the hundredth time since this crisis began, he looked up to glance at the cryogenic pods located just before him.

The three were identical. Large and industrial gray, all stood rooted side-by-side before everything else in the crammed cargo bay. They looked like mirrored images of each other.

The machines had the same dials and buttons, switches and gauges, perfectly matched, and the exact, various-sized hoses and insulated wires protruding off in all directions. The units, self contained, massive and still, were perched abreast each other, facing Archie's desk. Above the control panels, each held a frosty window taking up the upper third of the pod's coffin-like door.

Pods were a bold technological statement, but always looked to him much like run amuck video games stuck on a tank chassis.

His emergency instructions had arrived the day before, literally out of the blue. He was advised in curt language of the immediate, pressing need to revive two of the three well-frozen occupants of the pods. It seemed that those two were essential to containing the still unknown, but ever looming and growing crisis that was unfolding at their approaching destination.

But Archie, as Captain of the Deferent, instead had made a contrary command decision. He was reviving all three of his sleeping passengers. He knew this was a selfish action on his part but it was a move already made and he didn't regret it.

This was because a beautiful woman was cradled within the third pod. He could just make out her striking face through the icy glass on her unit, and that fact had only increased her allure for him. Archie had first noticed her some six weeks prior, while supervising the loading of his ship's cargo, and he'd been having difficulty since then not thinking of her, dreaming of her really.

For some time now, Archie had known that he was fed up, and not only with his dull, daily grind of a routine, but also with his total life in general. Of late, he had been wondering if he should just hang it all up and get a real job, and one with a real life attached. Maybe he should just drop everything, sell the ship, and stop traveling alone across the vastness of the cold universe.

If only, Archie thought, he had a woman like this one by his side, he would do it, and in an instant. If it weren't such a hassle to pressurize the huge bay, he would have already spent much of his time down here just staring at her. As it turned out, he had settled for her image via the bay's security camera, and, after six weeks of looking, he could see her haunting face with his eyes closed.

Archie was dying to know if she was anything at all in the flesh as she was in his imagination. Now he would have her awake for some well-deserved good-looking company and find out. The others would no doubt be consumed with the emergency situation unfolding on the planet beyond, still two days away.

He knew that he could always report his instructions had been garbled. Anyway, talk of tactics and strategy had never failed to numb him. Not beautiful women though, and not such a woman on a now-exciting deep space voyage.

All that Archie knew about her was contained on his trusty clipboard. According to her bill of lading, she was a social anthropologist, whatever that was. Her name was Doctor Judith Hall, and she was some sort of Historian, he guessed.

Well, not much to go on but no matter. In his own personal history he'd known less about other women and now he would have two days to get to know her better. Of course, she may not be too talkative, but that wouldn't bother him much.

He still could look at her even if she didn't speak to him.

The next pod contained a time jumper by the name of Jonus Welleb. He seemed to have dark hair and plain features, although it was kind of hard to tell. His image behind the frosted glass, as the woman's, was somewhat distorted.

He was of no concern to Archie anyway, for this man was just a technician, and they were, as a rule, a pretty dull lot. The ones he'd known in the past had always lived inside their own little world. Archie was bored enough, thank you.

But the last unit, now that was a different story. According to his clipboard, it contained a very important person, the new top man in fact. Archie couldn't ignore him.

"Commander Morris," he read aloud, to no one. No less than the incoming Commandant of the isolated outpost of Station Forecast, their final destination. The installation was located in a far-flung solar system near the very edge of the galaxy on a smallish planet designated on his star charts as A-RA.

The Commander was literally crammed into his pod, Archie saw, for he was a very large man. He could just see his chin through the glass of his unit with the rest of his head and shoulders hidden from view, above. As a rule, Archie steered clear of military types, for he was somewhat unstructured in his own lifestyle and they tended to be professionally rigid in their well-set routines.

Somehow this one's glaring size gave Archie an odd feeling. Apprehension? His own overbearing father had been a large person, very large, as Archie remembered him.

But what the hell, Archie thought, he's not my old man, and I'm no longer just some punk kid either. No, old Archie had gotten around some since then. Still, he felt uneasy.

As he sat thinking and looking at the pod, the seal of the heavy door of Morris' unit broke open, letting out the normal blast of cold, hissing air as it did so. Archie stood, and crossing to the machine he opened the door as wide as it would go. The full view he got after was almost comical, for the large Commander seemed to take up every available inch of the space within the pod.

His knees were bent to accommodate his massive bulk and his heavy arms were compressed against his oversized frame. The military man looked like something within an egg just before hatching, thought Archie, which in effect was just what he was. The thawing occupant of the still-chilly pod then started to move, and Archie reached out and touched him on the arm.

"It's OK, Commander Morris," he said. "Just take it easy. It's normal to be disoriented for a few minutes when you come to but I guess I don't need to tell you that."

He then helped the big man out of his unit and, steadying him as best he could, the two crossed the short distance to a stout metal bench bolted into the bulkhead next to Archie's desk.

Commander Morris sat dumbfounded, dazed and staring around with his small, black eyes opened widely. Both eyes were also bulging profusely. Archie knew that this was normal, and only temporary for one just awakened from induced deep sleep, something or other to do with the pressure differential.

Still, the effect did look rather comical on the big man. Archie had a difficult time not saying something snide that alluded to the

Commander's present, distorted condition. After all, the still disoriented man before him was huge, a professional soldier, and he might not have a well-developed sense of humor.

A few seconds later, Archie saw from the slowly-changing, but still surprised look on the Commander's face, that Morris was trying hard to clear his long dormant brain.

"Just take deep breaths, in and out," Archie said, trying not to be too intrusive. "You'll be fine in a few minutes. I've got plenty of hot coffee here when you're ready."

Morris smiled, as if pleased by this warm thought, but still his opening words were directed elsewhere. Although he was plainly confused, he was first and foremost a military man, and he was now fighting hard to understand. This was outside the normal operating procedure and he needed to know why.

"Where am I," he asked, and then he added, as he struggled to focus on this tall, thin man before him, "and just who are you?"

Archie handed Morris a mug of steaming coffee as he answered, "I'm Captain Spume, and you're on my cargo ship, the Deferent. You're on the last leg of your journey, but I've been directed to wake you earlier than planned. Just take a minute or two and clear your head and then I'll try my best to answer any questions that you may have concerning the situation."

The second pod's seal then opened and Archie went through the same process with the time jumper. All the while, Morris sat drinking his coffee, observing the scene before him as if it were some play in progress. By now, his eyes were popping only a bit.

When the third pod opened, Morris stood and crossed to help Archie with the door of the unit. The Commander then lifted the beautiful Doctor Hall, cradling her in his massive arms as he carried her to the bench. This time it was Archie and the technician who watched the scene in silence.

Now, Archie was a laid back and lazy man, but he was also observant, and he recognized a tenderness the big man employed toward the still-stupefied woman. These two were not just strangers thrown together on a chance journey across deep space. He supposed that the pair shared a history of some kind or other.

However, Archie had little time to contemplate this mystery, for once she was situated on the bench, the now-awakened Commander turned his overly-large frame to him.

"Well, Captain Spume," Morris said tersely, "just what is the situation here? Why have we been cracked open so soon? And what's the status on Am-Rif Arret?"

Archie had known these questions were coming and he'd been prepared to give what limited answers he had in response, but now he was the one feeling cramped. The hulking Commander was just too close. It reminded him of his childhood.

Archie was considered by most to be a tall man, but he was a full head shorter than the agitated giant now looming before him. The young Captain was fighting off a flashback of his overbearing father peppering him nonstop for answers that he always knew were never good enough to satisfy. He didn't like the memory.

Then the time jumper broke the tension by saying to the Commander, "Come on now, Moe, this isn't one of your normal back room interrogations, you know."

Both men turned and looked at the technician.

He was sitting with his elbows on his knees, a coffee cup now cradled in both hands. His face, newly revealed to be handsome, held an impish look. His smile was broad, and his dark eyes already had shrunk back to their normal size.

Archie realized that these two passengers also shared a history.

"Hey, it's OK," he said, 'I understand. The Commander's got every right to know what's happening at his station. The problem is, I just don't know too much."

"Start at the beginning," Morris said. Before Archie could, the big man looked to the time jumper and added, "And you, Jonus, just keep your trap shut." The Commander would never have put up with such a performance if the players involved had been in the military and he had little patience with civilians.

"We're now less than two days out from Station Forecast," Archie began. "Yesterday my detection screen picked up something sufficient to set off the alarm. It was a standard identification beacon, and it was coming right for us."

Morris raised his eyebrows at this news. Archie just nodded. At the time, he'd had much the same reaction.

Archie continued his briefing, saying, "It took me nearly six hours to maneuver close enough to intercept it and bring it aboard. It was tricky though and I almost missed it. It contained an encrypted message from the station."

"They sent a message in a beacon?" Morris asked, shocked. He hadn't expected that. "Why would they do such a thing?"

"That's what I wanted to know," said Archie, "so I tried to raise them on the horn." This referred to the Deferent's communication system. It was old equipment, but still dependable.

"But I couldn't," Archie continued, "for it seems the whole planet is surrounded by some sort of interference. No conventional messages can get through, and I guess that's why they sent the beacon. They had to punch their way out, don't you see?"

But Morris refused to see anything without first sizing up all the available information and the big military man knew that he had yet to be apprised of the whole situation. This was typical for civilians. For a briefing, it was piss poor.

"And the information in the beacon?" he asked.

In answer, Archie tore a sheet from his ever-present clipboard.

"Just that there's an emergency at the station," he said, "and that I should open up you two posthaste."

The technician stood and crossed over to his big friend's side, in order to scan the paper Morris now held.

"I guess they want you both up and ready to go when we get there," Archie added, thus completing his briefing.

All three of them were startled to hear another voice in the bay.

"But you opened all three pods," said Doctor Hall.

Archie hadn't the time to respond to this, for swifter than he would have thought the transit even possible Morris dashed over to the bench and knelt beside her. He was so tall and she so short, that from this position his eyes still looked down on the sitting woman. The contrast between them could not be missed.

"You all right, Julie?" he asked her with real concern in his voice. "Take a minute. Do you need something?"

She answered him first by reaching out to touch his face, and only then did she say, "I'm fine, Morris."

At this, he beamed.

She smiled at him and added, "Just give me a moment."

As Archie stared open-mouthed, the technician asked him, "So Captain, what kind of equipment do you have on this boat?"

When the stunned Archie just looked at him in response, Jonus first cocked his head, then slapped the taller man on the back and added, "I'm a pretty fair hand with machinery. Let's go check it out. Maybe I can get us a closer look."

Archie, after realizing that Jonus wanted to give the other two some privacy, said, "Oh sure, yeah. Just come this way, and call me Archie, if you want." Both then exited the bay by way of the tunnel heading toward the command center.

The Commander was already fretting over the woman.

"You sure you're OK, Julie? Your eyes look fine but it always takes some time to clear your head. Just breathe deeply, in and out," he said to her in one lengthy breath.

"I've done this before, Morris," she said, laughing. "I know what to do. But thank you all the same for being concerned."

Then, at once she became rigid. Too late the diminutive woman wished she had not spoken the words. They were, under the circumstances, a bad choice for her.

Commander Morris looked crushed by her changed demeanor. He glanced to the floor but then, his broad, round face became focused, and he looked up again, resolved. He realized he might have limited opportunity to press his desperate case.

The Commander had thought of little else for a long time now. Only cryogenic sleep had slowed his obsession for her, and he was now wide-awake. And, like a military campaign, he had already planned his entire strategy to finally win her heart.

Morris was confident in the soundness of his presentation. He had worked it all out to the slightest detail. He was sure of which points to stress first and which ones to touch on later, what to allude to now and what to omit altogether, and so forth.

The Commander had known Judith a good while now, and he thought he knew her pretty well. In fact, he hoped that he knew her better than she knew herself. That was his premise anyway, upon which his grandiose plans were based.

She had been confused and upset, that was all, he was convinced of it. He would make her see that. It was only a matter of time before he'd bring her around to his way of thinking.

Morris had believed his presentation well reasoned and to the point, but once he looked at her, he found to his consternation that he didn't know just where to begin. Now, he wasn't so sure of his opening, and with her attitude of late that could be quite a large negative factor against his elaborately planned tactics. Still, having to say something to her, he bumbled on.

"I didn't think we'd have a chance to talk before we arrived at the station," he started. He should have phrased his statement better for it was a bad choice of words for him. Without hesitation she cut him off, her face now hard and her manner stern.

130

"We don't have anything to talk about, Morris," she said. "We both know that's true. We've discussed it."

Under normal circumstances, there was nothing he would not do for this striking woman, but now Morris did not heed her wishes. The fight was currently on and he wasn't going to lose. He pressed forward with a fixed determination.

"You know he doesn't love you, Julie," he almost spat, at once forgetting all his well-laid battle plans. "That's more than obvious. He's too self-absorbed to love anyone."

She answered him with equal vigor, "He does love me and I him, I've told you so before."

At this, the big man looked away from her piercing glare and stared at the metal grid of the cargo bay's floor.

"But I love you too, Julie," he said under his breath. When he looked up, he had tears pooling in his eyes. Judith Hall was touched by this heartfelt display, but she knew that the unfinished business between them had to be resolved.

She also knew that it had to be done now. The hulking man had already pursued her halfway across the galaxy. His fixation with her had to end, and here, not later on the planet of Am-Rif Arret.

No, on the planet below, she knew she would have enough to deal with without this hanging over her.

She had put him off when they met, unexpectedly on her part, at the loading docks now several star systems distant. This was before they were placed into induced deep sleep for their long journey across the universe. She had been unaware until then that Morris had even put in for the position of Commandant of Station Forecast, the location of her estranged husband, Spencer.

She and Spencer, the distant station's Chief Engineer, had been separated for several long years. Before he departed, things had not gone well between them. But now she wished only to reconcile, and save their struggling marriage.

131

Judith had married young, and to an older man, to boot. Soon the freshness and vitality of their relationship had worn off. The hardworking Spencer Hall, ever the professional, had been consumed only with his career, it had seemed to her.

He appeared to have less and less time for her or their life together. Judith had felt empty. She had wanted more.

Morris had become a good friend, someone to talk to, to confide in. And then, he had become that proverbial more. And he had been a carefree jump from the blandness of the conformity, the stilted routine of a life married to the eminent engineer.

And so, she was consumed for a time with Morris. She had thrown herself into a secret life with the younger military man. Morris certainly had been worlds away from her dull, forever working and mostly absent husband.

Here was no bookworm, she had thought, no constant overachiever, as Spencer was. Here was someone who loved life, someone who loved what she had, in fact, given up. With Morris, Judith had given up nothing, or so she thought at the time.

She had felt reborn. Their relationship had been intense. Sad to say, the moment did not last.

As time progressed, she came to realize that she was receiving from him only an artificial feeling of release, and nothing more. Judith had loved being with Morris, but she had never been in love with him. He was not her answer.

Once returned to her senses, Judith realized that she simply had used Morris, and without shame. She hadn't thought in the least about his feelings in the matter. It could have been anybody.

She hadn't been proud of herself, but she had acknowledged the situation and faced Morris head-on with the bitter truth. Morris did not listen. Even now, he still would not hear.

No, Judith knew she had to be brutal, for she understood that nothing less would be effective with this determined man.

"Yes," she conceded. "You do love me, but you don't need me, Morris. We both know that you don't need anybody."

He began to respond, but she plowed on, unmoved.

"Oh, you may be sad for awhile," she said with resignation, "and you'll think of me with longing. But you'll carry on nonetheless. Your life will still be a full one."

Again Morris started to argue, but again she cut him off, this time with a dismissive wave of her hand.

"Sometime in the future you'll realize that it would have been, what," she asked, "nice? Yes, nice, but in the end you'll know that I was not as important to you as you had thought. You'll move on with your life with little problem, you'll soon see that's true."

Morris didn't know how to counter this rigid position. He had always known that she was strong-willed, but she never had been so scathing toward him. He felt wounded.

Judith didn't care about that aspect of the situation. She knew it had to be done. At this point, that's all that mattered to her.

She therefore added, "You won't be devastated, not for long, that is. Maybe, after some time passes, you'll even be a bit relieved. You'll move on, and you should, Morris."

Her words cut to the core, and were too painful for him to take. He abruptly stood and turned, in essence building a wall between the two of them with his massive frame. He was as strong as they come, but now his head was hanging low.

Still, being now quite resolute, she would not stop the onslaught. She didn't have the luxury. This had to end.

Judith continued with a steady voice, "But Spencer does love me and more. He needs me. He needs me more than I can know."

She knew that her husband had strong feelings for her, but he was an overly proud man. He wouldn't beg to be loved, nor should he have to. It was all so senseless.

"Now I realize," she said, "how much he needed me and just how hard it was for him to let me know. And I devastated him, Morris. I've hurt him deeply, and in the most terrible of ways."

The Commander recognized the truth of this pronouncement, but his only response was to hang his head further, while making and unmaking giant fists with his big fingers.

Morris had lost his fight, and he knew it. He also knew that he didn't like to lose. Judith was aware of this as well, and when she spoke next her voice was tender.

"I know you love me, Morris, but you will love again," she stressed. "Spencer would never love again. Opening up to me as he did was a great leap of faith for him, perhaps the greatest he'll ever make, and he would just give up on life."

Her eyes began to tear. How did it come to this, she wondered? How did it ever become so complicated?

"I can't allow that," she continued. "I won't allow that, I never will. Spencer is much too important to me."

Morris did not speak to this, but his eyes also dripped tears. What a waste, he was thinking. What a terrible waste.

The Commander, to calm himself, then attempted to control his breathing. He began blowing in and out deeply with an even cadence. He sounded like a blacksmith's bellows.

Judith, still distracted, didn't notice.

She continued, quietly now, as if to herself, "Oh, he'd go on with his life, but he would be dead inside. And I'm horribly afraid that I'm already too late, that I've already crossed the line. I have to know if there's any chance to make things right, if there's any way left open to patch up our life together."

She waited for some response from Morris, but when none came, she sighed a heavy sigh and closed her eyes.

She persisted in a weak voice, pleading with him, "If you truly love me, then let it go. Just let me go. Please."

In the Deferent's command center, Jonus had completed his ad hoc but professional survey of the ship's systems. It hadn't been difficult, for there weren't many. It was an old, well-used cargo vessel and the nerve center was small and cramped.

There was a limit to what instruments one would want or could afford to have on such a commercial ship.

On the other hand, all of the equipment was in excellent operating condition. Jonus could see that Archie fine-tuned it with exacting precision, for each system aboard was calibrated to a pinpoint. Then again, the time jumper thought, what else was there for Archie to do on such long, drawn-out missions?

Still, the technician didn't like what he saw.

Well, you called it true, Archie," he said. "The Deferent's power is insufficient to break through the planet's interference. I guess we'll have to wait to learn what's happening down there."

"I guess," Archie said in a serious tone, "the Commander's not gonna like that assessment very much."

Jonus laughed.

"Moe's OK," he said. "I know him well and he grows on you. He just takes some getting used to, that's all."

"Well," Archie commented without any trace of humor, "it's an easy thing to see that he's true to his clan."

Jonus laughed again, and responded in the affirmative.

"Yes," he answered, "he's a military man through and through, all right. It's literally in his blood. He's born and bred."

"You've known him long?" Archie asked of him, for the young Captain was eager to learn what he could about the big man. As Morris did, he preferred to know all of the available facts in any unknown situation. Sadly for him, poor Archie's big adventure was not unfolding in the way he had envisioned.

At the question, Jonus looked up from the Deferent's hardware and gazed through the portal built into the command center's

135

bulkhead. The approaching planet of Am-Rif Arret loomed large even though it was still a good day and a half away. Looking back through the years, Jonus didn't notice.

"I've known him a long time," he said at last. "All my life. We grew up together, ever since we were little kids."

This bit of information surprised Archie.

"You're from the Military Clan?" he asked. Jonus looked plenty strong enough, with broad shoulders and well-built arms, but he was shorter than Archie and much shorter than the hulking Commander Morris. Jonus smiled at the inquiry.

"My father was military," he said, "but he wasn't a fighter, far from it. He was true to his clan just like me. I'm a technician through and through, just like the old man."

He hunched his shoulders, to say that the fault was not his.

"Yes, I know, it's true," he continued, sheepishly, "we're everywhere, right? We're almost as bad as the damn bureaucrats." He then added, "Hey, you're not a bureaucrat, are you?"

"Oh no, not me," answered Archie, shaking his head. "Don't worry about that. I come from the Production Clan, although I haven't produced all that much of late."

Both were laughing at this exchange when Morris entered. The Deferent's control room was small. It soon became cramped by the added burden of the giant Commander's bulk.

"Can I assume that there's some good news here?" he asked.

"Sorry, Moe," said Jonus. "The interference is total. There's no way to get any information from Am-Rif Arret until we land."

The Commander, true to Archie's prediction, was not happy with this information. He needed answers, and wanted them yesterday. He had new plans to formulate.

His large, round face was scowling as he next asked, "What kind of interference is that, in the name of Primus? And how can it surround the entire planet? I've never heard of such."

"You got me," said Archie, "I've never seen anything like it."

"I have, though," Jonus offered. "The interference has the exact electromagnetic signature of the Time Fistula's containment field. But how the field has grown to surround the place is beyond me."

"Are you saying," asked Morris, incredulous, "the time-viewing machinery on the planet is responsible? I thought the time technology was well beyond safe. Tried and true through the eons, handed down from Primus Himself, and all that."

Jonus looked at both men before answering.

"Hey, I'm not of the theology clan," he said. "I'm just telling you what I know. It has the signature of the Fistula's containment."

"Just what is this Fistula?" asked Archie.

"It's the hole in time," Jonus answered. "The window through which you view the past. The containment holds it in check."

But not now?" asked Morris, trying to understand.

"No," answered Jonus. "Now the field is everywhere, a tight wrapping. That's not supposed to be possible."

"Explain yourself," ordered the Commander.

"Yeah," said Archie, also trying to follow, "just how's the time viewing machine work, anyway?"

"Well, it's like this," began the time jumper, "all matter is made up of molecules, and that means us, this desk, the air, everything. In turn, all molecules consist of atoms. Of course, beyond that you come to the various subatomic particles."

Morris and Archie looked at each other. If things progressed much further along these lines, in no time the pair would be in over their respective heads. Jonus saw they were close to being lost, a fact that was obvious by the looks on their faces.

He laughed at them, although at first he tried not to. Then he gave up trying. Morris thought this briefing was also piss poor.

"Oh, no," Jonus said holding up his hands, "it's not that bad. The point is that atoms, all atoms, in us, this desk, the air, are in large part all the same. Mostly they're composed of empty space."

Jonus paused here a few seconds for this to sink in before he continued, "So why is this desk harder than the air?"

The time jumper meant it as a rhetorical question, one set up to be answered by himself, but Archie blurted out, as if once again in his high school physics class, "Because there's more of them and, you know, they're packed in a little tighter?"

At this response, the Jonus laughed again for it was plain the young captain had flunked physics.

"Well, not so much," Jonus said with kindness. "It's that, but also it's the different speed of the particles involved. Some atoms are naturally more excitable than others are."

"So that's the only difference?" asked Morris, wanting to get to the point. He still needed some answers and he wasn't getting any. Besides, he hadn't done so well in high school himself.

"In a basic way, yes," Jonus told the two, but seeing their blank faces, he carried on. "Look, what it all comes down to is harmonics. Every atom, and therefore everything in the universe, is always vibrating, moving at its own set frequency."

"Uh huh," said Morris, as if he had heard all this before.

"Always," Jonus continued, "the outside particles in any atom are flying about the center ones. But the center is also moving, jumping around a bit within its space. So, nothing's ever static."

Their faces conveyed to Jonus that neither one of them was following any of this. He was sure. In the past, he'd seen the same blanched expressions many times before.

Undaunted, he continued with, "And these different rates of movement, different rates of natural vibration, in essence account for all the differences that we perceive."

"Yeah, so?" said Morris, still waiting for the point.

"So," answered Jonus, "Primus taught us that if you slow down the vibrations, then you in turn slow down time, that is, what we perceive as time. And further, if you can stop the harmonics altogether, then you can stop what, for us, is time. That's the general theory behind the machinery on the planet."

"So?" Morris said again, as if he knew where this was going.

Jonus carried on, "Well, in practice, it's not that simple, after all. Of course, the machine hasn't the power to slow down, much less stop time itself, but it does work in the same way, on a much smaller scale. The hardware was designed by Primus to focus only on an exact piece of time, and when you're able to stop the vibrations at that certain point, that's all you need."

This time, Archie spoke. So far, he didn't understand any of this, and he doubted that he ever would. Still, he was trying.

"What's all you need?" he asked.

"A portal," Jonus answered. "You've created a hole you see, a window in the fabric of time. It's called the Time Fistula."

Morris had gotten this point at last but it didn't help him much.

So how come there's interference around the planet?" he asked. "Because now these vibrations you've been talking about have been stopped? Is that what you're saying?"

The time jumper shook his head.

"This interference," he lectured, "comes not from the Fistula itself, but from the containment room that houses the machine. I'm sure of it. The signature doesn't lie."

Here we go again, thought Morris.

"The containment room?" he asked, still lost.

Jonus knew he was close now.

"I was taught," he said, "that the Fistula was not viable outside its containment, or vise versa. One won't work without the other and that's the beauty of the system. It's the built-in fail-safe."

"Yes, and that means?" asked Morris, trying to hold on to his composure. He still needed an answer. He still wasn't getting one.

Jonus knew this but he couldn't change the facts.

"In simple terms," he said, "there's no way that the field can act in this way. It's not possible. Not in any scenario that I can see."

"The station is pretty old," offered Archie, trying to be helpful.

"That shouldn't matter," said Jonus. "I mean, it doesn't explain the unexplainable. The hardware on the planet either will work or it won't, and it shouldn't create this interference in any case."

Once more they were startled to hear the voice of Judith Hall.

"Perhaps it's the prophecy," she said.

Again all turned to look at her. She was in the tunnel, leaning against the bulkhead with her arms crossed. She didn't try to step in, for the command center was already quite full.

Before anyone could speak, she spied, via the portal, the planet floating large. Its surface was almost covered by wispy white clouds, with a peek of deeply blue ocean showing through here and there in defiance. Not large, it was a typical example of the oxygen-bearing planets flung throughout the cosmos.

Judith nodded her head at the scene.

"It sure looks the part," she said. "And it is in the right place. Perhaps the appointed time has come at last."

Both Jonus and Morris seemed to understand this cryptic bit of information for their faces blanched after she spoke. Archie was lost, however. He had no idea to what she was referring.

"What do you mean, Doctor?" he asked, employing her official title. At this point, they had not been introduced, and one thing his father had beaten into him all those years ago was correct manners. After all, they were sometimes good for business.

"She's talking heresy," said the time jumper. "The 'Unspoken Prophecy' they call it. Don't listen to her," he warned.

Jonus then looked to Morris, as if for confirmation, but the Commander remained silent. He'd already had his fill today of arguing with this headstrong woman. He couldn't take much more.

"Come off your high horse, Jonus," said Judith without a trace of malice. "I'm an Historian. I'm only being true to my clan."

No one spoke for a moment, certainly not Archie who was not about to jump into the center of this one. Something beyond the obvious discussion at hand was going on between these three. At last, though, the tension was broken.

"I thought, Doctor," said Morris, but without looking her, "that the prophecy was prehistory. It comes from The Before Time. And I also thought," and here he gestured with his beefy hand for emphasis, "that nothing much was known for certain about anything that happened before The Golden Age of Primus."

Judith pursed her lips and shook her head, acknowledging this new boundary between them. Well, what could she expect? Her movement was lost on Morris for he was still looking away, but the other two observed the resigned reaction.

Relax, Commander," she said in a tone reminiscent of one lecturing a child, "I'm not a free thinker and I do believe Primus is supreme. Historically speaking, though, we do know certain things about The Before Time. Many things."

"But when Primus came, He destroyed all that was before," Archie said. He knew this part of the ancient story well enough. Most people did, but he'd never heard of any Unspoken Prophecy.

"Yes, that's true, of course," continued Judith, "and we don't, therefore, have any hard records of The Before Time. Yet there were accounts, contemporary accounts, of the way things were then. We have many descriptions."

"From people alive when Primus came?" asked Archie.

"Yes," she answered. "And Primus Himself permitted these accounts, or at least He didn't forbid them. That, gentlemen, is historical fact, you can look it up if you don't believe me."

Nodding to Archie, she explained, "Most everybody knows something of The Before Time, at least in general terms. It's common knowledge. That's where the various stories come from."

"You mean the various fables and tales," said Morris, sourly.

Hot on his words, the time jumper added, "Yes, Moe, all the various tall tales and doomsday heresies."

If this discourse was meant to give offense, it didn't. The woman dismissed it. She pressed on, unfazed.

She said, "All right, it was just an idea. So any of you have a better one handy?" They didn't.

No one spoke for a moment, and then Morris jumped in.

"Well Captain," he said, changing the subject and addressing Archie, "we're still a day away from the planet. This is your ship. You assigning us a billet or what?"

"Yeah, sure," Archie responded, "the Doctor can take my berth. I don't much use it and I do have some clean sheets aboard." He paused a second, then addressed the men.

"We," he said, "can crash in the bay cause it's pressurized now. There're hammocks and such stowed in the cabinet above the computer. The head, er, the bathroom is located on the port side."

He turned, and pointing to his quarters, said to Judith, "Your bathroom is on the far wall of my berth, Doctor."

"Thanks," she answered, "and call me Judith if you want to."

Archie did. As he grinned in response, he paused and thought of anything he'd missed. He'd covered the mission and the crisis.

"You people hungry?" he asked at last.

Their reactions were all in the affirmative, and he added, "Just let the computer know what you want, but be aware that it's programmed by me so it's on the spicy side."

"Well, we can't all eat in here," Judith reasoned. "I say we backtrack to the bay and after dinner, Archie, you can show me those sheets." She then turned and disappeared down the tunnel.

That was fine with Archie for his cheeks had gone red, and it was just as well that she hadn't seen his reaction. Both the men had, though. They weren't going to let it pass unnoticed, either.

Morris and Jonus eyed each other, and both started chuckling. The embarrassed Archie soon followed suit, what else could he do? All three men then broke out laughing.

"Women," said Jonus, and the three of them laughed the harder.

After the meal, when the others were hanging their hammocks in the cargo bay, Archie and Judith were topside in his berth, and indeed, he was showing her the sheets.

"Just how much is known about The Before Time?" he asked her. "And why would Primus let us know about the era? I mean, if it was forbidden to record anything from before He came?"

"As I said earlier, we have a great many accounts," she answered. "Yet all of the reports are in general terms. Primus permitted us the larger story, but He held out on the details."

Archie was listening as he retrieved the clean bed sheets from a small closet mounted in the bulkhead. Religious issues had never much interested him. She was very interesting, though.

"Why we don't know," she continued. "However, we do know that the history of our Alpha planet is a very long one. All the accounts are most emphatic on that point."

As he handed her the bedclothes, their hands touched. They both smiled. Then he started stripping off the used sheets.

"You mean the history before Primus is an old one?" he asked.

"Yes," she answered, "but that's not the correct way to put it. I mean, Primus was always there, He just didn't let Himself be known to all people before His Golden Age. To be precise, the era is referred to as 'The Golden Age of Primus', you know."

"Right, right," Archie said. He did know that much. "But what about this Unspoken Prophecy stuff?"

The two began to make the bed, and she answered him by delivering an abbreviated lecture. She liked to lecture. Archie found that he liked hearing her lecture.

"Well, it's like this," she began, "the history of our Alpha planet is old. From the early accounts, we see that it's very old. It's been estimated our species was seeded there hundreds of thousands of years ago, maybe even millions, there's no way to know."

"Wow," he said. That covered a large amount of time. How many people had lived, he wondered, in such a block of years?

"If true," she noted, "then our species has been on the Alpha planet at least as long before The Golden Age as we have after. It might be longer. Perhaps a lot longer."

"Wow," said Archie again. "What was it like back then, I wonder? Way different, I'd imagine."

They were on either side of his berth, now stripped, and she flipped him the end of a clean sheet before continuing.

"The numerous accounts," she explained, "say that through the eons, great civilizations, one by one grew from nothing and were in turn destroyed. It was a continuing spiral, a never-ending phenomenon. The poor planet was endlessly wracked by war and famine, and diseases of all kinds were rampant."

"Now, that's not good," he observed with distaste. He had been thinking in rosier terms. But life had been tough, he guessed.

She said, "Primus, during this time, would reveal Himself to someone or other, sometimes to some group or other, but the result was the same each time. It came down to the 'haves' and the 'have nots.' With no Mandate, they were lost."

"Wow," Archie said for a third time. She smiled as they tucked in the sheet. He was interested, she thought, and following well.

144

Archie was interested all right but she was his interest, so what she said was secondary. He was drinking up her entire persona, and he felt great. He couldn't believe his luck.

"There was," she continued, "constant social unrest, and the next civilization would fall. In time the growing population overtaxed the exhausted planet. By then, pollution had spoiled what little good land and water that was left."

The two were finished with the bed but not the lecture, so both next sat on the bunk, as she resumed with, "When things were at their worst, Primus revealed Himself to all and took total control. Enter The Golden Age. He soon gave us the technology we enjoy and the sweeping Mandate He desired."

"About time," said Archie. "We needed the Mandate." He meant it too, but in an overall, detached sort of way.

"You said it," she concurred. "Of course, the history of The Golden Age is known. Primus lived on the Alpha planet for twenty thousand years showing us the way to fulfill His Holy Mandate."

"Always building, ever growing, forever expanding?" he said, offering the standard line that everyone knew and recognized.

Judith agreed, and added, "And what was the end result? No more 'haves' and 'have nots.' No more wars."

"It must have been interesting to have lived back then," Archie mused. "What do you think, Judith? To have known Primus in the flesh must have been something."

"I've often thought so," she agreed.

She leaned back against the bulkhead and pulled her well-shaped legs up to her exquisite chest. She wrapped her arms around her knees and looked quite coquettish without trying. School was never like this, thought Archie, while cracking a smile.

"The first thing He did," she continued, "was to show us how to colonize the Cosmos. This had some immediate effects. It depopulated our depleted Alpha planet and opened up other worlds that began to raise food for all."

145

"Quite a solution to the 'have nots,' you have to admit," said Archie smiling. "Just give them their own planet, complete with plenty of elbow room. And there's lots of planets out there."

"Oh, come on now, Archie," she said, good-naturedly. "Don't belittle the vastness of that accomplishment. Just think, interplanetary space travel and all that comes with it."

"Hey, I agree," he admitted.

She persisted, saying, "The technology was handed down from Him alone. He taught us how to colonize the grunts, and He gave us the time-viewing equipment to help them along. There's no doubt, He provided us the ultimate purpose of our lives."

"Yes, yes, I know all that," countered Archie, with some impatience. "I know how He established all the clans to implement His Great Mandate, and how after a time, entire worlds were given over to each clan. So now, the Theology Clan is based on the Alpha planet, but what about this Unknown Prophecy?"

Judith smiled. She liked his enthusiasm. He thought she was as beautiful as anything he had ever seen.

"Yes, I'm coming to that," she said, not wanting to be rushed. "I'm getting to it. It all has to do with The Great Mandate."

"The grunts?" he asked, surprised. "What could they have to do with the prophecy? They weren't even around then."

"No," she agreed, "but the meaning does deal with them."

Archie groaned with good nature and rolled his eyes, which she realized were a rich hazel color. Then he leaned back against the bulkhead next to her. She didn't seem to mind in the least.

"I don't understand," he declared.

Taking pity on him, Judith reached over and patted his arm. She couldn't help it. He was pitiful.

"OK," she offered, "this is it, cut and dried."

"At last," he said, mocking her. Then he laughed, giving his strategy away. He was having a great time.

She ignored his jibe. It didn't bother her at all, as she knew it was given without malice. She was enjoying herself, too.

"The Before Time," she said, "lasts we don't know how long, but a long time, in any event. Then comes The Golden Age of Primus, which lasts about twenty thousand years. That's ten thousand or so to instruct and educate the populace and ten thousand or so to set up the various clans on their various planets."

"So that's how it happened?" Archie observed.

Judith ignored this lame attempt at humor.

"Next Primus leaves the Alpha planet," she announced, "and we have The After Time, also known as The Age of the Great Mandate, with another hundred thousand or so years then dedicated to seeding grunts throughout the cosmos."

"Which brings us back full circle," said Archie laughing. "We're in The After Time now." He was lost and confused.

"Perhaps," she said, "but perhaps not."

At this, Archie stopped laughing.

His eyebrows were raised now, his eyes opened in wonder. From this vantage, she saw their color was almost brown, but with tiny bits of cherry-red pigment placed throughout his irises. These small but striking specks, floating against the brownish background, cast the hazel tint in Archie's friendly eyes.

She asked, "What do you know about these Ages of Time?"

He said, "Let's see, there are four of them, and they're known as The Before Time, The Age of Primus, The After Time..."

"Or the Age of The Great Mandate," she interjected.

"Yeah, right," he agreed. "We're in that one now. And then," he asked, "next comes The New Time?"

"Correct," she concurred, "when Primus will reveal His plan for all of the evolving grunts. But there are those who believe we are now approaching the end of The After Time. That would mean the beginning of the next Age is near."

147

"And why think that?" Archie asked.

"Because now," said Jonus, who was standing in the hatchway, "the seeded grunts have made it all the way across the galaxy."

Archie and Judith both jumped at the sound of his deep voice. Neither of them had known he was there.

"And that means The Great Mandate is completed," the time jumper proclaimed with heavy sarcasm. "Amen, brother. Grunts aplenty, from one end of space to the other."

Addressing Judith, he added, "Isn't that what you meant before, about the planet being in the right place? It's across the entire galaxy from the Alpha planet. It fits the prophecy to a tee."

Without waiting for an answer, Jonus wheeled a chair from the command console to the opening of the doorway and took a seat.

"So, Judith, do you, in fact, fill your students' heads with such mush," he asked of her, "or do you save it all up for the extra-gullible people like poor old Archie here?"

"Hey!" Archie said with true offense. "I don't like your tone." He didn't care for the added company either.

Jonus had been looking at Judith, but now he turned his head to stare at Archie. His face was deadpan. His eyes were dull.

"Forget it," the time jumper said. "She's not impressed. She's not impressed easily and better than you have tried, believe me."

"That's enough, Jonus," Judith snapped. "We're just talking. That hasn't been forbidden yet, has it?"

Jonus leaned forward and placed his elbows on his knees, his blunt fingers interlocking. He looked like a man just taking a break from his daily labors. In fact, he was.

"Of course not," he answered, "but Commander Morris requests the presence of the Captain here for a little chitchat. Since all three of you won't fit on that bunk, I guess Archie will have to go down to the bay, and before you can tell him the really good part, too. Sorry, Archie, maybe next time."

148

At this crude dismissal, Archie jumped to his feet, his body tense with anger. Yet his big moment of bravado was lost on Jonus, who all but ignored him. The time jumper, still very much at ease, just slid his chair backwards to let him pass.

After he left, tromping down the tunnel muttering to himself in fury, Jonus stayed where he was. He had a good view of Judith as she sat, her arms still wrapped around her knees. She stared at him with a piercing, fixed glare of her deep azure-blue eyes.

He had no reaction at all to this but to stare back at her, as if he were bored by the whole situation. After a beat or two, she looked away and started smiling, in spite of herself. It was a fact that she didn't like him, but it was undeniable that he was persistent.

"So, Jonus," she observed, "it's good to see you've mellowed. I always hoped you would. How in the hell did you wind up here?"

The time jumper sat contemplating. It would have been easy to give her some flippant answer, and the two of them could pass some sharp-witted barbs, but that seemed like too much work. Instead he spoke the simple truth.

"J's on the planet," he said.

"J?" she cried, throwing her head back in unbridled laughter. "Who'd of thought? He's sure run a long distance to get away from you this time, hasn't he?" she asked.

He didn't react to this for he knew that she was just goading him. He also knew that she could do much better. She tried.

"Yes, little Jarvus," she said as if in a dream. "Don't you think it's time to let him grow up some? Without you, I mean."

His response was little more than a grunt. He knew it was so. He also knew that she knew he knew.

She didn't let up.

"You must admit," she added, "that's what he wants, Jonus. That's what he's always wanted. We both know that."

Jonus didn't bite. He hadn't the inclination. He didn't move.

Still holding his calm demeanor, he casually asked, "Do you honestly think it's the prophecy, Judith?"

His question was so simple that it threw her off her stride. She delayed a moment to compose herself by dropping her legs and sitting forward. Her dainty hands then started rubbing some life back into her now-uncomfortable thighs.

"So what are you after now, Jonus?" she asked him. "You're not going to sit there and plead Moe's case for him, are you? He didn't send you up here to do that, did he?"

"Moe's a big boy," Jonus said, adding as an afterthought, "to put it mildly. He can handle himself. He always has."

This time she said nothing and, at length, he added, "Gee, I've never heard you call him Moe before."

Now Judith was growing exasperated with this whole conversation, and she was never one to waste time.

"Come off it, Jonus," she said, anger in her tone. "No one calls him Moe but you, we both know that. Just what do you want?"

The time jumper sat in place for just a moment more. Then he moved only a little, but nevertheless his chair slid closer to the hatchway between them. It was his attempt at being intimate.

"Spencer's on the planet," he blandly stated. He leaned in some and added, "So is Jarvus. We need to work together here."

"Why's that?" she asked, really wanting to hear this one. Her husband and Jarvus had little connection that she knew of. Yet Jonus was here for a reason, so what was his point?

"Look," he said, "here's the situation. Moe's below decks right now grilling our young Captain for any pertinent background information. It turns out that this Archie Spume was the same hauler that dropped off the others early last year, and besides that, there's nobody else left on this tugboat for Moe to grill."

150

Jonus paused and stroked his chiseled face before continuing. He knew that she might misinterpret his next point, and probably would. It didn't matter, he continued just the same.

"Moe's, how shall I say it," he asked, "frustrated?"

Judith looked away. It was too fresh. It made no difference.

"And I'm sure on the planet, the military's doing the same thing to everybody they can lay their hands on." Jonus added. They'll be excitable, overly so given what's happened. You know how they are, the Civil War's barely ended."

"You mean the Holy War?" she corrected him.

"Whatever," he answered without rancor. "The point is they always concentrate on the worst-case scenario first. Only then do they look around for other explanations."

This comment was preaching to the choir as far as she was concerned. She had never much liked the military nor their agenda. Morris had been an exception for her.

"They'll be searching under any rock they have to," he said. "It's their job, and they can't afford to look bad at it. Before long, they'll find something and well, it might not be very pretty."

He had her full attention now, but she still didn't understand his overall thrust, if there even was one. What was he after, she wondered? What did he need from her?

"And?" she asked, trying to find out.

Jonus leaned back in his chair before answering. He had a faraway look in his eyes. Judith didn't like the look.

"Moe thinks there's a spy," he stated, with no trace of emotion.

"What?" she asked, not believing what he had said. "A spy on this meaningless planet? The war never reached this far out in the galaxy, and besides, the war's over, it's finished."

Jonus hunched his broad shoulders.

151

"Moe thinks it's sabotage," he said, "and I can hardly argue against that premise. Something out of the ordinary has happened there, and I sure can't explain it. I do know that this is not an everyday, run-of-the-mill system breakdown."

"And because of that you think Spencer is a free thinker?" Judith asked him, incredulous. "Or Jarvus? Get real, Jonus, mostly Jarvus doesn't even think at all."

This time, it was the time jumper who bolted up. He shot his chair backwards with enough force to propel it crashing into the command console. She had gotten to him, and without even trying.

He turned and looked through the portal. The planet was growing ever closer. He had to make her understand.

"They're down there," he said, fighting to hold on to his composure. "Spencer and Jarvus, both. And they're both alone."

Then turning for emphasis, he added, "I've known these types all my life, I grew up in the military. They don't like to lose, and they stick together. They'll pin this on somebody if they have to."

"You think so?" she asked him. The idea was absurd, but that didn't matter. If the powers that be needed scapegoats, then both her husband and his brother could fit the bill.

"Spencer and Jarvus are outsiders," he stated. "They have no protection. We need to work together, for their sakes."

Below decks, Morris was not through with the hapless Archie.

"And nothing out of the ordinary occurred," he demanded, "when you landed with the station's original complement?"

Archie was well past being tired of this whole episode.

"Beyond the fact that the station had been sealed off, no," he answered. Then he had a sudden flash of insight. Could it be?

"Maybe that's it," the young captain said. "Because of the war, the station had been shut down for twenty-five hundred years. Maybe the grunts themselves somehow are responsible, maybe in the interim they somehow got inside and did something."

152

"Negative," stated Morris. The big man pointed at the bay's computer console that now displayed a superimposed map over the planet's topography. Both men were bent over looking at it.

"The station is here," said the Commander.

"Right," said Archie, "I've been there before, remember?"

Morris ignored the sarcasm.

"The planet's grunts are all located further away, here, here, and here," he said, using his huge finger to point out the different placements. "And besides, the grunts are incapable of such convoluted doings. According to the first contingent's reports, they were not even evolving on schedule."

In fact, Morris had considered this possibility, but had rejected it. It didn't fit the circumstances. There had to be another plausible explanation and he was going to find it.

"That's why Jonus and Julie were sent for," he continued. "He's to run the equipment to view the past and she's to observe and give her recommendations. That's their jobs."

This reminded Archie of the two in his command center.

"What's the story on Julie and Jonus, Moe?" he therefore asked. "Seems they have a history. You know them both, right?"

The big man straightened, becoming very tense.

"Her name is Judith," he said, "and mine is Morris, Captain."

Archie's eyebrows went up at this.

The Commander soon relaxed and continued.

"But, yes," he then returned to the point, "and we've all known each other for a long time now. The two of them go way back. The fact is, Jonus introduced me to Doctor Hall."

Archie didn't know how to respond, so he said only, "I see."

"Both are upset," explained Morris, "and it's a natural reaction, as they both have family on the planet."

"I see," again said Archie. Yet he was confused. After a pause, he asked, "What's this Unspoken Prophecy thing?"

The Commander then turned and sat in Archie's well-used chair. If Archie hadn't seen it done, he wouldn't have believed it possible, but it was. The giant crammed his frame into the seat with relative ease and looked pretty comfortable after he did so, although he resembled a grown man in kindergarten.

"Oh, I wouldn't put any stock into that one," he offered. "The prophecy is just an excuse used by the heretics, these free thinkers, to wage their infernal war. If they didn't have it, they would just come up with some other pretext."

"It has something to do with these different Ages of Time, I take it," wondered Archie, his bland tone contrived to convey that he didn't care one way or the other, although he did.

Morris nodded at the question.

"It's the 'Trinity Heresy,'" he said. "It states that there are only three Ages of Time, not the four Primus dictated. It's an absurd position, but it's what they believe."

"Only three?" asked Archie. "How does that work, if we're in the Third Age now? Does nothing come after us?"

"Oh, sure," said Morris, "there's always something different that's gonna happen. Otherwise, why have a prophecy? But these heretics think we're still in the Second Age now."

"Still in The Age of Primus?" asked Archie. He was confused. He had thought that he'd been following pretty well up to now.

Morris nodded again, looking as if he were a world away.

Archie realized he was, in a manner of speaking. The military man was thinking over the tactical situation. The young Captain was irrelevant to this procedure, a nothing, just a mere detail not worth any consideration, but he didn't impede the process, either.

154

"Primus, after all, is still with us," Morris stated. "Every aspect of our lives is dictated by His principles. The Great Mandate drives our every move and has from the very beginning."

"And now we've come full circle?" asked Archie. "Is that what you mean? The grunts have made it across the galaxy at last?"

Morris cocked his head at this observation. It wasn't what he'd meant, but it did put an interesting tilt on things. It was a very compelling scenario, now that he thought about it.

The Commander's expression was currently so lifeless that he appeared demented, as if in a trance. He looks really stupid, Archie thought, but his next words betrayed that bogus concept. Morris was considering the situation still, and any outward sign to the contrary was just a by-product of that process.

"We started out on one end of the galaxy, and all these years later," Morris almost whispered to himself, "we've finally reached the other end. As such, the Second Age is only now playing out. It all makes sense in a crazy sort of way."

"And next comes the Age of The After Time?" asked Archie.

"No," stated Morris, in a louder volume. "Now there's no After Time nor no New Time, either. According to the prophecy, the next stage will be The Age of Real Time."

Archie said nothing to this, but he continued gazing at Morris, for the Commander's demeanor was quite mesmerizing. Then, so swift was the change in the big man's expression that Archie jumped when it occurred, and in an instant Morris looked engaged, his visage sharp. With little trouble, Archie could tell that the man had finally ceased his ponderous martial considerations.

Here it comes, he thought.

Morris cut his dark, beady eyes to stare Archie in the face.

Leaning back in the now-straining chair, he said in a normal tone, "But my bet Captain, is not to dwell much on the loftier motives. No, don't get caught up in the why, but look instead to the how and the whom. It always pays in the end."

155

"Uh huh," Archie grunted. He was leaning his tall, slender frame against his metal desk astern his computer screen, with his thin arms crossed against his chest. What could he say to that one?

No, the young Captain had figured it out at last. He now had a good guess on what was coming. Morris didn't let him down.

"I believe there's a spy about," the new Commandant of Station Forecast announced with a glum resolve. Commander Morris then slowly stood and stretched to his full, awe-imposing height. He looked as big as a mountain to Archie.

"Or spies," he added. "Spies of the free thinkers, these idiot heretics. And I think they've sabotaged my station."

Morris then pointed to Archie's battered clipboard, resting on the metal bench next to the desk.

"I want a full report on all cargo stowed aboard the Deferent," he ordered, "everything we're hauling."

"Uh huh," Archie said again. He had seen this development a mile away, too. Still, he knew there was more to come, and again the new Commandant didn't disappoint.

"I believe, Captain Spume," Morris said, thus ending his terse summation of the unfolding conditions on Am-Rif Arret, "that the long war is not yet over, my friend."

CHAPTER EIGHT

OFF TRACK

On the planet of Am-Rif Arret, Commandant Longley was impatient. Being an impatient man generally, this was his normal condition. Often in the past, he had used this facet of his character to his advantage, as a tool as it were.

He therefore never viewed his impatience as a flaw. Indeed, he never thought in such terms at all. But of late Longley's current, agitated state of mind had grown quite beyond the pale, now compounded by acute circumstances exceeding even what he would consider the ordinary possible boundaries.

And it kept piling on, with a vengeance. At present, Longley was worried that he might be close to his own, private breaking point. Of course, he wasn't sure of this, for the man had never before been anywhere near that unknown point before.

Then again, never before had he been this exasperated, either. He was working against time. They all were.

"Well, Doctor?" he asked, trying to stay calm. "Your briefing, if you please. Like you, I have other things to do."

He was addressing the station's Chief Technician, and he was having a hard time prying any kind of information, useful or not, from the woman. In fact, he was having a damned hard time getting her to talk to him at all, or worse, even getting her to acknowledge him at all. This was not the norm.

Longley seldom failed to command respect but now, for the better part of the day, all of his repeated calls and hand-delivered notes to her had gone unanswered. He wasn't used to such shabby treatment and he couldn't condone it, not under the present conditions. He felt exacerbated, and he didn't like the feeling.

The Commandant did know, and all too well, that the technician had her own staggering problems to deal with. But this time he had come to her, and by Primus, he was not going to settle for anything less than the whole truth, no matter how bad that truth was. And it was bad, as he would soon find out.

"There's been no change, Commander," she said, employing his official rank instead of his position's title.

With little effort, Longley could see that she was tired. Under normal conditions, with her flaming red hair and her very freckled, pale skin she had always appeared to him as extra-animated. He often had observed her more manic, zesty nature, even while she performed mundane daily tasks.

Her big blue eyes were always darting about, as if anxious should they miss any insignificant thing, and her pretty smile had always been present. It varied only in degree, from small and impish, to large and infectious. Not now, he saw.

She continued, "I've told you before, Commander, that I would let you know if there was any change. There is not. Now, I must get back inside, it's critical that I do."

"Negative, Doctor," Commandant Longley almost screamed.

They were standing in the narrow hallway just outside the containment lab, in front of the lab's large double doors. His sudden outburst had been amplified along the corridor's bare walls but, as luck would have it, no one was about to witness his behavior. He cursed in silence his failure to hold himself in check.

After a beat, he continued in a normal tone, "I'm sorry Rosemary, but I do need some answers, even if you are pressed. I've got to know where the station stands at present. t's my duty, you understand, I must be kept abreast of any developments."

She took a deep breath and looked him in the eye, having to gaze up to do so, although she was rather tall. True to his name, Longley was taller. She knew that he was correct, of course.

158

As acting Commandant of Station Forecast, the Commander had not only the right but also the responsibility to know all there was to tell, but the plain truth was that she couldn't enlighten him much. Rosemary just didn't know the answers he wished to hear. What's more, she felt guilty about not knowing them.

She was the resident expert after all, but she was also the only expert Longley had, and he was not about to be dismissed.

"You've had no time to check out my idea?" he asked her. He was probing this time, with no trace of the earlier passion in his voice. Rosemary looked away, thinking of just how to answer.

She had failed to give him what he wanted, she knew. Proof of sabotage was what he was after, and she had none, and no spare opportunity to look for any, either. Rosemary's entire being, her every effort and all of her concentration, were now consumed in just containing the unfolding situation.

At this juncture, why the original incident had occurred was an indulgent luxury in the mind game of problem solving, and she had no time for brainteasers now. Rosemary did wish to be truthful with the Commandant on that point. Still, if he thought she was being evasive he would view that in a most serious vein.

Longley might even think she was responsible, or at least duplicitous. She had the access, after all, and he obviously was desperate, but she also knew that the Commandant was now lost in the overwhelming technology of the situation. He had no idea if the facts, as she portrayed them, were indeed accurate or not.

The consequences were dire. A wrong move now might prove disastrous later to the whole planet, and that was the key. Her key.

No, Commandant Longley would not commit any rash action as long as he thought he needed her to contain the all-consuming and still-growing incident. She was sure. At least, she thought she was.

What she now needed most was to convince the man that she was indeed on his side, but that she was almost as lost as he.

Rosemary again looked him in the eyes and noticed for the first time that they were not the same color. One was a dull, pale gray and the other a very fair, light blue. They were close to an exact match, but they did have a small variation in hue, and one had to look hard to notice any difference at all.

"I've no time for, nor expertise in chasing spies, Commander," she said, adding, "I'm just trying to do my job, and I've told you the situation is unchanged. Why the time stream is accelerating is still unknown at the moment. But nonetheless, the stream proceeds to accelerate, and into the future at that."

"It's forbidden to view the future," the Commandant added with an inbred bitterness. He needn't have bothered to voice this view. They both knew that well-known dictum.

Rosemary continued as if he hadn't spoken.

"On the other hand," she said, "the machine's Fistula, a simple static field, is now refusing to act like one. And we still don't know why nor how the machine's containment has escaped. It's being projected somehow, which shouldn't be possible."

She noticed Longley scowled at this news, but she didn't acknowledge the fact. It would be useless. She knew that making faces would change nothing, so she resumed her briefing.

"We do know that the three conditions are somehow feeding off each other," she reported. "The faster the time stream goes forward into the future, the further into the past races the Fistula. And somehow, as a consequence of this phenomenon, the containment field grows proportionally, as well."

The Commandant did not react at all to this information, but she knew that he understood this crucial point. They had discussed this aspect of the incident soon after it had occurred. Still, she wished to be candid now, with no room for misjudgment later.

"The situation is nearly critical," she therefore added. "For the moment, we're on top of it but it's an ever-changing thing, you understand, very fluid and also growing. It's safe to say that at

160

some point the containment field that now surrounds the entire planet will exceed its threshold and burst."

The phrase, 'Passing Beyond the Elastic Limit,' was the standard employed to identify this phenomenon.

"And time itself will explode," said the hard-pressed Commandant with a defeated sigh.

Rosemary turned and looked through the window of the door in front of her. Beyond was the containment lab. The matching door and the one next to it, the door before Longley, were thick and neither permitted sounds to penetrate from the lab.

The frantic action inside reminded her of an ancient silent movie that she had seen once, a rendition of a mad house. Only now, it was no film playing out before her. It was her technicians in white smocks running about frenzied and without respite.

The muted scene inside looked like near pandemonium.

"The only solution we have," Rosemary reported, still looking ahead and not at the Commandant, "is to shut down the reactor and we both know that's not an option."

Longley raised an eyebrow at this, the one over his blue eye.

"Not a viable option, you mean?" he asked her.

Both knew that the antique reactor was his direct responsibility and that his crews were having less luck with this aspect of the volatile incident than she and her crews were having with theirs.

She did know the Commandant was now sure his reactor's computer had been tampered with. The machine's controls had been fused, and in such a way that the raging mechanism could not be shut down without a meltdown resulting. The possibility that the crisis was the result of a freak equipment failure was there but, at best that was a minuscule statistical chance.

What Rosemary didn't know was whether the flaw in the machine was just a related mishap, an unrelated mishap, or perhaps the planned result of more treasonous tampering.

She surprised him by laughing at his question.

"I'm no judge, Commander, believe me," she said. And then feeling better, as if some proverbial ice had been broken, she followed with, "I've no proof that it's not sabotage, you see, but none that it is, either. I'm just dealing with what I can at the present and that's only good enough to contain the situation."

Longley did believe her, even though at first she wasn't sure if he had. His face gave no indication either way. She never could read him with certainty, no one at the station could, but she knew the moment was past when he continued.

"It's the damn water line," he fumed. "It always comes back to the water. If only we could find the missing pipeline, we could easily shut off the water to the reactor."

Both of them knew that the fused reactor's core, once stripped of its cooling water, would soon overheat and the stubborn thing would then just automatically shut itself off. With no power, the timeviewing machinery located on the station's next level would then stop as well. The disaster would be ended.

The problem then became the water cut off itself. No one knew where the elusive junction was located, although two of Longley's men were out in the field now trying to find it. They had a general idea of where it was, where it had to be, for in the final analysis, the water table was dictated by the surrounding geography, but no one knew for sure the ancient pipeline's specific location.

What was known was that the long Civil War, or Holy War depending on one's view, had required the complete abandonment of the station. For tactical reasons, the outpost, having been sealed, was ordered deserted. The planet's seeded grunt populations, further by far from home than any other such endeavors yet attempted, had been left to their own primitive devices.

To Longley, it was evident that at the time the job of evacuation had been rushed. Not a surprising event, given there was a war raging. But now, after twenty-five hundred years, the original plans of Station Forecast were found to be at best incomplete.

The massive installation was eight stories square and included a landing field and several smaller support buildings. It was based on the same standard design personally given by Primus eons ago, but all such installations varied somewhat in order to accommodate for any differences in terrain found on any particular host planet. The building itself was intact, Longley and his crews had discovered, but the records of any modifications made were not.

All electrical lines, or lines of any kind, such as plumbing and communications, had to be tracked and inspected in a meticulous fashion. This included the giant nuclear reactor and its many accompanying systems. It powered the entire station and so it had been investigated first, and with much rigor.

It was of an ancient design, but still reliable. The same model was used on all monitoring stations placed throughout the galaxy. It had passed inspection with no problems being found.

However, the massive underground pipeline that fed the reactor its cooling water had not been investigated at all. Longley had held many heated conversations with the station's Chief Engineer over this. But at the time, the pipeline did not seem so important.

If the line failed, the reactor would simply shut down, or so the Commandant had believed. The place would not blow up or anything. Now, he wasn't so sure.

He had thought why spend valuable time on something that didn't need immediate attention when plenty of other nagging problems like his phones or the toilet or a few hundred other things at the installation were still not working properly?

"There's no word from the men in the field?" Rosemary asked.

The two men now were missing and out of contact, although they had left the station well before the incident had occurred.

"None," he answered, "and I don't like it. True, the containment interference could be blocking the pair's transmissions. Or they could be," and here he stood straighter before continuing, "simply not answering of their own accord."

She hadn't thought of this possible dimension to their problem, and it opened up some interesting trains of thought. They were trains she didn't wish to pursue, however. She said nothing.

Longley continued, looking very distant.

"Standard procedure dictates backtracking if there's a problem with communications," he said, "but who knows with that Spencer Hall in charge. The man's obtuse. You can't tell him anything."

The Commandant pursed his thin lips, remembering some incident or other concerning his absent Chief Engineer.

"I should never have let him go," he said in a stern voice. "Never. Anybody can dig a hole, but he knew this station."

Longley now looked very strange to Rosemary, almost as if he were in pain, or rather as if he were experiencing that shock one feels when, out of the blue, one has a sharp pain. It was disconcerting to see. Nevertheless, the man continued.

"Nor that other one, either," he emphasized. "He was good also. What's his name again, the assistant?"

Rosemary didn't know how best to answer this question. Her reply could easily degenerate into a rather complicated scenario. As it turned out, she didn't need to formulate a response.

The Commandant added, "You know him, yes? Doctor Hall's assistant." And then, "Welleb, yes, that's it, Jarvus Welleb."

She took a deep breath and crossed her arms.

Rosemary was torn. Should she tell him or not? And, should she tell him everything, or just enough?

And what was just enough, she wondered?

Still looking inside the lab, Rosemary could now see only one thing. The situation was clear. It was going to be awhile before she returned to her demanding workload.

Meanwhile, the Deferent was making its final approach to the imperiled Station Forecast. It wouldn't be long now. Archie and

Judith were in the command center strapped down for the descent, with Jonus and Morris below decks doing the same.

Judith had never before seen the landing of such a massive ship. In the past, whenever the procedure had taken place with her aboard, she had been unconscious, in the frozen state of induced deep sleep. Now she was wide-awake.

"They do know we're coming?" she asked of Archie.

"If they didn't before, they will now," he said.

The Deferent was moving at a fast clip, cruising a few hundred feet in the air. The vessel then dropped below the heavy cloud cover. The resulting panoramic view seen through the command center's portal was revealed to be quite breathtaking.

"The interference might well play hell with all airborne communications," he said, "but the phone lines should be OK 'cause they're all underground. We're a couple of hours behind schedule, but they'll be waiting, keeping a few eyes out for us. They're wanting those two below decks in a bad way."

Archie was grinning and very much at ease, sailing the massive ship by hand, shunning the automatic drives. The past two days had not unfolded in quite the way he would have wished, but nonetheless he was now pleased with himself. At long last, Archie Spume had come to a definite and far-reaching decision in his heretofore haphazard excuse for a life.

Hanging just over the horizon, big changes were in store for him, and as a consequence, he felt rather good about himself for it had been some time since he had decided on much of anything.

"How much longer before we land?" asked Judith, keeping her eyes forward, glued to the ever-changing topography. The Deferent was leveling off over an ocean, heading toward a large landmass. The deeply blue water underneath them was racing by.

"Only a couple of minutes to go," he answered, pointing out the portal. "Just a few hundred miles up the valley between those two big rivers." He added, "Once we set down, we can disembark right away 'cause I guess you're anxious about your husband, eh?"

Archie noticed that she wasn't very talkative about this part of her life. She remained silent. That was OK, for he had always preferred his women to be mysterious.

He grinned some more and pressed the point. He didn't care. What difference would it make now?

He asked, "You gonna get back with him after all this is over?"

Now it was Judith's turn to do some grinning. He was, after all, very persistent. She never stopped looking through the portal, but she did answer him, and with a question of her own.

"Well, first you tell me, Archie," she said, "what are you gonna be up to after all this is over, eh?"

Archie, casting his hazel eyes forward while banking the giant vessel, laughed aloud at the question.

"Oh," he said, "I got me some really big plans."

What he didn't say was that now his schemes included her.

When the ship had landed and all aboard exited, they were met at the foot of the Deferent's stairs by none other than the besieged Commandant Longley. However, his stiff military bearing failed to portray anything other than cool and professional resolve. Outward appearances were always important to him.

In fact, he was striking, extremely tall, thin and straight backed. His hard facial features were sharp and framed by cropped, steel gray hair. His uniform was flawless and he wore it well.

"Welcome to Station Forecast," he said to them, adding, "although everyone here seems to call it Point Zero."

After quick introductions were made, Longley began a briefing starting with the words, "People, we're in some real trouble here."

He turned first to Captain Spume, whom he had met before, after his own crossing to Am-Rif Arret.

"One," he said crisply, "the entire station must be evacuated. All non-essential personnel have been ordered to assist you in dumping sufficient cargo to make the necessary room aboard the Deferent. After that task is accomplished, they will board, and, for safety's sake, embark for orbit until further notice."

"Why?" asked Archie. He shouldn't have, although the question was innocent enough. After all, he only wanted to know what was wrong at the outpost.

However, currently Commandant Longley had other priorities, and sad to say for the hapless Archie, those plans were on a strictly need-to-know basis. There was no time to waste on anything or anyone that happened to stand in his way. Longley's urgent business was beyond pressing and it wouldn't wait.

"Because," he answered, "I wish to kick some ass and get some answers from those left behind. You want to be one of them, Captain Spume?" Captain Spume didn't, and it showed.

True, Archie wasn't of the military clan, but the he understood what was happening here well enough. He just bobbed his head and turned around to supervise the unloading of the Deferent's massive cargo holds, every one crammed full of equipment and provisions. Some big adventure this is, he thought, knowing that he would need his battered clipboard for this one.

The rest of the group started walking in order to keep up with Longley, who led the way, talking as he went.

"Two," he said, "Commander Morris was supposed to be my replacement, but under the circumstances that's out, and he will, for the time being, assist me in kicking some ass and obtaining some answers until we are out of this unholy mess."

Longley turned his head, awaiting Morris' reaction to his new demotion. He could have objected, but he didn't. He just nodded his approval while keeping a stern look on his massive face.

167

At this, Longley permitted himself the beginnings of a small smile. At least he knew someone around the damned station recognized his duty. Things might be looking up.

"Three," he continued, "my station has gone to hell and with the answers I have, I cannot rule out sabotage."

"The war?" Morris asked him.

Jonus groaned after Moe's question, and Judith started in with, "Oh, really, Commander," but Longley now saw that he had an ally in Morris. As a consequence, he was not moved from his summation of the situation and, without doubt, his assessment was the only one that counted. Others could think what they wished, but in the end they would do as he directed, he'd see to that.

"The war, people," he continued, "was in most part fought over the time technology. These free thinkers think it's a weapon, for the sake of Primus, and where better to obtain it than here on Am-Rif Arret? You have to admit, there's no place in the galaxy any farther off the beaten path than this insignificant planet."

"Why would the heretics restart the war over that?" asked Jonus. The premise was absurd in his view. "After all, we didn't use the time technology as a weapon then, when we could have, when doing so would have been more than advantageous."

After this statement, Commandant Longley stopped his advance. This also forced the others to halt. Longley then turned and looked down on the shorter time jumper.

"I thought," he said to Jonus, "that it was forbidden by Primus, Primus Himself, to use the machine in any way, and I mean in any way other than the purpose He had deemed acceptable."

That official maxim was true enough, and everyone present knew it. Jonus didn't answer, but he did flash his dark eyes up at the Commandant's. Longley held his stare.

"If you believe it possible," Longley slowly theorized, "for the time technology to be used as a weapon, then why shouldn't these damn heretics believe so, as well?"

"Why look elsewhere, you mean," snapped Jonus, "when you can just explain it away in any fashion that happens to be handy?"

But Longley was a cautious man, and this might be war. In his book, that meant spies would be about. He cut his eyes to Morris.

The time jumper was excitable, the big man knew. He was a long-time friend, but Jonus was a hot head and a general pain, even on a good day. With a look to Longley, Morris tried to convey to the older military man that the time jumper was, in fact, a well-meaning guy, but that yes, he should know better.

By now, Judith was about to burst for news of her long-absent spouse. All this talk of treason and warfare was fine and good, but it didn't push her personal agenda any. The woman had another priority and his name was Spencer Hall.

She took this opportunity to ask of Longley, "Excuse me for intruding, Commander, but do any of your various numbers apply to me and my husband? We haven't spoken in some time, you understand. Is it possible that I might see him soon?"

To this injection Longley raised an eyebrow. Again, it was the one over his blue eye. He didn't like to be interrupted.

It wasn't done in the military and it showed bad form during such a discussion. However, Longley didn't mind letting someone know that fact by demeaning them in front of others. He did so.

"I'm sorry, Doctor Hall," he said in a caustic voice, "but I'm afraid that we're not up to your number quite yet. I'm not finished with the time jumper here. We've not discussed the crisis at all."

Judith, understanding her position, bit into her tongue and shook her head, just as she had done earlier onboard the Deferent. She was way past her fill of military types. As well, she could easily see how this one and Morris would get along famously.

As if on cue, the new Subcommander Morris asked Longley, "Sir, just what is the current status of the station?"

The simple question placed Longley back on his proper track.

"The main reactor has been sabotaged," he answered, a scowl on his long, narrow face, "and that's not all. The station's time-viewing hardware has now malfunctioned as well, and in a new, heretofore unforeseen manner. At least, I've been told so."

He then began to walk on but Jonus quickly stopped him.

"How?" the time jumper asked.

Longley looked to each of them in turn, then over his shoulder toward the station, which was still more than a hundred yards away. He also noticed a fair outcropping of large, gray-blue boulders, not far from the path they were on. It was as good a place as any, he supposed, given they all wanted some answers.

He could empathize. The station itself could wait. He led the way over to the boulders and began to bring them up to speed.

"The time machine was being fired just to test the system," he started his briefing. "My engineers tell me this is a standard thing, a basic assessment, etc. Would you agree?" he asked of Jonus.

"It's the normal procedure, yes," the time jumper said.

Longley grunted, remembering.

"About the same time," he said, "the main reactor's controls were found to be fused, and in a very complicated fashion. They cannot be altered on threat of an immediate meltdown, although I do have people working on it. They've informed me there's a problem with the reactor's core computer program."

Of course, Longley believed that sabotage was the only explanation, but now, feeling somewhat better about the overall situation, at this point he didn't press this position.

"Meanwhile," he continued, "the time stream was then found to be going haywire, racing faster and faster into the future."

"The future?" gasped Judith, unbelieving, as if she hadn't heard him say it. But she had, and it was a shocking thing to hear. After all, it was forbidden by Primus Himself to view the future.

The implications were not lost on any of them, but Jonus, a time jumper, was the expert on hand, and he wanted to know more.

"And what about the Fistula?" he asked Longley.

"It's racing as well," was the answer. He wondered just how good this man was at his job. He didn't wait long to find out.

"Racing in the opposite direction?" Jonus asked him, and Longley was impressed with the time jumper's instant command of the volatile situation. He hadn't expected it, given the complicated nature of the crisis. The startled Commandant raised both of his eyebrows at the technician's question.

"Yes, in the opposite direction," Longley agreed, and then he added, "and both of them racing at the same exact speed."

"You mean the speed of each is the same," corrected the time jumper, "but both rates are also increasing."

Longley nodded his head in acknowledgment before agreeing, "Yes, yes, that's what I meant to say, of course."

"Why would that be?" ventured Judith.

Jonus shrugged his shoulders.

"I don't know why it began," he said, "it shouldn't be possible. But once it's started, the standard rules would then apply. For every action there is always an equal and opposite reaction."

"I thought the Fistula was the time machine," said Morris, confused. "Just what is this time stream? It's not the same thing?"

"No," stated Jonus, who now began to give the standard lecture on timeviewing for novices that all time jumpers held in reserve.

"Normally a hole in time is created," he said. "This is the static electromagnetic field called the Time Fistula. It's generated by the hardware, the machinery in the lab."

His shipmates nodded, all understanding.

"It's also highly controlled," he added, "manipulated within containment, so that past ages can be viewed and studied in detail.

171

But this only can happen when the Fistula itself is projected into an equally controlled flow of past time. This flow of the past, also generated by the machine, is the so-called time stream."

Again, they all nodded.

"These two," he added, "the Fistula and the stream, are the timeviewing machine. Use the two together, and it's like treading water while being pushed upstream against the gentle flow of a river. Against the current if you will, the flowing current of time."

"Well put," said Commandant Longley. Again he was impressed. Station Forecast's own Chief Technician had not explained the process with such elegance or simplicity.

"So why not just turn it off?" asked Judith.

"We can't," answered Longley with disgust. "The machine is now too hot to handle, drawing too much power too fast. It can't be shut down safely, and as I've said before, the power source, that is the reactor, can't be shut off, either."

"If the machine is drawing ever increasing amounts of power," suggested Morris, his big face pinched in thought, "then won't the reactor at some point just overheat and shut itself down?"

"That's the whole problem in a nutshell," answered Longley. "Not while it's being cooled. That's done via an underground aqua system, and I'm told the time containment will burst long before the reactor reaches its thermal threshold."

The Commandant then cut his eyes to the time jumper, and asked, "There's a term for that happening, yes?"

Jonus nodded, saying, "At the point of rupture, the containment passes 'Beyond the Elastic Limit.' And then," he added, "time itself will explode." It was not a good situation.

This was unbelievable, thought Judith. The answer was simple. So was the solution, or so she thought.

"Why not just turn off the water supply cooling the reactor?" she asked. "That would work, wouldn't it? At some point it would then overheat, just as Morris said."

"Yes, but we don't know where the cut-off junction is located," stated Longley, with a glum resolution.

He quickly recovered himself and added, "Which brings me at long last to your number, Doctor. Four. Your husband and his young assistant, whom I believe is your brother," and here he looked again to Jonus, "are out in the field now, tracking the buried water lines, looking for the main shut off."

Longley paused a moment, again remembering, but he had no time for second-guessing past mistakes now. He was planning only forward movement. He continued with the briefing.

"They had been out for about six weeks when the incident occurred four days ago," he said without emotion. "Since then we can't raise them, and I'm afraid I can't spare the manpower to look for them, either. Not now, at least."

At this distressing news, Judith looked over to Jonus, but he said nothing, and the Commandant continued.

"Perhaps they're on their way in, don't worry," he offered casually for Judith's benefit. "That is the standard procedure anyway, to backtrack if communication with base is lost, and that would take some time. Given the current, larger circumstance, any action now on my part concerning them would be premature as they're not, as things stand, a priority."

At this pronouncement, dissatisfaction showed on Judith's face. She started to respond, but Longley saw it coming and took quick, decisive action. Before she could speak, the Commandant stepped forward and silenced her with a glum look.

"Focus on other matters why don't you, Doctor," he said, with obvious condescension. "I know. Now that you're here, you can prepare me a report, posthaste, on the grunt population."

No one present spoke to this.

Everyone knew that the grunts could hold. They could be dealt with once the crisis was over, so Judith saw the order as made up work to keep her occupied, and thereby out of everyone's way. She realized that such a report was just a convenient way out for the smug Commandant and in a flash hated him for it.

Meanwhile Longley, who had been leaning against a boulder while speaking, straightened and held forth both his long arms, indicating that it was time to proceed to the Point. The others, who had been sitting on, or leaning against the various boulders, also stood. As before, Longley then led the way.

"Five," he barked as soon as they had fallen in behind him, "I want a feasible plan formulated straight away that will save not only my station, but the missing men in the field and the grunt population, as well. They are the reason we are all here, you will recall. The Great Mandate of Primus remains unchanged."

"Forward ho," Jonus whispered to Moe, who winced.

"And you, time jumper," Longley added, "Consult without delay my Chief Technician and figure out a solution."

The four of them then advanced toward the beleaguered Station Forecast, standing boldly in the near distance. The trio of newcomers was soon struck by the same exact thought. With such a slow approach, one could not ignore the blunt fact of just how massive an edifice the huge station was.

But, all knew also that this view was deceiving, for only two of the station's eight stories were visible. The other six levels were located below ground, buried deep within the encircling strata, much as the looming bulk of an iceberg remains hidden from view beneath its surrounding cloak of liquid camouflage. Still, what could be seen of the giant installation was imposing enough.

Constructed of heavy, gray reinforced concrete walls over eight feet thick and spanning almost five hundred feet across, the station no doubt dominated the landscape.

Inside the structure, the floor plans of the building were much the same as all other such outposts spread throughout the galaxy. This was a common occurrence, and never before had there been a problem with this standard arrangement. After all, the whole concept had been designed and presented to their ancient forebears by none other than Primus Himself in the flesh.

The first level always housed the standard reactor and its accompanying power plant, needed to fuel the station and several outbuildings. On Am-Rif Arret, this floor had been constructed six stories deep, in order to reach the abundant underground water supply located at that depth. It was ironic now, but for safety's sake, the subterranean river, ideal for cooling the reactor, had in the past been harnessed into a large pipeline.

The time-viewing laboratory filled the next level. The bulk of this lab was not, however, the viewing machine, per se. That hardware was located within the heavily constructed containment room and this structure was not in itself large.

Most of the floor was taken up with monitoring stations and bulky back-up systems, plus the considerable power feeds needed to run the machine. Several viewing rooms, where the image from the Time Fistula could be displayed and studied, competed with a few offices, each housing a bulky wooden desk and bookcase. Both of these were often spilling over with various technical manuals. There was also a reinforced room, the Library, wherein the Time Fistula data was stored for later use.

On the story above were located the various computer labs. These were small in size, but not in function. Computers ran everything at the massive station, from basic needs such as lighting and ventilation, to broader concerns like communications and weather projections. Each section had a substation, but all were connected to the main computer housed in the central lab.

The fourth level was the housekeeping floor. It contained vast storage areas as well as the ventilation machines, and the heating and cooling systems. In one corner rested the secured armory that contained the station's stowed weaponry.

The remaining four stories were divided into offices and sleeping quarters, with the kitchen, cafeteria and main conference rooms all being located on the ground floor.

As if the newcomers were not sufficiently impressed with the awe-imposing size of the station, Commandant Longley then led them through the building on foot to the Containment Lab five levels down, eschewing the many elevators available. This odyssey, starting in the marbled lobby, then traversing long hallways and never-ending descending staircases, took a good ten minutes to complete. At last the team arrived at their destination.

After entering the lab, the newcomers stared with disbelief at the bewildering scene before them. The place was in chaos, or so it appeared. This was containing the situation?

Frenzied personnel dressed in work smocks, most waving clipboards were running about like so many ants here and there between the crowded workstations. The technicians, while dashing, were also screaming at the tops of their lungs. Bits and pieces of pertinent but disjointed information flew without letup, barked to each other or, it seemed, to no one in particular.

To the newcomers, the lab staff acted as if they were possessed. Even worse, no one present in the morass seemed to care or even notice what it was that the others were shouting. Commandant Longley was nonplused by all this activity.

While he surveyed the room looking for his Chief Technician, he said, by way of explanation, "Don't be alarmed, this is only my department head's idea of emergency protocol. Somehow it works, if you'd believe it. And in truth," he continued, still scanning about, "it's in far better shape than it has been of late."

The Commandant at last spotted Rosemary in her office, the largest one on the floor, located against the rear of the lab. Although the room had a glass wall, no one but Longley had noticed her. The place was soundproofed, no doubt, for she was calmly sitting at her desk looking over a huge stack of paperwork, oblivious to the loud and constant cacophony in the lab proper.

Longley led the way and walked in unannounced. The others, looking bug-eyed around the lab, followed suit. The lab workers, absorbed in their labors, hadn't even noticed their passing.

Jonus entered the office last and paused to close the door behind him. By that time, Rosemary had stood to greet the group. When he turned around, Jonus was flabbergasted to see her.

The woman before him was none other than his estranged lover. Jonus had had no contact with her for many, long years. In fact, the hapless time jumper had believed that he would never see her again, and certainly not here on Am-Rif Arret.

At first, in a state of near shock, he refused to rely on the evidence of his own eyes, but without a doubt she was there. Suddenly, the scene changed, becoming surreal and incredible to him, unbelievable. He was too stunned to respond.

"Well, Doctor," said Longley to his Chief Technician, missing the frozen mask that was now Jonus' face, "as you can see, the newest contingent has joined us safely. Primus be praised for that blessing. I guess some introductions are in order."

Before he could continue, the new Subcommander Morris swept Rosemary's dainty hand into his own large and beefy one.

"That's all right, Commander," he said. "I've known this woman for a long time." Both Longley and Judith seemed surprised by this statement, but neither commented on the fact.

"How have you been, Doctor?" Morris said, smiling at her, which under the dire circumstances seemed inappropriate.

"I'm fine," Rosemary started to answer, but she changed her rejoinder to, "I'm holding up OK." This was not altogether a candid statement. She was trying hard not to let the others know.

In truth, Rosemary was keyed up by more than just the present crisis. Unlike Jonus, who had walked in unaware, she had known that the time jumper would be arriving, but she wasn't so sure what his subsequent reaction would be. She still wasn't.

On the other hand, she had expected Jonus. With the additional arrival of Morris, however, she was now feeling like the one being blindsided. Her heart, already beating fast, began to race but she tried her best to look unconcerned.

Rosemary knew that she had not been forthcoming about the time jumper in her earlier conversation with the exasperated Commander Longley. She had implied that she knew Jonus only in passing, through his younger brother Jarvus, thereby committing herself to her own private agenda. The determined woman was already walking a tightrope, and now she didn't know how to handle the added twist of Morris being present.

Morris knew each of them, Jonus, Jarvus, and herself, and all very well, too. Yet, the big military man was delighted to see her and wasn't concerned about showing it. It had been ages.

He didn't drop her hand and so she added, "And you?"

"It is," Morris answered, "a great pleasure to see you again." His dark beady eyes were boring into hers, which under normal conditions were large and a lustrous deep blue. Now, after her last week, they were very tired and bloodshot.

"Well, yes," snapped Longley, cutting him off, "and here is the time jumper we've so been awaiting, Jonus Welleb. I think you told me that you knew his younger brother, the missing assistant?" he added, thus letting Rosemary off the proverbial hook. Provided Jonus caught on, that is.

He did. Even in his state of near stupor, the time jumper did cope well enough to speak. But talk about understatement!

"We've met before, Commander, yes," he managed to utter.

Judith was about ready to burst. These idiots never got anywhere fast, she thought. She extended her hand.

"I'm Judith Hall, Spencer Hall's wife," she said.

"And the new grunt expert," added Longley, as if to remind her of her priorities and her present placement within the station.

Undaunted by this intrusion, Judith continued, "Even under the circumstances, it's nice to meet you, Doctor."

The Chief Technician laughed and said with good nature, "Understood, and just call me Rosemary, if you like."

These simple words almost caused Judith's eyes to pop out of her head. She stopped shaking Rosemary's hand although she still held on to it. Was this 'the' Rosemary? Judith thought, as she fought the urge to cast her eyes on Jonus.

Could this woman be Jonus' own Rosemary, the Rose that Morris had told her about so often? The one he had alluded to, that is, whenever he was attempting to explain his errant friend's sometimes over-gruff and rude behavior. And, if she was the same fabled Rose, then what was Jonus also doing here?

According to Morris, the time jumper couldn't bear to be anywhere near Rosemary. It was just too painful for him, too scalding to endure. Indeed, she'd heard Jonus barely could compose himself during the few, infrequent times Morris had gotten his distraught friend even to speak of her.

Judith then became aware that all of them were waiting for her to continue in some fashion, for the introduction had ceased in an abrupt and stilted manner. Trying as best she could to recover, she quickly shook Rosemary's hand several times more, and after, let it go. Her curiosity would have to wait.

Still, she knew in her heart of hearts that the woman before her was in all probability 'the' Rose after all.

"Well, if that's over," snapped Longley, not attempting to hide his acerbity. Civilian niceties always irked him. He then turned his head and indicated the two technicians, the resident experts.

"I want a plan of action formulated ASAP," he stated, "that will save not only the station but the grunt population as well."

The Commandant, at last issuing some meaningful orders, was within his element once more. He reverted with ease into his standard, controlled demeanor. The feeling didn't last long.

"And what about the missing men?" interjected Judith.

Longley turned to look her in the face. He had had just about enough of this strong-willed woman. Judith Hall was cramping his style, his well reasoned if unarticulated plans, and his ultimate authority over the unfolding, critical situation.

Still, his starched military deportment now was composed, and so he stated only, "Of course, Doctor Hall, that goes without saying. They are, after all, both assigned to this station." And then, leaning closer he added, almost whispering, "Unless, of course, you know something of which I am unaware?"

At this, Judith bit into her cheek to stop from saying anything further. What would be the point? She withdrew a few paces.

"Well, then," continued Longley, "we'll leave you to it. Subcommander Morris and I will be in my office conferring. Perhaps the idiot crews I have working the reactor sabotage somehow have stumbled onto something useful."

Next he looked at Morris and stated, "Although I doubt it." Then glancing at Jonus, he added, "Henceforth, full security is imposed." His eyes shifted to Rosemary as he said, "I will, of course, expect timely updates on the situation."

In response to him, both technicians only nodded their heads.

Longley then turned while saying by way of dismissal, "Fine. Let us know what you come up with." Once he had spun upon his heels to leave, however, he found his egress blocked by the determined Judith Hall, her arms crossed, waiting her turn.

He stopped, true, but the Commandant didn't miss a beat. The pressure was off and the man no longer felt besieged. Command was a joy after all, he remembered.

"Too bad Doctor," he said, "that you're not of the Technical Clan. I could use that. Still, we all do what we can."

He then placed his hands behind his back and stood more erect. This was going to be a formal rebuke. And appearances were always highly important to this regimented man.

"The Fistula Library is located on this level," he said. "I assume you can find it unaided. I'll await your report on my grunts." After this sharp rejection, Judith looked down.

It was apparent the man had no use for her or her lost husband. For all she knew, Longley believed that she and Spencer, and maybe Jarvus as well, were all in cahoots with the enemy, the dreaded free thinkers. Just a few heretics still fighting the insane war, and oh, by the way, Primus is only a fairy tale.

Judith was astounded, and she couldn't believe her position.

Once again, Jonus had been right all along. The military now had a renewed and separate order of the day. Commandant Longley was quite free to do whatever he wished.

He could look under any rocks he wanted to, and Morris, she knew, would back him to the hilt, if only out of spite.

Judith was lucky he didn't take sterner measures. He could and with no consequences for him. Who would argue with the man if he thought that she and Spencer had turned?

As things stood though, Longley had chosen to ignore the lot of them. At present, they didn't rate any of his precious tactical consideration. He wasn't going to waste his time, and there was nothing Judith could do or say to change that fact.

Her only option, and she loathed the position in which she now found herself, was not to rock the proverbial boat further. She didn't for she couldn't afford to. She stepped aside.

Longley quickly marched out of the office followed closely by Morris, who ignored Judith as he walked past her. Before he exited, the new Subcommander turned to cast a brief glance at Jonus and Rosemary. Then smiling broadly at the pair as he left, Morris began to think of these two finding themselves alone.

Talk about going beyond the Elastic Limit!

Judith offered the two technicians a somewhat awkward smile and hunch of her shoulders. Her situation was painful and also very apparent. Dejected, she turned to leave the office.

At the door, Jonus stopped her by saying, "Relax, Judith. We'll get them back." But Judith was torn.

She had loathed Jonus for a long time, and she knew he was aware of that fact. He knew her well, and what she thought. In her eyes, he was nothing more than a useless excuse for a man.

Jonus long ago had thrown away his very promising career in the military, even though it had sickened him at the time to do so. His stormy breakup with Rose had come after, a long and drawn-out affair. It also had been far too public, Judith thought.

Now he was soured by the dull life he lived because of those fateful decisions, and as a consequence, he felt sorry for himself. Worse, like a sloppy drunk, he didn't seem to care who happened to notice his misery. And the man didn't even drink anymore.

It seemed the time jumper's real problem, according to Morris at least, was Rosemary. Jonus could never really be happy without her, his big friend knew. But Jonus, Morris firmly believed, had been afraid of pulling Rosemary down.

She could do better, Jonus had said. Life itself was hard enough, even a good life. Even if you're a normal person, it was still hard, and he knew for a fact that he was far from normal.

No, Jonus had thought Rose was just wasting her fine potential, only throwing away her excellent chances for finding a good life with someone else, and someone worthy of her, instead of the sorry likes of him. He had then progressed from crushing heartbreak to simmering anger when things didn't quite go as he wished. What was wrong with her, didn't she get the scenario?

Why wouldn't she just let him go? Rose should just get over it and move on, have a good life and forget all about him, it was all for the best. What a boring spectacle, thought Judith.

Oh yes, she remembered, Morris, ever the true friend, had always done his best to make Jonus sound selfless, even almost noble given his sacrifice was so painful. But Judith, without the benefit of friendship, saw no such thing. She saw only a lonely man, a coward at heart, afraid to face his own pitiful life, the aimless existence that he had brought on himself.

That was why, she had thought, Jonus was so obsessed with the life of his younger brother, Jarvus. Because of the time jumper's stubborn inability to face his own worthless, and according to Morris, wasted existence, Jonus now lived his life only through the hapless Jarvus. It didn't help matters any that Jarvus always ran away under the strain of his overbearing older sibling, or that Jonus somehow always managed to track him down.

Both were predictable, and Judith wasn't sure which of the two bumbling brothers was the most pitiful. But as things stood, Jonus lived just to change Jarvus' erring ways, period, and so nothing else mattered to him. It was an unhealthy fixation.

Judith's no-nonsense approach to life found such a scene distasteful, and such a man disgusting. She believed that if you didn't like your life you just got up off your butt and changed it. That was what she was doing now, and she had no time for those who wallowed in their own negative, self-made lot.

Oh, if it suited him, Jonus could act a good game all right, full of bravado and bold talk, but she knew him to be in reality a loser who just didn't care. He was not worthy of her time, nor Morris' overabundant attention. But all the same, she could not deny that he had been on top of this one all along.

She had no other ally in the galaxy and she knew it. She also knew he knew it. And yet, in spite of everything, the ever-smug Jonus now seemed genuine in his encouragement.

She turned her head and their eyes met.

Judith wanted to believe in him, to be able to rely on him, but she still did not trust his motives. Her face easily gave her troubled thoughts away She looked down.

To her surprise, the always-crafty time jumper this time failed to use the obvious advantage he held to goad her further.

He said only, "I'll get them back, Judith, in spite of what Longley may think, you can bet on it."

She looked up, and his brown eyes bore into hers, as if in reassurance. Jonus was nothing if not passionate, she knew. The problem was that his passion always got him into trouble.

This swift train of thought was also easily conveyed to him. He had never failed to read the slightest changes registering on her always-beautiful face. Jonus then softened his own handsome one and smiled at her in wordless reassurance.

Judith also smiled, as if warmed by the thought of his help. She nodded, and then walked out. Only afterwards did her expression demonstrate that she was not so sure.

The two former lovers now found themselves alone. At first neither looked at the other, in fear that would start things rolling in a premature and awkward fashion. They didn't want that.

The pair was uneasy, and with the delicate situation at hand, they first needed a beat or two to sort things out. Both were proud and neither wanted to appear stupid to the other. Still, the clock was ticking, and each knew the proverbial ice would have to be broken, no matter how hard it was frozen between them.

It was just a matter of time.

Jonus was looking through the soundproofed glass wall of the office, his broad back to Rosemary, observing with dispassion the still-active lab crews. They were unchanged. All fretted about, with their silent mouths always moving.

It was eerie and also very tedious to watch.

Rosemary found herself still standing behind her cluttered workstation, and in fact, she had not moved much since the group had first arrived. She crossed around and leaned against the front of her desk, her slim arms, freckled like her face, twisted before her. After a moment, she raised one hand and began to rub a small, silver pin on the lapel of her work smock.

She knew that Jonus would calculate the odds of this being just a chance encounter. They were nil, of course, but he would pursue the chances of such an occurrence to the bitter end, if only to put off for one second more the real and hurtful issues between them. Yes, Rosemary knew this man, and very well.

Still, the relentless clock kept ticking. As it did, each moment became more strained. Soon enough, she knew, he would be forced to acknowledge the reality of the situation.

She also knew that under such a circumstance, like a cornered and wounded animal, he would react with anger and lash out without regard to consequences. Because of this keen awareness, Rosemary instead was calculating how best to soften the oncoming tempest. She had few choices open to her.

She decided to use humor. That had always worked well for her in the past. In the good old days, before their breakup, she could usually make Jonus laugh with very little effort.

"So big boy," she asked of him, "you come here often?"

Meanwhile, Longley and Morris, riding in one of the elevators, were en route to the Commandant's office. As everyone was aware of the mission, Morris surmised excess walking was now deemed unnecessary. Having firmly established the new order of the day, the Commandant had no further need to waste time.

"What's the story on this time jumper?" the senior military man inquired. It was plain to Morris that he didn't care at all for Jonus, that he viewed him as a loose cannon in his domain. "They're usually at the bottom of the barrel, you know," added Longley, "in particular posted all the way out here."

"No problem, sir" answered Morris, "he's, if anything, overqualified. He knows his job. He also likes it."

"Yes, but can he be trusted?" asked Longley.

Morris hesitated. He answered with a statement calculated to be truthful while also sidestepping the general thrust of Longley's overall inquiry. At least he tried.

"Jonus is obsessed with his younger brother," Morris answered. "He can be trusted to do anything it takes, as long as it gets Jarvus back safely. You can count on that as a fact."

This was intended to pull Longley away from the idea that the errant time jumper might, in fact be a traitor, just another heretic and free thinker. It worked. Longley bit the dangling bait.

"Obsessed?" he asked, and this time Morris did not hesitate.

"Their parents were killed in an accident when the kid was just ten years old," stated the Subcommander with no emotion. "We were at the academy then, roommates. Jonus, being older, felt he had to drop everything and raise him."

Here Morris gestured with his large hands for emphasis, but not much, only an indication. The big man was good at this kind of understatement. He usually pulled it off.

"Now it's fifteen years later," he continued, "and he still feels the same." Again he gestured, just enough, and then dropped his hands. "Jonus won't give up until Jarvus is found."

Longley scowled while he considered this assessment, and Morris believed the hard-bitten Commandant would now pass on to other pressings items, but he didn't.

"And what about after the brother's found," asked Longley, "can he be trusted then, do you think?"

This was the singular issue, Morris knew. It all came down to this one inescapable question. How would he answer it?

Morris realized that Jonus was nothing these last years if not a clever opportunist. He never hesitated to jump into something 'iffy' should the potential payoff be large enough. He had to be able to drop everything and run off into the vast universe, just as soon, that is, as Jarvus had saved up enough to do so first.

But was Jonus really a traitor? Thrown in with that sorry lot? Rejecting Primus and all the sordid rest?

186

Morris couldn't believe such a thing, or at least didn't want to. Still, it was not beyond the realm of possibility. Morris knew that with Jonus anything was conceivable.

But Longley was after assurances. What the Commandant wanted now was nothing less than Morris' own personal vindication of the confused time jumper. Yet at that point the door opened and they exited before Morris answered.

In the Fistula Library, Judith was close to tears. Her desperate situation was not hopeful. The fact that in the past she had always relied on herself, and always to her advantage, did little now to make her current dilemma any more bearable.

Under the present conditions, the woman's incredible will power and fixed determination were impotent. She was at a loss, stymied it seemed, blunted at every turn, and she found such an assessment dismal and depressing. Her only hope, and it wasn't much of one, rested with the hapless time jumper.

She did know without question that Jonus was bullheaded and that he would never stop until he had found his younger sibling. But Judith gained small consolation beyond that fact, for she didn't trust his broader motives. Jonus was a lost soul, without any real purpose, without any real aim at all beyond his brother.

What would he do once he found him? Could she trust Jonus to help Spencer then? She had no idea.

And that wasn't the worse part of her position. She knew that the chance of any plan to save her husband, any plan at all, never would come to fruition without Jonus' first being able to work side by side with Rosemary. To pull off this colossal effort would take the best of both the star crossed experts, for there was no one else with the necessary expertise available.

So Jonus had to face Rosemary. There was no other way. Judith knew that meant the time jumper had first to face himself and that happening was a long shot at best.

In fact, at that moment, Jonus was ignoring Rosemary.

He hadn't yet turned to face her. He hadn't even laughed at her attempt at humor, although he did smile at her joke. She saw this by his reflection in the glass wall of her office.

It struck her that this situation was a good metaphor of their past life together. How many times before had he, in essence, turned his back to her, rather than turn to embrace her, and address the hard and pressing problems between them? And why did he always seal himself off, why could he not confide in her?

In truth, she loved him, and even he could not deny that. It would be so easy for him, she thought. He had only to talk to her, be open and honest, and she would always be receptive.

Why was it so difficult, so painful for him to do so? Why couldn't he just try? However could he justify such a stance?

Rosemary could understand if she had been at fault in some way. If she had used him, lied to him, failed at any time to believe in him, if she had declined at all to lift him up, or to support him in any way. Yet the woman knew that she had never done any of those things, not ever, not even once, not even remotely.

Why then did he act as he did? She couldn't fathom this troubling aspect of his complicated psyche, and it came close to driving her nuts trying, for she knew him so well in so many other ways. Better than anyone knew him, even his oldest friend Moe.

Rosemary was still staring at his reflection but she was not conscious of it. She was lost in her own thoughts, contemplating why Jonus never talked to her in such situations of great import. He then surprised her by doing just that.

"How long did it take you, " he asked, "to set this one up? This thing sure took some doing. You've outdone yourself this time."

Rosemary had not moved. She still leaned on the front of her cluttered desk. Her hand still fingered the silver pin on her lapel.

"Oh, it was easy," she replied. "No trouble at all. Once I knew J was coming, the rest was child's play."

Here Jonus turned his head and looked over his shoulder, not at her, but toward her general direction.

"You are quite predictable," she explained, "and I knew you'd come sooner or later, once Jarvus was here."

As if that satisfied him, Jonus turned back toward the main lab.

He was trapped. She almost felt sorry for him. Almost.

"So, do you think we can pull this one out?" he asked her at last. He used an offhanded tone that conveyed he didn't care one way or the other. However, he did care.

Yet she didn't know to what he was referring. Did he mean the staggering station crisis or the personal entanglement between them? After a beat, she decided that it didn't much matter.

"Not unless you talk to me," she answered him in truth.

Jonus knew that it was a fact. He then turned to face her, but did so as if he were made of stone, which was not in character for him. He had always been very graceful.

But Jonus now saw his true options, and that knowledge weighed him down. There was no turning back now. He had to set Rosemary straight with no room for misunderstanding.

He was engrossed and preoccupied now, engaged in his own personal quest. His newest Mandate was to save his kid brother, and his agenda did not include her. But when Jonus turned and finally looked her in the eye, he froze.

She was the most beautiful thing in the universe to him, and he realized in a flash how much he had missed her. The unexpected acknowledgment was easy enough, but it released massive amounts of pain, abrupt and burning, from that hidden, oppressive emptiness in which he had lived, in which without her in his life, he had forced himself to live. The time jumper was almost knocked over by the sheer volume of hurt that flooded over him.

The fact that she was smiling didn't help matters, either. That wasn't playing fair. He had missed her smile far too much.

189

His natural inclination to turn and run was powerful. Anything was permissible to escape the horrible pain. But he found, to his consternation, that he was unable to move even an inch.

His eyes fell from her freckled face, drawn to the collar of her white work smock by the casual movement of her fingers. She was wearing the silver pin that he had given her so long ago. It was just peeking through her dark scarlet hair.

It was simple, but beautiful in a way that was hard to describe. Small and unassuming, it was shaped into the image of a rose, the bud of which was on the brink of bursting open for the entire world to see. Jonus found that he had tears in his eyes.

"Why?" was the only thing he could muster the strength to say. Like a child he said it, as if afraid of the answer. He was, too.

"Because I still love you, Jonus," she replied with honesty.

"That can't be true," he stammered, now fighting hard not to cry outright. "Not after all I've done to you. You can't think that."

She knew she had to make him understand. To believe, to believe in her, and here and now, for this was the proverbial nick of time, and there was no better place. Nor would there ever be.

She had, at long last, maneuvered him to the near end of the very universe itself, and into a corner that he couldn't wiggle out of. There was nowhere else for him to go, if they didn't resolve this one, that is. They had to get beyond this roadblock.

It was a fact that there was no time left to spare, and she knew it would be easy if he weren't so hard on himself. If he only eased up a bit, not trying to change as such, but to move on in some positive way. If Jonus would just stop judging himself, she knew that change would then come as a natural consequence.

Rosemary crossed the two steps it took to stand before him.

"It is true," she said with determination while looking him squarely in the face. It was easy to do for she was almost as tall as he. She added, "You haven't ruined my life you know, Jonus."

"But I'm no good for you," he choked in agony at the strained confession. "Can't you see that? I'm no good for anybody." Rosemary would hear nothing along this ridiculous line.

"That's absurd," she countered.

Jonus, standing before her, looked to the floor. He didn't know what else to do. This was inconceivable, he thought.

He knew beyond any doubt that he had deeply hurt her, and more than once, too. It was this realization that had driven him, compelled him even, to avoid her. Jonus simply could not bear the thought of bringing any more pain into her life.

Not her. Not again. Not ever.

Rosemary deduced what was on his troubled mind and she acted to quell this faulty assessment. She reached out and touched his arm with a faint and gentle caress. The time jumper looked up, confused, and for once not caring if she saw that it was true.

"You're always too hard on yourself, Jonus," she said by way of explanation, "you always beat yourself so. Well, I was close to you then, so I got a little beat up too. That's all there is to it."

This statement was simplistic and they both knew it. He started to say as much, but Rosemary quickly cut him off before he could continue. She had thought of a better response.

"Well, OK," she said with resignation, "I was tenacious, and I guess I just wouldn't let go. When you beat yourself over that one, I was still in the thick of it. At that point it became my own fault." Her features hardened, remembering.

Then she added, "I could have left then, perhaps I should have, but I chose otherwise. Jonus, I was the one that wouldn't give you up. I was the one that chose to stay."

It was true and neither could deny it. Any self-respecting woman so spurned would have left long before. But she had swallowed that self-respect out of her great love for him.

191

"So I got hurt then, too," she said, "but so what? I've lived with my actions, and since gotten on with my life. It wasn't your fault."

Still confused, he didn't respond.

She smiled and added, "I've always known that it wasn't personal, I know that you'd never hurt me on purpose. Not in any way, I've always known that. I always will."

He still wasn't sure. It just couldn't be true, he thought. He had assumed that she had detested him for a long time.

He would have, in her place.

"Don't be hard on yourself again," she whispered, knowing now that she was close "What's the point. What good can it do?"

"You never give up, do you?" he then asked with unhidden affection. He was caving. He was caving fast.

He reached out and embraced her. He couldn't help it. It seemed the most natural thing to do.

At last, she thought, as he hugged her. No one alive could hug her like Jonus could. He almost squeezed the breath right out of her and she squeezed him back as best she could.

It had been a very long time.

"Oh, Rosie," he said, "I've been such a fool."

"It's all right," she cooed to him, "everything's all right now." "I've wasted so much time," he almost sobbed, "being stupid." "No," she said, pulling back and shaking her head.

Now she was seriousness personified and would not accept any setback to her well-laid plans. Her big blue eyes flashed with a hard intent. They bored into him, not letting him go.

"Don't beat on yourself again, Jonus, now don't you dare," Rosemary said, almost pleading. And then with an upbeat tone she added, "Just live your life from this point on to the fullest, now, today, and don't you dare look back. To hell with ancient history, Jonus, no one can change the past."

192

As soon as she had said it, they both froze. Changing the past was now very much the new order of the day, the officially sanctioned mission, and just what they were proposing to do. If the two ever got around to it, that is.

Both of them burst out laughing, a shared pleasure enhanced because the absurdity of the situation had at last broken the ice between them. Soon enough the raucous outburst transformed into diminishing grins, for each was contemplating the daunting path before them. It was sad, but the pair knew that they would have to wait to get themselves back on track.

They hugged each other tighter at the thought.

"It's OK," Rosemary reiterated, this time whispering into his neck. "We'll get through this, Jonus. We'll both get through this nightmare together, you'll see."

"Do you really think so, Rosie?" he asked her, with his mouth now buried in her flaming red hair.

"Of course," she answered him. "Anything's possible." Then she pulled her face back once more to look him in the eye.

"Anything's possible," she stressed, "if we're together. That's the important thing. That's the only thing that's important."

Jonus relaxed. Literally. Rosemary felt his strong body ease.

He smiled, and so did she. She drew him close and hugged away, swaying in his strong embrace. She was very happy.

Now she could carry on, she knew, no matter what it might take. No matter at all. And it had taken a whole lot already, not including the current crisis they faced, of course.

But it did loom, and what a disaster! Unlike before, this one bristled with dire consequences. Predicted by heretics in unholy doctrines, it was rife with intrigue of galactic degree.

The future looked doomed, yet Rosemary didn't care. She now had a renewed strength, and she had hope as well. Hope enough to take on anything that dared stand in her way, including every single law of physics, if need be, if that's what it came to.

She had told Jonus the simple truth, and for Rosemary, telling the truth always gave her some measure of peace, sometimes a large measure. And progress would come for them, she was sure. Progression was the natural order of things.

She believed that anything was possible for them now, despite everything in their mangled past. They could do it, the determined woman knew. If only they worked together, if only they took the time to be a thoughtful, caring team, a true partnership.

How simple. Just be truthful with each other. That's all it would take, that's all that was ever needed, if you truly loved.

She had always believed it could be so. That's why she had worked so hard to bring about this long-awaited reconciliation. Rosemary had put in years of effort to pull off this one.

She had laid out devious plans in meticulous detail, as was her style, and then carried them all out flawlessly. Now that the whole thing was accomplished, she allowed herself to see just how brilliant her overall strategy had been. At last and against all odds, she had reached her goal, and it had been worth all of her efforts.

Rosemary was the one who had gotten Jarvus his job at the station. That part of her plan had been easy enough, for she and Jarvus had always been close. In spite of everything, of her stormy breakup with Jonus and the terrible death of his parents, the young Jarvus and Rosemary had always liked each other.

She had convinced him to come, although it took some doing. She was going after all, and no one else would know him there. It would be a new start for him, a new beginning, she'd said.

Beyond that, Jonus would be forced to leave him alone, because Rosemary would let Morris know of their posting. Jonus, once told, wouldn't show up if he knew she'd be there. Of course, she never did such a thing knowing that he would naturally follow.

She had wanted Jonus to come. But she hadn't realized that Morris would also show up for she was unaware of the relationship between Jonus' big friend and Judith Hall. Rosemary had never met Spencer before they both arrived at the Point, and she hadn't known until today that the man even had a wife.

But none of that mattered at present, for Rosemary's plan had worked like a charm. It was a great relief. Jonus was now by her side, and after a successful mission conclusion, forever would be.

And she had caused it to occur. She had brought the wary time jumper across the vastness of the galaxy itself and she knew now, beyond any doubt, that it could work out for them. Finally she was sure they could be together, always.

And the best part was, at long last, Jonus believed it, too.

CHAPTER NINE
REDIRECTION

Dejected on level two of Station Forecast, Judith Hall sat alone in the darkness of the tiny Fistula Library. Her eyes were closed and she was rubbing small circles on her temples. It was a useless attempt to erase her dull but still persistent headache.

In general, Judith hated to wait for anything. It just wasn't in her nature. Now any other option had been denied her.

She felt lost, empty, and spent.

Worse, she felt powerless, for she knew there was nothing further she could do to rectify or even modify her desperate situation. Being in this ostracized position, tucked away in the library, was an agony for her. Yet, under the present circumstances, she knew that such discomfort was a normal enough reaction.

The strong-willed woman had been defeated in her attempts to help her missing husband and she was now out of the loop concerning his rescue. And she didn't trust the motives of those who were in charge. But that wasn't all.

The unavoidable summons from the determined Commandant Longley for her to board the giant cargo ship Deferent was sure to arrive, no way around that. It was the only thing about this crazy scenario that she knew to be a fact. And that fact meant more waiting still, in orbit about the imperiled planet of Am-Rif Arret.

The very thought increased the ache in her pretty head.

Judith knew that as soon as some plan had been formulated, without her input, she would be ordered to the ship with the rest of the nonessentials, to circle the beleaguered planet for the duration of the mission. What Judith didn't comprehend was the delay in the dreaded order to go. By this time, several hours since the degrading scene in the lab, the Deferent would be unloaded.

Archie and his ever-present clipboard would have seen to that.

She had finished her review of the planet's grunt population, an easy task taking little time for the data involved was minuscule. The seeded human population had been on Am-Rif Arret for less than three years when the evacuation of Station Forecast had been ordered and less than a year had gone by after the post-war contingent had arrived. Beyond that, there was nothing to go on, for without the time-viewing machinery up and running, the long intervening years could not be evaluated at all.

Commandant Longley knew this much already. He would have asked for and received a review of the situation as a standard matter after he and his crews had arrived, and in the interim since that arrival, Judith knew the grunt's status wouldn't have changed very much. Evolution was a slow process.

Longley didn't need her assessment. He never did. He had just wanted her out of his way, and Judith had understood that.

The nagging thought that no workable plan of rescue was possible was an idea she kept trying to dismiss. That was a no-win scenario. Judith had to just file that one away inside her pounding head next to the prospect of time itself exploding any second!

Perhaps, she had first hoped, the stiff Commander had just forgotten about her, that she was that insignificant, but such a situation was out of the question. Longley wasn't a man to forget much, she surmised. He was exactly the type to take delight in the finer points of tying up any loose ends.

He basically wasn't bothering.

She had toyed with the idea of just calling the man. She did have a legitimate reason, be it slight. Simply call him and report, to let him know that she was ready, at his leisure, to brief him.

She'd dismissed that possible route for it smacked of an in-your-face attitude and, at this point, she couldn't risk that. After all, it was not beyond belief that Commandant Longley thought that both she and Spencer were just a couple of heretics with nothing better to do but make his life miserable. What a crock!

No, it was much better not to rock the boat. To say nothing, do nothing. Just sit around and be a nothing.

So, Judith was forced to concede that she was less than useless in the current crisis, and that fact grated. Her report was not needed and, beyond that, she and her ideas were worth little to the stiff Commandant Longley. It was an unbearable situation for she had always been proactive in her attitude towards problems.

She had made mistakes in the past, plenty of them, but Judith had always sucked them up and carried on. It was the standard way the woman coped with tough issues in her life. In the main, generally there was nothing she feared facing, but now she was restrained from facing anything but her own helplessness.

No wonder her head ached. The more she dwelled on her no-win situation, racing from one desperate point to the next, from the first indignant position she found herself in to the last, the more the dull pain in her temples raged. Judith then changed her strategy, for the one she was employing for relief wasn't working.

She stopped tracing the small circles on her temples and tried instead another approach in attempting relief, by finding the tenderest spot on either side of her head and pressing down hard for a full ten seconds. The resulting pressure brought tears to her eyes. After letting up, she found the pain was decreased, but it didn't go away so she resolved to try again.

Then the monitor on her desk lit up with a squawk and, opening her eyes, she saw the grim face of Commandant Longley on the screen before her. Here goes, she thought. Bon voyage.

"Ah, yes, Doctor," he said, "I need a word with you."

"Sir," Judith said, blinking a few times to clear her head. She straightened up in her chair. "My report's completed."

This simple statement of fact seemed to stun the military man, as if it were preposterous to even acknowledge the worthless effort to which he had so easily consigned her.

"Well, yes," he said, "but I wish to speak of another matter."

"I see," Judith replied, "I'll report to the loading docks ASAP."

The Commandant now shook his head and looked away, drawing in a sharp breath as he did so. When he turned back to the monitor, he held a determined look on his face. Judith realized that he was trying to pick his next words with care.

This realization took her aback, and she wondered then not just what it was he wanted, but also why it should matter to him how he phrased himself. Why should Longley care if he was subtle? He certainly hadn't bothered to do so before.

Judith's thoughts next flashed on her husband. Could it be, she thought, news of Spencer? Had they found him?

But no, that couldn't be it. That would cause no hesitation on Longley's part. Unless, that is, the news was bad.

She panicked with a deep, sinking feeling rushing over her. Had something happened to him? Was he, in fact, dead?

"Is there some new information on the men in the field?" she asked, not knowing if she wanted the answer.

"No, I'm afraid it's not that either, Doctor," he began. "There's nothing current on that front, I'm sorry to say. It's something else altogether, something I believe that only you can help me with."

"Yes, sir," she said quickly, with a straight face. It took some doing to accomplish. What relief!

"I need some information on these free thinkers," he said. "The so-called heretics. Their overall agenda and so forth."

Judith didn't understand this thrust. What was there for her to know? The Commandant, as a military man, would understand far better than she any current threat from that corner unless he really thought she was in cahoots with them.

But if that were the case and this was just an interrogation, then how could he expect any truthful input from her about anything?

"I'm afraid, Commander," Judith continued, now being the one trying to pick her words with care, "that I'm not at all privy to any plans that the terrorists may have."

Longley smiled at that one.

"Certainly not," he said, "that's Subcommander Morris' and my department. What I want is an insight on what drives them, from a historic view, that is. What's their overall perspective and what's all this Unspoken Prophecy stuff?"

"That deals with the different Ages of Time," she offered, surprised that the Commandant was not familiar with the subject.

"Yes, yes," he said, now with some impatience, "I do realize what it is, but I need to know what it means."

Judith still didn't understand this line of inquiry. She wanted to be clear. Did he want a lesson on their religion or their tactics?

From his monitor, he could see that Judith was confused. He tried again, this time step by step. He didn't like it, but he did it.

He had hoped not to go to such lengths, for he hated giving briefings to underlings. He hated to explain himself to any one at any time, but this was no ordinary occasion. It had to be done.

"Doctor," he said, without emotion as if he were talking about something mundane like the weather, "some time ago the laboratory reported they've established a definite line on the situation. They stated if nothing's done beforehand, the crisis will commence in about," and here he glanced aside for some degree of accuracy, "in about three hours. Time itself will then explode." Judith felt her throat tighten at that one.

Longley continued to a new point, saying, "I've just been informed they've come up with a viable rescue plan."

At this, Judith held her breath.

"Finally, Subcommander Morris reports that the Deferent is shipshape and ready to embark," said Longley, wrapping up his onerous briefing. "We can have the entire contingent onboard in one hour. The order just needs to be given."

Judith became excited. At long last something was happening. She fought for some composure, taking in a breath.

"That's good news, isn't it, Commander?" she asked.

Longley nodded his head and replied, "It should be but I don't like it. Somehow it doesn't quite fit. It's just too neat."

"I'm afraid I don't follow, sir," she said.

Commandant Longley leaned in toward his monitor screen, which gave Judith a larger-than-life image of him on hers.

"No one's taken into account the free thinkers," he said. "No one can explain their involvement, if there is any. I need all the facts before I proceed and I haven't gotten them."

Again he looked away, as if embarrassed by such an admission. Nevertheless, he continued. He had no other course.

"Morris is unconcerned," he said. "He's of the opinion that any contest comes down to foe against foe and let the best man win, so to speak, but my nature is more cautious. Hard experience has taught me to understand my enemy."

That statement made sense to Judith. Generally, she thought in much the same way. She always had, it was only prudent.

Longley said, "I wish to know what makes these free thinkers tick. I don't care about what they believe in, but what they want. There has to be an endgame here or why cause all this trouble?"

The Commandant was a sly man, and had to be. He surmised that there was something afoot here beyond the current crisis. He wanted to identify what it was, and he needed to know yesterday.

"What drives them?" he asked. "There's got to be something, a reason behind all this action. Just what are they after?"

Judith understood and tried to comply.

"The main idea they hold is that there are only three Ages of Time, not the four we have been told of," she said.

Thinking that she still misunderstood his thrust, he cut her off.

"Yes, I know all that," Longley said, "but why throw the cosmos into galactic war over a mere difference in doctrine? There has to be a bigger incentive. What do they want exactly?"

The hard-pressed Commandant then took the time to rub his chiseled face with his hand, and Judith realized that the man was tired. It was easy to see, as his image was still overly large on her monitor. No wonder, she thought to herself, if he had been dealing with this mess for the better part of a week.

Tired or no, Longley proceeded.

"Subcommander Morris thinks they're nuts and like to fight, period," he explained. "As such, they will fight anywhere for any reason, but I think they're dealing with a more specific agenda. All the way out here, they must be after something more concrete and I can think only of the time-viewing technology."

"That makes sense, sir," Judith said, but he was still unsatisfied.

He took a deep breath and leaned back in his chair.

"Why," he asked her, "and to what purpose? Because they believe the machine can be used as a weapon? The time jumper doesn't seem to think so, nor Morris."

"Not entirely," said Judith. "The technology is just a means to an end, you see. What they really want are the grunts."

This got Longley's attention. He wasn't sure that he'd heard correctly. He bolted ramrod straight in his chair.

"What's that?" he almost barked at her.

"No one knows, Commander, the true purpose of The Great Mandate," answered Judith, "and the grunts are now spread throughout the entire galaxy. We all take that fact for granted because it's just our everyday jobs, but it's an astounding thing

203

really. Just look at the time involved, the continuous, enormous amount of manpower and materials committed to date."

"I suppose that's true enough," said Longley, "but there are other galaxies, Doctor, lots of them. The Great Mandate must continue. It will continue if I have anything to do about it."

"Yes," said Judith. "But technically, at some point The Great Mandate will cease. Primus Himself said as much."

"He did?" asked Longley, skepticism hanging in his voice. This was new. He'd never heard of such a doctrine before.

"Oh yes," answered Judith, "the Mandate is a task, albeit a huge one, but it's still just a task, not an end in itself. Now, I'm not of the Theology Clan, but I'd say that there must be a higher purpose involved. Of course," she quickly added, "only Primus Himself knows what that purpose is, or when it will be revealed."

Commandant Longley didn't buy it.

"Primus hasn't changed the rules yet to my knowledge," he said. "The Mandate is crystal clear and always has been. It dictates grunts throughout the universe and not just in this galaxy."

"That may be so," granted Judith, "although we always could waste a lot of time here arguing over semantics. Still, you miss my greater point. It's assumed that Primus will let us know the grunt's ultimate purpose at the beginning of the Fourth Age of Time."

The Commandant had never heard of this, either. Judith could see it by the look on his face. She continued.

"The 'Great Revelation' it's been called," she informed him. "The free thinkers, however, hold that there are only Three Ages of Time, and now, therefore, is the moment for the grunts to come into their own. Of course, it's officially considered a heretical position, but that in a nutshell is the Unspoken Prophecy."

At this, Longley blanched.

"But what does that mean?" he asked. "Even on the first seeded planets, the grunts are only now evolving into primitive societies. Here, on Am-Rif Arret, they're just out of their caves."

The man was having second thoughts. None of this was what he was after. Perhaps contacting her had been a mistake.

"Doctor, if the 'Age of the Grunts' is what's to come," he inquired, "then all of us are gonna wind up going backwards a few light years, wouldn't you say so?"

"Certainly," she answered, "all things being equal, I'd say yes."

Now it was the Commander who looked confused and Judith, this time, the one with the calm demeanor.

She continued, "But I would say, sir, that if the free thinkers, these so-called heretics, had the time technology and used it for their own devices, at that point, things would not be so equal. Anything might be possible for the grunts then. And now there are millions of them on hundreds of different planets."

Judith saw from his changed expression that the man had what he wanted at last. On her screen, his image now seemed both deep in thought and somehow relaxed, as if this information was the final piece of the larger puzzle. It was.

"Thank you very much, Doctor," he responded. "At last, some sense had been injected here. I'm in your debt."

For once, Judith believed him.

"I'll report at once then to the Deferent," she said.

The Commandant had another idea.

"I think not just yet," he said. "Report to the time lab instead. Morris is on his way from the loading docks and I believe that you should be there for the technicians' briefing."

This was a stunner for Judith, unexpected in the extreme. Before she could respond, he signed off. Her monitor screen shut down and the room was once again pitched into darkness.

Only then did she notice that her headache was gone.

205

Meanwhile, Subcommander Morris, with young Captain Spume in tow, was making his way back from the loading docks to the main time laboratory. The two had just entered the building, passing the first set of metal doors that sealed Station Forecast from the beautiful, but alien, world it sat upon. As usual, Archie was talkative but Morris, giving up little beyond the occasional grunt in response, was thinking only of the coming mission.

He couldn't wait for it, and he had no time for either Archie or his endless, homespun banter. After all, Morris didn't have to travel to the end of the galaxy just to wind up playing second fiddle to someone. No, he could have stayed right where he was for that life now that the long war was over.

The new Subcommander had missed out there, and that fact still grated. The man had spent years watching with envy as the skyrocketing careers of older military classmates were fueled by the raging war. Yes, they all had been good graduates, but most of them, in Morris' professional opinion, were far inferior to him.

Under the present conditions, with the war ended, he would have had little, if any, chance to catch up. And there was nothing like training your whole life away just to wind up being someone else's permanent underling. What a waste that was.

So, Morris had counted very much on his own command at Station Forecast. In truth, he saw the assignment as his only chance to relaunch his stagnant career and he didn't care at all for the way things had turned out since his arrival. That avenue now had been denied him and he was far from happy about it.

Commandant Longley and his agenda were wearing very thin on the new Subcommander Morris. By rights, he figured Longley should be answering to him and not the other way around. And Morris would have stressed that course of action had not the crafty, older military man first neatly outflanked him.

Longley, by issuing his orders as a matter of course, had effectively rendered Morris powerless to disagree. It would have been improper to do so, inappropriate and not in the least military. Such internal matters were never argued before civilians.

And besides, under the circumstances, questioning Longley's order wouldn't have advanced his career any. The stiff Commandant was the senior officer on duty and it would have been a no-win situation for Morris to rock the boat all the way out here on the very edge of the galaxy. With no one higher to answer to, the Commander would have had the last word anyway.

Nevertheless, Longley was due to be relieved and Morris still held the sealed orders. He would have felt confident in taking over, too. He had trained hard for the chance, for long years, and he knew he would have made the most out of his opportunity.

Yes, Morris thought Longley should have just stepped aside, period, offering only his services for the duration. That idea brought a slight smile to the lips of the big man but he shook it off. He had no time to waste on frivolous things like daydreaming now.

The fact that his well-laid plans surrounding Judith were also dashed only fueled his craving for release. He wasn't winning anything these days, Morris saw, much less the glory he so wished. In truth, he couldn't stand it any longer.

Morris felt like a caged tiger just waiting to pounce and he wanted change, with hope having some heavy action attached. He needed physical activity now, and lots of it, with copious amounts of motion and excitement involved. That had gotten him through before in similar heartbreaking situations.

This was not, after all, the first time in his life that someone had dumped him nor the only time his career had stalled.

Before this situation, intense action had always given him the time, valuable time spent without dwelling on his problems, that he had needed to adjust. Now that time, that very release, was all that Morris craved, and as such he wanted nothing more than the long awaited rescue mission to begin. This go-round, Morris vowed to himself, he would see to it that he played a major role and, if need be, Commander Longley be damned.

Of course, young Archie was oblivious to all this, and he just kept chatting away. That was natural enough. He was a chatty person in general, and more than anyone else, he had been kept out of the loop concerning the station's current crisis.

It wasn't so much that he wanted specifics or any detailed information, but that being bored stiff, he just wanted to talk. And, by this time, anyone would do. Solitude had its limits.

Morris was having none of it and let Archie in on that fact.

"Let's just can all the static for the present, shall we Captain?" he said as he jammed the elevator button with his massive finger. "I'm sure the Commandant can answer any questions you may have." Archie actually winced at the thought and the men pressed on to the second floor without further comment.

The laboratory itself was unchanged. Morris found the now familiar scene unnerving. Frenzied personnel were still screaming and carrying on with their never-ending tasks, needed no doubt to keep a lid on the volatile situation.

Longley, Judith, and the two technicians were already gathered in Rosemary's glass-walled office. Morris led the way over. Archie dutifully followed in his wake, with only sidelong glances at the bizarre happenings of the time lab.

Once everyone was seated inside the now-cramped office, Longley wasted no time. After all, in a literal sense there was none to waste. Everyone felt the gravity of the situation.

"Well, then," he said, addressing the technicians who were on the far side of the large wooden desk, "let's have it. What have you come up with? Just how can we stop time from exploding?"

Rosemary and Jonus looked to each other before Jonus stood and answered, "I'm afraid we can't, Commander."

"What's that?" Longley asked, as if his hearing were defective. "What do you mean? I was informed you have a workable plan."

"We do, yes," said the time jumper, "we have a plan to rescue the missing men and save the station, but the explosion can't be stopped, I'm afraid. It's inevitable. It simply can't be avoided."

"I don't follow," said Longley.

He turned to Rosemary and asked her, "Just how can we do anything for anyone if time explodes?"

Rosemary replied, "Because we can use the explosion, Commander, to our advantage. It's the event itself that will permit the rescue. Station Forecast will remain unscathed, and if all goes well, so will the grunts and the men in the field."

Longley did not understand this staggering input, and he wasn't alone. The technicians saw that everyone in the office wore blank expressions. Here we go, thought Jonus.

He jumped in determined to make them comprehend.

"Look," he said, "a time explosion is not like a conventional explosion. There won't be any physical destruction, no rubble and all that. After it happens, everything will look much the same."

The time jumper began to rub his palms back and forth, a habit of long-standing that he employed without thinking. It helped him think, though. He needed to be clear.

"Only time is affected," he explained. "Our perception of time, that is. That's what's shifted and merged, nothing else."

"So nothing changes?" asked Morris. "If that's true, then where's the crisis? What are we all doing here?"

Rosemary smiled and said, "Oh, things change all right, but not in a physical sense. It doesn't just follow, that is. The only direct change is in the time signature."

At this, Archie let out a groan, sinking back into his chair. He was lost. None of this made any sense to him.

Judith, on the other hand, leaned forward, in her chair, as if the posture would somehow help her follow better.

Longley and Morris said nothing, but their eye contact confirmed that so far this briefing was piss poor.

Jonus had seen such looks before. Many times. After all, being raised in the military, he had grown up with them.

"Look," the time jumper said, gesturing with his strong hands for some emphasis, "we're making this thing far too complicated. It doesn't have to be. Let's just keep it simple, shall we?"

He crossed his arms and took a deep breath, staring down at nothing, stealing a second to organize his thoughts. He and Rosemary had talked over what to say, but so far things weren't flowing as planned. He needed a logical progression that was not overwhelming for the nonprofessional.

Jonus knew that it wasn't an easy concept to grasp, but he was pretty good at this sort of thing. At the corner saloon over some liquid refreshments, when nothing of consequence was riding on it, he usually could explain the basic tenets of time theory with little trouble. That is, if whoever he was conversing with was even interested, which was not often the case.

Jonus no longer drank but he did hang out in bars and restaurants, always sipping on his ever-present ice water while chatting easily with no one in particular, usually over nothing important. He thereby carried on what had passed as his social life, and granted, it hadn't been much, but it was low-pressure and that was the feeling he needed here. Keep it low-key, he told himself.

He looked up and saw the four of them were all attentive, but Jonus had always hated giving lectures. He decided not to and sat down. He had no drink resting before him but now at least everyone there was on the same eye level.

"Remember what I said before," he began his briefing in earnest, "about the time stream flowing like a river?" They all nodded and he continued the theme. It was the standard model for the layman, the classic example of the time and space relationship.

"Remember also how I described the Time Fistula," he asked, "the hole, or window if you will, projected into the time stream?"

Again they nodded. So far, so good, he thought. Take it slow.

"Well, it's a delicate relationship," the time jumper explained, "very subtle and precarious. You have to move slowly and with finesse. It takes a discriminating touch."

He paused a moment, for the next connection was the most critical one. He had to make sure that everyone successfully made it. Unfortunately, he didn't get the chance.

"Yes, yes," the terse Commandant interjected, "I'm sure that all of us are aware of the many difficulties involved. To be frank, I don't care about that aspect, we all must do our jobs regardless of how difficult they are. What of the explosion?"

Rosemary knew that Jonus was only a hair's breadth from losing what little composure he had left with the gruff Longley, and it was just what none of them needed. She couldn't let this briefing degenerate into a jousting match between the two hardheaded men for everything they all knew and cared about was at stake. Their plan, the only one possible, had to be approved.

"Commander," she said, employing a soft but firm manner, as if addressing a small child, "I'm not quite sure that you do understand. This isn't an argument over semantics. Everyone here needs to know the basic facts involved before they can begin to analyze the consequences that naturally will follow."

The Commandant raised his eyebrow at this, but said nothing in response for it was plain that she was not finished. Yet unlike Jonus, Rosemary liked to lecture. She stood and began to do so.

"The time viewing machinery works like this," she began, building on Jonus' example. "The Fistula is like a rock that you put in the river, the river of time. As long as the current, the flow of time, is slow enough, then you can move the rock wherever you want, up and down or back and forth, anywhere in the stream."

"Back and forth?" asked Archie. "I thought it was forbidden by Primus to view the future. That's what I've always heard."

This got the others' attention, for two reasons. First, it was a good point. Second, it was the hapless Archie who'd raised it.

"Yes, that's true enough," said Rosemary, "but the time stream is also moving, and always against you, against the rock, that is. So the future is always coming towards you, don't you see? By going forward, you're just viewing the past."

She was holding her hands out before her, using them to illustrate her example. One hand was open and this represented the flow. The other, in a fist, was the rock, the Time Fistula.

The further you go upstream," she explained, "the more distant the past you see. But you can always go back to where you started, that's not forbidden. That would not be viewing the future, you understand, just the more recent past."

For a moment, none of them reacted to this. Yet, calmness settled upon the occupants of the room. This thing could be handled, they realized, and all was not chaos.

Then Commandant Longley asked, "And what of the present, Rosemary? Where are we now? What can we do?"

Rosemary nodded and continued her briefing.

"Like Jonus said," she related, "the whole procedure is a delicate thing. If the flow of the river, that is the time stream, becomes too rapid, or if the Fistula, that is the rock in the river, is moving too fast, then time itself will be affected. There's no way around it and both these things are now happening."

"Yes," said Longley, "and that means?"

"The river water is now violently splashing against the rock," Rosemary said, "instead of flowing smoothly around it. The image from the Fistula has become distorted because time itself is now distorting, and the speed of both the rock and the river is still increasing. The situation is just going to escalate."

Again the four nodded. They understood. Jonus smiled.

Leave it to Rose, he thought to himself. When would he ever learn? But Rosemary next took a lesson from him, so the Chief Technician sat down before continuing.

"None of this is supposed to occur," she said. "The system is designed so that it won't, but as we all know, the current crisis is a real one. It's obvious now that we're in uncharted territory."

Jonus said, "The Fistula and the time stream are held in check by the containment field, manipulated and controlled, but not this time. Soon the machine will exceed its threshold. When that happens, time itself will pass beyond the limit of distortion, 'Beyond the Elastic Limit' it's called, and explode."

"What about the explosion itself?" asked Judith. "What happens then? And how can we use it, as you said?"

This was a tricky point. The possibility had been dealt with in theory only. Time, after all, had never before exploded.

The ancient protocols given by Primus Himself were supposed to counteract such a thing. In the past, they always had and it hadn't even been an issue. Still, Rosemary and Jonus both agreed on what would happen after the explosion occurred.

"At the moment of the event itself, certain things will take place," Rosemary said, "two things, to be precise. For every action, you understand, there is still an equal and opposite reaction. These two things, the things that will occur after the explosion, then become the tools that we are forced to use."

She and Jonus had discussed this crucial point at length. The elegance of the situation was an easy thing to see. The solution would prove more difficult, however.

"We must use them," Rosemary continued. "They'll be, in truth, all that we have. And we think we have a workable plan."

"We're listening," said Morris, "let's have it."

Jonus took over, staying with the same example.

213

"The explosion will be like taking the rock and throwing it into the river," he said. "Two things will then happen. First, the river of time will be pushed backwards, how far we don't yet know, and second, certain drops of separate time will be splashed off, out of the stream and in the opposite direction."

"Where do they go?" asked Archie. And then, all of a sudden self-conscious, he added, "That's not a stupid question, is it?" In retrospect, it sounded so, but what did he know?

With a smile, the time jumper answered, "Of course not." Then he asked, "Where would you think they would go?" After a beat with no answer, Jonus added, "Just think of the rock and the river."

Archie thought but could not make the connection. Judith did though. She understood the point with ease.

Back into the stream," she said, as if to herself.

Jonus leaned into his chair, his fingertips touching.

"Yes," he agreed, "but things will be different then, in terms of time, I mean. Unless the separate drops of the time stream just happen to fall back in the exact place they were to begin with. That's not a very likely occurrence, I'm afraid."

Commandant Longley asked, "Why?"

"Because the rock and the river, remember, are racing in opposite directions," Jonus explained, "and the growing momentum gives each of them incredible built-in drive. When the Elastic Limit is breached, the two will be thrown back into one another, and the water that's splashed and the water beneath the rock will then go in opposite directions, too. There's not much of a chance that they'll match up when they flow back together."

"I see," said Longley, "as was said before, 'for every action there's a reaction.' But let me get this straight, what will I be left with here? What will then become of the planet?"

"Am-Rif Arret will continue on," said Rosemary. "Nothing will happen here to stop that. Time won't end or anything, it's an ever flowing continuum and has no ending or beginning."

All seemed to follow this point. Now comes the bigger picture, she thought. It might not be so easy, but they had to understand.

"When the stream is blown apart," she said, "it will hurl random pieces of future time back against the past. 'For every action' as we've said. You still follow this concept?"

They all bobbed their heads.

"After the blast," she said, "the separate futures will, like water, again flow together, now becoming one mixed future, and this new reality will consist of different parts of the original time flow."

Again they all nodded.

"And all of it will be in the past," she said, hoping not to lose them. "The planet will still evolve, but the evolved planet's future will also jump backward. Again, 'for every action.'"

No one nodded.

But Jonus knew that he and Rosemary were getting closer. He could see that on their faces. They just needed the smallest push and he proceeded to give it to them.

"The planet's future will still occur," he explained, "but in certain random places that future will now be in the past."

"So," said Morris, "what you're saying is that after the blast, we may well walk into a dinosaur or something like that?"

Jonus hunched his shoulders and said, "That's possible, yes. Or worse could occur. There's no way to tell."

He looked around at the group and added, "Anything could happen. Maybe the future's grunts will have evolved into great nations by then. Maybe, just maybe, they'll be the ones being terrorized by dinosaurs, who knows?"

"And the missing men," asked Judith, her back straight as she spoke, "they could wind up in another time as well?"

"Or each in different times," he said, "that's possible, too."

"What happens to the machine?" asked Morris.

"Nothing," answered Rosemary, "because nothing changes in a physical sense. The machine will still be running, at a slower speed, true, because of the energy release, but it's unaffected in any other way, given it's now in the past. But the crisis will still be there, still happening, only we can alter that."

"The speed of the rock and the river will again increase," said Jonus. "It'll take time, maybe even a long time. That all depends on how much energy the blast consumes but at some point, the same thing will happen all over again."

"Then again," added Rosemary. "If nothing's done, it will happen all over again and again. We'll then be caught in a loop."

"Forever?" asked Longley, dumfounded.

Rosemary answered, "Yes, sir."

And you're sure you can't stop the first blast?" asked Archie. He had real fear in his voice. "There's nothing at all you can do?"

Jonus looked to Rosemary before answering, "Not a chance."

At this, after a moment, they all nodded. Even Archie. Now all were cognizant of what they faced.

"OK," said Jonus. "So far so good. Now we can press on."

He stood before continuing. Low-key or no, his legs were stiff and he needed to move. He began to pace as best he could, before the bookcase, in the only space left in the cramped office.

"Before time explodes," he began, "the ultimate destination of the random pieces of exploded time cannot be predicted. Neither can we know how far backwards the river will be pushed. There's no way to know either, but both can be identified and coded by the main computer at the very instant of the blast."

"They can?" said Longley raising his eyebrow.

"Oh, yes," answered Rosemary. "The station's main computer is unaffected by the crisis. It can be done with ease."

That raised Longley's other eyebrow. He was surprised to find something in the place was still working. It had been a long week.

"We can track the men in the field that way," said Jonus, now leaning against the bookcase. "It won't matter where they go. The computer will know, regardless of where they end up."

"How could that happen?" asked Judith.

"Because their brain waves are on file," Jonus answered.

"How's that?" asked Morris. Like a shot, the big man was incredulous, and it seemed that he wasn't alone, either. Everyone besides the technicians was confused anew.

Again Rosemary stilled the waters.

"It sounds fantastic," she said, "but it's true. In fact, each of our brain wave patterns are already coded and compiled. All are filed upstairs in the personnel computer."

Reaching inside her collar and fishing about, she produced her identification tag. She held it out in front of her for a few seconds, twirling it between her fingers. It was the same type they all wore, a roundish, red crystalline device about the size of a large marble.

"It's what's stored in here, too," she said. "Once time is blasted apart, the computer will track any pattern to any particular piece. Such data would be listed as a matter of course."

"So were does that get us?" asked Longley.

"In theory," Jonus continued, "it's possible that anyone then in the containment room, at the moment of the blast I mean, could also travel in the exploded time stream, on the same random piece, if their brain waves also were programmed into that piece."

"And they'd both go to the same place?" asked Archie. In truth, he didn't believe a word of it. It was just too bizarre.

Jonus smiled and shook his head.

"Not to the same place, per se," he said, "but to the same time period. Now, bear in mind what we said before. Anyone within an exploded piece of time will go backward in the time stream, but also forward into the redefined future."

217

"And also remember," Rosemary added, "that we can't predict where any piece will travel. You may go far into the future or not so far, maybe somewhere in between. There's no way to know."

"OK," said Longley, "let me see if I understand this. Each of the missing men is going to be blasted off in a piece of the exploded time stream. That or pushed back into the stream itself."

The two technicians nodded their assent but neither spoke.

"Maybe both will occur," he continued, "who knows? There's nothing we can do about that, it's going to happen, period. But the brain waves of the missing men could be linked with the brain waves of the other two, and each of the linked pairs could then be programmed into the same piece of time."

"Yes," said Jonus, "we'd follow them there."

So what does that get me?" Longley asked, now the incredulous one. "How will that help? Seems to me that I'll just have twice as many missing personnel and an exploded planet, to boot."

Rosemary took that one.

"You must understand, Commander," she said, "that we know what's going on, but the missing men don't. They may figure out what's happened, but maybe not. Either way, they'll be powerless to correct the situation on their own."

She stood and crossed to Jonus, still leaning on the bookcase.

"We do have a plan, Commander," she told him, "but we have to reach the men in the field first to apprise them of the facts. They have to know what we're doing, the new order of the day. There's no way to do that without first contacting each one."

Longley grunted, but made no other response. It was obvious though, to all of them, that the proposal had merit. But there were still numerous questions to be answered.

"So what's the plan you've come up with?" asked Morris. "What can we do? How do we get everybody back in safety, and just how do we set time aright, if that's even a possibility?"

With a look, Rosemary led Jonus back to the desk and both sat.

"It's simple," she said. "Before the incident all nonessential personnel will board the Deferent. In orbit above the raging containment field, they'll be unaffected."

Here she looked to Archie who nodded but said nothing.

"After the blast," she said, "the planet's future will travel to the past, and in this new future, the station will still be here. The building and hardware will be intact, with the machine still running wild, occupying the same space. It'll just be in the past, as well."

"And so will the main water shutoff," added Jonus. "The one Jarvus and Spencer are out looking for now, the one they may have already found if we're lucky. That would simplify things."

"Why would that be?" asked Judith.

"Because," answered the time jumper, "then we wouldn't have to worry about finding the shutoff, per se. Just them. That would save us a lot of time in the long run."

"Remember," explained Rosemary, "they set out on their mission before the crisis developed and communication with them was lost after the incident began. They don't know that the shutoff is the key to stopping the crisis. They can't know the water cooling the reactor is the crucial factor in ending this mess."

"In any event, the main shutoff must be found," said Jonus, "it's the only way. Stop the water to the reactor, and the time-viewing machine also stops. That's all there is to it."

"What difference will that make?" asked Archie. "How will that help? Won't any damage be long done by then?"

Jonus and Rosemary glanced at each other. They were so close now and the basic point was so simple. Most good theories, in point of fact, were much like this.

Often for those not trained professionally, the simplest concepts were the most difficult to comprehend. Without exception, throughout history this had always been the case. Without the proper frame of mind, no one can see the forest for the trees.

"So," Rosemary said, "after the event, the future is in the past."

They all nodded. They had that much. What they didn't have was the connection, the bigger picture.

"And the shutoff is also in the past," she added.

They all nodded again.

"Turn off the water and the reactor overheats, stopping the machine," said Jonus, and then he added, "and because the future is now in the past, the crisis is avoided before it began."

"And that's it?" asked Longley, skepticism hanging in his voice. He didn't believe it, there had to be more.

There was.

"Well," said Rosemary, "the machine will be stopped, at least. But time, that is the planet's future time, is still altered. Who knows where it will be then, where it will wind up, I mean."

Jonus concurred with this assessment.

"The grunts," he said, "will be affected in some way. They'd have to be. If any are left by then, that is."

"Of course," said Judith, the gravity sinking in.

After all, she was the resident grunt expert and she was horrified at the prospect. The implications involved were obvious. They were also staggering, extremely so.

"They'll be at different stages of their normal development," she reported, "thrown into different time frames of their natural futures. There's just no way they won't be changed. Perhaps by then, they will have evolved off the scene altogether."

She looked to the Commandant and added, "This is not a good thing, sir. It's the worst-case scenario, in fact. It clearly goes against the Great Mandate of Primus."

All in the room knew that was forbidden.

"So what's to be done?" asked Longley.

"Once the machine is off and the crisis ended," said the time jumper, "everybody heads back to the station. Remember it will still be here. The damage to the reactor's computer, that is the sabotage, can then be studied and corrected at our leisure."

"We'll have all the time we need," added Rosemary.

"Right," Jonus concurred, "and after we do get a handle on the situation, using the station's backup generators, we can then re-fire the machine and reverse the process."

"How?" asked Morris. He now saw the plan had merit. However, he needed to know more before he'd concur.

"With the data of the first blast stored in the main computer," explained Rosemary, "we can duplicate the exact process, only this time in reverse. Understand, the parameters will be the same. The resulting blast should then send everybody back in time, to that point just before the original incident occurred."

"Before the original blast, you mean?" asked Longley.

Rosemary and Jonus nodded, saying nothing.

"So the grunts are back to where they are now?" asked Morris.

Rosemary and Jonus nodded again.

"And the men would be saved," said Judith. It was a statement and not a question. Still, the two technicians nodded.

"And none of this," asked Archie, "will have occurred at all?"

He still wasn't so sure. He needed one last push. He got it.

Jonus and Rosemary looked at each other. They both started grinning. They had done it at last, and at last they knew it.

"That's right," the time jumper said, as the Chief Technician concurred by saying, "Yes, very good." Each started to chuckle. Both began softly clapping their hands.

At this, the heavy tension in the room broke. The relief was immediate. Everyone felt the difference.

Archie started smiling. Longley and Morris exchanged glances, giving each other satisfied looks. Judith, too, seemed relieved, but she wasn't finished, not just yet.

"So, who goes after the missing men?" she asked.

The scene then seemed to slow. The levity decelerated as the seriousness of Judith's question sunk in. Soon all were pensive.

"The missing men," said Jonus, "may not be together. It's possible, but we can't chance it. Someone has to be paired with each one of then, if only to be on the safe side."

"That's two people that go then," said Morris, relieved. He knew he would be one of the two. No way he wasn't going to be.

"Actually," said Judith, "we need one more. The station has to be monitored, you see. This mission may last a while."

"Right," said Jonus. "If time keeps blowing up, then who knows how long it may be before the men and the shutoff valve are found? We have to make sure nothing else goes askew here."

"And that could be done?" asked Archie. He still didn't believe it. "Someone's brain waves could be paired with the station?"

"Oh, yes," answered Rosemary. "With all of its systems up and running, the station would be easier to track than a single person's pattern. And, being there will enable me to begin working on correcting the computer sabotage."

"Then, that's three," Archie said, but Morris cut him off.

"Wait a minute," he said, "Rosemary's raised a good point here. Suppose it does take a long time. I mean, if what you two say is true, then they could be anywhere on the planet."

"Yes, it's possible that it may take years," said Rosemary. Then she extended the idea. "It may take decades, in fact."

"Perhaps it may take eons," added the time jumper, "who knows? It doesn't matter. It has to be done."

"Eons?" said Longley. He was wary. He didn't like this input.

"No, it's OK," said Rosemary. "Anyone that travels through the blast will no longer age, they can't. They'll be out of phase with their surroundings, out of time phase, that is, which means..."

Longley had heard enough. There was no need for unimportant details now. The plan held sufficient complication as is.

He held up his hand, saying, "I'll accept that's a given, thanks."

"Hold it," said Archie, breaking everyone's train of thought.

"What about those aboard ship?" he asked. "In orbit, we won't be in the blast. If we're still aging, how can we wait for eons?"

"You won't have to," said Rosemary. "If this works, you won't have to wait at all. For you, it should be almost instantaneous."

"That's right," agreed Jonus. "No matter how much time it takes us to complete the mission, it'll take place in the past, in your past, that is. You won't know the difference, Archie."

That seemed to satisfy him and everyone else as well. All were thinking over the consequences. A short moment passed.

"Well," said Jonus, feeling relieved, "to reuse a bad pun, once we're blasted, we'll have all the time in the world to get back."

"By that," said Longley, "I take it you're volunteering to go."

Jonus stopped laughing. The assumption was obvious, and he didn't like it. He looked the Commandant squarely in the face.

"With great certainty," he said, "I was counting on it."

"Sir, I'll absolutely volunteer," said Morris, jumping in. He couldn't wait for the order to be given. He could almost taste it.

"And I make three," said Rosemary, "I'll mind the station."

She glanced to Judith, as if to reassure her, but Judith hardly noticed. Her mind was elsewhere. She had a sinking feeling.

She realized that if Jonus went after his brother Jarvus, which of course he would, then Morris would be the one sent after her husband. There was just no other way for there was no one else to go and she wasn't sure how to react to that knowledge. After all,

Morris might view Spencer as the one thing standing in his way, blocking the entrance into her own sealed heart.

Earlier, Judith had been quite ruthless in her attempt to cool Morris' ardor. Then it had seemed the right thing to do, her only viable option. Now she was having serious reservations.

At the same time, she felt she was being foolish. The big military man was nothing if not a professional soldier, and as such, he wouldn't jeopardize his mission by doing anything seriously stupid. Still, Judith wasn't so sure, and she didn't like the feeling.

There was nothing that she could do about it now. The game was afoot and this plan was already in play. She had to go with the flow of events, as everyone else there did.

Then, for the first time she glanced at Morris and said, "Well, I guess that's it." But it wasn't. Not quite yet.

"I don't think so," said Commandant Longley.

"Is there a problem, sir?" asked Rosemary.

"Yes," he said, "a big problem, I believe."

The technicians turned to each other, scrutinizing. Had they missed anything? They didn't think so.

Morris felt uneasy at this development. He didn't like it, not at all. He didn't understand it.

Archie was wary, as well. He felt that it was all too good to be true, anyway. He was squirming in his chair.

Only Judith seemed calm. She understood. It was easy for her.

"It's the heretics, isn't it," she asked, "the free thinkers?"

Longley ignored her. He was focused elsewhere. Instead, he looked to the pair across the desk.

"This," he asked, "is the only practical plan, correct?"

They both nodded, each wondering what he was after.

Longley turned to Morris and looked him in the face.

"Why would the free thinkers cause this fiasco?" he asked.

"What's their purpose? What would they get out of it?"

Morris didn't answer. Longley knew his position. He didn't think they were after anything more than a good fight.

Longley looked back to Judith. For all her faults, the woman saw things with clarity. He only wished the others were as succinct.

"The time machine," she said, almost under her breath.

"Yes, the machine, said Longley, "the very point of the crisis."

Again he turned to Morris, again looking him in the eye.

"They're after the time technology," he said. "There's no other credible explanation. And this plan takes no account of them."

The Commandant stood. It was now his turn to lecture. He stepped to the bookcase and began to do so.

"The heretics," he stated, "from what I understand, wish to set the grunts free. Free it seems, from the tyranny of Primus. Obviously, they believe the time is nigh."

The military man stood straighter, his hands behind his back. He was in his element. His professional bearing was flawless.

"Crazy?" he asked. "Who cares, it's what they think. We may feel they're all idiots, but at this juncture that's beside the point."

He was looking through the glass wall of the office as he spoke. In the lab, the crews were still moving about, without hope of any let up of their labors. It was still a tedious thing to watch.

"Somehow," he continued, "they need the machine to bring their designs to fruition." He spun about and added, "If this rescue plan is the only feasible one, as we've just heard, then who's to say they can't figure that out, as well? Who's to say that they won't be waiting for you when you get there?"

"But how could they do that?" asked Morris. "How would they get there? And they would have to be there to take the machine."

"Yes, they would," answered Longley, "but perhaps they'd be there already. They could be, you see. They could be if the men, our missing men, the men in the field, were, in fact, the heretics."

Jonus leapt to his feet. He couldn't believe this. How absurd, he thought, while also knowing that he should have seen it coming.

"That's plain crazy," he said, "my brother's no heretic."

"Nor my husband, I assure you," said Judith. The very idea of Longley believing such a thing was exactly her worst nightmare. She had thought they were well past such foolishness.

"Sit down," Longley said to Jonus, emphasizing each word.

Jonus didn't like it, but after a moment he took his seat. His eyes, however, never left the Commandant's. Rosemary reached out and placed her hand on his arm but it gave him little comfort.

"I have," said Longley, "no reason to believe either of them is a free thinker. I've also no reason to think they aren't. It's possible."

The man held his rigid stance, ever the proficient soldier. Appearances mattered. Command was still the only joy he permitted himself, and he was indulging.

"One or the other may be," he said, with a calm voice. "Perhaps both, whatever anyone here may think. And perhaps there are confederates involved as well, perhaps even here at the station."

"Perhaps even in this very room, you mean," spat Jonus.

The time jumper knew that the mission had to proceed. There was no other way, Longley notwithstanding. He looked to Moe.

Jonus wanted back up, and he expected it from his big friend.

Longley, however, didn't play his game, and thus let Morris off the proverbial hook. The Commandant, at ease now within his protocol, simply continued on, as if without interruption. At this point, he could afford to be magnanimous.

"What I do know," he said, "is that this proposed plan does not, in the least contemplate the possibility."

"So it's out?" asked Judith, not sure of his thrust.

"Of course not," answered Longley, "it's the only plan we have. But I must be prepared for any contingency. It's my duty to do so and I won't fail in my duty, I assure you."

That shut them up. Who could argue with such a statement? Who would want to under these dire circumstances?

"So what do you propose?" asked Morris.

The Commandant crossed to his chair and retook his seat.

"I propose to go as well," Longley said with a calm resolve. "My brain waves, as Rosemary's, will be paired with Station Forecast. In that event, any free-thinking heretic will have to go through me before he acquires the time-viewing machine."

Everyone considered this proposal. All realized his suggestion had merit. The mission had to proceed and anything that moved it forward was more than acceptable.

"Agreed," said Morris at last, looking at the time jumper as he did so. Jonus paused a moment, but then he grudgingly nodded. "Agreed," said Morris again, this time adding, "sir."

Longley looked to each of them in turn.

"All right," he said. "That's how it will be then. Let's review."

He was all business now, producing a pad of paper. He began to list the particulars. These would be the new order of the day.

"Morris and Jonus," he said, "will go after the men in the field and the water shutoff. Rosemary and I will guard the station. You two," and here he spoke to Judith and Archie, "will orbit the planet and wait it out with the rest of the contingent."

Everybody nodded. Longley smiled. Again he stood.

"Always remember," he said to them, "that come what may, we will prevail. I know this for we do the work of Primus Himself. The Great Mandate will always continue."

Again they all nodded, knowing it was true. The Mandate was paramount. The will of Primus remained supreme and unshaken.

"We have two hours," Longley continued. "There's much to do in that interim. I suggest we get a move on."

An hour and a half later, Archie and Judith were in orbit inside the Deferent. The rest of the station's nonessentials were aboard as well, billeted in the ship's last two cargo holds. The four remaining holds were packed full of supplies and equipment.

Archie was adjusting the view screen that was trained on the planet's surface directly at the imperiled station. Judith, her nerves tight with anticipation, was sitting next to him. Both were strapped in, awaiting the coming event.

"Won't be long now," he said to her, just making conversation.

Judith didn't answer. She wasn't so sure. It showed.

The other participants were crammed into the tiny containment room located on level two of the Station Forecast. Here they were tucked safely away from the run-amuck containment field that surrounded the planet. From here, they would be shielded, protected, and not randomly scattered throughout the time stream after the passing Beyond the Elastic Limit.

The room was heavily armored but designed for only one person, a single time jumper, and it was a tight fit. All of the usual equipment, save a countdown monitor, had been moved outside the sealed structure to give the four added space. The detailed instructions of the mission, including everyone's brain wave patterns, had been fed into the station's main computer banks and now there was nothing left for them to do but await the inevitable.

As zero hour relentlessly approached, Judith and Archie had their eyes glued to the view screen. They didn't know exactly what would take place after the time explosion, but neither wanted to miss anything. The anticipation was palatable.

"This is it," said Archie, keeping track of the time. "Something should happen...now." Nothing happened.

The image of the station was unchanged.

"Did they go?" asked Archie. Judith didn't answer him. She didn't know if they had or not.

In the containment room, Rosemary had been counting down aloud to the moment of the event. When the appointed time came and nothing occurred, she looked over to Jonus. The shock, written all over her face, was plain to see.

"Something's wrong," she said to him.

Jonus was stupefied. The blast hadn't taken place but he didn't understand why. What had they missed?

"Explain yourself," demanded Longley, "what's happened?"

"I'll check on the equipment," said Rosemary.

"No," answered the time jumper. He was wary and he didn't want her taking any chances. "I'll do it," he said.

But Rosemary was closer to the heavy, sealed door of the unit. Jonus was on the other side of the small, cramped room. Morris and Longley stood crammed between them.

"No, it's fine," she said, "I'll go."

She opened the door and exited, closing it behind her. She then crossed over to a mass of machinery that was connected by cables to the containment room. Once there, her mouth fell open.

A scan of the equipment was all that she needed to comprehend what had occurred. In retrospect, she knew that she should have seen it coming. Now it was too late for anything to be done.

"Oh, no," she said in disbelief and then she added, very calmly under the circumstances, "This is not good."

On board the Deferent, Archie was convinced that something was wrong. He was half considering just blasting out of orbit, taking the beautiful Judith with him, of course. To be on the safe side, he had prepared for this very contingency.

He had a plan ready, a secret agenda if things went astray. The details were finalized. And his agenda naturally included Judith.

He could always ditch the two cargo holds that contained everyone else. This would leave four holds full of supplies for only them. Then they would have the whole galaxy to themselves.

At this point, it seemed a fair idea.

Judith, unaware of this scheme, was absorbed by the image in the view screen. She was not convinced anything was wrong. She thought perhaps the onboard timer had been miscalibrated.

"They said nothing much will change, remember," she reiterated, trying to convince herself as well as the hapless Archie. She was far from certain though, and it showed. Her knuckles were white, her hands gripping the arms of her chair.

Then, in the blink of an eye, Judith realized the image on the view screen had changed. The surface alteration, true to prediction, had been instantaneous. The vast station had disappeared from sight, a huge mound of earth now taking its place.

"Look," she cried, "something's happened."

Archie looked, amazed, and exclaimed, "It's gone! That's not supposed to be. Something has to be wrong."

But now Judith understood what had occurred.

"No, look," she explained, pointing. "It's still there, just under that hillside. It's hidden beneath the bluff."

Archie looked. It was true. His equipment plainly showed the station was, in fact, there, just buried deeply within the planet.

"See how the surrounding geography has changed?" asked Judith, her excitement building. "It's not all that much, but it is different. You know what this means?"

Archie wished no riddles now and she knew it. He was wound up so tight that he almost twanged. She didn't wait for an answer.

"It's happened," she said, "the blast has occurred, just as they said it would. The station's future is now in the past. The terrain of the planet has changed in the interim, that's all."

Archie wasn't convinced. In truth, the young Captain had understood little of the discussion involving the event. His instincts were to cut and run, and he usually followed his instincts.

"They said it won't be long now," stated Judith. "Not for us, I mean. They said it would be almost instantaneous."

Archie didn't know what to do. He thought, was this it then? Was this the proverbial point of no return?

Yes or no, stay or go? Should he act now or not? He was torn.

Either way, unlike those now on their own below, he knew that he didn't have all the time in the world to decide.

PART FOUR – THE ENDING
CHAPTER TEN
THE END GAME

The beast in the dungeon was indeed dead. The old Crone, Sorbus, stood staring with mute wonder at the sight of it, silent and still. At the time she was in the very bowels of the ancient Fortress of Forecastle, which was to say that she stood on the deepest floor of the installation she also knew as Point Zero.

With the great beast dead, the imperiled station, now buried beneath the earth by eons of geologic action, was at last free of the errant time-viewing machine, located only one story above. Sorbus had waited so long for this very eventuality that she could hardly believe it, but it was true. The beast was dead at last.

When it died, that is, when the station's main reactor core overheated and shut down, the power feeding the raging machine on Level Two was instantly removed, and it also had died. As a consequence, time itself was again contained within the elusive Elastic Limit. To the bent and disfigured old woman, this meant that the looming and ever-growing crisis, the very crisis that had driven her for all these years, was thereby ended as well.

That fact, the very finality of it stunned her.

Their plan, conceived in haste so long ago, was working at last. An unnatural and continuing merger of the planet's different futures had followed the explosion of time. Now, the mixing of those future consequences, forbidden by Primus Himself, yet all set into play by that now-distant event, from the exact moment of the incident itself, was finally, undeniably over.

Her work, however, was not. Far from it, for Sorbus knew that the main task of her Mandate was now at hand. The mixing may have been over, but the merger remained, and with who knows how much damage to the planet's original future?

With the beast dead, the sabotage to the reactor could at last be studied, and with hope and enough effort, corrected.

Yet the back-up generators, not the reactor were her most pressing priority. This was because the station's sealed, internal ventilation system was now also without power, its oxygen scrubbers rendered idle, and already the air within the vast station was growing stale. Time, it seemed, was still of the essence.

It was a strange thing to be in the dead edifice without the constant and reassuring buzz of the building's venting system. But no matter, Sorbus thought, as she, without thinking, stroked the small rose medallion still pinned to her wimple. She knew the generators, aged as they were, would be easy things to deal with.

The crafty, old Crone had already sent her daughter, Lucid, to fetch the appropriate manuals. Together they should be able to bring the sleeping machines online with very little trouble and that would give them power and light. Then the dormant air conditioning apparatus on the fourth floor of the station, the so-called housekeeping level, could be restarted.

Only after that procedure would the now-deceased fortress be reborn and breathe anew. Sorbus felt reborn too, with a sense of purpose, a new beginning. It had been a long time.

Without the benefit of electricity, the scene in which the Crone found herself was eerie. A large part of the dungeon, that is the immense generator plant housing the dead beast, was bathed in a stark light from the battery-powered lantern the old woman had placed before the looming main reactor. Complete with dials and oversized gauges, the machine's broad face was pocked with shadows cast from the lantern's artificial glow.

The Crone, still fingering her pin, wondered which of the men in the field had located the elusive water junction. Someone had, for the reactor's cooling water had been shut off, no doubt about that. Yet it didn't matter much who had found it, only that it had been and closed, for that meant the next stage of the overall plan, the new order of the day, would be already started.

They would make their way back to the Point with dispatch, for that action was now their newest Mandate. How much time would that take, she mused? Primus Himself only knew.

The door to the reactor room opened, and Lucid entered, holding the manuals to the various generators circled in her arm, balanced on her hip as if she were toting a baby. All were needed because a separate back-up powered each internal system at the station. She held a powerful flashlight in her other hand, the better to make her way through the blackened building.

Lucid advanced toward the Crone, smiling as she made her transit, for she happened to recall one of her favorite childhood tales. It was the one of the young girl helping her mother, all the while traversing the dark and sleeping fortress with the aid of a magical torch. Somehow the Crone's original rendition of the story had omitted how hard the poor girl would work for the books she now carried were a heavy burden.

"Enjoying yourself?" asked Sorbus in dry humor, noticing the smile on the approaching girl's face.

"Not as much as you," answered Lucid, adding, "We were supposed to meet at the back-ups."

All of a sudden, the Crone looked like a child with her hand caught in the candy jar and she laughed outright throwing her distorted head back as she accomplished the feat.

"Yes," Sorbus answered, embarrassed. "I only meant to stay a moment or two, to see for myself that it was, in fact, dead. After all this time, I found it very hard to believe."

Lucid nodded and looked to the massive machine resting before them. She understood. However, time was ticking.

She said, "Mother, the air grows foul and we must not tarry."

The Crone knew it to be so and she reached for her ancient walking stick in preparation to leave. Lucid then handed Sorbus the flashlight as well, taking for herself the heavier lantern that her mother had earlier carried. The two then made their way toward the corridor, but before she exited, the ancient Crone turned and once more cast her gaze to the dead beast.

It intimidated her in a strange sort of way, a way that she couldn't quite explain, nor understand. The old woman sighed while leaning on her stick, knowing that she would need Spencer Hall and his cool professionalism to figure this one out. The man was a talented engineer, that was a fact, and there was no one on the entire planet that understood the ancient reactor as he did.

Still, all of that and more, she realized, would unfold only later, and perhaps much later. It depended totally on the missing men in the field and how soon they made their way back to Point Zero. The Crone had no control over that unknown time frame.

She did, however, control events here at the fortress now that the beast was at last dead. At this stage, it was her Mandate to direct the particulars, and she was most eager to begin her new labors, even if those labors were only going to grow in the future. Just how long had it been since she'd had any real work to do?

The back-up generators were her first priority. The rest would then follow. There was much to accomplish in preparation for the men arriving and the generators might take some time to fire.

Yet she was not intimidated, daunted, nor concerned in the least by that awaiting task. No, she could handle that situation and what was to come with ease, she knew, with the aid of her beloved daughter. For the old, bent woman, the distorted Crone known by all as Sorbus, in truth was the beleaguered Station Forecast's Chief Technician, and so her real name was Rosemary.

At last, she turned back to the exit. Shuffling with a temperate pace, tapping with her stick as she moved, she followed Lucid to the back-up generator plant, located in an adjacent room down the darkened hallway. Only after their work there was completed would the two of them make their ponderous way up to the oxygen scrubbers on the housekeeping floor, three long levels above the dungeon, and the now dead beast.

At that very moment, the engineer Spencer Hall, the object of the old Crone's thoughts, was displaying no amount of cool professionalism whatsoever. He was far too unnerved for that. His heart was at present pounding with such force that he could hear the beats pulsing in his ears and his rapid breathing, labored and haggard, was nonetheless insufficient for his current needs.

He feared that both of the exertions, heart beating and lungs pumping, were far too intense to go unnoticed. He was terrified that the very sounds of them would give his hidden position away, and he took a moment to try to combat them, to force them under control. He wished with desperation to control everything now, using the only tool that he had left, his sheer willpower.

Spencer began compelling his powerful mind not only to take command of his frightened body, which might be conceivable given time, but also to somehow change his current surroundings, which wasn't possible, regardless of interim.

The engineer was deep in the foothills, hunched low to the ground, hanging on the side of a steep ravine. His long body was entwined among the gnarly trunks in a dense stand of mountain laurel for the heavy pine forests of the higher peaks had given way of late to rolling hills covered with a more diverse canopy. He and Moas had been making good time since the ancient water valve, the mission's main objective, had been sealed.

They had been traveling without supplies and living off the land. The two were in the Piedmont Region now, crowded with large stands of hardwoods, oaks and hickories, and by equally tall softwooded trees such as tulip poplars and the occasional, towering sycamore. Growing among these were smaller dogwoods and wild cherry trees, maples and redbuds, with bushes and small shrubs, assorted mosses and ferns dominating the lowest niche.

Their camp was overrun just before dawn. The small clearing, cut off from the thick underbrush, had seemed peaceful enough the night before. Spencer was just awake, sitting up and rubbing his puffy eyes, with the giant still asleep beside him.

He heard a crashing noise, but in the distance. Then he heard it again, louder, a tearing, ripping, popping sound. It was sharp in a weird way, buffeted as it was by the thicket, but it was there.

He was fully aware by then, straining to localize the thrashing in the distance, when he heard more examples coming ever closer. At last he realized that several unknown somethings were heading their way, dashing at top speed through the wood. Always the coward, Spencer froze, incapable of moving.

The giant, however, bolted upright, alert in an instant.

"Run," was all the big man said, but in a calm, determined voice. He then rolled to his feet and scampered off into the misty morning. He was gone in mere seconds, leaving Spencer alone.

The engineer tried to move, hearing heated voices screaming behind him, but he didn't get far. A man, a desert nomad by the looks of him, dashing at top speed and with the benefit of a mad intent, chose that moment to break through the brush. He overtook the fleeing Spencer, who was just starting his bolt.

The man crashed into him, causing them both to fall. The tumble seemed to take its toll on the nomad, for after the collision he moved no more. Spencer did though, his adrenaline rush jumped into overdrive, once he tried to roll the nomad off him.

Small and thin and dressed in faded rags, the man was well bloodied about his face and neck. He was also obviously very dead. Spencer screamed and tried to kick him off.

Before he could, another nomad, younger, broke into the clearing. This one stopped, breathing deep breaths, leaning on the flaky bark of a wild cherry tree while looking over his shoulder, gauging the pace of his pursuers. They were easy to hear.

Turning his head in the morning gloom, he spied Spencer and the dead man before him. After a beat, he dashed off into the wood at an angle to them, intent but heedless of any consequences before him. Spencer realized that he had to move, and quickly.

He commenced to kick at the man atop him, hearing a new sound as he began. It was mournful, a kind of moaning intonation, and it grew louder, with a higher and still higher pitch, increasing as he thrashed his long legs in a mad frenzy. Only after extricating himself, did the final comprehension come.

He had been making the unnerving noise himself, whining like a baby while kicking away.

Spencer nearly crapped his pants at the revelation.

Trying to move away while still on his back, he pushed off with his heels but had more success with his palms, digging them into the dirt at his sides to gain traction. It was then that the next man appeared on the scene, stepping from the brush with an easy pace. Spencer's run of bad luck was still holding fast.

This grunt was different from the nomads, larger and more rugged looking. He was dressed in a different way too, being armored after a fashion, with thick leather slabs bolted together and hanging in rows to shield his tenderest spots. These protected his chest, stomach and groin, upper legs, shoulders and arms.

The man carried a short-handled, double-headed war axe. He held the implement with ease, hefting it deftly, displaying his practice with the tool. The head of the man's axe was large, obviously well used, and covered in fresh blood.

Spencer groaned, but pitifully so, in an almost inaudible gurgle from somewhere deep within his throat. By then his eyes were large with fear, his head jerking back and forth in stunned disbelief. Rooted to the spot, it was his only movement.

The leathered man grinned, pausing, looking around some, but soon enough he stepped forward. Directly after, Moas reappeared out of nowhere, somewhat behind the man. The soldier sensed a disturbance to his rear and turned to meet it, his weapon raised and at the ready, but the giant was faster in spite of his great bulk.

He struck the man with his fist, a clean blow to the chin, with plenty of follow through. Spencer was amazed at the sound it had made. First there was a loud pop, then a squishing, spongy noise. Bright red blood spewed everywhere.

The jarring impact had been square to the soldier's mandible, just below his front teeth. The joint on each side of his jaw had been snapped in an instant with the bones then shoved in a deep and neat upward thrust into the soft tissue of his brain stem. The force of the contact was such that the man in leather actually left the ground as he shot backward and he was quite dead before he hit the dirt with a thud, his axe falling haphazardly to the side.

The giant looked at Spencer who was still sitting. Stunned, he was clinging with desperation to his backpack as if he could somehow gain comfort from it. He was frozen in place, rooted to the spot, incapable of moving on his own volition.

"Now," Moas screamed, grabbing his arm, "run, damn you!"

Both had begun moving through the thicket, this time side by side, carried forward by the giant's momentum. Day was dawning as they made their way, tearing along as best they could. A scream was heard nearby, bloodcurdling and cut off, but in their own, desperate flight they paid it little heed.

Doubtless another nomad dying, no match for the well equipped and butchering warriors hot on their trail. After a few seconds, they heard excited shouting, not as close but near enough, in a position somewhere off their flank. Then more shouting, louder this time, closing in, followed by another scream.

The two had then begun to climb a steep, rise, with the sounds of pursuit still behind them. Near the crest of the ridge the earth beneath their feet, a soft loam wet from recent rains, peeled off and gave way. Both men then toppled from the high ground, each falling over to his separate side of the elevation.

Spencer, screaming at the top of his lungs, rolled a few times, but after sliding a short distance, managed to scamper to his feet.

He continued moving, however, running faster downward through the trees and scrub as the force of gravity pulled at him.

Approaching the bottom of the gradient, he ran faster still, the better to propel his body up the equally steep, opposite side of the ridge. He took the crevice at a bound, and pulling and kicking, he climbed his way towards the new crest before him.

It was then that he encountered the mountain laurel thicket. The embankment was a sheer one, but once inside the stand Spencer was able to haul himself up without losing his hard-earned purchase. As he was doing this, grunting aloud with the new exertion, he heard another piercing scream in the distance.

This one was different from the others.

This was not some terror-stricken cry nor one of desperation brought on by horror at the final, deadly moment. This one contained no fear at all. This one was a cry of pain.

Spencer knew at once that the bellow came from the giant.

Was he injured or worse, had their pursuers already wounded him? If so, then they would, without doubt, quickly close in and together they would bring the big man down no matter how tough he was. What would happen to Spencer then?

He began to climb into the thicket, curling his way among the closely placed trunks and low, intertwining limbs of the mountain laurel. He was trying hard not to think, concentrating only on his task, trying to gain distance. He was blindly moving forward, while bending lower on the ravine, almost crawling on the ground.

Soon, however, he was forced to stop. The choking stand of vegetation had become too dense to proceed. Spencer was pressed into the grove then, with nowhere to run, just like a snake that had slithered down an ever-narrowing pipe.

In the distance, he heard another doleful cry of pain.

How far away, he wondered? How far had the giant man gotten? Was he still on the opposite side of the ridge?

By the sound of it, he had to be or not much farther. How had it come to this? How was it even possible?

When he heard voices in the distance, gruff but calm enough, closing in on the giant's position, he started to lose what little composure he had left. He would be next, he thought. Terrified anew, he began to panic in earnest.

His body may have been stymied at the time, but not his frantic and overactive mind. It began to race. This was unhelpful though, for his calculating brain knew his options were nil and that knowledge only fired his fear further.

He began to shake then, his whole body trembling, with sweat bursting out of all the pores he possessed. He felt nauseated. His heart was beating with such fierceness that the organ seemed near to ripping clean out of his heaving chest.

Trying to slow the raging pace of his lungs only made his breathing worse. How could they not hear him? They would if they crossed the ridge, that's all it would take.

Closing his eyes and wishing with all his might to be anywhere other than where he was, fighting for his very sanity, he began to will his body to calm itself, but to no avail. The effort was quite useless. In his terror, his body would not heed his resolve.

Why was this happening? Why was something this awful even permitted to happen? What could possibly be the purpose?

More cries shot out, the meaning unmistakable, even from his distant vantage. The calls were excited, short and choppy, beckoning with a definite purpose. They had found the giant.

Would they kill him now, Spencer wondered? Would they do it in quick fashion like the poor nomads? How often in the past had he wished for this very thing, to have his wife's lover simply die?

An easy thing to do, he realized, when not faced with the reality of the deed. In his daydreams he had thought of that often, as a tidy end to all of his marital problems. What would it solve now?

On the other hand, grasping for another alternative, if the big man were injured perhaps he wouldn't fight them. Perhaps then they would only take him prisoner. He was a unique specimen after all, bigger than most and an odd catch, no doubting that.

Yet what would happen then?

Spencer was not like the giant. He wasn't from the military clan. He couldn't fight them and the very idea was ludicrous.

He knew that he was a coward anyway, powerless to act.

Spencer began to cry. He couldn't help it for he was now a broken man. It began slowly at first with only a few tears streaming, but later a flood, pouring, gushing.

He had already been chewed up emotionally by enduring long years of a failed and disconnected marriage. Affecting him more than he knew, touching every part of his day-to-day existence, this personal collapse had infected his entire being with sorrow. As a consequence, his lifelong profession, achieved at great personal effort, was no longer pleasing to him.

Worse still, it was now only a burden.

Next, ill equipped and unprepared, he was nonetheless engaged in a staggering effort to somehow save humanity as well as himself, only to have his every exertion in that regard also stymied. Now cut off and alone, he was surrounded by death and fighting for his very life. Spencer couldn't believe it.

And why? What was the point? How in the very name of Primus, he thought, could this be permitted to occur?

He then jerked up his head, his eyes open and no longer crying. The question had been rhetorical but should it be? His powerful brain began to reason, sharpening its focus, starting to hone.

Spencer had never spent much time nor deep thought concerning the deity of Primus. It wasn't a shallow thing, a dismissal on his part, for he did believe that Primus was God. Yet, as most people, he had taken that fact for granted, content that the bigger picture was entrusted to a greater, higher authority.

In his safe little world, it hadn't really mattered to him.

However, if it was true, that is, if Primus were truly God, then He controlled all events in the universe. A supreme being by definition was all-powerful. He wouldn't be supreme otherwise.

Given that assumption, then how could Primus condone or at least permit what was happening here?

Was there a greater, unknown purpose?

Of course, this wasn't the first time that such questions had been posed. Throughout all of history, people had wondered why a good God permitted bad things to happen. Often in the past, the point had been discussed in blunt terms, for example during the recent Civil War, because in warfare it was always beneficial for those in power to allay such moral concerns among the masses.

In fact, most of the people referred to the recent conflagration as a Holy War, with the implication being that defying the justly designated civil authority was tantamount to heresy.

The explanation given the masses then, during the war, that is, also had been discussed before, in other connotations for eons. The position had been scrutinized at length, and by the theology clan in particular. An omnipotent God, this well used explanation went, was naturally beyond any comprehension.

How could a human being understand everything there was to know? It was unfeasible, unattainable. It just couldn't be done.

As such, a simple being had to have faith, and that's what it all came down to, he knew. You had to believe or the whole thing unraveled. Once doubt crept in, then nothing was for sure.

That position was, had always been, the answer to why bad things happened. Yes, they occurred for a reason, but that reason, by definition, was unfathomable. It was beyond our limited scope, far beyond our capacity to comprehend.

In the final analysis, who were we to question?

It was a simple solution, but to one possessing faith it was enough. To one with faith, nothing ever happened without reason. His problem was that he had no faith.

Spencer had believed in Primus, but from afar.

He had never needed to do anything else, not since he was a youngster anyway. Spiritual queries for him, at least, had been only a childhood phase, left behind when he grew and pursued other interests. He still believed that Primus was supreme, but only because the alternative was foreign, unfamiliar to him.

Just then, he heard more screaming, examples of pain this time. There was a tinge of desperation, too. Next a cry of anger was heard, followed by more quick cries of pain.

Next something else was heard, a different noise altogether, lighter, airy, as if floating on air. It took a second to recognize it, but then he did. It was the sound of laughter.

Now Spencer had his answer, and in undeniable fashion. They would kill the giant, after all, but not without a little fun first. A little torture would be tossed in to pass the day away.

At last, Spencer became detached somehow. It was a blessing, for he was a beaten, as well as a broken man now, and had no viable options left open to him. He knew on his own that he could do nothing, for being alone he had nothing.

Alone or not, there was everything to lose now if nothing was done. His life was at stake but he was powerless to alter that situation. The man had nowhere to go, no plan of action if he went, and no end to his problems if he stayed.

Spencer Hall was lost, not only in a physical sense, alone and away from all he loved, but in a spiritual sense as well. He felt small and powerless. He was empty, spent, and had zero, he thought, to fall back on, but he was wrong again.

He did something then that he hadn't done or even considered doing in a long time. Something that never would have entered his mind had the circumstances been less dire. Something that was at first the hardest, and then, the easiest thing he'd ever done.

Spencer Hall, alone and finding himself at the very end of his proverbial rope, began to pray to his God, Primus.

At the time, the caveman Moas could have used a few prayers himself. Unlike Spencer, the giant did not right himself after falling over the steep ridge. He had rolled, his growing momentum such that he had easily crashed through the thin vegetation in his way, but that downward motion had stopped soon enough.

Moas caught his foot on a large, curved root, not far from the trunk of an upturned tree. The root was open and exposed in the middle, but firmly grounded in the earth on either side. Somehow as he tumbled, his foot had curled into the semicircle of the snag, as if threading a needle, and though it gave some, pulling against the giant's great weight, the stubborn root had held fast.

The big man had continued his roll but he stopped in a wrench, just after his lower leg bone snapped. The sound it made was both loud and nauseating. He passed out then, grotesque looking and hanging askew, with all of his considerable bulk pulling against his now pinioned and swelling, rigidly anchored foot.

Somewhat later, he came to announcing his displeasure by bellowing in pain. This was the cry that Spencer, clinging on the next ridge, had identified as his. It wasn't his last.

At once, Moas understood what had happened and he began to draw deep breaths, girding for what he knew must come next.

With a jerk, he leaped up, bending at the waist. He then grabbed the root on both sides of his foot. He didn't scream then, just bit through his lip, but he did cry out next after first digging in with his good leg and throwing himself backward.

Then he screamed, snapping the root apart as he did.

He slid down the hill some and passed out a second time. It was short respite. Again he regained consciousness, his broken leg burning now, feeling on fire only worse, inundated with pulsing throbs and stinging, electric shocks.

Nonetheless, exposed as he was, he realized that he had to move. He began to crawl on his back, dragging his lower trunk behind him, but he didn't get far. The agony was just too intense.

He settled for what cover was available. He pulled himself up against the dead tree's upturned and decaying root ball. It was then that he heard the voices of his pursuers.

It was easy to judge that they weren't far away.

At first Moas tried his best to blend in with his surroundings by hunkering down and shuffling his broad shoulders, like a big bear scratching his back, but he soon gave it up. He was not going to disappear into the landscape no matter what he did. The giant man then took a moment to assess his situation, eyeing his disposition as he squeezed his great hands on his leg, trying to find the proper pressure points to ease the searing pain.

As he surveyed the scene, he tasted blood and realized for the first time his bitten-through lip was bleeding. His wide brow was also streaming a cold sweat. Next he noticed his foot was twisted in a stark and unnatural angle to his leg.

His situation was untenable and he knew it.

When the giant heard voices in the near distance, his life flashed before his eyes. Not his entire life, just the failures it had contained. He saw them all, as if detached and from afar.

He had failed many times during his span, in myriad ways.

Despite the circumstances, or perhaps because of them, Moas started to smile at the irony of his dire situation. It was ironic, and on many levels. Here he was failing once again, even though he had been raised since childhood to succeed, raised only to win.

And yet, even here in this dismal downfall, his greatest to date, he was still true to his clan and always would be. He was a military man through and through. He was, in fact, the new Subcommander of Point Zero and so his true name was Morris.

Morris knew well that both his professional and personal existence had been failures. He had no love life to speak of beyond

247

the short encounters that made up his sorry history. There was nothing but lots of dead-ends there.

Julie, Doctor Judith Hall that is, was just his latest and most grandiose example. And yet, with every successive relationship he had tried harder, fallen deeper, bet everything on a larger and larger hope, but all to no avail. Failure.

Somehow, every woman in his life, each different in so many ways, had been the same, sad story. They hung in there just long enough to get to know him, then boom, to a one, they were gone.

Just how many had it been, he wondered?

Morris couldn't remember the true tally, and he didn't want to try anyway. What was the point? Still, it would have been nice to have someone special to think of now.

His professional record was just as bleak.

He was strong and intelligent, could be overpowering or clever, but his timing had always been bad. He had lost out following the academy, as older classmates had already taken the best postings. With the end of the long, Holy War, only diminishing opportunities of advancement had come his way.

Despite his huge bulk, at the time Morris had been little more than a small fish in a very big pond.

For this reason, he had jumped for the open assignment on far off Am-Rif Arret, only to have it jerked out from under him once he got there. He didn't even find Spencer. No, the grunts had located him, drawn by the bizarre sound of his chainsaw.

To top things off, when he arrived on the scene, the bumbling Spencer had already found the elusive water junction. And now, broken and cornered, Morris knew that he would never find the traitor, his last secret plan to save his dying career. In the end, he wouldn't even be able to save himself.

Despite all of his training and fine preparations, the only thing going for the man was something that he had no control over. Having traveled through the time stream he didn't age, thus giving him plenty of chances to fulfill his Mandate. But this was no guarantee against personal injury or spoiled stratagem.

Poor Morris was now batting a thousand, because his mangled leg was still killing him despite his desperate ministrations. However, as a highly trained tactician, he knew that his situation would only get worse. His fears were soon confirmed.

There were three of them in the brush, signaling out, closing in. He could hear their positions as they converged, localizing as he listened, shifting his eyes between their calls to each other. They were tromping through the wood at leisure, tracking now, understanding from his earlier cries that he was wounded.

They moved forward with a slow pace, knowing that he was down, but not perhaps without some mischief left.

They were dressed, he saw at last, much like the one that he had already killed. Two of the three wore crude helmets, a metal cap with rivets around the base. One helmet had a length of fine chain mail attached at the rear, hanging down protecting the neck, giving the appearance of long, silvered hair.

Each of them looked serious, intent on business. They were all well armed, the giant saw. He had no weapons.

One was equipped with a mace, complete with small, sharp spikes. Another had a long sword and short knife. The last one, the one with the chain-mailed cap, carried a war axe much like his now dead comrade had possessed.

As they came forward, Morris suddenly thought of his long-lost friend, the time jumper. After all, the man had been thinking of his life, and the two had known each other since childhood. The giant, squeezing his leg in vain, wondered if his old buddy had done any better in answering his own Mandate.

He knew him to be tenacious and single minded, strong, and sly as a fox. Then again, he was hardheaded and could screw up royally, given half a chance. But upon reflection, Morris figured his cohort had to be doing better than he was and the big man smiled once more, somehow comforted by the thought.

At that moment, the Traveler was deep in the hilly forest, some three days distant from Point Zero, unaware at the time that he was only a few miles from the giant's present position. Still, he couldn't have helped the big man even had he known of his lethal predicament. Onus was then fighting for his own life, in fierce hand-to-hand combat with a larger and more powerful opponent.

He was struggling with a solid caveman who had jumped him from behind, taking him by surprise as he had moved through the thick underbrush. It seemed to be a fatal mistake. The caveman was very intent in his task and the Traveler had so far denied him a kill only by using his own superior wrestling skills.

Just the same, Onus knew that he was deferring the inevitable because he was tiring fast while his primitive adversary was not.

Onus wasn't doing any better with his Mandate either, having separated from the object of his quest in short order after their passage into the foothills, following a direct but harsh traverse through the desert. At first, the two of them had evaded detection in the ever-thickening forest, but this became more difficult to do the closer they had come to their final destination. The countryside was swarming, alive with grunts of all descriptions.

As far as Onus could tell, miscellaneous groups of them, all from different periods of the planet's future, were now in open conflict. The reintegration of time, only theory before the fact, was now accomplished and with deadly consequences. Currently, the populace was very busy and killing was everywhere.

Of course, Onus knew that all this chaos was a direct result of the planet being blasted Beyond the Elastic Limit. He understood well enough that everything had changed in the interim since the containment field exploded, and in drastic ways, too. Yes, the Traveler knew all of this and much more.

His grasp of the situation was quite clear, perceptive, and keener than most, for he was Station Forecast's currently assigned time jumper, and so his real name was Jonus Welleb.

However, official titles were at present worthless for grappling with a primitive grunt in the forest was not just an intellectual exercise with no tangible result. Jonus knew the endgame to this encounter was to be real enough and he groaned with a new effort to force the outcome his way. The exertion was wasted.

The caveman had a firm grip on him, something that the larger combatant had accomplished again and again, after each time that Jonus had managed to slip away from his stronger grasp.

The two had been fighting a good ten minutes now, thrashing about, in and out of this or that hold, followed by this or that response. By now, it was plain to see that the grunt warrior was a seasoned fighter experienced in close-quarter combat. Of more importance to the Traveler, he was a competent warrior at ease with himself and his considerable killing skills.

The caveman was in fact enjoying the joust between them, grinning at the exertion, boring his eyes into those of Jonus, confident in the final outcome of their encounter.

He had been surprised at first, when the time jumper had eluded his grip with a quick burst of action. But with each progressive move, Jonus had seen this response turn into a kind of grudging admiration, an appreciation of one pro for another. However, the result was clear, a foregone conclusion.

The grunt warrior was struggling but he was not giving an inch, and Jonus was aware that the situation was more than desperate. Yes, he was holding on but soon enough he would tire to the point that the contest would then become uninteresting to his opponent. After that, the end would come with dispatch, almost as an afterthought to the original purpose of the encounter.

After all, why dawdle if you're not having a good time? Oh, no. It was much better to get it over with and move on.

The grunt clutched Jonus by the shoulders, grasping the material of his tunic while pushing against him, pressing him into the trunk of a large tree. The Traveler had tried kicking at him, but the caveman was taller and this tactic had failed. His bigger opponent could effectively avoid the intended blows by bending and holding Jonus somewhat to the side, at his longer arm's length.

Next, Jonus had tried pounding away on the outside of the grunt's arms, then on the inside of them, but all to no avail. His adversary withstood the onslaught with ease for the impacts administered had no follow-through. The Traveler's considerable strength was thus rendered useless and his blows ineffectual.

Jonus was close to panic but his former military training held, and his sweating face showed only determination. He was far from done yet, anyway. He just needed to employ a different strategy and he needed to do so sooner than later.

Jonus knew that he had a good sense of timing, and he also knew that misdirection was in large part successful only if it was timed well. Struggling away while looking the caveman in the face, he chose a moment at random and then made his move. He glanced to the right, somewhere behind his foe, and in an instant his demeanor changed, his countenance showing horror.

Despite the caveman's grip, Jonus shifted to the left as if turning to flee. In doing so, he flung his arms out in the same direction, ignoring his adversary. This placed the Traveler's right arm between the two arms of the primitive grunt.

The action took only a moment, but together with a pitiful moan on his part, it had the desired effect. The warrior broke his concentration and looked over his left shoulder to gauge the perceived threat. It was all that Jonus needed.

He smashed his right elbow, hard, into the exposed side of the grunt's face. At first the movement had no tangible result, save the caveman's grip became tighter. Jonus struck again, delivering a blow to the man's jaw, and this time the grunt was clearly dazed.

The Traveler pummeled away, delivering with his elbow several quick shots to the man's eye and cheek. Still his stubborn foe would not fall. At last, after a final smack to the ear of the warrior, Jonus managed to twist away from his tormentor.

The caveman staggered backward a step or two and sank to the ground, a look of confusion on his now-battered face.

Jonus should have run then, making the best of his opportunity, but, despite his frenzied condition, his energy was drained and his breath was labored. He stood over the beaten man, a little dazed himself, trying to assess his next move. Breathing deeply, his hands on his knees, he glanced around the forest.

Jonus judged it to be midday and wondered just how far his missing brother had gotten since that morning.

At sunrise he had awakened to find Jarvus gone, just like that.

What's worse, he knew that he should have seen it coming. It's true that the two had been drained after crossing the desert, but in the time since, both had recovered well enough.

They had begun to argue at least, and Jonus had thought that was a good sign. After all, you couldn't debate with someone without their first speaking to you. Now the time jumper realized that you couldn't debate with them if they weren't there either.

Talk had been tight between the two them in the desert, for without question, Jonus had known the most direct route, and the arid conditions permitted little energy for idle chitchat. However, once in the forest, with less heat and ample food and water available, things had changed. The normally reserved Jarvus had opened up at last, just as his older brother knew he would.

The Great One had raised considerable objections to their new Mandate. The rescue plan was ill conceived, he thought, and he wasn't happy with such direct action on their part. Who were they, anyway, to fight against the way things were?

Jarvus hadn't relished his life in the desert, but his situation there was cushy enough given what had happened. And who could say what Primus really wanted? The brothers weren't from the Theology Clan, so who knew with clarity?

Yes, he was verbose enough then, quibbling over everything, arguing over whatever he could think of. He just wouldn't let up either. Talk, talk, talk, that's what living alone gets you.

At the time, Jonus had thought that he was upset only with the company forced upon him, not their mission in general. Now he wasn't so sure. His brother was hardheaded and sly and Jarvus had sufficient courage to follow through with any bizarre plan, if he thought the payoff was satisfactory.

He was just like Jonus and that's the part that galled the most. The Traveler should have seen it coming. Now it was too late.

In the big picture there was the traitor to worry about but that wasn't Jonus' present concern. Jarvus was no spy, he was sure. For one thing, he hadn't the necessary personal convictions.

Politics had always been meaningless to him. Self-interest had always been his only concern. Also, the payoff, living the life of the 'Great One' in the desert, had never been his desire.

Rather, he had made out as best he could, given the conditions available to him after the incident had occurred.

But rejecting Primus, now that was possible. Jonus knew Jarvus was just irate enough to do that. Why follow God when He screws up your life and when He does so for no reason?

One could always handle a fair fight, at least one could try to, but who doesn't resent a mismatched contest? And why beat up someone, when you're already all-powerful? What would be the higher purpose in such a pompous position?

From Jarvus' point of view, under the circumstances, who wouldn't be angry? In other words, at this stage, the Great One wasn't a traitor, but then again he might be a heretic. Either way he was sick of Jonus, and that much was certain.

Regardless, Jonus knew his man, for he had raised him, or tried to anyway, and he knew his brother's current motivation.

Jonus saw that Jarvus was past being fed up, and because his life had been turned upside-down, he felt abused as well. He only wanted to be free, with nothing to bind him. He just wanted to disappear and be left alone, not caring that Primus had never promised anyone an easy life, just one with a purpose.

He wished most of all to be free of Jonus. The Traveler could see that well enough. It was strictly personal between them.

Still, the two brothers were bound together in more ways than one. Jonus couldn't bring himself to let him go, he just couldn't. Not with what had happened to their long-dead parents hanging over them, still splitting them in two.

The fact that the brothers had been so close before the tragedy only made it more painful for both of them.

Just the same, it was plain that Jarvus wanted his freedom, period. He would think, Jonus reasoned, that he'd earned it after everything he'd been through. An ideal life of leisure, with no ties or responsibilities was what he was after, and his sibling could only get that if he headed back to Point Zero, Mandate or no.

He had to, Jonus was sure of it, for there was no other way to get out of this unholy mess. They had discussed these things in detail the night before leaving the desert city of Arret while the two were eating suckling pig and talking strategy in the water tower. He just would be traveling on his own now.

What it all came down to then was, on the one hand, his brother was still true to Primus, and his duty sends him to the station, only alone, without the Traveler. On the other hand, he's a heretic, but even then, if you go to the trouble to reject Primus, why not do so in the real world if you can, at home as it were? At least then you'd be free to damn yourself in familiar surroundings.

Yes, Jarvus had had enough of living lost forever in a displaced time stream, never aging, and spending eternity in a gilded, desert cage without any say in the matter. He wanted out all right. Jonus knew that he wanted out above all else.

So either way, heretic or no, it seemed that his brother had to be traveling towards the station. Still, with so much hanging in the balance, the Traveler was concerned. This was a rather large assumption, but was it correct?

He knew he had to be sure, but the answer then became moot.

The battered caveman had regained his wits while the Traveler had been lost in his contemplations. The angry grunt's face was now swollen and bluish but he was rested and composed. What's more, again he had the advantage of surprise.

From a crouching position, he sprang with alacrity to his feet, hurling his bulk towards the unsuspecting Jonus.

The warrior's placement was perfect to his task, and his shoulder struck his quarry square in the ribs. Following through, he then body slammed Jonus into the tree and pinned him there. The ferocity of the assault was so fluid in motion that the Traveler passed out before he realized what had happened.

With one long, blown-out breath, as if aiming for the candles on a birthday cake, the air was pushed from his lungs.

But before his vision blackened, his thoughts were for the Great One, his little brother, now on his own at last.

In actuality, Jarvus was no longer on his own. The Great One had been taken captive while making his solitary way towards the Point, rounded up by troops of the Empire of Am-Rif. A foolish move on his part, but it was done.

Jarvus had made good use of his time since morning, hiking with gusto to put distance between himself and his overbearing older brother. Nevertheless, he had traveled only a few miles when he heard voices in the distance, and then the sounds of livery creaking and armor clanking. Next, after hiding in the foliage, he spotted a mounted knight arrayed in full battle dress.

Clomping along astride a massive war-horse, the warrior led at leisure a company of ordinary foot soldiers. These in turn were herding a large group of misplaced grunts through the forest. The prisoners, mostly men but with a few old women and children tossed in, were a collection of nomads, farmers, peasants and desert city dwellers, all looking stunned and dejected.

Jarvus had decided to trail along, flanking the sluggish, unhappy throng at a short distance. At the time, he reasoned they might be heading toward the station, as he was. If so, he thought they would cover his surreptitious, parallel movements.

After a while, the lethargic troop had come to a path, a crude dirt thoroughfare cutting into the now-thinning woodlands. This in time had led the prisoners to a small, rustic encampment hacked out of the surrounding countryside. The place was filthy and you could smell it's stench from a fair distance as you approached.

Here the captive grunts were deposited within a holding area, a corral of sorts, alongside a couple of battered tents and lean-tos. A few bonfires smoked up the place. Jarvus, hidden at a distance, had observed the compound but only for a while.

The Great One had resolved to press on.

Instead, however, upon turning he'd come face to face with a few of the periphery lookouts of the camp, all of them grinning at his now untenable position. They'd assumed him to be a straggler and, without ceremony, threw him in with the rest of the captive grunts, just another collateral loss for the enemies of the empire. Now Jarvus waited for his turn to be interrogated.

Every few minutes, a few captives were prodded into a tent next to the corral. After a while, they trickled out, one by one, into another primitive pen. He didn't like the way some of them looked, seeing that they had been roughed up during their interview.

As he stood waiting, he noticed a plump, short man ahead of him. The little grunt was dressed in what at one time had been a fine set of clothing. He was agitated, and speaking to those around him with an animated gesturing of his hands.

Jarvus thought he recognized the man, but he couldn't place him. He was from the desert city of Arret, no doubt. After a few minutes, the man was among the next group hustled into the tent.

Jarvus didn't know what would become of the prisoners. They might be held here or sent elsewhere. Worse, they might be disposed of altogether, here or somewhere down the line.

He didn't like any of those options.

Surveying the guards, he saw they were numerous and mostly idle, standing around with nothing much to do. Under the circumstances, the chances of escape seemed slim at best. The inactive soldiers would jump at some action.

He had to stall, therefore, and hope a chance for freedom occurred during that interval. It seemed the only way left to reach the station. What the Great One needed then was a cover story, something that would be interesting to his captors, making him somehow important enough to be shuffled up the chain of command but also one that would not reveal his true mission.

Only then would future flight be possible. His trouble was that he had no such story ready. Nevertheless, he was soon pushed into the tent with the next group of prisoners.

They were led before a greasy flap that chopped the tent in two. Several soldiers stood sentry there, each one looking more bored than the next. Jarvus saw that they were all well armed.

The stains on the flap somehow reminded him of the large tapestry that had hung in his water tower back in the desert city. It held the same hues and tones, and the smudges flung in the distance conveyed an equivalent state of vastness. So, in spite of his grim circumstances, Jarvus smiled a bit at the recollection, at the irony of the situation, but not for long.

Loud lamentations then shot out from beyond the tent flap, the sobbing and wailing of an old woman crying, no doubt unhappy with the result of her interrogation. Jarvus was empathetic and this was not a normal reaction for him. After a bit, she was dragged off, screaming outright now, the sound of it accompanied by the laughing of her tormentors as she was led away.

The next session soon began.

By the overheard exchanges, Jarvus knew it was the little, round man's turn to be questioned. Having lived so long among the desert grunts, the Great One knew and recognized their speech. He even understood the many outlying dialects, and he grasped with ease the gist of the poor man's examination.

The soldiers indeed were culling the captives, hoping to find someone of strategic importance to the empire, someone with enough stature to break their tiresome, repetitive routine. Such a find would insure for them a hefty reward, but so far they had been denied any extra compensation, for most of these prisoners were of little value to anyone. But, the fat man was different.

Seeing him earlier in such a dilapidated state had been a strange juxtaposition for Jarvus, for unlike the other prisoners, this grunt clearly had been someone of caliber. But the short man's station had been much reduced of late, his once fine garments now a shambles and he hadn't looked like himself. As a consequence, when he was seen outside, no placement had come.

Now out of sight behind the tent flap, Jarvus recognized the sound of his voice and at last identified him. As a loading dock manager in the city of Arret, the man had held considerable prestige among his peers, although he had little real power in the bigger scheme of things. The Great One didn't recall his name for at best he had been only middle management.

Nevertheless, the little man had attended numerous ceremonial functions within the water tower, the mystical inner sanctum of the fabled desert city. Holidays and celebrations of all kinds, each involving high pomp and pageantry, had been copious in Arret. Jarvus himself had seen to that.

Over the years he had instigated them all, the better to relieve the usual repetition of his long, drawn-out days. Such grand festivities were one of the few things the Great One had actually enjoyed during his long captivity. Thankful for some time off, the city's population had taken great pleasure in them, also.

The manager's position must have become perilous, thought Jarvus, once the water in the lake was depleted. He must have run off after realizing that Rebus had disappeared, taking his chances in the desert after the Great One vanished without a trace. After all, abandoned and alone as they were, the grunts of Arret would have been powerless to alter the plight they had faced and life in such harsh conditions without water was just not possible.

Soon the flap was forced open by a guard beyond, and Jarvus and a few others were ushered forward. The little man was there all right, balanced on a small stool placed before a crude, rough-hewn table. Behind this were two seated soldiers, who were, by the look of things, in charge of the proceedings.

Plenty of other soldiers stood guard nearby, fanned out around the edges of the tent. The fat man was leaning forward, his plump arms outstretched, as he tried to explain his dismal situation. The two men sitting behind the table were unimpressed, and having their own agenda, weren't cooperating with him.

"Tell me again," one of them said, "what was your service?" The interrogator then sat back, pulling at his long mustache, looking hard at the little man. After a beat, he added, "Something worthy, I would think, to deserve such fine clothing."

"Yes," agreed the other soldier, "not just anybody dresses this well. You were an important man, that's easy to see. Tell us now, did you serve the false god, Rebus?"

The fat man was exasperated, with nowhere to turn. He was also afraid. He was more afraid than he'd ever been in his life.

He knew that he was of no real consequence, that his job had not been an important one, per se. He had served the Great One, as all did but he had been only a functionary at best. At any rate, now in desperation, he wished to speak of other things.

"I was a businessman, that's all," he sputtered. "I shipped water to the outlying farms but I didn't know that our chief god was false. You must believe me, please, I was deceived, as all of us were."

He looked down to the ground then, as if embarrassed.

"It's true," he said. "All of us were lied to, but you must realize that at the time our lives were good. We lived well under Rebus."

The man's face crimped up in anguish, remembering, and then in a whisper, he added, "We were happy in our ignorance." Looking up, he blurted out, "Just tell me of your gods, and I will worship them instead." This made the soldiers laugh.

"Serve our gods?" said the mustachioed inquisitor. "What would that accomplish? Would you then tell us the truth?"

The other questioner was impatient for an answer. The day, already long, was growing old, and others were awaiting their turn at torment. He smashed his fist on the desk.

"Who are you?" he barked.

The little man was frantic. He scanned the tent, looking first to the guards, and after that to the captives, as if somehow to find some succor there. Then his eyes fell upon Jarvus who was standing to the side with the rest of the prisoners.

The Great One was picking at his lip, his attention elsewhere. Escape was all that he was thinking about. His mind was racing, mulling over options that were hard in coming.

Then a change came over the fat man's face, by holding first an appearance of shock, and next, one of recognition.

"Ask him," he screamed, pointing to Jarvus. "He would know me, I'm sure of it. Just ask him."

Everyone then looked at Jarvus, all of them waiting for some response to this outburst. The Traveler's brother was mortified. The little grunt couldn't possibly know him, he was sure.

True, the man had been in the water tower back in the desert city, but at such times the Great One had always taken pains to remain in the shadows, seated upon his raised, marble throne. Even so, ever since his capture, Jarvus had been trying his best to blend in, trying to be inconspicuous, and this wasn't helping any. It was difficult to be innocuous with everyone staring at you.

Jarvus tried to shake off the remark as ludicrous by hunching his shoulders and looking incredulous, but the man would have none of it. He was sure. Flailing his arms, he jumped to his feet.

"Tell them, tell them, you," he screamed.

In his excitement he tried to make his way over to Jarvus, but a nearby guard grabbed him and pushed him back into his seat. Then the soldier cuffed him on the back of the head for his trouble. The room fell silent, the occupants amazed by this turn of events.

The questioner with the mustache looked at Jarvus.

"Well," he asked, "do you know him?"

All present awaited his answer, now interested in what it would be. All awaited but the little man, who jumped up once more. This time, to avoid aggravating the guard, he didn't move around much.

"Tell them," he now begged of Jarvus. He added, "You're a north side water bearer, aren't you? You know me, don't you?"

At first, Jarvus didn't understand this cryptic bit of information but then he realized that the man had only recognized his tunic. It was that of a water-bearing slave, and one from the north docks, as well. He and his brother had stolen the uniforms and all the water they could carry before absconding through the desert.

Dressing as water bearers had ensured the two easy movement throughout the city. At the time it had been a simple thing, out in the open, right in front of the unknowing citizenry. In broad daylight, they had toted their precious, purloined liquid past virtually everyone, but in the interim, Jarvus had forgotten that he still wore the now-battered and ragged tunic.

"Well?" the same interrogator asked again.

Jarvus didn't like this situation, for it was fraught with peril. He didn't want to be involved. To confirm the man's identity would somehow link the two of them, he thought, and he preferred at this point to remain anonymous in the minds of the guards.

Despite his earlier assessment, the chances of escape now seemed better if he were a nobody. As just one of the crowd, his sudden absence might not be so quickly noticed. On the other hand, to deny that he knew the grunt was just as bad for the little man would no doubt make a further scene if he did so.

Jarvus didn't know what to do. He began to pick at his lip, performing this personal, time-worn function without thinking as he thought over his predicament. He didn't pick for long, though.

A nearby guard, tired of waiting for an answer, grabbed him by the neck of his tunic. To get his attention, the guard shook him up some before letting him go. This movement parted Jarvus' uniform, exposing his red identifying tag.

"What's this?" the soldier said. "Jewelry? Is it real?"

"Wait," said the little man, aghast. "That's the ruby stone, I'd know it anywhere." He stepped back as he said this, not caring that he might be beaten again as a consequence, as if the sight of the amulet itself would bring more harm to him than the guard.

He looked at the seated soldiers and explained.

"Rebus, our false god," he began to explain, "always wore the ruby. The existence of the stone is legendary to the citizens of Arret, and it's been described often. Over the years, many of his concubines spoke of it and I myself have even seen it flash through the shadows, as the Great One sat his throne."

The little grunt, smiling now, looked back to Jarvus, the picture now emerging more clearly in his mind.

"Yes, and you're the right size, too," he added, starting to add it all up. "No wonder I didn't recognize you. You're no water slave." He then clapped his hands together, completing the scenario.

263

"Don't you see?" he asked the solders. "The false god Rebus disappeared after he was proven powerless. But before he vanished, I often observed him inside the sanctum."

The grunt then nodded his head, pointing at Jarvus, as a witness at a trial would have done, to distinguish the guilty perpetrator.

"He was just your build," the man said. "I'm sure, I saw him many times over the years. He even picked at his lip as you do."

Everyone again looked to Jarvus. Too late did this realization come. He was still picking his lip.

"Two of my north dock water bearers were attacked," the prisoner continued, while bending low and pointing, still accusing, "and their uniforms were stolen. And you wear the stone." Standing erect, the little man then stated with pride in a loud voice, "He is the false one, the city's deposed god, Rebus."

The man was beaming now, certain that his efforts would be rewarded. This could only help his perilous situation, he hoped. Sadly, in his present state, he had nothing else to offer.

"It is he who led us astray," he therefore said, "the 'Great One' we loved so much, the very one who abandoned us. He must be. No other would dare wear the stone."

"Is he now?" said the soldier with the mustache.

He stood and crossed in front of the table, and once there, with a gentle motion he placed his arm on the little man's shoulder.

"You're quite certain, are you?" he asked him.

"Oh, yes," the other answered, eager to please. He could almost taste his coming leniency. Yet his effort was not rewarded.

The soldier looked to one of the guards, who then grabbed the little grunt, pulling him from the tent. Before he could complete this task, however, his fat charge somehow managed to break free. He ran to the soldier's side and there he went down on his knees.

"Tell me of your gods!" he screamed. "Please, tell me and I will worship them instead. Just tell me what I must do."

"What you must do?" asked the soldier, laughing, his hands on his hips. "Why, you must die, as all the rest of you heretics will." This caused the other soldiers to laugh as well.

The little man was then at last led away, crushed and sobbing.

After a glance from the interrogating soldier, the guard that had manhandled Jarvus pushed him onto the now-empty stool that rested before the table and then stood behind him.

The now-satisfied soldier then walked back to his seat, retaking his original position next to his comrade.

"So," he said at last, "you're the false god?"

Jarvus laughed at the inquiry, but no one else did.

"Tell us of the stone," commanded the other questioner, leaning in for a better look. "Is it a real ruby? You never said before."

Jarvus took a deep breath. Here we go, he thought. Time had run out and he had to face his perilous situation.

"No," he said, "and I'm no god, either, not even a false one."

"Who gave you the stone, then?" asked the first inquisitor.

Jarvus then had an idea. It wasn't fully formed but because of the circumstances he went with it. He'd just have to improvise.

"My master gave it to me," he said, "the one the old fool called his god. That much is true, but he wasn't a god at all. Still, he was a great magician, a powerful sorcerer, and I was his apprentice."

That got everyone's attention. No one had expected such a strange tale. Some looked nervous and uncertain.

Jarvus continued in an offhand way, as if remembering.

"He was forceful," he added. "Very much so, in fact. His magic was such that the gods came to fear him."

Jarvus paused and looked about the tent in a way construed to include them all. He needn't have bothered for they were hanging on his every word. This was a good development, as it demonstrated that his story was at least gripping.

"The sorcerer," he said, "in time became so strong that he built a great palace, a fortress in truth, to keep the very gods at bay."

Here the two, seated soldiers glanced at each other. Jarvus missed the import of this silent exchange. The Great One didn't know that recently the mysterious Fortress of Forecastle had come to be most significant to the once-struggling empire.

He would learn soon enough, though.

"At last," he continued, "the gods came together, and banished him to the desert city of Arret. His great palace was locked away forever. Of course, as his apprentice, I was banished, too."

"But the false god fled," said the soldier with the mustache.

"Yes," agreed Jarvus. "That is why two tunics were stolen. We both escaped the desert city in defiance of the gods."

At this shocking news, the crowd of prisoners stepped back in horror. The guards became agitated, mumbling to each other. Regardless, they each stood their ground while glancing to their betters for guidance in the face of such discovery.

"And what of the sorcerer?" asked the same soldier.

"He was destroyed, of course," answered Jarvus, as if it were only a foregone conclusion. "He was killed for defying the gods. He was annihilated in the desert wastelands for his sins."

This reply gave his questioners pause. If the gods did indeed pool their powers, the resulting force would be a mighty one, no doubting that. Even the grandest of wizards, with all of their secret knowledge, would succumb to such potency.

The one without the mustache then asked, "And the ruby?"

Jarvus reached up and rolled the amulet between his fingers.

"It's not a ruby," he said. "It's not even a stone, although as a subterfuge it looks like one. My cunning master created it in such a fashion to conceal its true purpose."

He leaned in, giving them a better look. Both were drawn to scrutinize it further. They couldn't help it.

After a bit Jarvus leaned back and continued.

"My master was angry with himself," he said, "for the gods had tricked him into leaving his grand palace. Indeed, had he stayed there they would never have captured him. Its powers were so strong the gods could not destroy it, only hide it away, and hope that without my master it would never bother them again."

His interrogators said nothing to this. What was there to say? Such detailed information could not be lightly dismissed.

"As well," Jarvus added, "they hoped that without its great powers, my master would remain contained within the desert city, but here they were wrong. The sorcerer was too strong to be held against his will forever. He was displeased with his banishment and plotted revenge upon the gods."

One of the prisoners, an old woman in the rear of the group, had heard enough. She began to wail. Others were openly distraught.

"Out!" screamed the soldier with the mustache, "everybody out!" He jumped up for emphasis, and the soldiers on duty burst into action. It took but a few moments before the tent was cleared.

However, most of the guards stayed behind. The questioning soldier sat and beckoned Jarvus to proceed. He did so.

"One day," he began, "after countless years of exile spent in Arret, the sorcerer told me that at last he had succeeded in his devious plans. Despite his long banishment in the desert city, his power had grown only stronger. He now knew a way, my clever master said, a magic way to locate his hidden lair."

"You mean the fortress?" asked the puzzled guard, still standing behind the prisoner. He had been trying to follow the tale but was having trouble keeping up. The soldiers at the table glared at the man, and now embarrassed, he shut his mouth.

"Yes," Jarvus agreed, "the fortress, his home. With his new magic, he said that he could now cause it to call out to him, and make the fortress itself lead him there as if following a songbird through the forest. He was very excited and would hear of nothing else but his plans, even though I tried to dissuade him."

Jarvus paused, as if remembering the episode. This gave his tale the air of reality. He was a good liar and always had been.

"Soon we left the city," he said, "but before we did he gave me this." He stopped once more, and indicated his amulet. It flashed between his fingers as he twirled it about.

"What is it then?" asked the one without the mustache.

"It's the key," Jarvus said, "the key to the home of my master."

This was an unexpected development, and the inquisitors were more than interested now. It was well known that the old Crone had trouble controlling the many mysteries contained within the mighty fortress. Perhaps this key was the answer.

Jarvus was unaware of any this, of course. He was just spinning a tale, building as he went along. He was good at it, too.

"My master was very cautious," he continued, "and feared that if he carried the key himself the gods would find him, and so he gave it to me for safekeeping. It will unlock all the secrets of his home, the palace, that is, the fortress, but the magic involved is very strong. It cannot be taken from me, for whoever tries to remove it will be struck down, I assure you."

The soldiers grinned at this, now unbelieving.

"We could get a grunt to chop off his head," said the one on Jarvus' left. "I'd wager the old man outside would do it," answered the other, laughing. Both looked at Jarvus to gauge his reaction.

"The key will be destroyed if it's taken by force," he said, looking quite solemn. He shook his head for emphasis. "My master was a sly one, I tell you, and only I can use it."

"What happened to your master?" asked the one on the right.

"He was struck down by a lightning bolt," said Jarvus, "while crossing the desert. The gods found him there in spite of his many precautions. Now the key is all that matters."

"A lightning bolt in the desert?" asked the mouth below the mustache. It seemed absurd. Jarvus lifted his hands.

"Who are we," he said, "to question the gods?"

Both interrogators leaned back then, to consider. The story sounded feasible enough but was it true? They needed proof.

After a moment, the one on the left, who was the one with the mustache, asked of him, "What about the woman, Sorbus?"

Jarvus knew nothing of any Sorbus. Still, his poker-face was unchanging, his eyes unmoving. He stalled for time, his standard procedure in such cases, in hopes that he could wiggle through.

"What about her?" he asked.

"Who is she," demanded the soldier, "I mean, who is she really?"

Jarvus, naturally, didn't know. Nevertheless, he had to say something, as there was no alternative. It was fortunate that bald faced lying was second nature to him.

He paused a moment, as if remembering.

"Well," he related at last, "my master also had a young servant girl but that was a long time ago."

After this response, the shift in the soldier's aspect was palpable. His eyes darted to the side and he almost turned to his partner before catching himself. However, the other man already had raised his eyebrows in stark surprise at the revelation.

Jarvus understood that something important had registered, but he didn't know what or why. Without letting on, he decided to embellish some, fishing along the same line. This was also his standard ploy in such circumstances.

"By now," he added, "I guess she'd be pretty old, though."

It was enough, he saw. The tension in the tent, before so tight, broke and in a big way. Again, the two men faced each other.

269

"No wonder she fights for control of the fortress," said the clean-shaven one, "she doesn't have the key. The old Crone is strong but not strong enough. The key might prove the solution."

"It's true," answered the other. "The squire must be told of this at once. Only a knight can approach the king."

The guards murmured their agreement with this observation.

The inquisitor with the mustache stood once more.

"Yes, only a knight will do for such news," he said again, adding, "since we have no bastard baker handy."

Everyone present laughed at this line, including Jarvus, even though he didn't begin to understand what it meant.

At that time, the bastard baker was himself in the field, some distance away to the north, awaiting an audience with King Invar. However, the fact that the beast in the dungeon had died had altered somewhat the Crone's devious scheme. Now it seemed that grand subterfuge was no longer required.

At present, Pliant need only inform the monarch of the demise of the great beast for Sorbus was sure that such news would itself compel him to return at once to the fortress. Then, their original design would play out as planned. The old sovereign would be held fast, incognito, within the fortress, for, according to the Crone, he was now a stumbling block to her ongoing Mandate.

This plan was a huge step to take, dangerous for him and his confederates alike, but Pliant had a mighty trust in the old woman. As well, he loved her daughter, Lucid. He did believe in his heart that their current labor was now paramount but just the same he was uneasy about what was to happen.

Unlike any other peasant of whom he knew, Pliant had worked at many differing tasks during his span. He had labored hard at several vocations, seeing multiple changes in his life along the way. This had given the common man an uncommon insight.

He had been a miller's apprentice as a boy and a miller as a young man. Next a bureaucrat had been his position, as the manager of all the royal bakeries within the ravaged city of Am-Rif. After that, he had been a functionary for the king himself, first as a trusted go between in search of the fortress, and later as a competent ordinance instructor for the imperial troops.

Through dedicated exertion, Pliant had reached a point where he now enjoyed a sweeping freedom to complete his tasks. The peasant should have been content with his lot, so superior to others within his station, but he was not, far from it. For never before had this diligent man been a traitor to his empire.

But the Crone had convinced him of the prominence of her Mandate. She believed with her whole heart in the mysterious new god, Primus, and her faith had carried great weight with the simple man. The bent, old woman had stated her belief without flourish, without any grand tales of His higher power, but her acknowledgment of His omnipotence had been total.

For her, there was no other way but His way, and to Pliant this grounded conviction had held great sway.

Being a member of the lower classes, he had never been concerned with the theological realm. He had offered his personal sacrifices to the gods, of course, but his day-to-day existence had never dwelt upon the bigger picture. As most peasants did, he had left the particulars to his betters, the nobility and the imperial bureaucrats that controlled the feast days and festivals.

The sacrifices had been his, but without any real thought on his part. The man had only been going through the motions. Now that he did consider it, however, he considered it well.

Pliant knew that belief in gods at all, in powers beyond those of normal mortals, was a great leap in itself. Nonetheless, if you believe in anything that is bigger than your own comprehension, then by definition you have to believe in something that you can never hope to understand. It wasn't possible.

This dichotomy of reason had been dictated to the masses during ancient times, by those then in control, and all had long ago accepted it. In fact, it had been an easy thing to do. The sweeping belief in gods had firmly grounded everyone, explaining away the mystic unknown, the unattainable knowledge of everything that was, whether it was physical or not.

But now, after reflection upon the Crone and her Mandate, Pliant saw the folly of multiple gods. True, Sorbus had spoken only of Primus as the 'highest god,' but he knew her better than that. Without being boastful, she was a wise woman, and she abetted nothing that wasted her time or energy.

He could see that now with undiluted clarity. She wouldn't cling with such tenacity to a god that was not omnipotent, and why should she? Why should anyone, he now thought in retrospect?

The old Crone hadn't spoken in such terms, but Pliant knew just the same. He had divined rather than seen that her Primus was all powerful, not just more powerful. While traveling the countryside, that knowledge had steeled him for his approaching task, but now that his journey had ended, he was again uneasy.

He currently stood within the king's campaign tent, awaiting his sovereign. The king himself was somewhere about the imperial camp, Pliant had been told, inspecting the preparations of his various commanders. The baker had been offered food and drink but he had refused them, for he was too upset.

Soon enough he heard a commotion outside, a noisy retinue approaching. He supposed the king was nigh. It was so.

The tent flap was opened and King Invar entered, accompanied by a few retainers. After seeing Pliant, however, these were dismissed by the king, leaving him and the baker quite alone. The simple man had gone down to his knee in the presence of his temporal lord, but soon he was instructed to rise.

"Ah, Pliant," the king said in good humor. "What news from the Crone? More exploding stones to use against our enemies?"

"Alas no, my King," answered the peasant, realizing that he was shaking in his boots. It was a disconcerting action as it was something that he had never done before. Not during a royal audience, or anywhere else that he could recall.

"Sorbus bids me here for another reason," he explained.

The king's demeanor changed at this. In an instant, he was suspicious. His face reverted back into its old, familiar hardness.

"Well?" he commanded, not wasting his words.

Pliant took a deep breath, hoping this would cover his nervousness. It did not. He began to speak but he had to stop in order to clear his now-tightened throat.

The king, born impatient and humored ever since, brooked no such delay in any underling. Because he was also very tall, only a few strides were needed to close the distance between the two men. Once the transit was accomplished he loomed large over the much shorter peasant still shaking before him.

"Out with it, man!" he barked.

The poor baker was flustered. He began to tremble in earnest. The old Crone had told him to act as if nothing was amiss yet under the present circumstance that was an impossible task.

"The beast in the dungeon is dead," he blurted out.

King Invar was not prepared for such news. So intent was his concentration that even his breathing momentarily stopped. His Majesty was stunned, his eyes opened overly wide.

Because he stood so near, Pliant noticed for the first time that each of them were slightly different in color. They were very near in hue, although not an exact match. You had to look hard to see the discrepancy hiding between them.

Regardless, the king seemed frozen in place, stiff, debating in his mind the import of the old Crone's message.

After a moment, he relaxed a bit and without speaking further, he crossed to his well-used campaign desk. This was a portable but highly impressive affair, ornately carved and stained to convey a grandiose hunting motif. He then sat, his regal head held in his hand, contemplating this momentous development.

Pliant didn't know what to do. He felt out of place but he had not been dismissed. He stood his ground and waited.

"Well, well," stated the king at last, "this changes everything."

His royal impatience then returned. He began to rifle the many sheaves of parchment stacked on his desk, sending a few of them flying off in the process, grunting to himself as he did so. He paused enough to call out, "Guard," before resuming his rustling.

Many regular soldiers were posted about the perimeter of the royal pavilion but the king's own guard, charged with his protection, stood duty at the entrance to his campaign tent.

In response to the summons, one of the pickets stationed there entered, and standing just inside the opening, he awaited in silence the bidding of his sovereign. This particular man had done as much many times of late, for in the field, the king often employed his sentries in such a fashion, to dispatch messages throughout the camp. On this occasion, the man would receive different orders.

The king indicated Pliant with a nod of his imperial head.

"Arrest him," was all His Majesty said.

Back at the fortress, the Crone was also experiencing impatience. Unlike the king, it was something that she had not felt in ages and the long-unused emotion surprised her. Somehow the old woman had forgotten the real passion involved, the sensations of agitation and helplessness the feeling generated.

To be fair, the interim since the explosion of the Elastic Limit had been great, and from that point on the old Crone had not aged.

So, Sorbus always had plenty of time at her disposal and impatience on her part had not been necessary. But beyond that, just remembering the dormant feeling was a shock, for it was a shocking thing that she had ever forgotten it in the first place.

It was a strange sensation to experience because it was so unexpected. It was like one day, out of the blue perceiving that you had forgotten your own name or the fact that you had a sister or brother. How could you not recall that?

The beast dying in the dungeon had undeniably changed everything. Yes, that was it, the situation in a nutshell, she now saw with clarity. Before then, before the reactor shutdown, that is, if some task had not been completed as scheduled, it could always be done later and with no negative consequences to speak of.

The best example of this was her personal Mandate. The Crone knew that her part of the now ongoing mission, her new order of the day, could take vast amounts of time to accomplish but that cold fact had never mattered to her in the least. No, long ago she had been assured of all the time that she would possibly need, and all that she had ever required she had indeed received.

Things were different now. Of course, time had a new meaning but there was more to it than that. There was also a much broader implication, one quite beyond the moment itself, and this revelation, too, was unsettling for her.

Her life since that distant time explosion, Sorbus realized in retrospect, had given her an attitude of indifference when it came to her daily tasks, to her daily existence, really. Her true life had been wrenched away by the incident. And, that authentic existence was unattainable to her, even now.

She wondered how long had it been. How many years between the explosion of time and the main reactor shutting down? She didn't know, not off the top of her head, anyway, but at the very least, it had been centuries since the original incident.

In hindsight, her situation hardly seemed strange but it felt so, nevertheless. As predicted, the time explosion had released great amounts of pent-up energy and that energy had hurled her past the point she knew as the Elastic Limit. But once this fantastic feat

275

had been accomplished, an unforeseen but equally tangible consequence of the procedure had occurred as well.

She had been rendered powerless to proceed with her own part of the new Mandate. True, she had helped draft the strategy employed, but she had not realized at the time how, once it was in play, her life would be changed, thrown into a holding pattern beyond her control. Even if she had found the hidden station on her own, the others, her cohorts now in the field, first had to deal with the hidden water system cooling the raging reactor.

That was the idea, and at long last the plan seemed to be working. Yet, before then she had no real role. Regardless, from then she had been left to her own devices, living in a span of years the length of many a normal woman's life, forced to bide her time until the station was found and the reactor shut down.

To her credit, she had lived that extended life to the fullest, not wishing to squander a second of the rich experience this time around. Wasting so much of her original life had taught her that very valuable lesson. She had learned it well.

Given this premise, she had lived her new life with boldness and passion enough under the bizarre circumstances. For the most part she had enjoyed herself. However, somewhere along her journey, without her realizing it at the time, something else had happened, something that had become all too pervasive.

As the years passed unabated, the old woman had somehow forgotten her true purpose. She had grown to overlook the fact that her new life, her life as the Crone, would always be only secondary to the genuine life that she had to inevitably lead. A gradual, imperceptible drift had occurred and she had become lost in the very enormity of her current existence.

While treading the choppy waters of the time stream, floating there as time itself flowed about her, she had migrated unaware into a daze. Until her confederates in the official mission became involved, she had held no immediate aim in her life, and as so much time had passed by, it was not such a strange thing for her to have forgotten her fate. Still, it felt as much.

She knew better, of course. Her Mandate was undeniable and her future agenda unstoppable. But just the same, she had given little thought to her great work yet to come.

Through the years, she had chafed for something momentous to happen, some signal to action that would end her rut of routine, but long ago the effort had grown as old and stale as she.

Her duty had reduced her life to a giant waiting game, and although she did not age, the passing time had worn her down just the same. Well, her waiting was over now, and boom, with no warning. It was like awakening from a deep sleep after having had an engaging dream, yet knowing at once that you have a full schedule ahead of you, prepared and all ready to go.

With the sabotaged main reactor staring her in the face, the Crone at last had a real problem to deal with and it was galling that the solution she needed was eluding her, despite her many labors to the contrary. Hence, her impatience and her epiphany of feelings felt long ago. In retrospect, it all made sense.

She did hit the ground running, so to speak. Just after the station's backup generators had been restarted, she had begun her investigation of the main reactor's vast computer program. After such a long time with nothing to do, the Crone had relished the new labor but now she feared she was unequal to the task.

The old woman, not a programmer, per se, was and always had been a competent technician, and in that respect her stubborn efforts had not been a total waste of time. Through dedicated exertion, she had gleaned a good deal of information about the errant program and that was something. Under any circumstance, it was always a positive thing to learn something new.

But the answer itself, the larger, overall solution that she sought had not been learned. How to correct the sabotage to the reactor's computer was still hidden, and hidden very well, it seemed. And the deeper she had probed into the machine's program, in order to unravel the mystery, the more complicated that program revealed itself to be, confounding her at every stage.

It felt like a personal thing between them. On one side stood the cold and unfeeling, calculating piece of hardware and on the other side she stood, mentally alive and still kicking, despite her great age and abundant deformities. But by any reckoning, the indifferent device was winning the battle, still protecting its inner secrets, and it soured the Crone's disposition to have to acknowledge that fact.

Still, she persisted. She had to. It was her Mandate.

She did know more now than she did before, even though this added input wasn't helping her much. The reactor's original computer program had been altered, no doubting that now. And the design of the alteration was pure genius.

The whole thing was a work of art, beautiful in its own way, and she knew of few people at the station capable of such finesse. But it was also a maddening thing, bewildering in its levels of complexity. The reactor's sabotaged program was more intricate than anything that she had ever encountered before.

As such, it was also unyielding to any but her crudest assessments of its parameters. The layers it possessed, as those of an onion, were deep. Peeling them away was no easy thing.

The program had several, differing codes, but somehow they understood each other. All passed throughout the system, each connected at some point, and this arrangement made them difficult to track. Also, every now and then, each spun back into itself and sometimes this occurred more than once.

The ramifications of all this were boundless. She couldn't begin to grasp the overall picture. It seemed the more she learned, the greater her understanding of what she did not know.

In and out this information, these coded bits of programming, were woven to and fro like a bird soaring, or back and forth like a fish darting, and identifying any one of them was reduced to little more than a guessing game. Yet, she knew of no better way to solve the puzzle than by picking away at the stubborn thing. Doing so was the most taxing assignment that she had ever undertaken.

The old woman leaned back in her chair, moving away from her computer screen. She was sitting at the cluttered workstation in her former office off the main laboratory, and she knew becoming exasperated now would accomplish nothing. Being so distracted was out of character for her in any case.

She began to finger the silver pin on her chest, without thinking, as was her habit. No need, she mused, to get carried away. Under normal circumstances she wouldn't have, for it had always been more natural that she take things in stride.

In the past, she had attacked any substantial problem before her bit by bit, by whittling away until the solution eventually appeared. Her history had always been one of a conscientious and hard worker, and being transformed into the Crone had not changed that part of her character. But she was perturbed.

There was something more that bothered her now. It was something beyond her Mandate, something that she had avoided thinking about since being blasted Beyond the Elastic Limit so long ago. And she felt guilty about being bothered by it, given that it wasn't, after all, a bad thing in itself.

She was thinking of Jonus, the errant time jumper, and the love of her life. The two had been separated once their mission had begun, and since then she had put him out of her mind with relative ease. Doing so had not been a sign of less interest on her part, nor a hardening of her feelings toward him, but a real recognition that, as things stood, he was unattainable to her.

Tucked away as he was somewhere within the time stream, he had been only a distant memory. The fact that one day she would see him again had steeled her against wondering every day what had become of him. Now things had changed.

This ability to compartmentalize different parts of her life had always worked to her favor before, enabling her to concentrate using her entire being. It had always been easy, a natural proclivity. So it was now, or at least had been until lately.

The fact that the mission was currently at a new stage, groping towards completion, had triggered all kinds of thoughts of Jonus, but they weren't helping her any and she knew it. Much remained to be done at the station and it might be a long time before she laid eyes on him again. Daydreaming about him was premature, to say the least, a giant waste of her now-precious time, and, as such, an annoyance that she didn't want nor need.

Still, the thoughts were there. They were real. She couldn't deny them or, it seemed, escape them.

Sorbus shook her head to clear it. She needed to think, but not those thoughts, for they were unproductive. Once again the old woman leaned in to her computer screen, weary but defiant.

"Back to work," she said aloud to nobody, next adding with a sigh, "Where is Spencer Hall when I need him?"

Spencer Hall also was thinking, again racking his brain for all that he was worth, but the effort was no longer painful or frightening to him. His present attitude and demeanor were far from the frayed and jagged disposition displayed earlier. He was quite altered now, a different man altogether from the tortured one before, when he'd found himself so lost and confused.

Praying to his God had redeemed and also calmed him.

There had been no revelation from above or anything like that. No bolt out of the blue had come his way or voices whispered in his ear, conveying with crisp inflections of authority, an answer to all of his problems. There had been no chorus reverberating from the heavens either, thundering oracle-like advice.

Yet, praying to Primus had steeled him nonetheless. He was still lost and on his own but Spencer was convinced that things would somehow work out. After all, the Mandate was paramount and Primus would show a way, he was sure of it.

Spencer had doubled back from the mountain laurel grove. He stood hidden in the brush at the edge of the hillside opening that contained the injured Morris. The giant was down, propped up against a large tree trunk, surrounded by several grunts who were poking at him with sticks and small limbs.

The grunts, enjoying themselves, were judging his reaction to their efforts at torment, laughing as the big man responded with a jerk or a grimace. At least he was still alive, thought Spencer, but what would happen now? He could follow at a distance if they hauled him away but that seemed unlikely, given the giant was far too large to manhandle over such hilly terrain.

Spencer was concerned but, in view of his revelation, not panic stricken. Quite the opposite was true. Finding strength in his faith, he knew that Primus would provide him an answer.

Spencer became aware that something had changed to his left. He was surprised to see a caveman standing a few yards away, eyeing him with a strong intent. He'd heard nothing of his approach even though the forest floor was littered with debris.

The grunt was young, not much beyond a boy, but he was lean and strong, an adolescent well on his way to adulthood.

The two stood still, caught in the moment, but then the caveman raised his finger to his lips indicating silence. Spencer reacted as if in a daze, bobbing his head to show that he understood the unspoken message. The grunt smiled and pointed behind Spencer.

The lone researcher glanced over his shoulder and saw another grunt standing there. This one was different, older, but there was something else about him that made Spencer stare. He looked familiar, although that seemed absurd given the circumstances.

After a beat, the new grunt raised his hand to his throat and tapped a few times. Spencer didn't understand this gesture and it showed. The grunt tapped again, nodding encouragement.

Spencer raised his hand, mimicking the action, and in doing so he touched his id tag hanging about his neck, hidden beneath his

281

shirt. The grunt then smiled, a satisfied look on his face. Now Spencer smiled as well, in recognition.

The primitive warrior was older than the last time they'd met, but the new grunt was Jargon, the caveman from the pit.

Jargon next quickly indicated with a movement of his hands that Spencer should stay put. He then turned and darted silently away through the brush. Spencer slowly turned his head and saw that the other caveman had vanished also.

Well, well, he thought, something was happening now.

"Hold on, Morris," he said under his breath, "just hold on."

In the clearing, Morris was holding on, but only by the skin of his teeth. His abundant strength was gone, sapped by exhaustion and pain. The only thing fueling him now was his anger.

He knew that he was finished, but by Primus, he wanted to go out fighting, not by being picked to death by a bunch of ignorant grunts. But they had no sense of honor, and any sense of fair play was wishful thinking under the circumstances. He just wanted them to rush him en masse and get it over with.

Then a scream shot out of the forest, somewhat down the hill to the right of Morris' position. The tormenting grunts all turned and looked. Morris just cut his eyes.

A figure leaped from the brush brandishing a crude stone dagger. He screamed once more, then turned and retreated whence he came. Spencer, who was observing the action from above, recognized the primitive warrior as the younger caveman.

After this strange happening, the three soldier grunts looked to each other, gauging reactions. The one with the war axe, the same one with the chain-mailed helmet, pointed after the retreating caveman. The other two laughed, knowing there would be quick action now regarding the beaten giant.

More game was afoot, more fun in the offing.

The giant knew this too, and he tightened his grip on the biggest limb that before he had wrenched from his tormentors. Morris was eager, impatient even now. Bring it on, he thought.

The warrior raised his well-used axe.

Another cry pierced the air. This time it came from the opposite side of the forest, to the left of the last ones. The same caveman jumped out and again he screamed his same scream.

Everyone was stunned, including Spencer still watching from the scrub above. No way the caveman had moved so far, so fast through the wood. Yet there he was for all to see.

Not for long. Soon he came running towards the soldiers. He was screaming in earnest this time, still brandishing his knife.

The solders never had a chance.

From his vantage, Spencer saw the swift action unfold. The timing of the attack was perfection. While attention was drawn towards the warrior on the left, a figure broke from the forest scrub above and another from the original position on the right.

Quickly and in silence, the second one dashed down the hill, along the fallen tree, and over the huge root ball where beneath the stricken giant hunkered. Soaring head first above Morris, Jargon pounded into the soldier with the axe, catching him unawares. At the same time, the third figure, soundless as Jargon had been, attacked from the rear the soldier without a helmet.

All of this shocked and dazed the last grunt standing. Seconds later, the caveman on the left engaged and took him down. The attack was over almost as instantly as it began.

The slaughtered men had reacted with haste, but to no avail. All of them had been crouched and ready, weapons drawn, focused on the oncoming attack. But stung from the side and the rear, they were disoriented only seconds before being struck from the front.

One, two, three, and each was dead in quick order, and all with military precision, Morris observed.

The attacking cavemen stood, a little dazed themselves, but still full of the thrill of the hunt. They were smiling as they turned and looked at Morris. He recognized them with ease.

"Well, Jargon," he said in the caveman's language, "looks like you've gotten your dreaded beast after all."

"There's more," Jargon retorted, wiping his knife on his animal skin vest. He wasn't overly content. It had been too easy.

The giant now glanced to the other, younger cavemen. He loved them both. They were mirror images of each other.

"Boys," he chuckled, despite his present condition. "You've grown so." And then he added, "Where's that father of yours?"

"Here," cried a voice from the forest, and all turned to see who had spoken. Steadfast emerged from the bush and he wasn't alone. An unconscious man was slung over his shoulder.

By this time, Spencer had succeeded in scrambling down the steep hill into the clearing. He crossed to Morris and crouched beside him. His concern was genuine and heartfelt.

"You OK?" he asked the giant.

"I've been better," Morris said. "It's good to see you made it, though. I was wondering what had happened to you."

Spencer looked to the two brothers.

"They're twins," he said, astounded.

"And good boys," agreed the giant. "I've known them all their lives. Judging by their handiwork, I'd say they're both men now."

"And I'm their father," said Steadfast, who by this time had joined them, still holding his unmoving burden over his shoulder. It was just another day in the forest for him. He said, looking at the dead, "Good hunting, it seems."

Morris' laugh turned into a groan, and squeezing his broken leg, he answered Steadfast, again in the warrior's tongue.

"An interesting day all around, I'd say," he agreed.

284

Steadfast was now the one grinning. His handsome face was bruised, with dried blood evident, but it didn't seem to bother him. All in all, it had been an eventful morning.

"The day's not over yet, my large, old friend," he said.

Grunting some, he stooped and put down his load, saying, "This one has your neckwear, Moas. Lucky I saw it. Friend of yours?"

Morris looked at the unconscious time jumper and raised his eyebrows in astonishment. This was an unexpected turn of events. He then looked to Spencer and translated the exchange.

Spencer didn't know Jonus. The man looked familiar to him in a vague sort of way, but there was no recognition. Perhaps he'd seen him in passing before, at the station maybe.

"One of your team?" Spencer asked him, after checking the id tag around the man's neck.

Morris nodded, his eyebrows still raised.

"Yes," he said, "I haven't seen him in a long time. He's your assistant's older brother. He's the one that went after J."

"J?" asked Spencer, but then he added, "Oh yes, Jarvus."

Then he looked to the giant and asked, "So where is he?"

By then, Jarvus was being shoved into a rickety wagon for transport. He didn't know where. He had told his story twice more, once to the captain of the guard and the next morning to the knight who was in command of the detachment.

The knight sat unmoving during the interview and showed little interest after. Without comment, he nodded to the soldier in charge. Jarvus was led out and his wrist bindings were removed.

Next, however, his legs were chained together, a loud and pinching process that would assure his compliance.

Then came the wagon, a large wooden crate with wheels. He could see the countryside through gaps in the wall. At least there was a layer of straw to cushion him on his ride.

Jarvus wasn't alone in the wagon. A man was there, seated with his back to a corner. A hefty peasant, he looked absurd.

He was wearing an uncomfortable yoke of wood about his neck, binding his wrists on either side of his head. With such a stance, the peasant appeared to be giving himself up. He eyed Jarvus with curiosity, but he didn't speak to him.

The horses were whipped and the wagon lurched forward.

"And I thought I was dressed well," Jarvus said to the man as he jingled his chains, "but I've got nothing on you."

The man did not answer. Instead he smiled at the irony of the remark. It was the only enjoyment he'd had in a while.

"Where we going?" the Great One asked.

Again the restrained prisoner said nothing. He looked as if he didn't care where he went. It didn't matter anyway, his eyes conveyed, as they were both going regardless.

After a time spent bouncing around, Jarvus tried again. He had nothing better to do. Besides, he needed information.

"Are we heading to the fortress?" he asked.

The yoked peasant then spoke.

"I'll tell you nothing, spy," he said, with a glum resolve. "Don't bother yourself. You'll not trick me into speaking."

The Great One was amused by this interpolation.

"A spy?" he laughed aloud. "Me, a spy? Now that's a rich assessment, next you'll call me a heretic."

"As you say," answered the man, sticking to his opinion of the situation. It was easy to see his agony, constrained and jostled as he was. No wonder he was in a bad humor.

Jarvus, usually indifferent to the plight of others, felt for him.

286

"I'd say we're both in the same position, you and I, that's all," he responded. Again he rattled his chains. "I'm not after any information, friend, just conversation."

It was apparent that none was forthcoming. Jarvus gave up the effort, but he did wonder where they were going. He hoped it was closer to the station, for that would help, at least.

He had to get to there before the others. It was important. Without his getting there first, all would be lost.

That hardheaded brother of his wouldn't have believed that, however. Jarvus knew this for it was indicative of their whole relationship. It had been the same story between them since their parents had died so many years before.

No, his big brother would have jumped in and taken charge, as he always did, but in this case, Jarvus knew that such action would just doom them all. Yes, on this occasion Jarvus had the inside track, and not the overbearing Jonus. This time he knew better, despite what his older sibling might think.

And, without Jonus even knowing, the Great One was going to act on what he knew. He had to. That's why he'd run away.

He looked to the restrained man riding with him. The peasant's eyes were closed, but he wasn't sleeping. The grimace on his pained face was evidence enough of that.

"I must get to the fortress," Jarvus blurted, although he was speaking more to himself than the man.

The peasant opened his eyes at this revelation. They were hard as steel and betrayed nothing of what he thought. He sat silent.

Undeterred, Jarvus continued speaking aloud even though he knew the man would not comprehend the meaning.

"I must get there," he persisted, "I must. Only I can save the Mandate. Only I know who the traitor is."

This input caused the peasant to cock his eyebrows although he remained mute. Now the Great One felt foolish. He gave it up and with a grunt he leaned back and began to pull at his lip.

They plodded on without comment, minus the occasional groan due to the bumpy trail, for about an hour. Jarvus tried to sleep, but the chains on his ankles chafed too much for him to drop off. He continued picking away with his fingers while thinking.

Sometime later, the wagon creaked to a stop. They heard several horses approaching, with voices calling out, hailing the wagon master. Soon they were surrounded.

"Do you have him?" one of the newcomers asked. A mumbled response followed from the wagon's seat, too dim for the men inside to comprehend. Jarvus assumed that the disembodied voices were speaking of him, but he was wrong.

"Well, my good man, open up then and let's see him," called out another rider. At the sound of this new voice, the yoked peasant stiffened. He stared, eyes wide, through the slits of the wagon that heaved as the wagon master descended from his perch.

As footsteps crossed to the rear of the wagon, the yoked man, as best he could, leaned in to Jarvus.

"I must get to the Fortress as well," he hissed. Keys then rattled in the latch. Just before the door was opened, the bound peasant whispered, "Only the Mandate is paramount."

This time Jarvus raised his eyebrows.

The wagon master's form then filled the doorway, but he soon stepped aside, creaking the door back as he went. Beyond, Jarvus noticed several knights on horseback. One of these warriors, dressed in splendid attire, slowly clomped forward.

Jarvus could see that even his horse was clad with a fine livery. A few feet away, the knight bent in his elaborate saddle, the better to gaze inside the wagon. He liked what he saw.

"Ah, good Baker, that is you," said the young Duke of Fervent, speaking to the man in the yoke. "My, how the mighty have fallen. What a shame it is, what a tragic loss for the Empire."

This assessment caused the knights with him to laugh. The duke then leaned back, casting a superb image astride his snorting steed. Smiling as he turned the huge war-horse, Fervent quickly gestured for the wagon master to close the door.

"On to the Fortress," he commanded his men, "the day grows old and the Crone's wench awaits me."

At this, his henchmen laughed all the more. Then the group galloped away, stirring up a cloud of dust in their wake. As soon as the wagon master retook his seat, the horses were whipped and the bumpy journey resumed as before.

Jarvus glanced at the fettered man across the wagon. His peasant face showed not fear, which Jarvus had expected, but anger. He wore the look with fierce determination.

"Well, Baker," the Great One said, as they jolted along, "what we need is a plan and we better cook one up fast."

In the hillside clearing a plan was also being discussed.

The rest of the team members still had an agenda, but the newest particulars had to be taken into account. Like Jarvus, they all knew they had to reach Station Forecast. Yet their current problem, unlike his, was getting there undetected.

Morris' condition complicated things.

Increasing numbers of grunts were roaming the countryside and most were hostile. Soldiers, cavemen and desert dwellers, displaced farmers and city folk were all killing each other with apparent abandon. It seemed the planet's entire population, unaware of the many events that had led to this point, was unprepared for the dire consequences that followed them.

Jonus had regained consciousness, although he felt battered and exhausted by his vigorous romp with Steadfast. He was lucky, indeed, that the strong warrior had seen and recognized his identifying tag. Many times in the past, Steadfast had seen the one Moas always wore and, since then, Jargon had informed him that the strange man at the pit had worn one also.

Jargon's tale of the pit and the true nature of 'the beast' there was laughed at by most of the tribe, but Steadfast had not scoffed. The giant was still a friend and his loss to the tribe was not insignificant. Steadfast had taken Jargon aside, and after much discussion, had believed his bizarre account.

Jargon, so full of bravado as a growing boy, was now quite altered by what had occurred in the forest. As a result, the formerly brash youngster had matured. And the older warrior understood firsthand, from his own personal history, how an extraordinary experience in the hunt could achieve such a change.

Besides that, Steadfast was a good judge of character and he knew the import of the situation was not lost on Jargon. This was not one of his normal stories with no consequence. Big things were happening in the forest, big, unexplainable things that had never happened before the advent of the beast.

The twins facts that the giant could converse with the man at the pit and that both of them wore the same type of amulet was significant. Steadfast knew that it all tied together, somehow, although he didn't know just how. He, Jargon and the two boys had soon set out in search of some answers.

They hadn't informed the elders of the tribe, however, for they would have been too cautious and slow moving with their assent to such drastic action. Steadfast, on the other hand, had no time to waste. His yearly crop of grubs was almost ready to harvest.

The warrior had been scouting alone when he had spotted Jonus. The beast, it seemed, came in many forms. About the same time, the others had encountered Spencer and the giant.

Morris had been lucky too, that the bumbling Spencer had somehow carried his backpack with him when they had run from the camp that morning. It was the only thing that they had taken with them from the pit. Spencer had insisted for it contained his first aid kit and since then he had put it to good use.

The giant was now sleeping under a heavy dose of narcotic. Once he was out, Spencer and Jonus had then straightened and bound his broken leg. Now the two strangers were engaged in quiet but animated discussion, the cavemen saw.

The warriors were huddled a short distance away, eating some dried grubs. All were patient. The hunt had been good that day and they were content to wait and see what tomorrow would bring.

Steadfast was most pleased that his giant friend had been found. Once Moas was better, some answers would come, he knew it. However, the strangers were not so sure.

Jonus had conceived a plan, or rather a strategy that he wished to employ. Spencer was against it. The time jumper wanted to involve the grunts' unwitting help to achieve their mission but instead, Spencer wanted to leave them out.

He wanted to proceed alone with no further help of any kind from the locals. He felt as though they had polluted the grunts enough. But he was losing the argument, or rather, he was failing to bring Jonus around to his point of view.

The point, according to Jonus, was logistical.

Their position was evident in the time jumper's view. The giant's condition hindered moving about without being detected. Yes, this was true but it was a moot point, according to Spencer.

They could afford to wait for him to heal. After all, they didn't age and so they had all the time they needed for him to recover. The station would still be there, no matter when they arrived.

Yet they were throwing away a valuable, available tool if they failed to use the grunts, was the rebuttal of Jonus. There were great numbers of them in the area and the team members were

291

vulnerable where they were. They might be set upon at any moment, from any quarter, and that would end their mission.

They needed eyes and ears in the forest region to pass undetected. It was much better for them if the grunts were allies. There was safety in numbers and it was foolish to assume success before the many obstacles in their way were overcome.

"Create an army of them then, to do our bidding?" asked Spencer. He was incredulous. "That's what you mean?"

Jonus held no such scruples, he couldn't afford to.

"If need be," he answered. "If we have to. It's in their interest in the long run, surely you can see that."

"It's not their fault," countered Spencer, "and to involve them is dangerous as well as immoral. The Mandate is ours, not theirs. They're unaware of that aspect and should remain so."

"I'm not of the Theology Clan," spat the time jumper. "And we can't be bothered now by such lofty ideals. We've got to move, and move fast, or we're dead, and where's the Mandate then?"

"But to deceive them so," said Spencer, sticking to his guns, "to feed them some bull, just so they'll go along, is wrong,"

Jonus had heard enough. He didn't care what it took or who they used. He had to find Jarvus, in his mind, to ensure his safety.

The Mandate included him, no matter what his hardheaded brother might think. And the Mandate had to continue, there was no other option. Duty compelled it, or religion did, or both.

It didn't matter to Jonus how it was justified. It had to be done, that was his quest now. Completing the Mandate was the only way he'd have a life with Rosemary, once all of this was over.

"Look, it's nobody's fault," he said. "We're in the middle of a whirlwind no matter how much it insults your sensibilities, and we've got to get moving as soon as we can, period. I've got to find my brother, and I say we use what we have to get to him."

This reference gave Spencer pause. He had sent the brother away in the first place. Jonus, however, didn't mention this point.

"Anything we have to do to achieve the Mandate is acceptable," said the hard-pressed time jumper.

The Great Mandate, Spencer thought, it always came back to that well-known dictate. Well, it was paramount, and there was no doubting that. So, it all boiled down to how it was carried out.

Could one justify any deed to realize the objective? Was anything acceptable then, given the end result? Could one turn a blind eye in order to better things in the long run?

Just chew up a few grunts now for the good of the many later?

Spencer didn't think so and he never would. The very idea soured him. More so, it sickened him.

Now that his personal crisis was over, he preferred to trust in Primus and let the events unfold from there. Still, there was some time left to change things, change minds. The giant was incapacitated and would be for a while yet.

"I don't agree," he said, stating his position, "but I guess we'll wait and see what Morris has to say."

That was satisfactory. Jonus knew his big friend very well. He was sure Moe would agree with his assessment.

"I'm going to talk to the grunts," he said. "We need information. They may know how close we are to Point Zero."

"You understand their speech?" asked Spencer.

"Sure," Jonus answered, "so will you, given time. At some point in the future, the two languages will just merge in your head. It's a natural turn, a by-product of the event."

Spencer might have been a great engineer, but he was no time jumper, and his face showed his skepticism. Jonus had seen the look before, many times, and he laughed in spite of himself. Then he realized that he hadn't laughed in a long, long time.

Spencer wasn't a bad sort, he judged, just confused. He didn't understand the marshal implications involved or the real danger that all of them were in. Yet Spencer did understand.

He just didn't care.

Nevertheless, Jonus tried to explain.

"The time flow first blasted apart," he lectured, "but later reintegrated after you closed the water valve. Then all the blown up bits of time once more came together. But time is currently different, or it's blended in a different way, that is."

Spencer nodded, now following. This wasn't his specialty, but being a well-trained engineer, the phenomenon was familiar. At least he was on the most general, theoretical level.

"Time overlapped its original sequences," he said. "Now it's kind of meshed together. That's why Jargon is years older than when I met him only a few days ago."

"Right," Jonus agreed, "and your brain merges too, and it eases into the new time frame and sucks it up like a sponge. The language is identical, you see, it's just from different time periods. Now these periods are in the same sequence, and your brain, being blended, will gradually adjust for the difference."

He looked to the warriors and pointed with a flick of his hand.

"They'll understand you soon enough as well," he said.

The engineer again nodded, satisfied.

"It'll be OK, Spencer," Jonus said as he stood. "I'll get you back to Judith, don't worry. I told her I would."

The time jumper then walked away.

Spencer was stunned. He hadn't thought of his wife in what seemed like ages now. What a strange occurrence, he mused, given that he had done little else before the incident had occurred.

He looked to the sleeping giant. Moas loved his wife, he knew, or rather the man Morris did. Did she love him back?

Was it too late, he wondered? Spencer sighed, not knowing. Trust in Primus, he thought, just trust in Primus.

At this point, Jonus preferred to trust in something more tangible. He sat down between Steadfast and Jargon, but he looked to the boys. After a beat, he raised his hands and started to rub his sore ribs, slowly, while making a tortured face.

The twins enjoyed this act. Both burst out laughing. Jonus looked to Steadfast, not so sure of his reaction.

The warrior, making the same face, touched the still-swollen features on the side of his head. The boys laughed louder at this, smacking at each other a bit to demonstrate their enjoyment. Steadfast laughed too, while handing Jonus a fistful of dried grubs retrieved from an open sack before them.

The Traveler munched and nodded his thanks. The grubs, the last of the previous harvest, were very tasty. He looked to Jargon.

"Your brothers?" he asked him, indicating the boys.

"No," replied the young warrior, "Steadfast is not my father. I have no parents and haven't had for a long time." This was said as a matter of fact with no shame held in the statement.

"No," Steadfast agreed. "Jargon is not my son." Then he added, "But I would be proud if he were."

Jargon slowly drew a deep breath at this, to still his own pride at the remark. To his memory it was unprecedented. No one had ever before paid him such a wonderful compliment.

Jargon knew that Steadfast had always liked him, despite his brash demeanor as a boy. As well, while growing up, he had always loved hunting with the renowned Steadfast. The attempts they shared were never very productive when he tagged along, but that fact had never had mattered to either of them.

The fault was his, for he had been too noisy, or he had moved too fast, or he had done something else detrimental to the outcome, but in his arrogance, he had never admitted it. Yet Steadfast had been patient with him, and Jargon learned much from the older man. Now he knew he was respected and loved by him, too.

"I have no parents either," Jonus said, "but I do have a brother. He's part of our team. He's missing and I've got to find him."

He again looked to Steadfast, without doubt the elder here.

"Do you follow?" he asked him.

Steadfast nodded, all seriousness now.

The warrior glanced to Jargon and his sons. While holding their attention, he tapped his throat to indicate the id tags the strangers wore. They all made the connection.

"I'm pretty sure he's close by," Jonus continued, "because he's heading to a place, a special place we need to find. This location may be hidden now but I'm not certain, it's been a long time since I've seen it. All of us are heading there."

"This place," asked Steadfast, "is home to your tribe?"

He spoke with a soft voice, and the others leaned in to hear the Traveler's answer. Here it starts, Jonus thought. This crossed the proverbial line, and there was no going back once it was done.

"Not our home, exactly," he explained. "It's more like a well used base camp. It's similar to a winter hunting site far from your village that you go to again and again."

Steadfast nodded, easily following.

Jonus continued, "We have to get there but it's dangerous now. The big one is hurt and I have to protect him. I also need to find my brother so he can help us once we get to our camp."

Steadfast grabbed a fistful of grubs and handed them around.

He considered some, then asked, "And once we have your brother and once we're at your camp, what then? How can we fight what has happened to our world?" His eyes were sad.

Jonus glanced over to Spencer. The engineer was still sitting at a distance next to his sleeping friend, both in the shadow of the upturned tree. He appeared to be sleeping too, unmoving, with his head tilted back into the tree's huge root ball.

"There's a way," said Jonus, "but it won't be easy."

"A good hunt never is easy," said Jargon, slowly chewing a grub. The twins grinned, thinking only of the adventure to come. Steadfast, however, was quiet, thinking of other things.

He was a brave fighter, no doubting that, but he wasn't foolish. This competent warrior never rushed headlong into imminent danger if it could be helped. The man didn't mind dying in the hunt, but he didn't relish dying for no reason.

He wasn't opposed. He just wanted more details, the bigger picture. The fact was evident by the look on his face.

But he was patient, waiting for more input.

At this point, despite his earlier, feisty exchange with Spencer, Jonus was hesitant to go any further. The grunts seemed willing and that was enough for now. Any sticky details could wait, and he'd work that out with the others later.

He said, "What we need is information. We need to know about the lay of the land and what ground comes next." They all nodded.

"I need specific details concerning the enemy," he continued. "They have greater numbers. We must know where they are and where we need to be to avoid them."

This also made good sense to the warriors.

Jonus added, "They'll try and stop us, you see. They don't want things changed back and they'll fight to stop us. But getting to the camp, all of us, is the only way we can settle this."

Here Jonus paused and looked to each of them in turn to better gauge their reaction to his request.

"I need information and friends that I can trust," he said.

297

In the fortress city of Am-Rif, some twenty miles away to the northeast, Lucid had just received some information of her own. As well, the effort had come from a friendly source, although one the young girl hadn't thought would assist her in such a manner. Yet the captain of the tower guard had sought her out as she had roamed about the city running errands.

He had delivered the distressing news of Pliant's arrest. The old soldier's bushy eyebrows had twitched constantly during the exchange. Pliant was safe enough, he had reported, but now under lock and key by the king's own command.

It was presumed that he was on his way back from the field.

Such news spread like wildfire through the army. It also spread through the substantial peasant throng that accompanied the ranks. Soon all would know that the bastard had fallen from grace.

She had to inform her mother.

Lucid was terrified. She loved the shy peasant and worried for him, but there was more to it than that. The fact that her mother's plan was now in disarray bespoke a larger problem for her.

In the past, the girl had always taken for granted her life with the Crone. For as long as she could remember, Sorbus had clearly stood apart, solid and sure, despite her slight frame. Never before had the girl ever questioned her judgment, never had she wavered in her belief that the old woman knew all.

Now that faith in her had been dashed, shattered in an instant. This piercing insight had left her cold and stunned, for the revelation signified a further implication. It was one that the girl didn't want to face, but she had to, regardless.

As she hurried back to the fortress in search of the Crone, she wrung her hands. If it were true, she thought, that her mother was as fallible as anyone else, then what of her mother's belief in the all powerful God, Primus? Was Sorbus wrong to cling to Him so?

The girl tried to dismiss such thoughts. To think in such a way would undermine all that she had lived by. Still, she couldn't help it for the doubt was there, despite what she wished.

But no, her mother was different from everyone else, and that much was evident. She knew things that others did not. There was no denying she always saw things on a much broader scale.

The fact that the old Crone did not age was proof enough that she possessed powers far beyond normal understanding. Her knowledge was commanding, ubiquitous and unique. She also knew the outcome of any situation before it came to be.

Then why had Pliant been taken prisoner? Would he be executed? Could they save him, just the two of them, alone?

And what did his capture mean to their ultimate strategy, to the Great Mandate of Primus so important to her dear mother? Was this occurrence part of His overall plan? Lucid didn't think so.

In her youth, she had never heard such a story.

The poor girl was upset, as upset as she'd ever been in her life, and she didn't like it. It ruined her well-ordered world, the only existence she'd ever known. Such doubt had never bothered her in the past, and as she rushed to the fortress, she now fought the strange feeling with every fiber of her being.

Still in all, what if it was true, she wondered? What if they were doomed despite all efforts otherwise? Lucid didn't want to change her name now, and certainly not to Morbid.

Suddenly, she was cut off by a figure darting in front of her.

"Ah, just who I was looking for," said the young Duke of Fervent while seizing her slender wrist. The peasant girl, unlike most, was unmoved by the duke's higher station. She was indignant at such treatment and struggled to break free.

However, he was stronger and grabbed her other wrist with ease, jerking her about some to emphasize the point. Lucid froze. The gravity of the situation was evident to both of them.

The duke leaned in, whispering, "No bastard now to come to your aid. You're all alone. It's just you and me, my pretty one."

He laughed, satisfied that she was powerless. How smug he was, Lucid thought, standing there for all the world to see, without a care, rough handling her in such a cavalier fashion. This Fervent was contemptuous and base, as well as dangerous.

He was also well known for his vanity, and had changed his wardrobe yet again, having shed his magnificent but heavy suit of armor. He now wore a rich outfit made with several layers of fine fabric, each one stitched with silver thread, and wrought with care into puffy gathers at his sleeves and breeches. These abundant spheres of dazzling cloth had slits, which showed a different, but complementary color of fabric underneath.

The duke also wore high riding boots of the finest leather, and a great, fur-collared cloak was pinned to his wide shoulders to better frame his person. A stylish cap topped him off. This ensemble was offset by many pieces of glistening jewelry.

He spoke the truth, though.

Pliant at first, and then her mother had protected her once the king had left the city. She had thought the duke absent, too, but she had been wrong. Now she was alone.

She lowered her pretty head, as if in resignation, and the arrogant royal smiled widely at this unexpected turn of events. He was only sorry his retainers were absent and could not witness his triumph in person. But they would know soon enough for they were close by drinking in a peasant alehouse.

He had just left the place himself to go out and pee in the alley. His unplanned timing had proved perfect to the task. Luckily for him, he had seen her in the street, and luckier still that the Crone was absent and the bastard baker arrested.

It was true that the girl was in great danger, but she hadn't lost her wits. She wasn't called Lucid for nothing. She jerked up her head, her green eyes flashing and her blond curls dancing.

It was a striking thing to see, and the duke looked down on her with open relish. Lucid's eyes met his, unafraid now and determined. She then kneed him as hard as she could, shooting her lower thigh into his perfectly embroidered codpiece.

Fervent turned her loose and sank down to the ground, his legs giving out beneath him. He didn't scream, there was too much pain, but he did let out a mournful groan as his eyes bulged. He slowly slid into the muddy street, tightly gripping his arms about his knees, and assumed a twitching fetal position.

Lucid ran away, thinking of her Pliant.

The duke was struggling to breathe. He groaned some more, trying to focus. Then he pissed his beautiful pants.

Pliant was thinking of her also, and he wasn't that far away.

The peasant was still riding in the wagon, still heading in her general direction, but his situation had changed and for the better. He no longer wore the bulky and uncomfortable wooden yoke about his neck. Instead, the wagon master did.

The man in the chains had picked the lock on the yoke with little trouble, after plucking a large, hand-poured nail from the wagon's rickety wall. Unfortunately for him, his own chains were riveted together. He had been attempting to pick the lock that held the door with his hands stuck through the gaps in the wagon when, once more the wagon stopped, ceasing their journey.

The wagon master, it seemed, had to relieve himself.

Jarvus, after first smiling at Pliant, started screaming to the driver that the man in the yoke was choking to death.

"Hurry, hurry" he bellowed, "he's turning blue."

As keys were jingling in the lock, Jarvus added, "I was asleep and didn't notice. Hurry, he may be dead already." All this time he had masked the view of Pliant with his animated body movements.

From there, it had been easy thing to overpower the man. He was no match for the both of them. He had no fight in him at any rate, once his position had become clear.

The outlaws had decided to continue on their way using the same transport for it was a safe cover for them as they moved. Who would be looking for the two, if no one knew they were missing? That was their combined reasoning, anyway.

The driver, unhurt save his pride, had been placed in the yoke to keep him restrained. He had been assured that no ill would come to him if he gave them no trouble and he showed little sign of trying to alter his present lot. He knew that he would have trouble enough trying to explain things to his angry superiors once he was finally let go somewhere closer to the city.

Jarvus, wearing the driver's over shirt for subterfuge, now drove. It was a beautiful day and he was enjoying himself. His leg chains were hidden from view in the bottom of the driver's perch.

As his companion changed his garb, Pliant had easily seen his identification device hanging about his neck. It was the same amulet that the Crone wore, the baker noted with interest, although he didn't mention it. Nothing beyond the briefest of plans had been discussed at the time for others might have come down the path at any moment and the escaping pair had to keep moving.

But now, again on their bumpy way, his thoughts once more fell to Lucid and to the detestable young Duke of Fervent. Was she safe from him? And if she were, for how long would she be?

And what of the old Crone's devious plans now, he thought with disgust? What of her all-powerful god, Primus? He was as worthless as the rest of them as far as Pliant was concerned.

He couldn't believe the current turn of events, even though he knew that they were genuine enough. The girl's position was perilous at best, yet he was unable to aid her. His current lot was tenuous as well, so what could he do?

The realization that Sorbus, in spite of her vast abilities, could be defeated with such ease stunned him to the core. What would happen to the girl now? Was she, the one true love of his life, just a sacrifice to the old woman's damned Mandate along with him?

It was a fact that Lucid's affection had made treason more palatable, but now the taste was sour in his mouth. He wished he had never left the walled city of Am-Rif. What would happen to Lucid now without him to protect her?

And who else was there but himself? Was Lucid to rely on a bent old woman or on a defeated god? Was the fortress itself mighty enough against everything that was to come?

None of this made any sense to the poor baker. He was tired of trying to figure it out. The mental activity involved, as he racked his brain over and over for an answer, was just too taxing for him.

Pliant was a simple man at best, and he knew that he had no head for such lofty ideals. They were far beyond his limited reach. No, he had been more than content to leave those concerns to Sorbus but look where that strategy had gotten him.

So, a broken, mysterious fortress and some quest with a higher purpose were no longer important to him. He just wanted to make his way to the girl and to save her from any harm. That was his only Mandate now, rigid and unchanging.

His first concern was the strange man in the chains. He was a crafty one, no doubting that, and it might not be such a bad thing to have so determined a confederate but could Pliant trust him in the long term? He didn't know the answer.

Their Mandates were different. That might come into play later, one never knew. What then, thought Pliant?

Also, although Pliant had worked well with other people in the past, for the most part he had been in charge of things when he did. But from what he'd seen of this man in action, control was not an option there, certainly not a viable one. Yet the man was able, they were still some distance from the city, and who knew what changes had taken place there in his absence?

Pliant looked through the slits in the creaking wagon and saw the countryside was changing, opening up into outlying farmlands. After a while, the crude path they traveled would merge into a real road and congestion would then follow. The peasant knew that the time had come so he banged on the roof of the cage and shouted for the man in the chains to rein in the horses.

Next the two were crossing the cultivated fields on foot. Riding would have been faster but less safe from detection, in particular when viewed from a distance. The wagon master, yoked, gagged and locked inside the conveyance, was left in a thick stand of trees not far from the path where soldiers backtracking the missing trio would find both him and the horses soon enough.

They were making good progress despite the chains bolted to Jarvus' ankles. He simply ran with petite steps while holding up his burden of iron links between his short but strong legs. However, it was tiring for him and so, as they moved along, the two looked for an empty barn or isolated farmhouse.

They were wishing to find some tool they could appropriate to break him free from his bonds. Then they would make even better time. It was all they could hope for at this stage.

Somewhat later, they came upon a horseless cart half filled with hay, not far from a lazy stream. A young farm worker was taking a break from his labors, swimming in the nearby water, having left his pitchfork stuck in the haystack. A pitchfork wasn't the best tool for the job but it would have to do.

The bound man watched as Pliant crossed unseen to the cart, en route to steal the implement, but once there, the baker instead found an old axe in the cart's well. He took it and retraced his steps, still unobserved. Rejoining his comrade, they again took off heading once more towards the city, and after losing sight of the farmer, the two then stopped in the cover of more heavy trees.

304

Seeing a large, flat rock Jarvus hiked his leg upon it and said to the peasant, "I hope your aim is good, my man." He was smiling as he spoke. Things were looking up.

Holding the axe, Pliant also smiled.

"You sure are a trusting sort," he answered, and then he added, "What's your name, my newest friend?"

His newest friend laughed out loud before responding, "Things haven't been going very well of late, so I guess my current name should be Jaded, but just call me J."

"For me either, J," said the troubled baker. "My life used to be rather routine, but I find it grows more and more bizarre as each day passes. Now I find it quite out of control."

Jarvus grew philosophical.

"You are what you've been," he said.

"Perhaps that's true," answered Pliant, "but I've been lots of things in my life and changed my name many times."

He handled the axe thoughtlessly as he spoke, moving the tool from hand to hand without a care.

"And in that case," he continued, "I guess my name should now be Amalgam, but I've grown weary of changing it somehow."

Before Jarvus could respond, the baker hefted and brought down the axe, splitting the iron shackle off with a spark.

The action had been so swift that Jarvus had to look twice to make sure he still possessed his foot. He did though, and he removed the heavy iron band with alacrity. He then started rubbing his chafed ankle with alacrity, too.

He looked up, again grinning. Pliant was getting used to the sight. He liked this man, in spite of his earlier reservations. "Next?" the baker asked, referring to the remaining leg iron.

"Give me a minute," said Jarvus, relishing the feel of his scratching. "So," he next inquired, "who's this wench that knight spoke of? You know, earlier in the wagon."

At mention of Lucid, Pliant's demeanor changed. He froze becoming stiff, but, after a moment, he relaxed some and tried to answer. It wasn't an easy thing to do.

"She's," he started, but then he stopped. The baker didn't know how best to describe the entangled relationship they shared. At last, he decided that brevity was the best course.

"I love her," he answered.

"I see," said Jarvus. After a beat he added, "We need to get to her then. That'd be better for both of you."

The other man did not reply to this, but his hands were still working away, gripping and ungripping the axe handle. It was disconcerting to see. Jarvus changed the subject.

"So," he asked, "just who's this Crone that everybody's talking about? What was her name again? Sorbus?"

This question confused the baker.

"You don't know her?" he asked.

"Should I?" was the other's retort.

Pliant sat down beside Jarvus.

"She has your neckwear," he said, pointing to Jarvus' throat. "Are you not a believer in Primus, as she is? And does this not signify your servitude to Him, as the one she wears?"

This answer confused the Great One for the grunts were not supposed to know of Primus. None of them was, not here, not on any of the seeded planets flung throughout the galaxy. Not now at any rate, that's what the prophecy said.

But this grunt did know about Him and he knew about the standard-issue dog tags also. What other knowledge did he possess? Had he knowledge of the station?

Jarvus said, "I'm part of her team." This was a assumption. At this point, he didn't know who she was and so he moved on.

306

"But then again it's this way with me," he continued. "I leave all that theological stuff to the experts. I'm only concerned with the task at hand and I have enough trouble dealing with that."

"I can relate," said Pliant. "I know nothing but my love is in danger and that everything I trust in fades away. I've been beaten down by belief in things I don't understand, and to no good end."

The peasant was pensive. The situation baffled him. He had no idea what he should do, or what would happen from this point.

He shook his head in never ending amazement and grunted, "I used to rely on myself, but now I'm afraid. I'm afraid that now I may do something to make matters worse. It's a bad feeling."

"You're not alone now," said Jarvus, trying to make him feel better, "and I'll help you help the girl but first you need to tell me what you know. I have to know all that you know about the fortress and about everything else, Sorbus included. Then I'll explain some things to you and we'll go on from there."

The baker stood at once, instantly resigned. The plan was better by far than anything that he could come up with on his own and he knew it. He looked to the other man and nodded.

Jarvus placed his other leg on the rock. Again the peasant's aim was true. The remaining shackle also sparked.

Sorbus herself had some explaining to do, to her daughter. Like a cyclone Lucid had burst in with news of the baker's arrest. However, Sorbus having her own sources, had already known,

The two were safe enough inside the fortress, the Crone had seen to that. She had locked down the entire structure, every level and every door. It had been done with the flip of a switch.

This was a normal operational precaution built into the ancient building. Each station throughout the galaxy was so equipped. Calming her daughter was not as easy.

All was not lost, the Crone knew, but things were now becoming more complicated by the minute. There was no time to waste. The plan was in play and it could not be halted now.

A new force was forming in the countryside, but not like any army heretofore. This time, all factions of the planet's displaced grunts were joining against the kingdom with any old animosities or mistrust now forgotten. And, for once, they had a coordinated plan with leaders who knew what they were doing.

Somehow these new leaders understood that the station was at the bottom of all their problems. The Fortress of Forecastle and its mysterious secrets were now well known throughout the huge continent. Of course, no one knew for sure what it was or where it had come from, but not having it for themselves, they wanted it destroyed and, it seemed to the old woman, at all costs.

Reports from her many sources, who were by and large well placed peasants, said the fighting so far had been equally brutal and barbaric with no regard for the weak or innocent. Thousands had been lost on both sides. A trial by fire to burn clean the entire planet was now not only raging, but steadily growing, feeding on itself and all others to increase the conflagration.

Yet there was hope.

One of her team had also been taken prisoner. Accounts of his id tag confirmed this for what the hapless Jarvus had told his interrogators had been true. If a tag were removed, it would be destroyed for it drew power in part from the electrochemical processes unique to the person for whom it was programmed.

Once that power source was absent, compounds released broke down the structure of the tag and then it literally faded away. There was no mistake, she was sure. If the tag was present, then the prisoner had to be a member of her team.

From the detailed description given by her spies, Sorbus judged that prisoner to be Jarvus. This naturally meant that his older brother, Jonus, the love of her life, could not be far behind. The

Crone would have to keep a sharp eye out in order to assist him once he arrived at the city, and this action would not be easy.

The king's armies were once more retreating, and again the walls of the citadel had been sealed against the onslaught, but she knew that Jonus would somehow find a way to gain access. Then she would take over, but she still needed the assistance of her beloved daughter. The Crone couldn't do it alone.

The young girl was calmer now. Lucid already had one cup of hot tea down her, and another was cradled in her hands. Her green eyes were large with trepidation, but she was listening to Sorbus, giving her mother a chance to explain.

The old woman didn't know where to begin. The true state of affairs was convoluted to be sure but that wasn't the problem. The situation was complicated by her love for the girl.

She had never lied to Lucid, but she had imparted ideas to her in simplistic forms using metaphor and allegory. At the time, it had seemed the natural thing to do. It had been effortless, too.

When the Crone found herself in a medieval world, she had leaned upon the social contexts of the period. Before she had joined forces with the king, in order to search out the station, she had prepared the young girl for what was to come with sweeping stories of adventure and intrigue. That part she had enjoyed.

But because she knew the girl so well, Sorbus also knew that, for Lucid, the simple tales were not just stories anymore. They were now her personal mythology. The well-loved stories grounded her daughter, explaining her world to her, and as such, they satisfied her inner being and gave her peace.

They were her foundation.

Should the Crone now lie to her? Even if it was for her own good, should she? It would be a simple thing to do.

Some mystical explanation would be easy enough.

But what, in the long term, would such an action accomplish? What of her personal mythology then? Should Lucid live her life based on make-believe and fairy tales, ignorant of the real world, just to let the Crone off the hook?

And what of Pliant?

On the other hand, telling her the truth also had its drawbacks.

It was against the Great Mandate for one thing. True, Primus Himself had prophesied that the time would come for such a revelation, but this wasn't it. And she couldn't cause the appointed time to occur now, just because she wished it so.

Another concern was Lucid's future. It was uncertain. Once the present mission was accomplished, the original time flow would be restored to the planet and the six members of the team blasted Beyond the Elastic Limit would then return to their former lives.

It was sad but neither her daughter nor the baker was one of the original six. As such, Lucid or Pliant or both, might not even be present in the reconstructed time sequence once it reached the point for them to naturally appear. Lucid, for all her preparation and expertise, was unaware of this part of the scenario.

Knowledge of that kind, of a possible negative future, might have a drastic effect on the girl. Would she cope, could she live on with such an insight? Or, was the proposition that what she didn't know couldn't hurt her the better idea?

That was the crux of the matter, Sorbus saw. It all came down to how much of the truth to tell her daughter or whether to tell her at all. This girl was not just some grunt to her, not just one of many to be used up now for the salvation of the planet later.

No, she was the girl the Crone had raised, and Sorbus loved her beyond what mere words could convey.

"My child," she said to her, "I know this is difficult for you. I know that you fear for Pliant. But there are things at work here that are beyond your understanding."

"Will he live?" Lucid blurted out. "Or are we all doomed?" As usual, her remarks cut straight to the heart of the matter, and this time, into the Crone's ancient heart as well.

The girl was named Lucid for good reason.

Sorbus felt for her, and the feeling was a heavy one. It was true that she didn't wish to deceive her daughter, but she didn't want to get into a weighty philosophical debate, either. There wasn't time.

The plan was in play, and things were moving at a fast clip.

The old woman leaned in closer, with one bloodshot eye overly open and the other one squinted almost shut.

"We must have faith," she said.

In the countryside, Spencer was facing his own philosophical debate and it sorely tested his newfound faith as well. He couldn't believe the recent bloody and escalating turn of events. Worse still, he was powerless to alter or control them.

The sleeping giant had awakened indeed, and as the time jumper had earlier predicted, Morris had quickly sided with Jonus' idea of how to proceed. Any action employed to hasten the Mandate was fine with the two of them, and the consequences be damned. For Spencer, it was a sickening thing to contemplate for the end result would be staggering to the whole planet's future.

Currently, the two determined men were waging all-out warfare with the ease of a casual chess game. And every day brought more and more grunts to their deadly cause, drawn by the hope that the growing multitude could do what they could not do alone. All were committed, at any cost, to defeating the enemy.

Spencer was horrified at the bloodbath that had resulted and concerned with his own damnation as a result.

His tortured conscience, along with the rest of the planet's grunt population, was in open rebellion. His complicity so far, no matter how unwilling, already had contributed to thousands being slaughtered. Before it was over, thousands more would have to be sacrificed in order to achieve access to the stricken station.

At present, the engineer's sense of good and evil was very well defined and the failure to sway his team members to his point of view tormented him as nothing ever had. What was occurring now was definitely and definably evil. This could not be the will of Primus, yet it was happening nonetheless.

Why? What was the hidden purpose? What did it all mean?

Spencer's input had been listened to but ignored without hesitation. He was no military man and that was evident to his confederates. That snap assessment was true enough but the swiftness of it had still stung, nonetheless.

Now what bothered him more was the cavalier way in which the grunts had been persuaded to fight. They had been lied to, mislead, and with no shame, thought Spencer. All of their concerns, their well-founded fears, and their belief system itself had been harnessed and used by Jonus and Morris, as easily as any beast of burden would be to plow some field or carry a load.

And in this brutal war, the grunts were carrying the entire load for they were the ones dying left and right. How many more, Spencer wondered? But that wasn't all.

No one was concerned about the decency of the thing. The planet's grunts were expendable, and that was that. As long as the Great Mandate was achieved, anyone could be used as fodder, without compunction, without any second thought.

Spencer didn't understand such reasoning and never would. Nor could he condone it. To him, the ends never could justify the means even if the end product was a good one.

In any case, the grunt population and their continuing welfare was the whole point of the Great Mandate. Killing them in order to achieve their salvation was, to Spencer, ludicrous. And too overt, as secrecy was, and always had been, the order of the day when carrying out this portion of the will of Primus.

As the engineer stood in the clear forest night, he looked up and saw the stars shining above. He knew that other teams on other planets were engaged in surreptitious and quiet observation, waiting only to assist their grunts, if need be. That's what Primus wanted and demanded, and that alone was the proper thing to do.

That exactly was the Great Mandate's holy dictate.

Spencer's entire civilization had been geared to this function, and long had it prospered in the day-to-day acts of doing so. But what was happening, what this mission had become, was heresy. There was no denying it, not for Spencer, anyway.

The fact that he now understood their speech only made matters worse for he could now better comprehend their agony.

So, at present, Spencer was empathetic. He felt for the planet's grunts on a basic, but broad human level, yet he was powerless to alter the disgusting situation. Or was he?

He still trusted in Primus. For him, there was no other path. Perhaps, just perhaps He would still show a way.

Spencer was not far from their newest encampment. The army was near its objective, bivouacked in close proximity to the walled city of Am-Rif. He had walked a few hundred feet away for some solitude, but he could see the campfires blazing in the distance.

As he stood thinking, he heard someone approach. At first he saw only a silhouetted form moving towards him, but soon he made out the figure of one of Steadfast's sons. But, because he was a twin, Spencer wasn't sure which one of the boys he was.

Both were fierce warriors, despite their age, but on a personal note, Spencer couldn't help but like them anyway. After all, the fault was not theirs. They, like all the grunts, were being used.

In truth, these two were being used well, and to the best advantage of the army as a whole. They were not just common soldiers. Jonus and Morris had employed them as their personal runners, sending them between each other's position during the heat of the battle, the better to coordinate the ongoing carnage.

The twins were perfect for this task, each agile and swift, and both relished the important duty they held. The only drawback was that now they saw very little of each other. Yet, undeniably, it was an exciting life they lived, full of adventure.

Both the boys, in fact young men, were intelligent and quick learners. It was a sad thing, thought Spencer. The pair were learning too much of slaughter these days.

Although they were mirror images of each other, Spencer knew the duo was quite different in temperament. One was calm and introspective with the other being a hothead, blurting out his feelings with little prompting, leaving no doubt as to how he felt. So, although the boys looked alike, they were polar opposites.

Their father had deduced the cause of this difference early on by referring to their birth order. The calm one had come first. The hothead, born next, had been impatient ever since.

The calm one was also pensive, and this tentative trait often had been misinterpreted as hesitancy, and so his name was Timid. His twin brother held no such demeanor. He could explode at any moment, and so his name was Tempest.

In general, it took Spencer a while to figure out which one was which, but tonight the choice was easy. This twin carried a steaming bowl of stew with him. He handed it to Spencer.

"I saw," he said, "you took no dinner before you walked away."

"Thank you, Timid," Spencer said, accepting the bowl. The choice had been clear. Tempest would not have made the same gesture, had his observation been identical.

"You're troubled," Timid said, as a statement, not a question.

"Very," answered the engineer. The stew was good, and he hadn't realized how hungry he was, but he kept speaking in between chews. He wanted to talk to someone, needed to even.

"I think we're making a big mistake," he slurped, "I think things could have been handled in a different way."

Timid considered and said, "The two are not the same. At any time there are different choices. Is this not always so?"

314

Choices, thought Spencer. It always came down to choices, regardless of what was mandated from above. Even men of good conscience differed, and he did know the two new generals were only doing what they thought was best given the circumstances.

From their point of view, it was incumbent on them to act, no matter how bloody it became. The two stubborn men were just using the tools at hand. Might makes right.

He saw it from the other way around. He now was grounded, steeled in his belief of how things should be. Right makes might.

Primus never said it would be easy. The fact that it had been was of little solace to him now. There had to be another way.

Then it came to him, just like that. In an instant, he saw the proverbial light. He realized that he had his own choice to make.

"Yes," he said to Timid, "there are always different options." Spencer returned the now-empty bowl to the twin and slapped him on the back. "Thanks," he said, moving towards camp.

He realized that his choice was already made.

Pliant also needed to make a choice. He and his companion were holed up within the city of Am-Rif, in the storeroom of his old mill. The baker might have been a wanted man, but he still had some trusted friends willing to assist him.

These had transported the two fugitives through the gates by way of a cart loaded with wheat bound for the mill. It was easily accomplished. With the fighting now raging in the countryside, bread for the masses was again the basic staple for all, and the grain cart had been waved through without a glance by the numerous guards on duty.

Pliant had been apprehensive, to say the least, hiding under the freshly cut stalks, vulnerable to detection. Afterwards, relieved by their success at the subterfuge, he had felt better, but now, with his confederate asleep on a pile of empty wheat sacks, he was again agitated. He needed a plan, a workable plan.

315

He had to breach the fortress in order to get to the girl, but he was well known in the city and traveling through it was a dangerous proposition. He might make it with the aid of a disguise or some other ruse but if not, if instead he were apprehended, all would be lost. His confederate, on the other hand, was not known, and this would grant him freer access among the populace.

But his aim was not the girl, per se, but the building itself. Could Pliant trust him, he wondered, once the fortress had been breached? Could he trust him before then?

They had discussed tactics previous to Jarvus' nodding off, but how they were to proceed was still unresolved. Jarvus had offered to reconnoiter alone, but Pliant was leery of this. If he left the mill unattended, he might not return of his own volition.

The man was nothing if not self-reliant, and he might think that he could do better without assistance. Pliant couldn't have that, as on his own, he had no other options. The baker, always cautious, wanted to be sure of Jarvus' continuing help.

The sleeping man knew the fortress well, the peasant had learned. In their talks, first in the grove of trees and later as they had crossed over the farmlands, he had described it to a tee. And J was sure that he could gain access once he knew the location of the main entrance, for he was aware of how the installation's septic system ran in relation to it, only a short distance away.

A tunnel could then be dug surreptitiously to gain entrance. From there it would be easy. It sure sounded so.

Jarvus hadn't bothered to tell the frustrated baker that his first job at the station had been cleaning out the ancient sewer. Pliant was skeptical, nonetheless. He wasn't sure of the story's validity, but more so, the whole thing might be just a convenient ploy to get away while the poor baker sat alone in the mill's basement.

No, the choice was clear. Pliant would have to accompany Jarvus on the morrow, no matter the risk to himself. If he were detected, he would just have to deal with the situation.

Yet he didn't get a chance to make that choice. Awakening the next morning, he found himself alone. Jarvus had left the building.

Spencer almost missed the chance to implement his own choice, the one that he had made earlier while talking with Timid. After leaving the young caveman, the engineer had sought out Jonus, eager to confront him with his new idea. In spite of himself, Spencer had begun to get excited for the more he had turned it over in his mind, the more his plan had made sense to him.

Beforehand, his views had been dismissed outright because he had disagreed with the military objectives of the team. He had argued against the idea of a grunt army, and did so on many fronts, starting with theology and its application to the Mandate. He had been quite verbal but this argument had failed.

Jonus and the healing Morris had been unmoved. The mission counted more to them than did the will of Primus. Forward ho, and they couldn't be bothered with all that heady stuff.

Next, Spencer had appealed to the humanity of the thing, but again to no avail. Who cared how many grunts were butchered now, if in the end, you could start back at the beginning? No, nothing he had said, no point that he had broached had worked on the hardheaded men, but now he had them.

His new idea would change everything. This time his objective would be the same as theirs was, breaching the city. Only the means was different, and with hope, less brutal.

Spencer believed his plan would work, and better still, he saw no reason why his team members wouldn't agree with him. So perhaps there was not only a way to win the station, but also to win it without further bloodshed. He had seen enough of that.

However, upon arriving at the new general's tent, Spencer was informed that the time jumper had moments earlier quit the camp. Jonus was off to confer with the giant, established somewhere

317

further north, and no doubt to coordinate with him the final assault of the besieged city's wall. The game was on in earnest.

Spencer set off at once. It was dark, but there was a nearly full moon to illuminate his way. And there was other light, as well.

He made little progress at first, for the entire army was now moving, engaged in drawing up and encircling the battered city of AmRif. Evidence of the siege warfare to come was pervasive. Grunts of all persuasions were working in a coordinated effort, hauling battering rams and catapults, and driving crude wagons piled high with pieces of armor and weaponry.

Various kinds of livestock and dogcarts of fodder were being driven amongst the crowd with assorted domesticated fowl left to follow the slow-moving migration on its own.

The crowd was thick and everywhere there were blazing torches waved about to help advance the action. In their determined toil, the grunts never noticed the hubbub. The atmosphere was resolute but festive also, and many of the laborers were smiling and laughing as they spurred each other forward.

Unlike his mission cohorts, Spencer hadn't been trained as a military man but he understood well enough why this march had been ordered at night. The very sight of it from the ramparts as it converged about them, approaching and undulating as a single living thing, would horrify the city's citizens and demoralize the imperial troops. After all, holed up within in the walled capital, they were rooted to the spot and, as such, they couldn't run away.

Everyone in the throng knew Spencer, or at least knew about him, and some there had grown to know him well. This was because he had assumed control of the wounded once the outbreak of hostilities had begun. He had established crude field hospitals and organized a system of sorts for nursing the injured.

Most of those struck down during the fierce confrontations died later from infection if not from the horrid injuries themselves, but Spencer had done what he could and everyone there knew it.

With the enormous number of casualties so far, it was a losing effort to be sure, but he had tried to persevere, and was universally respected because of it. So, some he passed by graciously offered him a ride on one conveyance or another, but he turned them all down with a wave and a smile or a nod of his head. The crowd was so thick, that he made better time on foot.

Then Timid overtook him. The twin rode a massive war-horse taken earlier in battle, and there was plenty of room to share the oversized, wooden saddle it bore. The engineer pulled himself up and seated behind the twin, the two rode off.

Cutting through the crowd, they soon outpaced the slower moving grunts. Once in the open, their speed increased. Even given the hour, it was easy to see by the light of the moon.

"The hunt continues," said the young warrior over his shoulder.

Spencer knew that this was true, but the man was deep in his own thoughts, and so he said nothing in response.

The imperial hunt was continuing also, because the king had been more than furious upon learning of the baker's escape. His devious plan of action was to use the man as leverage against the Crone, but now he was gone. At any cost, the two of them could not be permitted to join forces against him.

No, the crafty old woman alone would be enough for him to deal with, safely hidden as she was within the deep fortress.

The search for the baker was both ongoing and far-reaching, and involved much manpower needed elsewhere for true to his name, the king was a rigid man. But he was crafty, too, and he knew that Pliant was headed for Sorbus. He had to be, for he was impotent without her and he loved her comely daughter.

Nevertheless, so far the pursuit had been fruitless, the baker still at large, and King Invar most displeased.

The fault was his. The king should never have let the bastard out of his sight, but, at the time, he had been stunned by the

319

unexpected news of the beast. After he had received it, developments in the field had deteriorated, and with a vengeance.

His bivouacked forces had been attacked on three sides at once and by a coordinated, determined force. Only with the greatest of effort had Invar retreated to the walled city with his bloodied army intact. By the time conditions were under control, the king had discovered that the baker was already missing.

But perhaps the peasant would never reach the Crone. The fighting had been fierce during the forced retreat with many dead on both sides of the conflict. Perhaps he was cut down already, while making his way across the countryside.

However, the ever-cautious king could not count on this. No, he always planned for any contingency. So the city was now sealed and the entrance to the Fortress of Forecastle also well protected.

In addition, there was a reward posted for the baker's return but one never knew about these commoners. They stuck together, despite incentives. He could not count on the likes of them.

Still, events were moving apace and other game was afoot. What the king needed now was more weaponry to beat off his enemies and Sorbus stood in his way. But, unlike a standard siege, the old woman inside the fortress could not be starved out.

The supplies she commanded were too vast. In any case, he didn't have the time. Invar should have arrested her, seizing the place long before this, but now no such option was left to him.

Action of another kind was called for and he had already issued the new decrees. With his troops consumed by the city's defense, crews of ordinary citizens had been pressed into labor. The conscripted workers were now excavating a massive trench, exposing while also flanking the ancient stronghold.

The crafty King Invar planned to breach the naked wall at several points at once, in order to rush the old Crone en masse. Even Sorbus, with all of her abundant abilities, could not resist that approach. At least he didn't think that she could.

It was too bad that he didn't have the baker to once more direct the diggers. That blunt fact stung Invar's royal pride but it could not be helped now, and therefore another had been placed in command of the laborers at the wall. Still, the king was concerned for he had employed his nephew to the task.

The vain royal would be pleased, Invar knew. Once more, he'd be free to give orders left and right. On the other hand, the king knew that he'd have to keep his eye on the young Duke of Fervent.

The king wasn't the only one concerned with the duke.

Pliant, his shaggy beard shaved clean and his thick hair cropped short, was watching him as well. The peasant was hard at work digging in the trench, one of many doing so. As a consequence, he was covered with mud from head to toe.

Somehow this feeble attempt at subterfuge had worked. No one in the trench, or in the city for that matter, had recognized him. He was a good digger too, yet he wasn't giving it his all.

His pace was slowed by his continuous observation of the duke.

The arrogant noble was supervising the ongoing labor as if he knew what he was doing. How smug he was, safe within his lofty station. His attitude was appalling, but his wardrobe still flawless.

Pliant hated Fervent beyond what mere words could convey. The peasant had never known such hate in his life. He never took his eyes off him, scheming all the while.

Any hopes of help from Jarvus were gone. The man had not returned to the mill, and the poor baker had been forced into making other plans. They weren't too elaborate, either.

His Mandate was to protect the girl, and the trench had seemed a decent idea, the better to be close to the action when the wall of the fortress was breached. If he could gain entrance among the first attackers, he stood a good chance of reaching her before they did. Unlike them, he had been inside the structure many times and the floors and corridors it held would not be surprising.

321

But, as he glanced at Fervent strutting about, he thought a better idea would be to kill the young duke first. The digging would continue, the hard-pressed king would see to that. Pliant could still gain entrance later, when the wall waned.

The peasant was armed. He had a bodkin in his boot, and the thought of pushing the sharp blade through that royal heart made him smile. And his chance could come soon, for his shift was near to ending and the insufferable duke was still about.

The baker, after calculating his limited options all day, knew that he might not get a better opportunity.

Replacements began to arrive. Those in the trench exited and lined up for their payment, a small loaf of brown bread. In all likelihood, it was employees from one of Pliant's former bakeries charged with distributing the compensation.

As the muddy peasant stood in line awaiting his bread, the duke started to make his way over. Fervent would pause here and there, while leaning over the trench, imparting orders to the fresh diggers. His back was facing the line of workers.

Closer, closer, thought Pliant, just a little closer.

And the duke did come, shortening the distance with every step.

Pliant's only hope of escape was to run away in the confusion after the deed, but that didn't matter to him. He had to protect the girl and this would go a long way towards that goal. The baker would have preferred to stare the duke in the face as he murdered him, but now he would have to take what he could get.

He bent down and played at adjusting his boot as his prey approached, his hand almost touching the hidden dagger. He was surprised by how calm he was, given that he'd never killed before. Closer, just a little closer, and it would all be over soon.

"Your bread," said a voice that seemed far away, even though it wasn't. It was Pliant's turn to be paid, and the peasant doing so held out the loaf to him. Pliant didn't want to look at the man, for fear of being recognized by a former co-worker from the bakery.

More to the point, the duke's person was almost upon them. He stood, yet issuing his damn orders, just a few feet away. His back made a fine target and Pliant was willing to oblige.

"None for me, thanks" he said, still tugging at his boot, but the man with the bread would not give up.

"Oh, but I think you'll like it, my friend," he persisted, and in such a way that the baker couldn't help but gaze up at him. The deliveryman then stepped in front of Pliant as the duke passed them by. His hand extended the small loaf.

"It's very tasty," he added.

"Thanks so much," said Pliant as he straightened and took his payment. They looked at each other and smiled in recognition. The man with the loaf was the missing Jarvus.

As the two walked off, Pliant began to munch his dinner. The brown bread was indeed very tasty. He was pleased that the bakery still produced a quality product.

"You've found the sewer?" he asked of Jarvus.

The Great One nodded in response.

"It will be an easy thing, too," he answered his partner. "With all the digging at the trench, no one will even notice another hole in the ground. But it will take both of us."

Pliant nodded this time, still chewing.

"Good thing you saw me," he observed.

Jarvus laughed aloud at this comment.

"It took some doing," he replied. "Locating the sewer was an easier job. I hardly recognized you with your new hairdo and all."

Jonus and Morris hardly recognized Spencer, either, although in a physical sense he appeared much the same. It was his personality that had changed, and they didn't trust the stark difference. It seemed too total, a complete turnaround.

The three of them were in a huge campaign tent, embedded in the throng surrounding the walled city of Am-Rif. Spencer had been, and was still trying to sell his cohorts on his big idea. The grunt army stood in position, now just awaiting the permission needed to attack the wall, and it was eager for the action to begin.

Spencer's plan would avoid the need for such proactive orders. Still, all three of them knew that the command would come if he failed to convince the two generals. But he didn't intend to fail.

"What are you saying, Spencer?" asked Morris. "The will of Primus, the Great Mandate and all, that's just worthless now? You don't care anymore, is that what you mean?"

"Yes," said Jonus, "why the sudden change of heart? You were so sure of yourself before. But now, your position's quite the contrary from what you've said in the past."

The time jumper looked to his old friend, Moe. The skepticism on his face was easy to see. He didn't try to hide it.

"I don't like this," he said, with a glum face.

"Look," said Spencer, trying again, "I've told you that I haven't changed my mind about Primus. I never will. That's just not possible for me, after what's passed since the incident."

This was a true statement. Currently, Spencer was immersed in his personally overpowering, newly found faith. It steeled him, and he had never been so sure of anything in his life before.

"It's just that now," he continued his explanation, "after all that we've been through, I see you're both right. Anything that gets us back to square one is permissible, it has to be. We are all here, and there's got to be a reason for that, plus it's forbidden by Primus not to try to get back, you both think that's so."

This line did not sway the two generals, for that premise was their original position, and just stating it didn't explain the diametric change in Spencer's character nor his outlook.

He knew this, too, so he carried on, "I'm not of the Theology Clan, none of us are. I wasn't even religious before the incident. I'm just a normal guy trying to do what's right in a bad situation."

"And we're not?" asked Morris, looking him in the face.

"No," retorted Spencer, at last seeing an opening that might persuade them. "You two are military, trained to fight, trained to win. Any moral factors are thereby of no concern to you."

"Gee, thanks," said Jonus, again looking at Moe. "We're just a couple of godless killers on a rampage. I feel much better now."

Spencer ignored the retort. It didn't move his agenda any. He continued, pressing forward and not giving up.

"What it all comes down to," he said, "are the tactics involved. I didn't want them to be bloody and I didn't want the grunts involved, but the facts are the facts. Both of these are happening now and, if I'm to be true to my God, I have to believe that He's still in charge, no matter how much I wish it otherwise."

The lone researcher looked away, shaking his head in exasperation. He had spent countless hours trying to understand, to comprehend, thinking of all that had happened, and not just what had occurred after the incident, either. No, the man's entire life had been on the table, his failed marriage as well as the dismal professional decisions that he'd made in the past.

The ramifications of all this were boundless, as they would be in anyone's life. There was no way he could ever totally fathom the convoluted content. Trying to do so had only beaten him down.

He had to let it go, the poor man had to have faith.

"I believe in an ordered universe," he said, "and I believe that nothing happens without a reason. I think that Primus Himself has placed us here now, each of us for His own purpose. I can think no less and still keep my faith in Him."

He sighed a big sigh, now resigned.

"My Mandate is to fix the computer sabotage," he said, "that's now my only job. First we must be inside or that will never happen. Your Mandate is to get me there."

This argument also failed to sway the other two.

"I've always known it," Spencer added, "I just didn't like it."

This was also a true statement. The current state of affairs had tortured him as nothing had before. Even now it was distasteful.

"But at this point," he confessed, "I know that my Mandate is not to understand the bigger picture. After thinking it over, I see that I'm just a piece of the overall puzzle, as both of you are. And now I believe that's what Primus Himself wants me to be."

"Well, gee, Spencer," said Morris, openly feigning admiration, "who could argue with that lofty sentiment?"

But Jonus ignored his big friend and instead addressed the point at hand, Spencer's new plan of action.

"It's one thing to shift your position," he said. "It's another to advocate open heresy. And with your normal, holier-than-thou attitude, I'm just skeptical, that's all."

"I told you before," said Spencer, "it's not heresy. It's no different than using the grunts in any other way, it's just a matter of degree. It's a tool that we can employ to achieve our mission and it will save grunt life in the long run, not squander it."

"Look, Spencer," said the giant general. "It's not that I disagree with your plan, per se, it's just that it's a sweeping tactic. Don't get me wrong, I love a fanatic usually, but now I want to know exactly why you don't think this action is heresy."

"It's pretty ambitious, you have to admit," added the time jumper. "And it takes some guts to interpret the Mandate in this way. It actually takes a lot of guts, if you ask me."

He leaned in, resting his elbows on his knees, his palms rubbing back and forth between his fingers. Moe had seen the display often over the years. It was an old habit.

Jonus continued his thrust, "Now, we use the grunts, it's true, but we don't interfere with their core beliefs. That's uncalled for, in my opinion. They have their own gods and for our purpose that's just fine, it's no stumbling block to our strategy."

"Sure," chimed in Morris, agreeing fully with Jonus, "the forest people alone have dozens of them."

"And to fill their heads with forbidden knowledge," said the time jumper, "does seem uncalled for, given it goes totally counter to the Great Mandate. I mean, talk about taking advantage of them. What good could it do at this point?"

He looked Spencer in the eye, silently calling for an explanation. He wanted to understand, he needed to if Spencer's plan had any chance to proceed. He wasn't convinced.

Spencer tried again. He had to. He had no other choice.

"But, if we bring them over," he said, "then they'll just give us the station. We won't have to take it by force of arms. If that happens, then there's no more killing, and everybody's happy."

It all made perfect sense to Spencer. In his eyes, it was a simple thing. Of course, now they were the ones who had to see it.

"The mission goes forward," he said. "We go back and set things right, and that's what we need to do. In the long run, the planet's grunts will never know the difference."

Jonus and Morris considered this. It was their own position after all, and they couldn't deny it. Neither of them wanted carnage and both knew an assault on the city would be bloody.

Sure, it could be done, but at a high cost.

On the other hand, if the empire did just open the gates, then no doubt things would be easier. Little blood would be spilled, too. The question was how to accomplish it.

Morris leaned in next to Jonus, who was still rubbing his palms.

"And you're convinced?" he asked Spencer. "There's no other way it can be done? Without the one god part, I mean."

"Belief in one god will bring them together," said Spencer, "and they'll never come around otherwise. Not all of them would, at any rate. And we'd need all of them, or it wouldn't work."

He started to get excited, in spite of himself. He knew he was right. He also knew it was the right thing to do.

"There's no incentive without it," he added. "It's them against us without the concept, just their gods against someone else's. But give them the idea of one, all-powerful God, and it can happen."

He was close now, and he could feel it. They weren't opposed, just cautious. Closer, he thought, just a little closer.

"If we show them the folly of having multiple gods," he explained, "then they'd join us. Why wouldn't they? Who among them would fight against the one true God?"

Morris leaned back, propping his foot on a stool. The broken bone had long ago mended, but his leg often ached, especially after a long day. As of late, all of his days had been long ones.

"I don't know," he said with a sour tone, "It's not time for the grunts to learn of Primus, and it's not our job to clue them in on that point. It's not our call, at any rate. That revelation should come much later, according to the prophecy."

"I'm not suggesting that," protested Spencer. "And there's no reason to go that far. It's not the knowledge of Primus that we need to use, just the idea of a single, all-powerful God."

"So anyone will do?" asked Jonus. He now leaned back too, considering this aspect. He saw that it might work, but it would take a lot of finesse to successfully accomplish.

"I don't like it either," said Spencer, "but I see there's no other way to avoid a bloodbath. After the mission is over, it won't matter anyway and you both believe that. The original time stream will be replaced and no one's the wiser."

"It would be simpler," said the time jumping general, "no doubting that. And we could always attack later, if it didn't work." He looked to his big friend, admitting the value of the scheme.

"Now the battle is over worldly concerns," he said to Moe. "Our grunts want their world to be the way it was, and the Empire's grunts want it to stay the same, but if we escalate the debate, well, it's always better to have God on your side. People always fight harder when there's a higher purpose involved."

"Ok," conceded the giant, "so we give our grunts the one true God. That's the easy part. They follow us without thinking, but how are we going to convince the Empire's grunts?"

The three sat and considered.

"It would have to be dramatic," said Jonus, "something they couldn't argue with, something very persuasive."

"Amaze them, you mean?" asked Morris.

The time jumper nodded, thinking hard now. Morris was pondering, too. Spencer relaxed at last.

He knew he had won. He also knew that the two generals before him would figure something out. After all, it was evident that they were an amazing pair themselves.

Jarvus and Pliant were pretty amazing as well. At least they thought so. They had dug their hole as planned, and in front of everybody in the castle's courtyard, too.

No one there had asked their purpose or bothered them in any way. Everyone had assumed they were just ordinary workers, employed in some ordinary labor. They even received a daily ration of bread for the loaf bearers had thought they were just citizens pressed into duty like everyone else.

The two had dug all day. In the late afternoon, with a swing of his pick, Jarvus struck through to the ancient septic system. The game was afoot in earnest, no doubting it now.

"It's there?" said Pliant, in amazement. He hadn't been so sure, although he hadn't voiced his concern. At this point, the man had been operating on little more than faith alone.

329

"Oh," answered Jarvus, "I knew it was." He looked up, adding, "I guess we should try to hide the opening so no one will follow us." Pliant concurred, and the two sprung into action.

They stacked some stones and dirt behind a few logs, holding the mass upright by a piece of jagged wood. Once inside the hole, Pliant held up the shorter Jarvus and he reached through and snatched away the piece of wood. The mass then tumbled over and covered the hole, plunging them into darkness.

Pliant struck his flint, lighting the snub of candle that he always carried. They looked to be in a cave of sorts. They were.

"This way," said Jarvus, and the two set off. Both of them were pleased. All in all, it had been an easy thing to accomplish.

They didn't know that it had been too easy.

Another pair was pleased at the time. For them, also, it had been easy. Very much so, they believed.

From the ramparts, the two had watched as the baker and his confederate had dug their deep hole. Yes, they were both satisfied now. The taller of the two spoke first.

"Well, well," said King Invar, leaning against a wooden ballista, "things are progressing, and in timely fashion, to boot."

"Yes, uncle," said the young Duke of Fervent, gesturing with his ornately gloved finger. "The trenchers have almost achieved the wall and now we have a secret gopher hole to use to our advantage." He laughed with gusto at the very thought.

"Patience," stated the old king, stern as ever. "We must have patience." But then he laughed as well, adding, "You see, my nephew, it's always only a matter of time."

It was a matter of time for the Crone also, and she knew it. But Sorbus, full of resolve, was trying not to show her trepidation. She and her daughter sat in the small security office of Station Forecast, their eyes glued to the numerous viewing screens there.

The station was well equipped with all sorts of defensive snooping devices. Motion sensors and cameras and such, all up and running, were blinking warning lights while softly beeping away. Both were bathed in the hardware's glare.

The women were aware of the activity in the trench for the sensors had seen to that, but the Crone was unconcerned. Breaching the station's wall would not guarantee entrance into the fortress itself. This was because the rooms adjacent had been flooded, and after the breakthrough occurred, a strong electrical current could be generated into them with the flip of a switch.

That would give the attackers a shocking welcome. However, the king's diggers were nowhere near the point of attacking yet. The beeping machinery showed that this was the case.

No, the old woman was concerned about something else. Another breach had occurred, and at an unexpected point. It had to be one of her team, she was sure of it.

No one else in the city was aware of the station's ancient septic system. The odds were against such a thing being just a random happenstance. Was it her Jonus, she wondered?

An alarm went off, with its blinking light brighter and its beeping tone louder than those in the background.

Lucid leaned in and scrutinized the controls.

"It's the main lab," she said to her mother.

Moments later, another alarm erupted.

"Your office this time," reported the girl.

Sorbus grunted, saying, "That's where they'd go first, I guess."

She reached over and pushed the appropriate button on the console. Whoever was in her office was locked in now. The heavy doors would hold them, for a while at least.

"Let's go see," she said.

331

The king also wished to see something. Diggers at the trench, and there were none. They had abandoned all labor and run off to flock to the one, all-powerful God, the new god of the enemy.

That made this novel God his enemy, as well. What rubbish anyway, he thought with scorn, an all-powerful god that was everywhere at once yet nowhere to be seen. These grunts believe in anything, he thought with distaste.

Nothing had held them, not warnings nor dictates.

It had started as a trickle only. Once news of God was proclaimed, the workers had begun decreasing, sucked off in small numbers at first. But in the days since, the situation had escalated, growing at a progressive pace until no diggers remained.

The guards had become useless for they ran off as well. The only loyal troops now were the lowest sort of men. These were afraid of going over, for all feared reprisals and revenge for many prior atrocities committed against the enemy.

The king could not rely on the likes of them.

He was once again upon the rampart, looking outward this time. Arrayed before him was a view unlike any that he had ever seen before. Never in all of his long years of battles with standing armies had he ever experienced such a multitude.

It was a vast portrait. There were too many assembled to count, spread before him like a stain. They were a stain.

Footsteps approached from around the corner, a single pair. King Invar quickly placed his regal hand upon his bejeweled dagger. The meeting had been prearranged, a planned encounter, but one never knew and it always paid to be prudent.

His precaution was not needed, however.

The Duke of Fervent arrived. His face was blanched, although his attire was still flawless. But he was now a frightened, demoralized man, his uncle his only protection.

His dreams of becoming king or dickering with the enemy were dashed. Who wanted to be king anyway, with the world turned upside down? He would have left already if there were somewhere to go, but where was he not known?

"It's worse than we thought," he said, wringing his hands, which were covered at the time in soft, calfskin riding gloves.

"Well?" barked the impatient king.

The duke jumped at the sound. His old bravado was long gone. He was a beaten man now, with little to look forward to.

"My Liege," he stated, thus beginning his briefing, "the grunts are planning a display tonight by bonfire to at last demonstrate the almighty power of God." That was the end of his briefing.

The besieged king thought the attempt was piss poor.

Yet, the facts were unchanged no matter their phrasing and Invar knew it. He had to act. He would act.

"The time is nigh," he said, "it's the gopher hole for us."

"Now?" asked his nephew, real fear in his voice.

"Not just yet," the king answered. "The gates will hold them back for a bit, I suppose. And we do have the best view."

His Majesty crossed his arms and sighed.

"Let's watch the show first," he decreed.

Steadfast wanted the best view too. He was a great warrior in his own right, and now he was well known for being one of the most effective commanders in the grunt army. This position assured him a fairly good seat but he wanted better.

He needed to have the best location. He had his own reasons, two of them, in fact. His sons were the centerpieces of the show.

The demonstration was a fake, of course, something dreamed up by the two generals. He knew their new god was also a fake but

333

that didn't bother him. He was happy with his personal deities and a single god held no sway over him.

Steadfast only wanted to hunt and fish, and grow grubs in his forest world again. He missed his old life. All of that would come in time, the caveman hoped, after this war was finally over.

Of late, he had directed the crews that had fashioned the towers. There were three, two of them constructed of stacked logs to the height of twenty feet, about fifty feet from each other. Between them was a third, somewhat taller, also created of stacked logs.

Many large piles of fodder for bonfires had been gathered, great groups of bound sticks and dry straw, only waiting to be lit.

All of this was before the city's wall, placed at a distance and well beyond the range of the now-unmanned catapults.

There were ropes staked out to mark the closest seats, but Steadfast wanted more. He needed vantage. He needed height.

He needed the wall.

He turned and scanned it. There were plenty of protrusions and small openings present, windows, he guessed. Was it enough purchase for him to climb, he wondered?

The Crone and her daughter were wondering something also.

They were approaching the time lab on the station's second level and both were wondering who was behind the oversized doors. Sorbus was armed only with her walking stick, but Lucid had two weapons. She held a pistol in one hand, and a revolver in the other, each at the ready as the pair moved ever closer.

Suddenly, with a crash, the double doors to the lab burst open. A strange-looking peasant was revealed. He stepped into the corridor before he realized the women were there.

"Stop where you are," barked Lucid, currently most serious. Yet the command was unnecessary. The man from the office had frozen in place at the sight of her.

334

He couldn't believe that it was she.

"I feared you were dead," he said, stunned.

The girl recognized the sound of his voice.

"Pliant," she screamed in unexpected joy.

She ran into his arms, hugging him about the neck with the weapons, all but forgotten, now crisscrossing his broad back.

"Well, my son," said Sorbus as she reached the embracing pair, "you look younger without your beard."

Still hugging, he just grinned in response.

"I don't much like the haircut, though," the Crone added.

"Mother," said the relieved Lucid, "his hair will grow."

She then burst out laughing at the comment, as if his hair were important now. Pliant and the old woman shared in her laughter. Soon, however, they stopped for time was ticking by and they certainly had none of it to spare for levity.

Pliant looked to the Crone, his face chagrined.

"Sorry about your doors," he said in a somber tone.

Sorbus shook her head in wonderment. It was good to see him. Still, how had he known to enter through the septic system?

"You're alone?" she asked, looking beyond into the lab.

"Yes," he reported, "but not at first."

"How so?" Sorbus inquired, now leaning on her stick.

"He showed me the way," he said, to Lucid, "and I'd have never gotten inside without him. Yet, I was excited for I knew the building. I told him to follow and then I ran off in search of you."

She beamed at this.

The peasant continued, "After a bit, I turned and he was gone, just gone." He then looked to the Crone and added, "A most interesting fellow. He said his name was J."

335

"Ah, Jarvus," said the Crone, "yes, I thought it might be he. And he's still in the station? That's interesting."

She moved towards her office, tapping her stick as she went.

"I wonder where he is now," the old woman mused, "but even more, I wonder what he's up to."

The king and the duke were wondering what the grunts were up to. Both still stood at the rampart, each looking down, but the scene there had changed. Now the masses were tightly crammed around the three towers, with all the bonfires lit.

The blazing piles illuminated the scene as if in a dream. Scores of drums were pounding, relentless in tempo, and as the sound of them drifted to the wall, it enveloped the two nobles. The Duke of Fervent was spellbound, as were the rest of the grunts below, but King Invar watched without emotion.

Then the king leaned forward, scrutinizing.

"Look there," he said, pointing, "at the tower on the right."

The duke looked. He saw only shadows within the well of the structure. Nothing there seemed out of the ordinary.

"I see naught, uncle," he said.

"I saw something moving," the king replied, "a shifting below the lip of the deck." They both stared intently, but saw no further disturbance. "Someone's there, I'm sure of it," Invar insisted, "hidden below the short wall on the edifice."

Someone was indeed atop the tower and had been for most of the day, stretched out on the concealed floor. However, the frenzied grunts packing the area were unaware of his presence. But all of them would see him soon enough.

The drumming stopped, announcing to the crowd that the ceremony was imminent. It started with a small procession leading from the tent of the two generals. Jonus would have preferred to walk the distance the better to whip up the multitude, but Moe's leg still bothered him so they rode instead.

They sat in a peasant cart and were pulled along by a matching pair of war-horses being led by a single man, a warrior from the forest tribes. The silent throng was awed. It parted before them, melting away in respect for the two generals and their new god.

On the wall, the king said, "So, that's where my best steeds went." He shook his royal head. "Pity," he added.

The cart stopped abreast the middle tower, the tallest of the three. When Morris and Jonus stood to step down, the grunts went wild. A huge roar erupted, piercing the air.

Everyone present began to jump about while waving their arms and screeching. Then, seeing those around them shouting, all in the crowd howled the louder. It did not let up.

With a look, Jonus asked Moe to lean closer, and he did.

The time jumper screamed, "I guess that riding over was a good idea." The giant barely heard him for all the noise but he nodded. The two then stepped to the ground, the grunts still cheering.

They climbed the tower, followed by the warrior who had led the cart. Many recognized him as the generals' runner, the young caveman that rode the huge war-horse. Because he was a twin, and because both used matching steeds, the same ones hitched to the cart, few in the masses knew that there were two brothers.

Of late, they had never been seen together except when inside a general's tent, and so most of the assembly assumed that there was only one runner. That's what the generals hoped, anyway. At last, they reached the top of the tower, the cacophony unabated.

Morris stepped forward and raised his huge arms. As if on cue, the crowd fell silent and the resulting diametric change in decibels was striking, compelling. The grunts to a person were riveted, not wishing to miss any part of the miracle to come.

"There are no gods," Morris bellowed, "only God."

337

Jonus stepped forward and raised his arms.

"He is everywhere," he shouted to the enraptured crowd, "all powerful and all knowing."

"God can do anything," added Morris, his voice booming.

At the foot of the tower, Spencer gave a signal to the drummers. They began to pound a beat, very softly at first, but ever increasing in volume. Spencer's hair stood on end for this was big, with implications that none could foresee.

It was Jonus' turn to speak, broadcast in his loudest voice.

"God has no need to prove Himself to us," he screamed.

"But He will," the crowd next heard Morris. "He will give you a sign. A miracle to comfort you, that you may believe in Him."

Timid, the twin that was on the tower with the two generals, first turned to the multitude, showing himself with arms raised, and then he dashed down the steps. Spencer smiled at him as he ran past. The drums were loud now, and growing louder.

The young caveman then raced up the pillar to the left.

Both of the shorter structures, the ones on either side of the middle tower, bore wooden scaffolding with ropes attached. When Timid reached the top, he found a short ledge at the level of his knees, surrounding him as he stood below the rigging. The over-anxious crowd could see him though and, all present, being eager for the coming spectacle, wondered what was about to happen.

At the wall, the king muttered, "Well, I'll be damned."

The young duke was near shaking in his high-top leather boots.

"What is it, My Liege?" he asked, almost breathless.

The king shook his head in bemused disbelief.

"This should be good," was his whispered answer.

At Spencer's signal, the drums again stopped, but they started up once more as soon as the two generals stooped down. Each picked up an axe and then holding them aloft, both slowly displayed his weapon to the multitude. Then they walked to opposite sides of the pillar, the drums pounding at full volume.

A circular curtain was hidden beneath the ledges on the two outside towers, connected to ropes on the scaffolding above. These lines passed laterally across the distance between the structures and were run through a loop at either side of the center column. They ran down from there, to a team of pullers on the ground, already holding on, just awaiting their cue.

Morris and Jonus stood by the loops, each with his axe.

At Spencer's signal, the pullers pulled. The curtains on both towers began to rise, concealing Timid as he stood on the left one. At the same instant, on the right tower, Steadfast's other twin, Tempest, began to stand behind his curtain.

The two were dressed identically, but it was Timid who had to be fast. Timing was crucial. The drums were at fever pitch.

As soon as the slowly rising curtain concealed him from the crowd, Timid fell to the floor, hidden below the ledge as his brother had been all day on the opposite tower.

From the rampart it was an amazing sight. Although it was a trick, it was still amazing for it was pulled off with perfection. Seeing that it was an illusion actually rendered it more impressive, although unlike the mob, the two there were not moved.

Just after the circular curtain hid Timid and he had fallen to the deck, Spencer again signaled the drummers. Once more the pounding drums abruptly ceased, and only a millisecond before the generals' axes struck home. All easily heard the resulting, sharp retorts as the weapons bit through the ropes and deeply embedded themselves into the wooden planking beneath.

Both curtains had risen slowly but they fell quickly for numerous, heavy stones had been sewn into their upper hems to give them weight. So when the ropes were cut, they dropped like a shot. Timid had disappeared but Tempest was revealed.

It seemed to the crowd that the young warrior on the left tower had been transported in an instant to the tower on the right over fifty feet away. The impossible had happened! The miracle had indeed occurred, and before their very eyes.

The grunt horde was completely stunned at first but, in short order, it became jubilant. Once more, pandemonium broke. The resulting noise was deafening, louder than before.

From above, the king observed all.

"That's it," he said. "Let's get going. It won't be long now."

The duke was aghast, but powerless to disagree. The two nobles turned to leave. It was then that they spied Steadfast.

He had indeed climbed the wall for a better vantage, and he had enjoyed the show. He would enjoy this too. He drew his knife.

The king and the duke stood their ground. Invar also pulled out his blade. Fervent just pissed his pants.

On the center tower, the two generals met, both surveying the frenzied multitude. The old friends had pulled it off, that much was evident. The miracle had been accomplished, the grunt horde converted, and at last, the station was within their grasp.

"Well," said Jonus, "they sure have God on their side now."

"Yes," the giant agreed, "but which one?"

CHAPTER ELEVEN
THE FINAL STAGE

The gates did hold, but just for a bit as the king had predicted.

The empire's remaining soldiers were nowhere to be seen, having fled their posts in terror. All had shed their distinctive uniforms, and once the city was invested, they planned to mingle unnoticed with the masses. It was their only hope of survival.

With no opposition, the grunts had little real trouble at the wall. The locked gates were broken open in short order. The grunt army then swept from all sides into the liberated city.

The generals weren't so sure about the station. It was not designed to rebuff a siege, but it was substantial and well constructed. Breaching its defenses might be more difficult than the walls, but gaining access there proved easy also.

The Crone had unlocked the doors.

The multitude was unconcerned with the fortress. The walled city itself was what mattered to them. All were busy sacking the place, lost in the euphoria of a bloodless victory.

The team members found the underground stairway in the castle courtyard, just where their many spies had said it would be. Jargon was placed in charge of a detachment of trusted warriors to stand guard at the entrance for no interruptions were wanted. Then Morris, Jonus and Spencer at last walked into Point Zero.

As the three advanced to the second set of oversized, metal doors, they were taken aback to see them both fly open. More surprising yet, they were met there by a beautiful young woman. However, she was not surprised by their arrival.

"Good day to you, sirs," she announced in a sweet voice. She then gave them a nod of her comely head and added, "We've been expecting you. Please come in."

"Who's we?" asked Morris as he scanned the corridor. He saw no one. There was no one there to see.

"I shall answer your questions, good gentlemen," said Lucid, "but to business first." She then shooed them away, as if they were mere children in her charge and after, relocked the doors using the Crone's key. Next the girl turned back to them and smiled again, all while placing the key into her apron.

Yet, when she withdrew her hand, the men were shocked anew. None of them had expected this. Lucid held a large pistol and she looked as if she knew how to use it.

"More business?" asked the time jumper.

"I'm afraid so, yes," she said. "I must be sure, you understand. Your identification tags, if you please."

Jonus and Morris relaxed.

"Standard procedure," the giant said to Spencer. Spencer nodded and relaxed some himself. Then they bared their necks to the girl and revealed the ruby-colored devices that hung there.

With a sure hand, Lucid twirled the pistol and offered the butt to Morris. He was surprised but gladly accepted the weapon. A long time had passed since he'd handled one.

"Perhaps you will remember this, Commander," she said. "I retrieved it from your office desk, but had to breach the lock first. I'm afraid I had no key, you understand."

They all laughed a bit at this report. The proverbial ice had been broken. They began to walk.

"There are three of us," Lucid began her briefing. "Myself, my betrothed, and my mother. It is she who commands the fortress."

"Your mother?" asked Jonus. The import of the question was not lost on the other men. Had Rosemary had a child?

Lucid understood their confusion, although she was unaware of the relationship involving Sorbus and the time jumper.

"I'm adopted," she said in explanation. There was no shame in her comment. In fact, she was proud.

They boarded the service elevator, after which Lucid punched the appropriate button, sending them on their way.

"There are others about," she continued to brief them. "Your brother," she said to Jonus, "came in with my Pliant, but he has since hidden himself. We don't know where."

"J's here," asked the time jumper, stunned, "in the station?"

"Yes," she replied. "But there are two more also, in before we knew it. Where they are is a mystery as well."

By now, the newcomers wanted a decent briefing, including all the stupefying facts, and soon enough they were going to get one. The elevator stopped and they exited, heading towards the Crone's office. The surprises were not over yet.

Meanwhile, a surprising turn also awaited the king and the duke. They were on the fourth level of the fortress, the so-called housekeeping floor, traversing a corridor filled with supply cabinets. Each was in actuality a small room, a closet of sorts, filled with the everyday necessities needed to run the station.

The king seemed to know where he was going. He scrutinized each numbered door as they passed, but the young duke, numbed by recent events, was undeniably lost. His well-ordered world had vanished, just crumbled away before his eyes, and, as such, his vaulted position in that world was now gone too.

Worse, his current lot was reduced to nothing more than following, as a blind man would, in the old king's wake. He didn't like it but it was all that was left to him. He had no other options.

"Are you sure it's here, uncle?" he asked, tentatively, and not wanting a negative answer. He needn't have worried. The king always knew what he was doing and, if his objective was achievable, he brooked no delay in getting it.

"It's here," said Invar, "but it's been so long, so very long."

He spoke no more, as if that settled the matter. He walked off, looking at the numerous doors in the corridor, remembering. It would come to him in time, he knew.

This response was mystifying to Fervent. It was plain that his uncle had knowledge of the fortress, hence their presence, but how had he first-hand information? The fortress itself had been only exposed of late, and its secrets remained well guarded.

"You've been here before?" asked Fervent, agog."

The old king was past being tired of his royal tagalong, tired of his whining, his incessant questions. Invar would have gotten rid of him already save he might yet prove useful. The caveman warrior on the ramparts was a good example.

He had bolted towards the king first, ignoring the frightened duke, for with a glance he had correctly surmised the situation. The young pisser was no immediate threat while the second beast was armed and clearly determined. But in the heat of the moment, Steadfast had made a fatal miscalculation.

The king had used the duke as a shield at the last second, tossing him into the lunging man. Steadfast, seasoned fighter as he was, had tripped and gone down, thus entangling himself with the screaming royal. He knew it was the end but he would die happy.

The caveman had lived a good life, had grown good grubs, and raised good sons. He had seen many wondrous things in his span, and had lived through many strange adventures. And now he would die in the hunt, not in his sleep like some toothless elder.

The king had not hesitated, but plunged his dagger deeply into his opponent's back, then retracted it and moved on. He had left his nephew to extricate himself as best he could. And who knew if some similar necessity might not arise again?

Therefore, the harried king allotted the time needed, although now there was little of it to waste. Invar, to engender calm, stopped and placed his majestic hand on Fervent's shoulder. The fabric there was soft and felt rich to his touch.

"All is not lost, nephew," he said, lecturing in his best regal tone. "In fact, things are progressing on schedule, appearances notwithstanding. Don't bother yourself with the details."

His eyes bore not malice but tenderness and the duke realized for the first time that they were of a slightly different color.

"We are far from being finished," firmly decreed the king, with a sweep of his hand. "I intend to leave you a vigorous empire, my sweet boy. One with no boundaries or unvanquished enemies, one that is worthy of our glorious royal lineage."

The duke's eyes pooled with tears.

What rot, thought the king, and how easy to accomplish. He hadn't even addressed Fervent's earlier concern regarding the fortress. What a moron he was, yet what could one do?

"We must find arms," Invar said, moving on. "They're here, stored away, but I can't remember the number. Ah, what's this?"

The king stopped. Fervent looked. The corridor was lined with doors on both sides but only one door stood at its termination.

"Yes," said Invar. "The end of the hall. How foolish of me."

He quickly made his way over and reached for the knob. The door was unlocked. He pushed it open and then entered, with the duke following closely behind him.

It was a linen closet, with shelves on three sides containing sheets and such. The now-impatient king lost no time. He began to rifle the bedclothes searching for weapons.

There was a closing sound, and Fervent turned in response.

He saw a man who had been hiding behind the door. The peasant held a piece of dull metal in his hand, pointing it at the newcomers. He was smiling, satisfied, but his hand was shaking.

"Uncle?" Fervent said. The young duke stood arrested, frozen in place. The king, still searching, paused and turned.

345

"Well, Commander," said Jarvus, "it's been too long. And what a nice outfit you've gained in the interim." He tightened his grip on the pistol he held, trying but failing to stifle his trembling.

"Do you want my briefing now," he asked, "you know the one, my report on Dr. Hall's assignment? That was my mission, was it not, the reason you sent me out with him? Just keep an eye open and check in, that's what you said."

The hand that held the pistol began jerking about, almost as if it had a mind of it own. Jarvus' voice began to strain. After all these years, he was having a hard time controlling himself.

"Or has the order of the day been changed of late?" he nonetheless asked with the sarcasm hanging heavy. "Command is a joy after all, is it not? Perhaps, just perhaps, it's changed because the planet's since blown up in your face?"

"My boy," said the king, who was, in fact, Commander Longley, the absent Commandant of Station Forecast, "put down your weapon, we're on the same side here." He looked to the baffled duke as if in confirmation, and then he grabbed him and tossed him into the unsuspecting Jarvus. The pistol fired.

No one else heard the shot for at the time the other team members were receiving their own briefing, two floors below in the Crone's office, with Lucid and Pliant standing guard in the hall.

Both well armed, these two were stationed just off the main time lab. They could see the newcomers through the glass wall at the rear of the room but, despite the broken office door, they couldn't hear them. All inside were talking in low tones, seated in the old wooden chairs before the Crone's massive desk.

Rosemary was explaining her transformation, but Jonus didn't need to hear. He was the resident expert after all, and upon seeing her condition, the time jumper had deduced the cause. He held her gnarled hand as she told her story to the other two.

Both Morris and Spencer had known her in the past. As best friend to Jonus, Morris had known her for years but neither he nor

Spencer could fathom the reason for her metamorphosis into the Crone. They wanted some hard facts.

"When we were in the containment room," she was saying, "the countdown to the event came without anything happening."

"Yes, I remember," said Morris, who had been there. "You left to see why. I've often wondered what went askew."

The old Crone nodded, calmly recalling the incident. Her distorted eyes were watery and sad. Spencer didn't know if this was bitter nostalgia or a byproduct of who she was now.

"I then crossed over to check the equipment," she continued her narration, "that we had retrofitted outside of the unit in order to make adequate space within the containment room."

"There were four of us," explained Jonus to Spencer, who nodded. As Chief Engineer, he knew very well the cramped nature of the room. But he and Morris still didn't understand what had gone wrong or what had caused Rosemary's alteration.

"When I looked to the instruments," she said, "I saw what had happened but it was far too late to intervene."

Here she sighed and Jonus squeezed her hand for reassurance. She looked up and their eyes met. Both knew her condition was not permanent and that she could be restored.

They knew, in the end, it would work itself out and at long last they would have their life together. However, the hardware had to be up and running first. Just a little more time was needed.

"Our preparations were flawed," said Jonus, taking over the briefing. That belated knowledge was a bitter pill for him to swallow. In retrospect it had been a giant blunder with the consequences that followed being both dire and far-reaching.

"We failed to realize," he said in a strained voice, "something that was bound to occur as the event drew closer."

"The time line itself slowed down," confessed Rosemary, "as the moment neared. We should have known that this would happen. It does follow the basic theory, after all."

"I don't understand," Morris said to her. He wanted to understand for she was a good friend and Jonus was as close as the brother he never had. Then the giant noticed the rose-shaped pin that the Crone always wore on her peasant wimple.

He was with Jonus the very day it had been selected. It now seemed like a million years ago. Perhaps it had been.

"You still have that thing?" he said, pointing.

Without looking, the bony fingers of her free hand sought out the silver piece. The movement was instinctual. She had performed it innumerable times through the centuries.

In answer, she only smiled, but she did squeeze the hand of the time jumper to let him know that she still treasured the memento.

"The explosion of time happened," explained Jonus, his tone now professional, more matter-of-fact, "but later than predicted."

"I would be unchanged," added Rosemary, "if I had stayed put a few seconds more. The Elastic Limit was exceeded as theorized but sad to say, it occurred after we had envisioned it would. It's a natural phenomenon but we failed to account for it."

"And you were outside containment," said Spencer, who now understood. "Your brain waves were sent like theirs," and here he indicated Jonus and Morris, "but, unlike them, you were unprotected. So you were pulled within the time stream without the normal failsafe, the built in system safeguard."

They paused then, each considering the deep implication. This was heavy stuff. All of their lives had been affected by the event but her duty had been bought at a higher cost.

"There is an upside," added Jonus. "The situation can be reversed. We know how it's to be done, we just need to do it."

"How?" asked Morris, eager for some good news.

"It's simple," Jonus told him. "We just replicate the process, like we planned all along. Things go back to normal then."

"But we need the computer up and running," said Spencer.

"And it still takes six brain wave patterns," added Rosemary, "to duplicate the procedure. There were three pairs sent and all six have to go back. There's just no other way."

"Longley," said Morris, in a glum but resigned tone.

"And J," the time jumper chimed in.

The giant glanced at his oldest friend.

"Jonus," he said, "I love you more than you know but I must be true to my clan here. I'm a military man through and through and there's only one way this thing adds up. I have to let the chips fall where they may, no matter how it pains me."

He then looked to each of them in turn.

"Longley's the spy," said the new Commandant of Station Forecast. "He's got to be. He's the one that's caused everything."

"I know, Moe," said Jonus, still holding Rosemary's bony hand. He looked her in the face, but he kept talking to his big friend. He hoped the unspoken point was not true.

"I know you believe Jarvus might be one, too," he said. "I don't blame you. But I don't think that's so."

"We need them both," said Spencer, stating the obvious. He could be forgiven for this. The missing men were his personal key to getting back to his own true love, as well as the only viable solution to righting the planet's staggering problems.

Spencer's mind then flew in a different direction. The man never stopped thinking. It wasn't in his nature.

"I wonder," the engineer asked, "do you think our esteemed Commandant is a heretic as well as a traitor?"

"From where I sit, that doesn't much matter to the bigger picture," grunted Morris, but Spencer replied, "It might."

"Longley's insane," stated Rosemary, as a fact. "I've known it for some time. He thinks he's a real royal, a great king."

She shook her head and added, "Sad."

"He's dangerous," said Jonus. "But we need him alive. J, too."

"Medical supplies?" Morris asked Rosemary. "We need some help here. We got a dart gun or something?"

She nodded. She had the answer. She always did.

"We are prepared for any contingency," she related. "Everything that you need is under lock and key, stored in the armory on level four, beyond the supply closets. Both Lucid and Pliant withdrew their weapons from there yesterday."

"That's it then," said Morris, without a bit of hesitation. "We need that dart gun." For emphasis, he slapped his service issue pistol, now in his combat holster on his hip.

"You should all draw arms as well," he advised, "but don't shoot anybody who's not expendable. Those two understand?" He pointed to Lucid and Pliant in the hallway.

"Oh, yes," replied the Crone, "she's told him the story many times by now. They know just what to do and what not to do. They're both good people, don't worry about that."

"Just where on level four is the armory located?" asked Jonus.

The old woman replied, "It's on the opposite side from the closets, on the eastern corner of the floor. The cabinet itself is reinforced and there's a locked gate around it. Take a left off the main elevator and you can't miss it."

"We need a team," said Morris, "to retrieve the goods. Then I'd like to reconnoiter the upper floors, one by one. We'll find them, it'll just be a matter of time and effort."

"That's three teams, then," said Spencer, "one to retrieve the required guns and one to search for the missing men plus the one that stays here to work on the reactor sabotage."

Morris smiled in spite of himself. Things had changed. Spencer was learning, but he wasn't a soldier quite yet.

"Well-laid plans take some time," he observed.

He then issued his commands, the new order of the day.

Jonus and Pliant were sent to retrieve the stockpiled weapons on the housekeeping floor, two stories above.

Spencer and Rosemary worked on the reactor's errant computer program. They sat at either side of a large double desk in the main time lab, shuffling printouts between them. They were engrossed and more than happy to be busy.

Lucid stood watch over the lab itself while Morris swept the area, guarding the stairwells against unwanted entry to the level.

He, Jonus, and Pliant would later check the upper floors, once they were armed with the non-lethal weapons. The missing men had to be found or all was lost. And they weren't that far away.

The pistol shot in the linen closet had killed only a stack of pillowcases. The gun discharged when it slipped away from Jarvus, having been knocked out of his hand by the force of the collision with the propelled duke. Longley, after tossing poor Fervent into the fray, had scrambled after the dropped firearm.

At the same time, Jarvus had scampered out of the door. He hadn't thought ahead and had no back-up plan. He just ran down the hall as fast as he could and slipped into another supply closet.

He began to pick at his lip as he cursed his failed attempt to rid Point Zero of its spy. True, in the past he had been in collusion with the now-mad Commandant, for Longley had recruited him before the incident had occurred, but at the time Jarvus had thought it was only station politics at play. What a crock.

For some unknown reason, the stiff Commander hadn't trusted Dr. Hall. He had wanted an inside source to keep an eye on him, an unofficial channel of communication, that's what he had said. But now, after piecing it all together, Jarvus knew better.

In retrospect, he realized that Longley had just used him. He had caused everything that had happened since too. Jarvus' troubles, as well the planet's problems, were all his doing and he hated the Commandant as a consequence.

Why had he dropped the gun? Why hadn't he retrieved more? He had hidden many there long ago, at Longley's personal order, but like a fool, he'd only taken one.

He had surmised Longley would head to the closet to retrieve them and he had been correct, but now he had lost his best chance to kill the man. Jarvus needed another weapon. That meant a visit to the armory, but first he would have to wait for the Commandant and his well-dressed friend to vacate the area.

He did wait, picking at his lip all the while, for more than an hour. Several times he thought he heard noises in the corridor, low mumblings and footsteps of someone moving about, but they had always died down without incident. At last, he decided it was safe enough for a quick peek outside but he didn't get his chance.

Gunshots rang out from down the hall. These were answered by closer discharges while excited shouts were being exchanged. Jarvus hunkered down in the corner and waited.

In the hall, Morris was returning fire while squatting behind a reception desk he'd overturned. He wasn't trying to hit anyone, just cover the retreat of Jonus and Pliant. They had already swept the lower floors, but had come under attack upon reaching this level.

At least now they knew where the missing men were.

It was lucky that Jonus and Pliant had succeeded in reaching, without incident, the heavily protected munitions store, but it was some distance from the closets, and their mission indeed had been accomplished. The team was now armed with both knockout darts as well as lead. Morris was using lead.

With his leg, he wasn't running anywhere, but he knew that Jonus would circle around soon enough. He would come through the ceiling in all probability for the far hall cabinet ended at the wall of the building thereby denying him a flanking maneuver. That's what he would do anyway if their situations were reversed.

In the meantime, he needed better cover so as he squeezed off some shots, he scanned for options. There weren't many so he took what he could get. As he emptied his pistol, he hurled himself across the hall and against the door of Jarvus' closet hideout.

It burst open with splinters flying. Both men were surprised to see the other one there. Neither had expected this turn of events.

"Well J," said Morris, as he retracted his spent pistol clip, "it's been a while. Quite a while, I'd say. Wouldn't you agree?"

Jarvus didn't answer. He had known Morris a long time and he knew that his demeanor could be misleading. Under the present circumstances, he wasn't going to rock the boat.

The big military man seemed unfazed, almost calm. He slammed home a clip and charged the weapon by pulling back the bolt. Sharp, metallic sounds of clicking and popping filled the air.

"Fancy meeting you here," was his bland comment.

He took a quick look out past the broken doorjamb, scanning the hallway. More shots followed this action. The game was on.

"Jonus will be glad to see you," Morris added with a grin. Then he asked, "Why aren't you down the hall with Longley? Shouldn't you two be devising some secret plan?"

"I'm no spy," spat Jarvus, compelled to answer the implication. He was trying to remain calm. He wasn't succeeding.

"I'm no heretic, either," he added.

Morris, without looking, stuck his weapon out and popped off a few rounds. He was enjoying himself. It had been a while.

"Just keeping him occupied," he explained.

"There's two of them holed up down there," said Jarvus, "he's got a grunt from the city for his new assistant."

"Is that so?" asked Morris. He fired again, still not looking. Now the big man was having some fun.

"Well, it doesn't matter," he observed. "Jonus is closing in." At the second mention of his brother, Jarvus bristled.

"Damn him," he said, before he realized it.

Morris had seen this animosity many times in the past. The two brothers were always at each other's throats. It was becoming boring, a stale retelling of the same old story.

Morris knew the gist, of course, but not the particulars.

"So, what's the big deal with you guys?" he asked.

The brothers had a long history, as any siblings would, but since their parents were killed, it hadn't been a good one. More like strained, pained, and pitiful. Jonus was obsessed and Jarvus was fed up, and Morris wanted to know why.

"Want to talk about it?" he asked in casual tone.

"Right," said Jarvus, "like that's gonna happen."

Morris, given the present circumstances, pressed the point.

He emptied his clip out the door, ejected it, and then reloaded. He used one of the thirty spares that he was packing. His movements were fluid and graceful, accomplished without thinking, a professional talent of long standing.

"I mean it," he said. "I've known you all your life, and where else are we going? You got other plans?"

Again he blasted a few rounds down the hallway.

"Are you afraid I'd talk to Jonus?" he asked. "Well, he doesn't tell me any more than you do. What a pair you two make."

Jarvus exploded in spite of his intentions.

From his tortured viewpoint, the situation with his brother had been festering for a thousand years, yet in all that time, he had never verbalized his feelings. It was too hurtful and to whom would

354

he have talked it over with anyway? He'd thought about it sure, but never before discussed it with anyone.

Still, Morris had known him all his life, his real life, that is. And he knew Jonus well. He had known their parents also.

It was too much. The dam burst. Jarvus, without knowing why, began to open up and tell his side of the bitter story.

"Why won't he just leave me alone?" was the first thing he screamed. "I have a hard enough time living with myself as it is. Each time he turns up, he just reminds me of the whole thing."

Heavy anger at his brother, but Morris knew there was more to it than that. There had to be more. Most siblings fought at some point but these two hated each other.

"I know they were his parents, too," added Jarvus, "but our situations are different and I can't stand the reminder, OK? But still he shows up, he always shows up. It hurts more each time."

Morris scanned the hallway with a quick nod of his big head and saw nobody. Interesting. They had retreated.

He shifted his frame and sat just inside the far end of the busted doorjamb. This gave him an easy view down the hallway with just a small tilting movement. He stayed on track, however.

"It hurts him, too," he said. "Losing your folks isn't easy, and not in the way yours died." He worked as he spoke, pulling out and making neat piles of pistol clips within easy reach on the floor.

"That's what I mean," Jarvus screamed again, "it's the whole point. Jonus loved them and I took them away. And the sight of him always brings the whole thing rushing back."

Morris didn't understand this response.

"How did you take them away?" he asked. "That doesn't make sense. The fire was an accident, that's the official version."

This was the heart of the matter, the terrible fire. Jarvus was no longer irate. He was introspective and still grieving.

355

Could he even say it, he wondered? After all the years that he had spent running from the fact, could he even form the words? Somehow he was compelled, unable to stop, in spite of himself.

"But I killed them," he choked, his eyes pooling. "I started the fire." Then he cried in earnest.

This was a new one for Morris. The account he'd heard was quite different. Could there be another explanation?

After a brief glance down the hall, the big man asked Jarvus, "How do you figure that?"

Jarvus became calm, no longer weeping but with his cheeks still wet with tears. His eyes were fixed, but staring off at nothing in particular. He took a deep breath, as if in resignation.

"I was in my rebellious period," he said in a voice just over a whisper. "My parents and I had a fight, and I'd gone to my room to listen to music. Mom had forbidden me to burn candles there because I always forgot to blow them out but I was so mad at them that I went down, holed up and lit a bunch."

He shook his head, speaking without thinking, as if in a dream.

"I fell asleep," he recalled, "and the next thing I knew, Jonus was pulling me out past the flames. You know how fast the place went up. Now they're both gone, dead, and it's all my fault."

Morris laughed, which jerked Jarvus out of his daze. His wet eyes were flashing mad. Morris, now knowing the truth, couldn't have cared less and met his stare head-on.

"You didn't start the fire," he said. "Jonus did. It was an accident but he caused it, he's told me so."

"What do you mean?" asked the unbelieving Jarvus. When Morris once more paused to scan the hall, Jarvus asked again, "Tell me what you mean, Moe. What?"

"We were out drinking," recalled the Commander. "Jonus, Rosemary, me, and what's her name, the one I was dating then. We had just graduated the academy, our careers only starting."

He shook his head, chasing away the nostalgia.

"Jonus and Rose were soon to be married," he continued, "at least that was the plan. We drank a lot that night, and Jonus was never one to drink a lot so he was trashed. So, I first drove each girl home, and then I dropped Jonus off at your parents' house."

Morris had finished making his piles of clips on the floor. He holstered his pistol and pulled out the dart gun. He checked its load but continued his narration without much of a pause.

"Jonus told me later," the giant reported, "that he had been hungry. Besides, he said his head was spinning, and he thought that food would help him. He said he put something on the kitchen stove to warm up and then went into your room."

"My room?" asked Jarvus. He was all attention now. Morris saw that this was so, for Jarvus was pulling at his lip.

"He said he threw a blanket over you," the big man replied.

Then he leaned in to Jarvus for emphasis. He didn't want to overplay the following point but this was important. More so, it was the linchpin, he now realized.

"Jonus said," Morris explained, "he blew out your candles."

Jarvus was thinking now, trying to remember.

He did have a blanket with him that night after his brother had drug him out of the stunning inferno. He had wrapped himself in it while watching the raging fire that soon completely consumed the house. And Jonus had smelled strongly of drink, too.

"Well," continued Morris, "Jonus went into the living room and passed out on the couch, completely forgetting the stuff on the stove. He woke up later and the place was on fire. He couldn't get upstairs to your parents but he could get to you."

Ever the true friend, Morris remembered this part well.

"He was devastated," the giant said. "He felt that he had to go on for you. He had to make it up to you, at least he had to try."

357

Jarvus was stupefied by this astounding news. This changed everything! Of course, Jonus would have felt guilty and Jarvus knew just how heavy that guilt could be.

No wonder his brother had never given up. No wonder he was so driven. Jonus had wanted to compensate for the horrible loss that he had caused the both of them.

"I understand now," said Jarvus quietly.

"I hope so," replied Morris. "And I hope you understand this, too." Then he shot the Great One with a medicated dart.

Down the hall in the linen closet, Longley was calm. The fact that he was insane helped his attitude. There was no way, he thought, that he would not win this contest.

"Just take it," he said to Fervent. "You may need it, my boy." The Commandant was holding out a revolver but the royal wanted none of it, not the gun and not the situation.

"But uncle," the duke said, "I am unlearned in such arts."

"No matter," said Longley, who wasn't, in truth, his uncle, "it's a simple thing, there's nothing to it. You just squeeze it like you do one of your wenches, eh?" He then thrust the handgun behind Fervent's wide, perfectly tooled leather belt.

"But how can we win?" Fervent asked. "How is it possible? Our enemies are more numerous and possess the same weaponry."

"Because they fear to kill me," decreed his sovereign. "You see, they plan to use my regal person to their devious ends, but I shall outsmart them." He laughed at the thought.

This was too much for the distressed duke. He knew that such a strategy was doomed to failure, but he had no other viable option left. He contemplated falling to his knees and begging, but Fervent knew he had no different course for which to beg.

The mad king would not be held back.

Longley threw open the closet door without visible fear, but just the same he had taken some prudent precautions. His medieval garb was now bristling, loaded down with every weapon that he could possibly carry. His rich tunic was crisscrossed with bandoleers of bullets, with numerous holsters cradling side arms, and spare ammo clips everywhere that were crammed alongside.

However, the demented man was not holding a mere handgun in his grip, but a loaded assault rifle set on full auto mode, and he looked as if he knew how to use it.

They found the hallway a shambles. Bullet holes were everywhere, with chunks of wall and pieces of splintered doors and jambs littering the floor. Even the ceiling tiles were ripped apart in places for Morris had fired blindly down the hall.

The waiting giant heard them coming, gingerly stepping over the debris. He held the loaded dart gun at the ready. Closer, closer, he was thinking, just a little closer and it would all be over.

At that moment, the floor above the linen closet exploded.

Longley fired his weapon while turning, peppering the corridor with fresh holes as he made his arching swing. The noise was deafening. The startled duke screamed and, holding up his empty hands, ran down the hall, a little mad himself.

Morris let him go. He could be dealt with later. Other game was afoot and he wasn't going to let it pass.

The king expended his rifle's clip in short order. He threw it on the littered floor and pulled a sidearm, laughing away. They thought they had him, but they were wrong.

He fired into the lock of the nearest door and then jerked it open. A wall of water knocked him over and came rushing down the hall. The Crone's defensive measures had worked after all.

Morris, who was now standing thigh deep in water, saw Longley float past, a stunned look on his face. The mad monarch was spitting and puffing, valiantly struggling but failing to right himself. His heavy gear prevented him from doing so.

Morris sloshed past the doorway, observing the scene.

359

"Sir," he said, "consider yourself relieved." He then shot Longley with the dart gun. "Mission accomplished," he added.

It was the most fun he'd had all day.

With a splash, Jonus dropped through the blown-apart ceiling of the linen closet. He made his way up the hall as Pliant jumped down also. The water was receding, but it was slow going.

"Good job, Moe," said Jonus. "You did it. Sorry I was late." Morris was elated but calm under the circumstances.

"You ain't seen nothing yet," he said with a toothy grin.

He pointed and Jonus looked. Inside the room, he saw his brother sprawled atop a wooden desk. What relief!

He glanced back to his big friend who was still smiling at him. Gratitude was written all over the time jumper's face. By this time, Pliant stood beside them, a rifle in his hand.

"Two for two," said Morris to the peasant.

But Pliant wasn't in a jolly mode.

"There was another?" he asked, fearing the answer. He thought he knew who the other was. He wanted to make sure.

"Oh, yeah," said Morris. "His new assistant. Flashy dresser."

This passing comment confirmed Pliant's worst fears. It was the duke he thought, it had to be. Yet, he said nothing.

"Let's get back to the lab," said Jonus. "Once these two are stashed we can look for the one that's missing. At this point, we don't want any added complications."

"Right," Morris agreed. "Not when we have all the team members. We need to protect our assets now."

He bent down, plucking the unconscious, floating Longley from the water, and tossed him over his shoulder like a sack of potatoes.

Jonus and Pliant took hold of Jarvus, and between the two of them they dragged him through the mire.

On the second level, Lucid was sitting in the hall when she heard the ping of the elevator tone. Rosemary and Spencer were still working inside at the double desk. The girl poked her head in and gave them a sharp whistle of warning.

They looked up, but by that time Lucid saw who was exiting the lift. The team members were returning and they weren't alone. Lucid signaled the all clear with a wave of her hand, and then she swung open the doors to the lab.

Both Jarvus and Longley were coming to, but they were still groggy. Pliant stood guard at the doors of the lab, relieving Lucid who was now in search of blankets. Jonus was ministering to his dazed brother, speaking to him in soft, reassuring tones as the Great One was slumped in a wooden chair.

Spencer walked over to Morris, who was busy fishing various guns from the Commandant's tunic. One by one, he tossed them into a nearby cabinet, which he then locked. Longley was on the floor, propped up against a desk, his long legs splayed before him.

"He'll talk," said the giant, standing upright, "I'll see to that."

"Doesn't matter," Spencer reported to him, "Rosemary and I have cracked the code. We don't need his help now. We can reprogram the reactor's computer on our own."

Jonus looked up from his brother.

"That's great news, Spencer," he said.

Rosemary had shuffled over. She was tired by her recent exertions, but pleased by the outcome. She placed her bony hand on Jonus' shoulder but she spoke to Morris.

"What a devious mind," she said, referring to Longley.

Morris was unimpressed, and it showed.

"He's a spy," he spat, "and a traitor to his clan."

"A heretic also," added Spencer, "still, the computer sabotage was ingenious, I'd have never thought he had it in him."

"How long to reprogram the computer?" Morris asked his Chief Engineer, serious now with the business at hand.

Spencer considered the parameters involved.

"We have to purge the system by dumping the old program," he said. "Then feed in the new one, then reboot. Maybe a day."

Now Morris was the one considering.

"Right," he said, quickly ceasing his consideration. "I say we stay put. We can defend ourselves here, and I don't want any accidents now that the team is complete."

"What about the other one?" asked Jonus. He was referring to the young Duke of Fervent although he didn't know who he was. Was the fancy dresser a problem or not?

"Safety in numbers," answered Morris. "We'll stay here and wait it out but I don't think we have much to worry about. This grunt is no fighter, that was easy enough to see."

Standing in the hallway, Pliant was listening to the conversation as he stood by the lab's open doors, tightening his grip on the rifle he held. The peasant wanted nothing more than to track the missing duke down and kill him, once and for all. Without Fervent dead, he would never feel that his Lucid was safe.

Still, he said nothing. The bizarre situation was beyond him. As long as the others were confident of their actions, he would do his duty as he had so many times in the past, but he didn't like it.

Lucid appeared with blankets. She gave one to Jonus, who then placed it around Jarvus. He was rousing but was still dazed.

He looked up at his brother and said, "Jo?" He hadn't called him that since he was a kid. It was good to hear it again.

"It's OK, J," said the smiling time jumper.

Lucid passed on to the deposed monarch. She deftly arranged the blanket around the still-propped-up man, as if she were tucking him in at bedtime. He was also beginning to recover his senses and recognized the pretty girl hovering over him.

362

"Thank you, my dear," he said with his finest regal air. The poor man was in his dotage. In spite of herself, she smiled at him.

"No problem, King," she said without flourish.

A puzzled look came over his face. He began to rise but was stopped by the giant. The new Commandant of Station Forecast squatted down and placed his beefy hand on the chest of the old one, pushing him back into position.

Rocking on his haunches, Morris looked like a bear at leisure. He was enjoying this. Enjoying it too much, maybe.

"I'm afraid," he said, "you'll have to stay put for the moment, Your Majesty. As soon as you're in a pair of cuffs, then I may let you walk around a bit, we'll see. It depends on how feisty you get."

At last, the dazed Longley realized his perilous situation, but he remained calm. Then he startled Morris by laughing aloud. He seemed to be enjoying himself as well.

"You haven't won," he said with a cheery lilt in his voice. "You may think you have, but I am invincible. No one defeats me."

"Primus can," said Spencer, "and will. With His help, we'll set things right. Nothing is beyond Him."

"Primus?" said Longley, and he laughed again, throwing back his head this time. "Primus is nothing. A myth, that's all."

Spencer shook his head at this pronouncement. It was almost amusing. The old man was mad, that much was evident, but the demented king was not to be stopped.

"You'll see," he said, "Primus holds no power over me. I know His secrets. I know what you don't."

By this time, Lucid reappeared, having retrieved the handcuffs. She handed them to Morris who put them on the raving man. He held his arms out, unconcerned as they were applied.

"Yeah?" The giant said. "How do you figure that? You're of the Military Clan, not the Theology Clan."

363

"Am I?" Longley continued. "No, I have been many people in my life, and so I come from many clans, and have changed my name many times. It always has been an easy thing for me."

Here he stood, for this was his final briefing. Because he was handcuffed, no one stopped him. He leaned an elbow on the desk and propelled himself upright as Morris also stood.

"When things are at their worst," he explained, "I act and step into the breach. These grunts are just worms, they know nothing. They want someone to tell them what to do."

He laughed again, agreeing with himself.

"They hunger for direction," he added, as a fact.

"Like Fervent's authentic uncle, you mean?" asked the Crone. "The real prince? Was he also hungry for direction before you exterminated him and assumed his identity?"

"As I said," Longley replied, "it was an easy thing to do for the prince had been in hiding for years, and all I needed was his signet ring. No one asked any questions. They all wanted me."

"Did they want this?" asked Rosemary, becoming angry. "Did I want this? Did any of us want this?"

She held out her bony arms, indicating everything around them.

"You're a heretic," said Spencer, cutting her off. "Primus never wanted this. It flies in the face of The Great Mandate."

"Ah, Primus," said the old king, unimpressed by this admonition. "Always Primus. That's ever your stance."

This contemptuous comment went unanswered so the mad monarch chose to continue his thrust.

"Think for yourself, why don't you," he added with a scowl. "But who cares for reality when Primus speaks? What rubbish."

"And you know reality?" asked the unbelieving Jarvus, coherent for the first time as he continued to sit in his chair.

"I know Primus," Longley answered, with scorn now in his tone, "for I come from the Alpha planet."

"A priest?" asked Jonus. "Then you are of the Theology Clan. So why do you reject Primus with such vehemence?"

This got the largest laugh from Longley so far.

"A priest, you say?" he uttered, amused. "No, my young friend, I'm just like you and your brother here, a technician through and through. For uncounted generations, my family has maintained the theologians' computers on our Alpha planet."

"And so," asked Spencer, "because of this you know Primus?"

Spencer didn't hide his skepticism but Longley was unfazed.

He had them now, he realized, he had them all. They were all the same. They knew nothing, but he knew everything.

"Oh yes," Longley said in his best lecturing tone.

The ruined king paused, glancing at each of them in turn, even Pliant, who was watching from the hallway.

"You see," he explained, "your precious Primus, the God you serve, the very One that gives your trivial existence meaning, is no god at all. He never was. He's nothing more than a computer."

No one spoke. They hadn't expected this, how could they? The very idea was stunning, and also unbelievable.

"That's absurd," Spencer at last blurted, "you're insane."

This retort amused Longley anew.

"Yes, I say," the demented traitor cackled, "it's true. He's the oldest computer there is. You see your Primus is nothing more than the Primary Memory User System."

Again no one spoke. They couldn't. They were dumbfounded.

This had to be false, patently untrue.

Still, there was doubt present, despite what they wished.

Pliant was the first to say anything. The peasant saw plainly that no one there knew the truth. This madness had to stop.

"Lucid," he called, as he held out his open palm. She came to him and they joined hands. He'd made his choice at long last.

From now on, he would rely on no one but himself.

Everyone had turned to view the pair in the doorway. Longley bent over and, picking up a stout, heavy wooden chair, smashed it over Morris' back. The big man was caught unawares, and he went to his knees, the breath knocked out of him.

Longley then leaned in and, using his cuffed hands, the insane Commandant drew the service pistol from Morris' holster. Then everyone moved. In an instant, the time lab was a blur.

Spencer dove for cover but Jonus jumped at Longley. The old king fired, but not before Jarvus had thrown himself between the pair. He took the bullet that was meant for his older brother, as had been his intent, once he'd seen him in lethal jeopardy.

The Crone had also jumped in to aid Jonus, but she was off to the side and he didn't see her. The thunderstruck time jumper was standing with his back to the others, staring only at Jarvus who was now clutching his bleeding chest with his hands while writhing on the floor. It had happened so quickly!

Longley was adrift in his madness. He fired again and shot Rosemary an inch below her silver pin. Her face held a look of surprise as she crumpled and went down.

Upon seeing Longley's first action, Lucid had pulled Plaint's rifle from him. As she was bringing the weapon to bear, Longley had begun firing. The girl knew that no one was supposed to die, that all of the team members were needed, but when she saw Longley shoot her mother, she screamed and authored a new story.

She pulled the trigger and shot him in the face. He never saw it coming. The rear of his once-regal head exploded, the blast propelling his now-dead body backward.

366

She dropped the rifle and tried to run to her mother's aid, but Pliant held her back, unsure it was safe within the lab. She turned to confront him and that's when she saw the young Duke of Fervent, standing behind them in the hall. Lucid screamed again.

The duke pushed the surprised Pliant to his knees and grabbed Lucid about the waist. He was brandishing the revolver Longley had given him earlier and he looked as if he knew how to use it. He began to retreat, now with Lucid in tow.

"Stay away," he ordered. "I want only the girl, but stay back or I'll kill you. I mean what I say, don't tempt me."

Everyone was frozen in place, shocked into inaction by what had occurred. Only Pliant was calm and he knew what he had to do. He stood and began to walk toward the pair in the hallway.

"Pliant, no," shrieked Lucid, ceasing her struggling with Fervent to do so, but the determined Pliant didn't stop. He came forward at a steady pace, one foot in front of the other. He was on his own quest now and nothing would halt him.

Because he was so intent, Pliant failed to notice that the chambers of the revolver were empty. Longley had only wanted the duke as a buffer. He hadn't trusted him with a loaded weapon.

"I mean it," Fervent again croaked. "Stop. Stop where you are."

In desperation he began to squeeze the trigger. The empty gun only clicked, the pin not contacting a charge. It continued clicking away as Pliant's hands closed around the throat of the duke.

The last thing young Fervent saw was the baker's steely glare. It did not let up until well after he was gone. When the peasant was sure the noble was dead, Pliant dropped him to the floor.

It was over, finally over. The girl was safe at last. The young Duke of Fervent made a richly-attired corpse.

It took a few seconds but, moving awkwardly, the stunned inhabitants of the lab began to react to what had just transpired.

Spencer crawled over and took Rosemary's hand. Her frozen face was still showing a look of surprise. Lucid and Pliant arrived and knelt down beside the stricken woman.

The three were staring at her, taking it in. The perfect circle of the bullet hole beneath her pin was small and barely bleeding. On the other hand, the growing red stain beneath her demonstrated the damage to her back was more considerable.

Then the old woman drew a sharp breath, bubbling crimson in the effort. Her eyes, before fixed, began to move. She was conscious, but unaware of what had happened.

"She lives," murmured Lucid. What relief! She bent low trying to give her mother comfort, but Spencer pulled her back.

"Not for long," he said in an intense whisper. "She's been hit in the lung. We need to apply pressure or she'll bleed to death."

While speaking, he handed Pliant the blanket Lucid had brought earlier for Jarvus. It had fallen to the floor during the melee. There wasn't much time to make a difference.

"Tear this in strips," he said, "so we can staunch the blood."

Spencer had been terrified when the shooting started but he was now in his element. He had ministered to hundreds of dying grunts.

He had thought those days were over, a vain wish now.

"Get the other blanket," he said to Lucid. "She's in shock and has to be kept warm. Hurry, we may be too late."

The girl scampered away as Pliant began ripping.

Spencer gently turned the Crone on her side. It didn't look good. The gaping hole in her back was bigger than his fist.

Jonus was preoccupied and unaware that Rosemary was even hit. As she was near death just a few feet from him, the time jumper was applying pressure to his sibling's wound. He knew it was a wasted effort but he had to try something.

His brother, his only family left, was slipping away and there was nothing he could do to stop it from happening.

"Jo," Jarvus sputtered. "I'm so sorry. It's all my fault."

"Don't talk J," said Jonus. "You're going to be fine, just fine." He was lying, but again he didn't know what else to do.

By this time Morris had recovered.

The giant bent down on the other side of Jarvus, watching his oldest friend tend to his dying brother. Blood was everywhere. He wanted to help but knew it was hopeless.

Morris had been trained to be stoic in battle but he was human. He felt bad for J. He hurt more for Jonus.

"I need to tell you something," Jarvus said between gasps.

"Don't talk, J," Jonus said again.

Morris soothed Jarvus' hair with a huge hand.

"Don't worry, J," he said, "I'll tell him how we spoke."

But that was not the Great One's intended message, so in desperation he continued even though it was a struggle. "I need to tell you," he said in a whimper, "that I love you." Then he died.

Jonus had no time to grieve. As he looked up, he saw Spencer and Pliant carrying the unconscious Rosemary out of the door, her body wrapped in the now-bloodstained blanket. They were taking her to the infirmary on the fifth level, passing the dead Fervent in the hall as they moved to the elevator.

Lucid had dashed ahead to make ready for their arrival.

Jonus and Morris followed and, in the lift, Jonus asked Spencer if she would recover. Spencer, however, didn't know. For all his expertise, he was no medical doctor.

"If we could get her back through the time stream, she might," he said, but all save Pliant knew this could not be done now. Two of the original six people flung beyond the Elastic Limit were now dead and all six had been needed to replicate the initial procedure. The vaulted mission, so close to completion, was finished.

The priority was now just to keep her alive so that she would heal on her own, but the fact that she was the Crone complicated the matter. Rosemary was no longer young and vigorous. The outlook was not good and everyone knew it.

Nevertheless, Spencer did what he could by cauterizing the wound, packing it with antibiotics, and stitching both holes closed. They gave her fluids and waited. Somehow, she survived the night.

Early the next morning, the wounded woman regained consciousness, but only briefly. However, in that short time, she solved the dilemma they faced. Leave it to Rosemary.

Lucid and Pliant sat on one side of her bed, Jonus on the other.

The Crone opened her eyes and looked around, seeing those she loved surrounding her. Jonus cradled her bony left hand in both of his while Lucid caressed her upper right arm. The girl couldn't hold the other hand because it was connected to several IV drips.

Morris and Spencer were in the infirmary, seated at a distance, discussing options. They were slim. Trying to carry out the procedure with only four brain wave patterns was suicide for the variables would be different and they were too vast to compute.

The only reason it could be done with six was because the parameters of six were already known, on file in the main computer. At the time, the particulars of the original six patterns had also been too vast to compute but there had been no need to do so. They had been fed into the computer by the event itself.

What about this or that, asked Morris, who was searching for a solution. No was the answer from Spencer for this or that reason. From across the room, the Crone heard them talking.

She squeezed Jonus' hand and he bent nearer.

"There's still a way," she whispered to him, "we just need six patterns." She turned and looked to the girl and the baker, smiling at them. She then squeezed the time jumper's hand once more, and again slipped into unconsciousness.

"That's it," said Jonus, "how could I have been so stupid?"

"What's that," said Morris, crossing over, "what do you mean?" Jonus turned to his big friend, but he still held his Rose's hand.

"Six brain wave patterns were originally blasted beyond the Elastic Limit," he explained. "All we need is six patterns to go back. They don't have to be the same six."

Morris didn't understand, but Spencer did. He was a good engineer and now he saw the elegance of the solution. He also knew, as Jonus did, that he should have seen it all along.

"We just need to program in a new pair," he said to Morris. But the big man was no scientist. He still didn't follow.

"The computer won't care," explained Spencer, widely smiling now. "It will still have three pairs to plug into the formula. The program should run without knowing the difference."

They all looked to Lucid and Pliant. The poor baker didn't comprehend the importance of the exchange, but she understood. She wasn't named Lucid for nothing.

"We will go back also?" she asked.

"Yes," said Jonus. "All of us will. It's her last hope."

Lucid looked to Pliant. He hunched his shoulders. He didn't care where he went as long as the girl came with him.

Lucid caressed the arm of her mother anew. She was the only parent the girl had ever known. The decision was not difficult.

"We shall go," she said.

"How long to feed the needed changes into the reactor's computer?" Morris asked his chief engineer.

Spencer looked to the time jumper saying, "I'll need help."

"Try and stop me," was the reply from Jonus.

"If we work all night," Spencer said to Morris, "we could be ready by this time tomorrow. Ready with everything I mean, the new pairings for the main computer plus the repaired program for the reactor's computer. It'll work, I know it will."

Morris nodded, satisfied.

"Let's get to it then," said the Commandant of Station Forecast.

The next day all were inside the cramped containment room.

Lucid and Pliant each wore a new ruby-colored crystal containing all of their pertinent information. Their brain wave patterns had been paired, as had the patterns of the time jumper and the still unconscious Rosemary, and each had been stored in the main computer. Those of Spencer and Morris were already filed together for these two had been paired all along.

Jonus threw the switch and began the standard countdown. The count soon fell to zero and nothing happened, just as before. Time itself had slowed outside the sealed structure.

"Just a moment more, a few seconds," said Jonus. "We're close now." Closer, closer he thought.

Above the station, the masses were still joyously rioting, not satiated with a mere three days of revelry. They were euphoric in their easy victory. Fires were everywhere and all manner of grunts ran to and fro carting the spoils of war.

The city itself was located on a high bluff and from a distance the smoke was thick and rising without letup. The horizon was black. The denuded countryside was razed, burnt and barren.

Then it all vanished, replaced in an instant by a different scene.

The first two stories of Station Forecast now stood above a flat plain next to a huge forest. The day was clear with not a cloud in the sky. There was no one about for the station's contingent was in a spaceship, circling high above Am-Rif Arret.

The reversing process had worked as predicted. The original time line was restored to the planet. The long mission was over.

CHAPTER TWELVE
THE HOMECOMING

Above the planet, Archie and Judith were seated in the Deferent's cramped command center, their eyes glued to the ship's viewing screen. While they watched, the image it held abruptly changed and the station was restored to its original configuration. As predicted, the conversion had been almost instantaneous, occurring within a few seconds of the first surface alteration.

"They're back," gasped Judith, "just as they said. We can land now. The team should be there, inside the time lab."

Before Archie could respond, a buzzer sounded and a printout began to spit from the communications console. He reached over, tearing it off. As he scanned it, his eyebrows shot up in surprise.

This was clipboard material, no doubt about it.

In the station, the occupants of the containment room looked to each other. Had the procedure worked? It had.

Lucid was the first to notice the change in her mother's appearance. Rosemary was restored to her former self, her flaming red hair once more framing her pretty face. Yet the stricken woman remained unconscious with grave injuries.

"Contact the ship," said Morris, "they have doctors aboard."

"They should know already," said Jonus. "I bet they're keeping an eye out for us. I would if I were them."

They rushed Rosemary back to the infirmary. She had lost a lot of blood, but she was now young and vigorous and she had always been a fighter. Jonus could only hope that, at long last, their life together would finally come to pass.

Lucid and Pliant could not believe the change in her. Spencer had explained what would happen after the procedure, but they were unprepared for the extent of the transformation. Her restored frame was tall now, and no longer bent.

The implications were not lost on either of them. These people indeed had strange powers, but did those powers come from their God as they had claimed? Or did the old king speak the truth?

They said that he was mad, lost in his demented fantasies. Had he been? The two peasants didn't know.

Morris and Spencer reported to the landing field just as the Deferent was making its descent. They both watched in silence. Each knew that Judith was aboard.

Spencer was excited but apprehensive as well. He wasn't sure of her feelings, but he was sure of his. He knew beyond any doubt that he loved her and he would let her know it.

Other than that, there was nothing he could do. He had to have faith. And, despite everything, he still did.

Morris was apprehensive also but not for the same reason.

He knew now that Judith had been right. They were not meant for each other and never had been. She was not his answer.

Yet Morris knew the woman well and now he realized that given time she would lose her bitterness towards him. He had lost his toward her long ago. It seemed like ages now.

But, the new Commandant was apprehensive about the war he suspected was currently raging elsewhere in the galaxy. Longley may have been insane but he was no fool. His agenda had been bigger than this puny planet and its grunts.

He had needed the time machinery for a reason and had gone to great lengths to get it. He had kept everyone busy before the explosion, steering the team with expert steps into doing his bidding. He'd failed in the end, but that didn't matter to the giant.

Something else was afoot here for nothing that had happened in the interim made any sense otherwise.

Yet, Morris was ambivalent about any war. Play-acting the military life no longer held appeal for him. If indeed hostilities were raging, then the Great Mandate of Primus was finished, and all of the various prophecies were rendered meaningless.

He would hold no allegiance to a lost cause. No, he wanted the bigger picture now. He wanted to know what was behind it all.

He was going to find out. He'd make sure of that. It was his new, self-imposed quest, his own ongoing and personal Mandate.

Once landed, the ship's door opened and the command center's steps deployed. Judith was the first one off and she quickly spied Spencer. She waved at him with a sweeping arcing of her arms as one would do on a deserted island to signal for rescue.

Spencer smiled, no longer concerned. Now he had his answer. Soon the two of them would rescue each other.

The couple met and embraced at the base of the huge ship. Morris held back but just a moment. He had other business, and as he approached the stairway, the demure woman grasped his hand.

"Thank you," she said simply.

"Take care of him," answered Morris. Then he added, "Take care of each other." He already knew that they would.

By this time, Archie stood at the base of the steps. As Morris walked up, Archie held out his clipboard. Morris scanned the communication it held but showed no surprise after reading it.

"We need the doctors," he told Captain Spume. "We have injured in the infirmary." He handed him back the clipboard.

375

"Yes, sir," Archie said, "right away." He turned and ran up the stairs in order to open the cargo bays that contained the station's contingent. He had held off performing that procedure until he was briefed on the status at Point Zero.

Morris turned. Spencer and Judith were still embracing, laughing and crying some. He felt good about that.

He and Judith would be fine, fast friends. He knew it. She and Spencer would be fine too, true partners, at last.

He walked back towards the station, pensive.

As he was doing so, a newly liberated medical team ran past him, but he kept to his pace, still thinking. All of Station Forecast's personnel would have to be dealt with, he knew. He couldn't just abandon them here at the very edge of the universe.

The planet's grunts were a different matter altogether. They would have to be left to their own devices. With their numbers, it was the only call that he could make.

Morris needed to see some star charts but he didn't want to board ship to do so. As the station's contingent was disembarking, from this vantage the looming vessel looked like a picnic basket swarming with ants. He wanted no interruptions.

Nevertheless, as he entered Point Zero he came upon Jonus. The med team was busy treating Rose, and the time jumper could not just stand by with nothing to do but watch and wait. He had sought out his big friend to plan strategy.

"The war's raging," said Morris, still walking. I just got it off the ship's horn. It didn't take long for all hell to break loose."

"How bad is it, Moe?" asked Jonus, working hard to match the big man's stride. Morris didn't notice. His mind was elsewhere.

"Bad enough," was the answer. "Massacres on every one of the seeded planets, each very bloody, and inside jobs. All of the viewing stations have now been destroyed."

The two old friends had reached the main elevator. Morris punched the call button. He was calm and focused with all of his extensive training now paying him dividends.

"Station Forecast," he said, "is the only grunt-viewing station in the entire galaxy that's been left untouched."

"There was another Mandate in play here," said Jonus, as they entered the lift. "Longley's true mission was to get the machine. I suppose that his confederates assumed that he would, and so the time was right for them to make their big move."

"They're idiots," said Morris, punching the floor, "but that's beside the point. The Alpha planet's been attacked, too, and with a large and coordinated force. Somebody sure knew what they were doing even if Longley's schemes backfired here."

The time jumper said nothing, but he was thinking. This was big news. The ramifications were big also.

"The computer complex has been hit," continued the giant. "The priests are powerless. No one's there to tell them what to do."

Jonus looked hard at his oldest friend, reading him. This war was against the rule of Primus, no more doubting that. And if Primus were not divine, then everything they knew would change.

After all, would fight for no more than a disproved theology or a demolished piece of machinery?

"The military's not much better, Moe," the time jumper said. "Now, who's telling them what to do?" He needn't have had concern for Morris agreed with him.

"You're preaching to the choir with that one," the giant concurred. "All the clans are going to love this situation. They won't know who to follow or whom to trust."

Hearing this, Jonus shook his head in open disgust.

"They'll start making their own pairings soon enough," Morris added. "It's a galactic blood bath just waiting to happen. The situation couldn't get any worse but it probably will."

They exited the lift, walking to the Commandant's office.

"I think we need a new order of the day, Moe," said Jonus.

"Count on it," he said, nodding. "But first I've got to deal with the staff. Where I'm going they can't follow."

"What's your idea?" asked Jonus.

They had reached the office. Morris kicked the door open, his injured leg no longer an issue. Star charts hung on the far wall.

"We can dump the contingent here," he said, using his huge finger as a pointer. "That's two star systems in from us, but still out of the way. No one would look for them there and we can give them the supplies from the ship."

Jonus wasn't picky, but then again, he couldn't afford to be. Not now, at any rate. The new game was on.

"I guess so," he said, looking at the chart.

Morris tried to sound upbeat.

"It's for the best," he reasoned. "And it's the best that we can do. If they hole up now, they can be picked up later."

"If there's someone left by then," Jonus said, "to pick them up."

The phone on the desk rang. The unexpected sound startled both of them. No one knew they were there.

After a few rings, Jonus said, "It is your office now, Moe. Maybe someone's looking for you. Go on, answer."

Morris did. He then shot his eyes to Jonus and hung up without a word. It wasn't good news.

"It's the doctor," he said, looking glum.

They rushed to the infirmary, and they were almost too late. Rosemary was near death, with a raging infection racking her body. She was too weak now to fight it off for the double transformation she'd undergone had been too much for her to bear.

378

Lucid and Pliant were standing by her bedside but they backed away when Jonus and Morris arrived.

Jonus approached her but Morris stopped to talk to the doctors in hushed tones. There was nothing to be done, they reported. With her condition, conventional measures had no effect and the unconventional ones they had tried were also to no avail.

She was dying and everyone knew it.

Jonus took her hand. He placed his other hand on her burning head, smoothing her red hair much as Moe had done earlier to the stricken Jarvus. Her pale, freckled face was tired and haggard, but she was still the prettiest thing that he had ever seen.

As he caressed her, she opened her eyes. His was the first image she saw. For once, he didn't know what to say.

"You come here often, big boy?" she asked with a faint smile.

He tried not to, but he started to cry.

"Don't," she said, gripping his hand in both of hers. "And don't you give up either. I wouldn't want that."

"Rose," he croaked, "it wasn't supposed to be this way."

"One never knows," she answered, waxing philosophically, "at least we found us again. At least now we know that we never stopped loving each other. That's something."

"It's not enough, Rose," he spat between tears. How could he go on without her? He had no idea.

"It has to be," she said, soothing him, "it's all we've had." Then she added, "You know I'd never give you up. I've always loved you, Jonus, and I've never given that up."

"I'll always love you," he cried. "My Rose. My sweet Rose."

They buried her the next morning with a brief service.

Jonus had lost both his soul mate and his brother within the span of two days. He should have been devastated but he wasn't. Instead, somehow, he was steeled with a new resolve.

379

Both had loved him, despite the long separations they endured. Jarvus had died for him and Rose had died fighting to get them back together. It wasn't the outcome that he had wished and, in fact, these were the two things that he had least wanted but that no longer mattered to the former time jumper.

He could go on with his life knowing that he had done his best. He was saddened, yes, but not defeated. The memory of both of them gave him strength, each in a different way.

No, he would remember them, and smile as he did so. That's what would matter. That was the important thing to remember.

"You OK?" asked Moe. He wasn't sure. He knew he wouldn't be, if their situations were reversed.

"I'm fine," was the reply, "I need to stay busy."

Morris nodded. He could relate. All of them could.

As acting Commandant, Commander Morris had already issued the new order of the day concerning the disposition of Station Forecast. The time machinery was being dismantled as they spoke. It was now the only example of its kind and Morris was going to take it with him when he vacated the planet.

It might prove useful if a power source could be had and there could be many unused reactors now handy on one of the increasing number of destroyed planets throughout the universe. Misuse of the machinery had been forbidden but now all bets were off. The vaulted Age of Primus was over, never to return.

Reports of the newest war were few, but they kept trickling in just the same, and all of the accounts were bad. With no Great Mandate to bind them together, the various clans were busy killing each other. It wasn't going to stop anytime soon.

Morris was lucky that his station was the furthest one out in the galaxy. Beyond Longley's doings, they were unaffected but that wouldn't last long. Sooner or later, someone would show up.

"Time to talk to young Captain Spume," observed Morris, considering all options. "We'll need a good pilot involved. Several are on staff, but I'd prefer non-military."

Jonus grunted his agreement. Except for Moe, he'd had his fill of martial types. They both had.

"If he's game," Morris added, "Archie would be easy to work with, but I've got to know if he's with us."

"He'll jump at it," said Jonus, "all he wants is adventure."

"Me, too," Morris concurred, with a sly smile.

Spencer was in charge of the demolition crews. He'd worked out the particulars to the slightest detail. There were teams on each floor of the doomed station rigging the explosives.

Station Forecast was to be destroyed, along with all of its outbuildings. Perhaps when someone did show up, they would assume another faction in the hostilities had wiped out the installation before they arrived. As a consequence, they might not search for the vacated personnel, thinking them already dead.

Spencer Hall found himself a changed man. He no longer followed with blind obedience the dictates from above, but he hadn't lost his faith either. The man just couldn't bring himself to believe in a random universe, it wasn't in his nature.

In spite of everything, he continued to deem that a higher power was still in control, just not the one that he had thought. At this point, he was past trying to figure out who was in charge anyway. In truth, the particulars no longer mattered to him.

Instead, Spencer was content to live as good a life as he could from this point forward, and take his chances hoping for the best. Judith concurred with this assessment. She was working on the logistics of the move to come, which were daunting.

In the beginning, she had been sent to the planet to help the struggling grunts, but that agenda had drastically changed. The station's contingent was aware of this and was eager for her expertise. They would need all the help they could get.

Who knew how long they would live on the new planet? The ship's cargo bays would be detached and converted into temporary housing. The limited supplies then had to be dispersed, and a new social order established that wouldn't squander them.

Judith also had changed. Her personal Mandate had been achieved and she was thankful for that fact. Her long-lost husband was safe and she was relieved that he still loved her in spite of the foolish way that she had acted in the past.

The fates of Jarvus and Rosemary were examples of how things could have been different, and Judith felt lucky in that regard.

She had always been a determined woman and now she was determined to move forward, despite the uncertain future. And, even with their present dire circumstances, she was eager to begin her new life with Spencer. She was more than eager, in fact.

As with everyone else involved, Judith had learned a great lesson of life from the recent events on the stricken planet. And she planned to live her new life accordingly. From now on, there was not, nor would there ever be, any time to waste.

Archie was in charge of the repacking crews.

The Deferent's bays were to be purged of anything not needed for the new mission. All foodstuffs were to be kept of course, and also any supplies or material that might prove useful on the new planet but no frills. Space was at a premium on the ship.

However, Archie Spume and his ever-present clipboard made an efficient, effective team. The massive vessel would soon be readied. Past that point, he didn't know what would happen to him or where he'd end up, once all was said and done.

As he was supervising the action, Morris and Jonus joined him.

"Captain," said Morris, "we need to talk, if you're free." Archie was. He was eager for news of any future strategy.

"We have some plans beyond the relocation," added Jonus, "and both of us want you to be a part of them."

Archie said nothing at first. This was serious, no doubt about it. The world order, set in place so long ago by belief in Primus, was being ripped apart as they spoke.

Archie's new life had already started, as had everyone else's, but he had no real direction beyond reacting to what might come his way. Yet these two knew what they were going to do, that much was evident, and now they wanted him to be involved. The details were unimportant to the formerly lackadaisical man.

Archie had spent the better part of his life as a loner, answering to no one, and he was well set in his ways. But he needed a change, had craved one for a long time, and big change was on the horizon, no matter what he did. And, it was true that Archie was not the same man that he had been before the incident.

The recent events had altered his outlook. He had matured and drastically so. In the past, he had wished for a new life, but now he wanted one containing real meaning.

After short consideration he said, "I'm in."

"But you haven't heard what we going to do," said Jonus.

"Doesn't matter," Archie said, "you're doing something, and that's enough for me. I want to do what I can. I want in."

Morris patted Archie's shoulder with his big mitt of a hand.

"Good man," he said to his new pilot.

"How long till you're ready here?" asked the time jumper.

Archie took a minute to scan his clipboard.

"They're loading the time machine now," he answered. "An hour, maybe two. Then the contingent can board."

"Right," said Morris, satisfied. "We'll see you in two hours, then." In answer, Archie only nodded.

The two ex-generals then walked off towards the station, soon overtaking Lucid and Pliant. They had lagged behind after Rosemary's service. The couple now considered themselves married, despite the absence of any official ceremony.

383

The girl was having a hard time being orphaned once again. Pliant didn't know how to console her in her massive grief, but this was not surprising. He would not have known how to console himself, had she been the one who died.

"Haven't changed your minds?" the giant asked them.

Pliant looked to Lucid, the true love of his life.

The sadness on her face was painful to see. For once, she was lost with no direction. He was the one making the decisions now, but in this case, both of them would have to live with them.

"No," he replied, with stiff determination. "This is our home. We'll stay here and make the best of it."

"But, Pliant, you don't understand that things have changed," stressed Jonus. "You two will be alone. The rest of the population is primitive now as well as far away."

Morris agreed with this assessment.

"You may never even see anyone else," he said.

Yet Pliant had already considered this. It didn't matter to him. From now on, they would rely on themselves.

"I have been many things in my life," he explained, "but never a husband. I look forward to it, and this is where we belong." He put his arm around the girl, to comfort himself as well as her.

In her grief, she didn't seem to notice the action.

"From now on, I am just a man," he added. "A farmer and hunter with my woman by my side. We'll get by."

"We'll leave what we can," Morris told him, "in the way of supplies and equipment. Enough to help you through a season or two, at any rate." He knew further argument was moot.

"I want to give you something more," said Jonus, extending his hand to the distraught girl. Lucid's green eyes widened at the sight of the silver rosebud pin he held. It represented a new beginning, a fresh, bold life elegant but strong.

"Of course," explained Jonus, "she'd want you to have it, I know that she would, she loved you so."

Three hours later, everything was readied. The station's staff was tightly stowed aboard the Deferent, billeted in two cargo holds. The remaining four sections were packed with all of the usable goods that could possibly be crammed into them.

Archie was in the command center, busy with his pre-flight protocol, but Spencer, Judith, Jonus and Morris stood at the foot of the steps, saying their final farewells to Lucid and Pliant.

"I wish you two luck," Spencer was saying, ever the optimist.

"We'll need some, I'm sure," said Pliant, now the stoic, "but we'll make it regardless, no matter the difficulties."

"Just a man and his woman, eh?" asked Morris.

He was in a buoyant mood, almost jealous of the pair, alone and together on a nearly empty planet, but it was a passing fancy. He had no time for such domestic pursuits. He was going elsewhere.

"Yes, we are," answered Lucid, "a husband and wife, at last." She now wore the small, silver rosebud pinned to her simple peasant dress. "Thank you for everything and good luck, as well."

"We'll need it," said Judith, taking Lucid's hand in one of hers. She swept her free arm about, indicating them all. She was determined, almost defiant, but filled with optimism.

"Even with the numbers we have," she noted, "in our new home, I'm sure we'll face a few challenges ourselves."

The two former generals exchanged a glance.

"Actually," said Jonus, "Moe and I aren't staying with you."

"What do you mean?" she asked.

"We're moving on," Morris answered her. "We have the machine. We may use it to find out what's really happened."

"That's forbidden," said Spencer, before he realized it. At this point, he didn't know if it was or not. None of them did.

"We'll just see," said Jonus philosophically, "and take our chances in the meantime. It seems to us that someone's responsible for everything we've gone through. We're both betting that it's not some higher power named Primus."

Morris concurred with this well-phrased outlook.

"I think we're all here for a reason, like Spencer said to us once," he related to them. "Now we've been given the hardware. Why shouldn't we use it get to the real bottom of this thing?"

Then Spencer added, "Maybe it's the prophecy. Maybe the New Age has started. Maybe it's the new Mandate."

"We're on a quest," said Jonus and, as if that settled the matter, the veteran Traveler turned and walked up the steps, soon followed by the other three, now-resolute passengers.

At the hatch, Morris stopped before entering.

"Remember to stay clear," he shouted, "we can give you only half an hour before we blow the station."

Lucid and Pliant wasted no time.

They hurried toward their supplies already cached at a safe distance. As they trotted off, the Deferent's giant engines began to fire. Soon they heard the huge ship lift from the ground.

Only after reaching their larder did they turn. The massive vessel was circling on the horizon, a small speck from their vantage, hovering like a honeybee over a flower. A series of explosions then occurred, reverberating through the countryside, and the resulting smoke and dust masked the scene.

When it dissipated, the sky was empty. The ship had gone. The man and the woman were alone at long last.

The couple was safe enough. Any hostile faction reconnoitering the site would not be looking for only two people, but the station's functioning contingent. And the planet's primitive grunt population would be of no interest to them.

They stood gazing at where the mysterious Station Forecast had once stood. There was now only a large pile of rubble in its place. In a year or so, the forest would reclaim the area after which no one would ever know that it had been there.

"We have much work to do," announced the man to his new partner. "We must have a hut. We need shelter and we have to protect these possessions from the elements."

The woman was unconcerned. She knew that the two of them would do what was needed. She was thinking of something else.

"Husband," she asked, "does this mean there is no God?"

He laughed aloud at the question.

"I am but a poor man, wife," he answered her. "I know not of such heady matters." It was the truth and they both knew it.

"But if," she persisted, not letting him off the proverbial hook, "God talked to you, then you would listen?"

The man laughed again and took her hand.

"Who am I," he asked, "not to answer God if He spoke to me?"

The woman smiled at him. It was the very reply that she had wanted to hear. If there were a God who wished to speak to them, then the two would be open and willing to listen.

And thus it was, and forever shall be. The far-flung planet of AmRif Arret had been completely turned around and so its name now became Terra Firma. And, as the two of them were the first of their kind, their new names then became Adam and Eve.

~The End~

ACKNOWLEDGEMENTS

Stephanie stuck with me from the very beginning, never failing

Her father also, who retrieved text from a doomed computer

Will ran off countless revisions, always quickly

Cort, Susan, Jean and Jim read first efforts, in bits and pieces

Virginia corrected for grammar and context mistakes aplenty

Becky first read the unedited work without previous readings

Lucy read my first self-edited attempt, and saw volumes

I talked plot with numerous interested parties;

Mike, Phil and Buster would be included in this group

Susannah edited this Edition, her insight a huge bonus

Rob's technical support remains unrivaled

None failed me in any respect

I know this and I am grateful

They know this and I am pleased

It's dedicated to Paul, who gave the most, freely and with a smile

Made in United States
Orlando, FL
20 September 2023

37119350R00213